To my dear departed father, M.N. Ayyar,

and to my mother, Kamakshi Ayyar:

The beacons of light illuminating my life.

# When the Lotus Blooms

A NOVEL *by*

KANCHANA KRISHNAN AYYAR

**When the Lotus blooms**

Written by
Kanchana Krishnan Ayyar
Copyright © 2011  Kanchana Krishnan Ayyar

Library of Congress Control Number:  2011935941
ISBN-13: 978-09838765-0-2
ISBN-10: 0983876509
Edited by Jim Fairchild & Indrani Chakrabarti
Cover design by Feroza Unvala
Author photograph by Daljeet Singh

Published By Kanchi Books

Kanchi
Books

http://www.kanchibooks.com

# FOREWORD
*by*
## Dr. Shashi Tharoor, M.P.

'*When the Lotus Blooms*' is a deeply arresting novel. The well-realized characters come alive from the very first chapter.

Set in Colonial India, the author vividly paints a picture of the lives of two child brides, Rajam and Dharmu, their trials and tribulations, hopes and dreams. She offers us a panoramic view of small town India, with its interesting collection of inhabitants, whose characters and concerns are depicted in subtle and varying shades. At times dark, at times inspiring, the chapters in this novel weave a tapestry of moods that ultimately beguile the reader into feeling a part of the lives of the protagonists.

For those of us residing in India, the stories of these women resonate with insight into the realities of a male-dominated society. But the strength of this book lies in the ubiquity of the characters, Rajam, Dharmu, Mahadevan, Nagamma, Kandu, Partha, Meera, Revathi and Swaminathan. We all have known people like them, loved them or loathed them, at some point in our lives.

A brave and bold attempt at a first novel. Well done, Kanchana!

*Dr. Shashi Tharoor is a renowned author, peacekeeper, human rights activist, and a member of the Indian Parliament*

"Kanchana Krishnan Ayyar's novel, *When the Lotus Bloom*s may well be the definitive record of life in India during the first third of the 20th century. It follows the arc of two Brahmin families and traces the lives of over a dozen characters. A born story teller, Ms. Ayyar dramatizes every incident with confidence and flair. Her characters are authentic and touching, and the novel teems with vital memories of Indian life under the Raj. She doesn't flinch at exposing the injustices of patriarchy, imperialism and caste prejudices but tells it all with love and compassion for the victims even though they may be pariahs. I was especially intrigued with the endless duties and rituals of the Brahmin caste and their individual struggles and sometimes failures to meet such high-minded responsibilities. Westerners may be shocked, for example, at the Indian practice of marrying off their daughters before they reach puberty. For once, this story is told from the perspective of an Indian woman rather than a conscience-stricken British male. Anyone interested in this historic period will find *When the Lotus Bloom*s difficult to put down."

*— Dr. James Fairchild, Associate Professor of Literature
Maharishi University of Management*

# AUTHOR'S NOTE

I first embarked on writing this book in 2008 for two main reasons. I wanted to share with the world the miraculous events leading up to my mother's birth, as a token of gratitude for being my constant inspiration and support. I also wanted to write a book that would be a legacy and a source of pride for my children and theirs, giving them a snapshot of the era in which their ancestors lived, back in India. Although I have used particular situations and simulated the locales in which my grandmothers grew up, the incidents and encounters are all a figment of my imagination, created fictitiously based on my mother's tales. The myth of the Brahmakamalam is also fictitious conceived to blend with the events in the novel.

Streaming through the book is a powerful feminist vein, highlighting the trials and troubles faced by the women of the time while searching for identity in a man's world. Some stories, like that of Revathi, a victim of domestic abuse, ring true even today. I have touched upon and moved on from the story of Revathi deliberately, mirroring the tendency of society to show fleeting interest and concern over tragedy, only to sink back into the comfort of their own numbing routines.

The book was conceived because of my dear mother, whose vivid stories allowed me to create a kaleidoscopic picture of 1930's Colonial India with its juxtaposition of cultures, customs and languages. I could not have finished this project without the constant support and encouragement from my darling husband Rajiv, and my lovely daughters Karunya and Lavanya. My gratitude to my friends Jayashree, Teva, Ann and Aditya who read the unedited version and offered valuable suggestion. Thanks Rita for your help with all my printing needs. A special thanks also to Janevi who created my glossary. I cannot forget the invaluable support of my book group, who taught me all I needed to learn about the publishing business. My earnest appreciation to Christine and Kitty and especially to my sister, Lakshmi, for proofreading. My heartfelt gratitude to Dr. Shashi Tharoor, who took time and effort to write the Foreword for a first time author, in spite of his busy schedule. I could not have done this without Feroza, my childhood friend, mentor and phenomenal graphic artist. Finally, a big thanks to my editors, Jim Fairchild and Indrani Chakrabarti, without whom the book would not shine as brilliantly.

# Rajam's Family

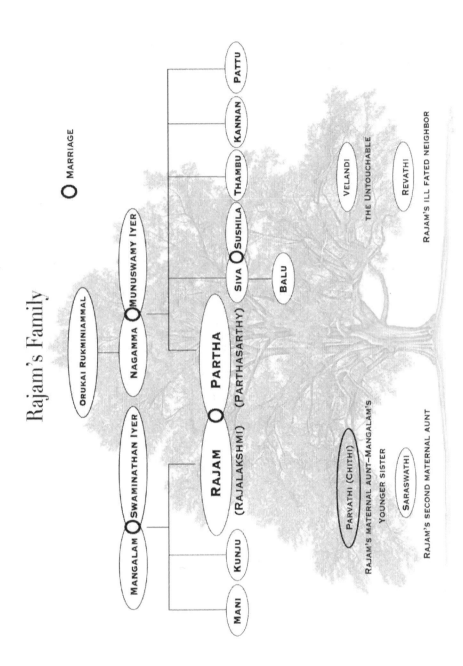

# RAJAM'S FAMILY

**Rajam:** (Rajalakshmi) A child bride

**Partha:** (Parthasarathy) Rajam's devoted husband

**Nagamma:** Partha's mother, Rajam's mother-in-law

**Munuswamy Iyer:** Partha's father

**Siva:** Partha's older brother

**Sushila:** Siva's wife

**Balu:** Siva's son from his first marriage

**Thambu:** Partha's younger brother

**Kannan:** Partha's youngest brother

**Pattu:** Partha's sister, Nagamma's only daughter

**Orukai Rukminiammal:** Nagamma's mother

**Swaminathan Iyer:** Rajam's father (Inspector)

**Mangalam:** Rajam's mother

**Kunju:** Rajam's older sister

**Mani:** Rajam's younger brother

**Parvathi:** (Chithi) Rajam's maternal aunt–Mangalam's younger
    sister

**Saraswathi:** Rajam's second maternal aunt

**Velandi:** The cleaner, belonging to a caste of untouchables

**Revathi:** Rajam's neighbor

# Dharmu's Family

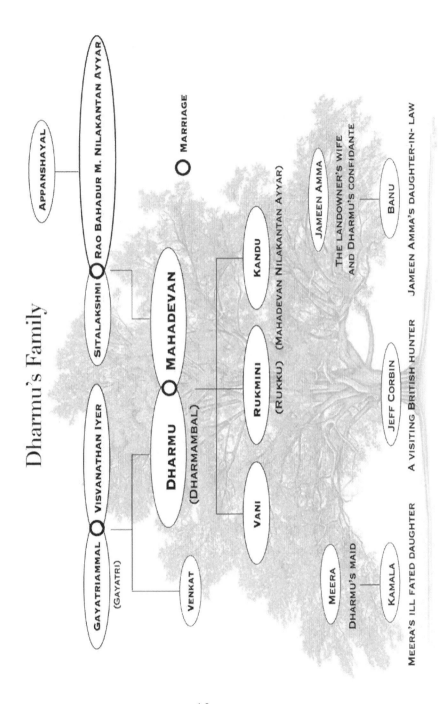

APPANSHAYAL

SITALAKSHMI ○ RAO BAHADUR M. NILAKANTAN AYYAR

○ MARRIAGE

GAYATRIAMMAL ○ VISVANATHAN IYER
(GAYATRI)

DHARMU ○ MAHADEVAN
(DHARMAMBAL)

VENKAT

VANI

RUKMINI
(RUKKU)

KANDU (MAHADEVAN NILAKANTAN AYYAR)

JAMEEN AMMA
THE LANDOWNER'S WIFE
AND DHARMU'S CONFIDANTE

BANU
JAMEEN AMMA'S DAUGHTER-IN-LAW

JEFF CORBIN
A VISITING BRITISH HUNTER

MEERA
DHARMU'S MAID

KAMALA
MEERA'S ILL FATED DAUGHTER

# DHARMU'S FAMILY

**Dharmu:** (Dharmambal) A child bride

**Mahadevan:** Dharmu's husband

**Kandu:** (Mahadevan Nilakantan Ayyar) Dharmu's son

**Vani:** Dharmu's oldest daughter

**Rukmini:** (Rukku) Dharmu's younger daughter

**Gayatriammal:** (Gayatri) Dharmu's mother

**Visvanathan Iyer:** Dharmu's father

**Venkat:** Dharmu's younger brother

**Rao Bahadur M. Nilakantan Ayyar:** Mahadevan's father

**Sitalakshmi:** Mahadevan's mother

**Appanshayal:** Mahadevan's grandfather

**Shankar, Dandapani, Ganesh, Kannan:** Mahadevan's brothers

**Meera:** Dharmu's maid

**Kamala:** Meera's daughter

**Jameen Amma:** The landowner's wife and Dharmu's confidante

**Jeff Corbin:** A visiting British hunter

**Banu:** Jameen Amma's daughter-in-law

When the Lotus Blooms

# When the Lotus Blooms

# Prologue

# RAJAM

The cramps began as a dull throb at the base of her belly and disturbed her sleep as they grew in intensity. Groaning aloud, she opened her eyes and sat up. The spasm had passed but she was wide awake. It was four o' clock in the morning. The sun had not yet risen but the air was hot and muggy, making rivulets of sweat run down her forehead, dampening wisps of hair that had escaped from her tight bun.

"Rajam, fetch the water." She heard the high-pitched drone of her mother-in-law, her daily morning alarm. Rolling up her thin mattress and blanket, she walked out into the courtyard. The moon was still visible low in the sky and she paused for a moment to admire the starry night. *The whole world is asleep, yet I have to awaken and attend to the morning chores,'* her mind protested. Rajam took slow, deliberate steps across the courtyard, breathing in deeply. She smelled the fragrance of the Night Queen still in full bloom, working to spread its perfume as she toiled to serve her family. Reaching the well, she picked up the bucket and guided it down until the splash of water broke the morning's silence. As she pulled up the bucket, the cramps in her lower belly intensified. She stopped to take a breath and heaved on the rope, praying she was only dreaming. The spasms were stronger, and then she felt the stickiness between her legs.

There it was again. Her dreaded monthly period. She filled a pot with water and crossing the stony courtyard, hurried toward the bathroom. Her breath came in sharp shallow gasps, with churning emotions pumping through her veins. Unwittingly, hot tears streamed down her cheeks and combined with her glistening sweat to create an ocean of disillusionment.

14

She was seventeen. Five years had passed since her marriage and she was still without child. Could it be true? Was she really barren? Maybe what her mother-in-law told her day in and day out was true. She was barren—as barren as a dry, dusty desert. She sank down onto her haunches, her tiny body racked with tears. She sat for what seemed an eternity, with her knees pressed against her belly, rocking back and forth. Then she stood and dragged herself to the dark and dreary room which would be her refuge for the next three days, with her agonized emotions as her solitary companion. Holding a pillow against her aching stomach, she rocked herself to sleep.

Hearing someone call out to her, Rajam stirred, slowly unfurling from the fetal position she had curled into to ease the pain. The whole room was bathed in sunlight that streamed in from the skylight. There was a hesitant knock on her door.

"Rajam, are you in there? 'Out of doors' again?"

"Yes," she replied despondently. She recognized her sister-in-law, Sushila's voice. Had she come to preen about her fertile womb? She was pregnant with her first child and her swollen belly impeded her ability to walk.

"I have some *upma* for you," she said, as she pushed the brass plate in. Sliding across the stone floor, it came to a clanging halt in front of Rajam. This was how she would be fed for the next three days. She was 'out of doors' and no one was allowed to come near her, lest her dirty presence pollute them. Rajam needed to use the toilet and announced her intention so Sushila could move out of her way. As she made her way back to the room, she poured water over the spots where her feet had touched the stone courtyard to cleanse the area, so other family members could walk through without fear of contamination. She sat down to eat breakfast, her mind protesting against being treated as though she were a leper. With a deep sigh she resigned herself to be alone: not talk to anyone, see anyone, or touch anything. On the fourth day, after a head bath, she would be permitted to reenter the house.

Ironically enough, Rajam smiled. At least she didn't have to hear her mother-in-law's annoying cackle. She could sleep all day and dream all night. She did not have to do any of her regular chores. Not clean the front porch with manure, or decorate it with a *kolam*, not cook in that steaming kitchen and not wash clothes. Nothing. Three days that

15

were hers to sleep, think and be herself. She reached out to the brass plate and put a morsel of the upma into her mouth. She could taste the buttery flavor of ghee on the roasted semolina, the onions and tomatoes. How nice to eat food cooked by someone else. These were times when she would make believe that she was a queen and the upma-servers her vassals. She would imagine that she was asleep on a velvet-covered *divan* adorned in the finest silks, bedecked in magnificently crafted gold and diamond jewelry.

The cramps were getting more severe now and she pressed her knees even harder into her belly. She began humming a lullaby her mother used to sing to her. It made the pain go away and when she closed her eyes, she imagined her mother's soft hands caressing her forehead, her face gleaming like freshly polished ivory, her twin diamond nose rings glimmering in the sunlight. Rajam almost smelled the fragrance of jasmine that had been braided into her hair. The haunting scent, combined with that of sandal paste, created a fragrance which she identified with Amma. How she wished she could go home and hold her for just a moment. That would make all her pain subside and everything would be fine.

But for now, the song would have to do.

# Part I
# Rajam

# CHAPTER 1 – RAJAM
## VIZHUPURAM – 1934

"Rajam… Rajam… *Shaniyane*! How much time will you take to bathe? You had enough time to rest and escaped working for three days last week. This is what annoys me about you. Rajam…do I have to call you five hundred times before you appear?"

Hearing her mother-in-law Nagamma's voice, Rajam froze, her heartbeat surging like a runaway train. She had enjoyed the respite for three glorious days without Nagamma to frighten her and make her jumpy and miserable, but now it seemed as though that had taken place a long time ago. Just hearing the sound of Nagamma's voice sent Rajam's thoughts into disarray. Completely confused, she dashed across the courtyard, hurriedly wrapping a towel around her wet hair. She was totally out of breath as she entered the kitchen. "Amma I'm so sorry…" she began.

Nagamma scaldingly interrupted her. "What do you mean sorry? Is that all you can say after my voice is hoarse calling for you? Go, collect the cow dung from the shed." Rajam hesitated, unable to bring herself to begin this distasteful chore, causing even more irritation. "What? Are you waiting for me to do it? Or shall I hire a servant for your majesty?" Nagamma stood up and walked over to her. Her taunting face towered over Rajam's diminutive form, making her shrink back in fear. She rushed out of the kitchen, utterly bewildered and nervous but grateful to escape from her mother-in-law.

Rajam's heart sank. She hated this task. She couldn't help wondering how it was supposed to be a privilege to collect cow dung and why it had to be her turn so soon. She had just bathed and her body shuddered in revulsion at the thought of the upcoming task. With great reluctance she opened the door to the cowshed. Immediately, her breath caught in her throat, her lungs overpowered by the strong

18

stench of manure. Unable to tolerate the smell, Rajam ran to get Partha's handkerchief, which she dipped in rose water. Then, tying it over her nose and mouth, she re-entered the cowshed. The task was vile but at least she wouldn't gag and retch while doing it. Lethargically, she picked up a basket and collected the droppings, shivers going down her spine, as her body reacted to its gooey texture. Scarcely breathing, she made her way out of the shed. Pulling the handkerchief off her face she walked to the entrance of the house for the second part of her chore: spreading the manure on the floor. She couldn't imagine how this foul smelling dung was a disinfectant, when it felt as though she was exposed to some infectious disease just by touching it.

She was almost done when Nagamma yelled out for her. A dollop of fresh cow dung flew out of her startled hand and landed on her face. Instinctively, she raised her soiled hand to wipe it off, spreading the greenish brown mixture all over her cheeks. Brown rivulets flowed down her neck and stained her blouse, as tears of frustration ran down her wet, dung-streaked cheeks. Just then, Nagamma walked out and looked at her. Rajam was mortified. She was assigned one task and even that she had messed up—literally messed up, and now she was staring up at her mother-in-law with cow dung all over her face. Nagamma sniggered in delight and called out to the family to come and see the show. "*Yenna Rajam, neeye moonjilai shaani pooshiniyaa?* Hey Pattu, Sushila, come here, you have to see this." Rajam turned her face away in utter humiliation and grabbed the basket in her trembling hands. It was uncanny how Nagamma always chose the most inopportune moments to appear. Fearing the shame from Nagamma's cruel tongue, she fled into the sanctuary of the cowshed, where she sat down and sobbed till her eyes dried out.

Rajam was so upset she hardly noticed the stench of the dung, which had been intolerable a moment ago. The cows looked at her with a bored expression, indifferent to her pain. "Stupid cows. Stop looking at me. It's your filthy droppings on my face. You think you're so sacred don't you? Well you're not. And your poop stinks." She paused, almost as if she were expecting a response and then continued angrily. "I hate her, I hate her I hate her!" Rajam ranted, completely out of control, pummeling the wall with all her strength. The cows merely mooed loudly, unaffected by her angry outburst. "*Nagamma, Snake Mother, Vicious Viper, Hooded Cobra, Striking Serpent!* I hate your large nose and your pock-marked skin. I hate you, do you hear me? And I hate your cows and I hate this horrible cow dung."

Rajam leaned back against the wall, her tiny body racked with tears. She had no idea why she was reacting like this. It was so out of character. Collecting dung was something she always did, so why was she feeling so overwhelmed? Venting her feelings felt good, especially with a mute audience. She could never dream of saying such things in anyone's face. If only she had the courage to say something to Nagamma; but no, that was not an option. To begin with, she was too timid and her upbringing didn't permit her to disrespect elders, even though it was warranted. Just seeing Nagamma made her shiver, and hearing her voice paralyzed her, leaving her tongue tied; so the question of replying to her never arose.

These last few years had been too much of a strain. She wanted so much to please Nagamma, to get one compliment from her but that never happened. No matter what she did, something always went wrong, and then there would be hurtful jibes. Adding to her already timorous nature was her obsession with her inability to conceive. She wanted so badly to have a child but her monthly sojourns to the back room were like clockwork. Now it had become a fixation which consumed her. Unmindful of her unhappiness, Nagamma always commented about her bleeding womb. She had become so attuned to Nagamma's reactions that even an exasperated look on her face, though unintentional, would set Rajam off, making her feel like a victim, the guilt overwhelming and the disappointment devastating.

She had to control her tears or else it would be one more win for Nagamma, not that she was counting. Thankfully, neither Sushila nor Pattu saw her looking like this. She still had one more part of this distasteful chore to complete and steered herself towards the back door. Still sniffling, consumed with self-pity, Rajam began the repugnant task of plastering the rest of the dung in large cakes against the back wall. She then peeled off the dry ones and carried them back to the cowshed to store for fuel.

Reaching the well, Rajam took a deep breath, determined to calm her nerves. She vigorously cleaned her hands and face with *shikakai* but no matter how much she scrubbed, her hands would smell of dung all day.

The kitchen was hot–very hot. It was two hours past sunrise but with the feverish activity in the kitchen, the heat was unbearable. The morning meal had to be ready at precisely 8:25 every day, when the men would sit down to eat heartily before setting off to work. By the time serving the meal was complete, half the day was over for the women of the household. Rajam hated the thought of working in the kitchen just after finishing the cow dung routine, but she had to help Sushila with the cooking or face Nagamma's wrath.

The menu was elaborate that day: drumstick *sambar*, tomato *rasam*, lentil *thogayal* (chutney), podalangai *poriyal* (stir-fry) and potato *masiyal* (mash). Rajam watched Sushila as she squatted on the floor with her left leg folded along the floor and her right leg propped up and placed on the wooden block to prevent it from moving. The blade was sharp and required a lot of skill to keep her fingers out of the way, but Sushila was an expert at cutting vegetables using the *aruvaamanai*.

Four women worked tirelessly in the kitchen with Nagamma acting the part of Master of Ceremonies. For Rajam and Sushila, the stress was unbearable. The rasam had to have a tangy lime taste with just the right amount of water, the sambar be thick enough and have the aroma of fresh curry leaves, and the vegetables cut identical, sliced thin and even, so no one could tell the difference between two slivers. In addition, there were a host of other chores they were attending to simultaneously. The two daughters-in-law complemented each other as they danced a *jugalbandi*: a dance duo, now stirring pots on the stove, then dashing off to the cowshed to make sure the milkman wasn't adding water as he milked the cows, rushing back to check the temperature of the bathwater and then squatting to cut vegetables on the aruvaamanai.

Rajam's heart was pumping extra hard in expectation of the 'Nagamma censure.' If Nagamma as much as whispered her name, it impacted Rajam like a deafening thunderclap, following which Rajam's heart hammered uncontrollably.

This morning Nagamma was relentless. "Rajam, did you heat the bathwater?"

Boom boom thump thump…

"Sushila, cut the brinjals thin and long, not round as you did the last time."

Boom boom thump thump…

21

"Pattu, stir the sambar. I don't want the vegetables in it to burn."
Only Pattu, Nagamma's daughter, responded by mindlessly humming a
tuneless song, completely unmoved by her mother's instructions. The
cutting, slicing, grating, stirring, pouring, mixing, running and
squatting, all in a hundred degrees temperature, created a total body
workout in this culinary spa. To make things worse, the kitchen had
just one small window on the ceiling for the smoke to escape. With
smoke and fumes everywhere, the soot blackened wall complemented
the soot blackened floor and Rajam's eyes watered incessantly, reacting
to the spice scented fumes.

It was 8:15. Time to add the finishing touches to the food. In a
small pan, Rajam watched the mustard seeds dancing in hot ghee and
sighed at the familiar sizzling *choiiiii…* when she poured it into the
sambar and the rasam. Now all that was needed was to add a squeeze
of lime in the rasam to end one morning's cooking. That only left the
afternoon and evening cooking but it wouldn't be as long, tiring, or
complicated.

Rajam winced as she squeezed the lime into the rasam. The acid in
the lime penetrated a small cut on her cuticle. But then, curiously, a
smile lit up her face. Her mind wandered back to when a lime had
changed her whole life. Partha had narrated the story to her many
times but he never changed a word in each retelling.

She was only eleven years old when, unknown to her, Partha was
loafing around on the field in front of her school watching the fanfare
of Sports Day. Partha was in his final year of school and had three
months of vacation to prepare for exams. Not academically inclined,
he looked for any excuse to abscond from the house and spend some
time with friends hanging around the *maidanam*, or drinking tea in the
market place.

On this fateful day he was with his friends cycling past the school,
when he noticed a lot of activity in the front field. Being Sports Day,
students dressed in white and green were marching in groups around
the field. Having nothing better to do, he propped his bike along the
wall and went to get a closer look.

There she was, with skin like a pearl, slanted almond colored eyes,
her hair in two pigtails, tied with a green satin ribbon. Her white shirt

22

was tight over her prepubescent chest and her bottle green *pavadai* stopped just short of her slender ankles, accentuated by silver anklets. Partha absorbed all this in one glance, drunk with the onset of love that would last a lifetime. Just then, her pink lips parted, giving a brief glimpse of perfect white teeth, as she threw her head back to laugh at something her friend said. Partha had to get a closer look. He pointed to her and asked his friends if they recognized her. Vizhupuram was a small town and most people were acquainted with each other. He was surprised he hadn't seen her earlier.

"Oh her? I don't know her name but I know she is Inspector Swaminathan's daughter. Her younger brother, Mani, plays with my brother," someone commented.

By now Partha was visibly shaking, heady with unfamiliar emotions and sensations. As he drew closer to her, she skipped away on hearing the announcement for the next race, the fateful 'Lime and Spoon race.' There she was at the start line, right foot forward, her almond eyes focused on the lime balanced precariously on a spoon, held firmly in place between milky white teeth. Off they went. As Rajam crossed the finish line, she was completely unaware of Partha's piercing eyes and his longing heart secretly urging her on. Whether it was Partha's energy or her own skill, Rajam came first in the race and won a special place in Partha's heart.

He had to meet her. But how? He was seventeen years old, definitely marriageable age. But how was he to approach her? He could not actually go up to her and speak with her directly; that wasn't acceptable behavior. Then how was he to meet her? His mind whirled with a million unanswered questions popping into his head every second. One thing he knew was, if he had to marry, then it would be to this girl. The 'Lime and Spoon' girl.

The next few days were long and weary, with strategies made, vetoed and then replaced, as Partha was consumed with finding the right course of action. He sat on the terrace with his math book open, rehearsing walking up to his mother and saying, "Amma, I think I want to get married." That sounded too brazen. Then he switched to a more casual tone saying, "Amma, do you know Inspector Swaminathan?" That was too random. No matter what he tried, it just did not sound right. He had to make sure that he had an impeccable Plan A, so he did not have to resort to Plan B, which was marrying someone else.

After three full days of practicing, he decided the best course of action was to confide in his brother, Siva, who had been married for many years, and have him plead and present the case to their mother. That night, Partha brought Siva to the terrace after everyone was asleep and talked to him. At first, he felt sheepish and awkward talking about marriage, guilty about being preoccupied with a girl when he should have been studying, but the nature of the problem demanded urgency.

"Siva, you have to help me. I am going out of my mind."

"Why? Did you fail your exams again?"

"No it's not about school. It's about…a girl."

Siva smiled. "What's up Partha, met someone you like?"

"Yes," Partha said bashfully. "And I need you to talk to Amma about it."

"Why me? Why don't you ask her yourself? After all, you are her *chella kutti*. I'm sure she would oblige."

"I may be her favorite but I feel nervous about asking her. You are older and married. Coming from you, it will seem as if the whole thing was your idea. You know how Amma feels about boys loafing around. She won't take me seriously."

For the next fifteen minutes, Partha talked non-stop about the pros of Siva talking to Amma, and the cons of talking to Amma himself. So intent was he on convincing Siva, he barely took time to breathe. After Partha's monologue, Siva smiled and patted him on the back, urging his brother to calm down and take a deep breath if he wanted to live to attend his own wedding.

Partha was overjoyed.

# CHAPTER 2 – RAJAM
## VIZHUPURAM – 1934

Rajam was jolted out of her reverie by hot rasam boiling over and spilling onto the flames, causing them to rise in an angry, orange, mini inferno. It was time to serve the men their meal and she had been lost in thought, filled with memories of her husband, Partha. Sushila brought the banana leaves in and was in the process of cleaning them before laying them out on the floor. The five men sat down. Following a routine typical of a Tamil Brahmin household, Nagamma began by pouring water into the brass tumblers and serving rice and ghee on the banana leaf so the men could perform the prayer ritual before commencing the meal. They initiated the prayers by pouring water around the banana leaf to prevent insects from climbing onto it. Then, putting one grain of rice in their mouths, recited each of the sacred names of *Vishnu*, thereby energizing the food with *prana* that would nourish the body and the soul. As they all chanted the sacred *Gayatri Mantram* in unison, Rajam and Sushila served the rest of the food: piping hot sambar, with drumsticks floating in its curried sauce, followed by rice with tomato rasam, and finally to cool the system down, rice with yoghurt. Vegetables: snake gourd stir fry, mashed potatoes and crisp fried appalaams on the side completed the meal. The men ate heartily and then got ready to leave for work.

Nagamma's husband, Munuswamy Iyer, worked as a clerk in a law firm and had to reach work by nine in the morning; so he left the house with Siva, who was a stenographer for a businessman and started work at the same time. Both offices were next to each other and only a short walk from the house. Partha worked at the local school as an elementary teacher after completing his Intermediate year at college and the two younger boys, Thambu and Kannan, were still in secondary school. Altogether, the men brought in a princely sum of fifty rupees every month. Now that Nagamma's daughter, Pattu, had moved away with her husband, there were fewer mouths to feed, yet the family was stretched for money by the end of the month.

Nagamma hailed from a very wealthy family that owned a lot of land in Vizhupuram. For several years before the boys grew up, rice and wheat from her fields kept their bellies full. Even the cows were part of Nagamma's dowry. Nagamma was stringent and somehow able to ensure no one ever went hungry. She controlled the income and saved whatever she could from the sale of produce to use in difficult times. Their lifestyle was simple and no extravagances were tolerated. Now Siva had taken on the family responsibility and it was largely his salary running the household. Of course, control of all family finances was still in Nagamma's competent hands. She took pride in maintaining the household on a shoestring budget and never let anyone forget that.

That afternoon, Sushila and Rajam sat in the back courtyard, the only portion of the house with shade from the blistering afternoon sun. Nagamma was asleep, as was Sushila's stepson, Balu, so the girls had the house to themselves. Rajam could not sit still; she kept fidgeting with the end of her sari, the constant movement a result of her overactive thoughts. Of late, she found it difficult to focus on anything, her mind racing ahead, thinking about the next chore.

"Hey Rajam, what's the matter? You can rest now; the serpent is asleep. Why are you so agitated?"

Rajam smiled, a little surprised at Sushila's insight into her mental state. "I just don't understand how a woman can be so domineering. I try so hard to please her, yet she is never happy with me."

"That's just it, Rajam, don't try so hard. Try and relax. Nagamma will never be satisfied, so no matter what you do, you will hear some comment. If you are so tense, how can you conceive a baby? I don't let her bother me. I just go about my work without thinking of her reaction. Try to be like that." Sushila gave her the same advice from time to time but Rajam did not know how to dissociate herself from Nagamma. "I wish I knew how to do that. I just feel terribly nervous around her. I don't want her to be angry with me all the time."

"Stop trying to please. That is how she is, and that is how she was brought up. She learned all of that from her mother. You know about her don't you?"

"Orukai Rukminiammal? Yes, Partha always talks about her. He is so proud of her, always saying how amazed he was that a lone woman could run the plantation singlehanded."

Orukai Rukminiammal. Everyone spoke of her with respect. Rajam had heard different stories from everyone in the family and in her mind pieced together a fine image of what she must have been like.

Rajam knew that Rukminiammal married into a very wealthy family of landowners, *Mirazdars*, who owned land as far as the eye could see. Rukminiammal was widowed early in life and her only daughter, Nagamma, with five children—four sons and a daughter—moved in with her. She ran the farm with an iron hand. She was everywhere: in the fields, in the cowshed, at the market, or handling the accounts. In addition, she cooked for her family and cared for her daughter, instilling in her values of honesty, diligence and the benefits of incessant hard work.

In spite of their wealth, the family lived a simple lifestyle. The house was large with ample space for everyone. Behind the house was a huge cowshed with thirty-forty cows. Till her last days, Rukminiammal milked the cows, even though there were many cowhands hired for that very purpose. Rajam wondered how she did that, considering she had only one hand.

Perhaps Sushila was right in saying Nagamma inherited this streak of dominance from her mother, whom she saw as the powerful matriarch, always in control. All this in spite of having only one hand, which was what gave her the name Oru kai Ammal — the one-handed mother. Rukminiammal was almost a legend in that area and there were many anecdotes explaining the mysterious loss of her hand.

"I say, Sushila, do you know the actual story behind her missing hand?"

"Hmm… not really; several stories float around but Nagamma said something about her chasing a thief through the fields, only to have her hand cut off with a giant *aruvaal* in the ensuing struggle. The curved knife sliced her arm below the elbow and it was a miracle she survived." Rajam winced at this new tidbit on the matriarch.

Sushila rubbed her swollen belly and straightened her back, grimacing in pain.

"What is it? Sushila; are you alright?" asked Rajam.

"Nothing. I thought I felt pain in my belly and back but it was just a spasm and it has passed now. Getting back to Nagamma, she may be strong like her mother but she is certainly not generous. At the plantation, on the front *thinnai*, there were three large earthen jars: one was filled with water, the second with buttermilk and the third with *pazhayadu*. Anyone passing by could drink and eat out of these jars irrespective of their caste, be they farm laborers, or visitors."

Rajam jumped to attention as she was reminded of an unfinished chore. "Thanks for reminding me. I have to soak the old rice in water for the men to have pazhayadu tomorrow." As she scampered off, Sushila muttered, "Rajam, Rajam, always worried about doing this and doing that. You can never sit still for a moment."

Later, the family was relaxing on the terrace after the evening meal enjoying the cool breeze and moonlight, a routine they followed before retiring for the night. Rajam could not focus on the conversation. She was anxious because she knew that tonight was her turn to use the bedroom. The house had only one bedroom with any semblance of privacy and the two brothers took turns using it.

While Rajam lit the lantern, Sushila rolled out the bedrolls in the central hall. Nagamma slept in the middle with her sons and husband on one side and the daughters-in-law and grandchild on the other. Rajam was sweating profusely. The humidity was high but more importantly, she was waiting for the evening drama to unfold. While everyone lay down, Partha stood in one corner of the room, fidgeting and edgy, waiting to catch his mother's eye for permission to use the room. Watching his discomfort, Rajam closed her eyes tight, wishing that magically she were somewhere else, not having to go through this. Nagamma was aware of Partha desperately signaling to her but took her own sweet time to acknowledge his presence. With a sheepish smile, he bent his head, his palms pressed together, almost begging for permission. Only his eyes reflected his embarrassment. Rajam noticed the two younger boys exchange meaningful looks.

"Hmm… *Pohalaam*," Nagamma said finally, to Partha's relief. Partha stood at the doorway of the bedroom, now signaling to Rajam. Her heart fluttering, Rajam raised her eyes to look at Nagamma for her consent. But Nagamma had turned her back to Rajam, and now she was forced to verbalize her request, which she did in an almost inaudible whisper. "*Pohalaamaa Amma?*" Pretending she didn't hear, Nagamma didn't reply, making Rajam repeat her question, this time a

28

little louder. The two boys sniggered, taking pleasure in watching her squirm. Beads of perspiration formed on Rajam's upper lip. She felt like a sparrow trapped in the coils of a boa constrictor, never knowing if she would be crushed or allowed to fly free. Would the serpent be in a benevolent mood and assent, or would she take pleasure in demeaning her? The silence in the room was deafening and everyone had their ears perked waiting for Nagamma's decision. "Hmmm…" Nagamma said at last, signaling with her hand that Rajam could go. Blushing in embarrassment, Rajam slunk out of her bed and headed towards the room. As she reached the doorway Nagamma added, "Only because I want that grandchild," reminding Rajam that sex was for procreation, not for pleasure.

Rajam's face turned red. She hated sexual references, especially coming from Nagamma. It took away from the joy of intimacy. She could hear the boys muffling their laughter and her shame was overwhelming. This was the only time she and Partha could be alone, and Nagamma controlled that part of their lives too. It was as if her whole life centered on Nagamma and not her husband. Amma was wrong. Your husband was not the most important person for a married woman; it was your mother-in-law.

As she closed the door behind her, she turned to Partha, "*Yenna*, please don't do it more than once. I have to go out and bathe each time. Last week after you made me bathe three times in one night, the boys were giving me looks the next morning, and Sushila commented too. I have been sneezing all of last week because of the cold water baths." Nagamma told her that it was divine punishment for her carnal sins but Rajam didn't want to complain to Partha about his mother and spoil a perfectly good evening.

But Partha did make her bathe twice that night, and as she walked to the well and stared at the cold water, she cursed her destiny. Crouching down, she poured the water over her body as silently as possible. Even so, each splash shattered the silence of the night, the sound symbolizing her shame. She was sure to hear a comment tomorrow about this, but that would happen tomorrow and she would deal with it then. She was too tired and needed to sleep. When Rajam crawled back into bed, Partha was snoring. Grateful for the reprieve, Rajam closed her eyes, hoping to get a few hours of rest before the activity of the morning began.

# CHAPTER 3 – RAJAM
## VIZHUPURAM – 1934

"Come on. Clean up. What are you dawdling around for?"
Nagamma's voice boomed. Not wanting to hear anything more, Rajam
quickly cleared the banana leaves and threw them in the garbage. She
swabbed the floor, making absolutely sure there was not one morsel
anywhere. Satisfied with her handiwork, she wiped her wet hands on
her sari and ran in to get a quick word with Partha before he left for
work.

Rajam watched Partha dress in a white *veshti*, the muslin lower
garment and a crisp white shirt. She handed him the *angavastram* and he
draped the top cloth on his wide shoulders. Rajam watched him apply
*vibuthi*, drawing three straight lines across his forehead with the sacred
ash. Fragrant *chandanam* and bright vermillion *kumkumam* he drew in
perfect concentric circles in the center of his forehead. Partha noticed
her looking at him and tried to steal a forbidden kiss but Rajam pushed
him away in panic.

"*Yenna*, can I go and visit my parents this month? I haven't seen
them in a while." Before Partha could respond, they heard a wail from
the kitchen. The family converged there from all corners of the house,
where, to everyone's horror, Sushila was supine on the floor, lying in a
pool of blood. She was only in her seventh month and the baby wasn't
due yet.

Nagamma took charge, ordering Siva to carry her to the room,
while Kannan ran to fetch the midwife. Amidst feverish activity
around her, Sushila was screaming in pain. Everyone was running
around trying to help but not managing to actually do anything. The
contractions had begun in earnest, and Nagamma was absorbed in the

30

task of cleaning her while Rajam prepared hot water as they waited for the midwife to arrive.

Vizhupuram was a small town and the Ayurvedic *Vaidhyar* was the medicine man for everyone, making potions, or *kashaayams*, out of different herbs. The midwife took care of all pregnancies, assisted ably by the older and more experienced women of the household. With no doctors nearby who practiced western style medicine and the nearest available hospital two hundred miles away in the city, there was no viable option other than calling the midwife. It was a long two-day trip by bullock cart to see an 'English Doctor.' Siva knew they didn't have time to make that trip. Instead, they would have to rely on the midwife's expertise. He was afraid because he knew childbirth was the most common reason for mortality in women, especially after delivery, when they were particularly vulnerable to many infections after giving birth in a dark room with no fresh air or sunlight. Siva lost his first wife during childbirth. When the baby was born, her grandmother insisted that she not bathe for eighteen days, as this was considered to be an unclean period. Especially weak after childbirth, this increased her propensity for disease and infection, ultimately resulting in her untimely death.

Once the midwife arrived, everyone was shooed out of the room. It did not look good. Siva was silent, staring out of the window. The death of his first wife made him more afraid for Sushila. He closed his eyes and prayed she should not follow in her sister's footsteps, who died under most unfortunate circumstances. Balu, his first-born male child survived, and Siva was forced to remarry so this child could get a mother's love. After a lot of pressure from his mother, he married his wife's sister Sushila, so there would be no jealousy if the new wife had other children. And now this. Would Sushila survive? The neighbors were already gossiping in hushed whispers about Siva being a wife killer. Siva thought to himself: *Jackals may howl but why should the moon care?* Sushila took very good care of Balu and now she was eagerly expecting her own children. She was patient and loving and did not deserve a miscarriage.

Siva marveled at destiny. He was only twenty-three years old and already married twice. He must have done something awful in his previous life to deserve so much heartbreak. Times were bad in Vizhupuram and it was difficult to get a well-paying job. He could not

31

think of moving away, as it was his salary that largely contributed to the family income. Partha did not earn very much as a school teacher, and the other brothers were still too young. His father lacked initiative, content with the job he held for years. The morning had taken off on an even note and in minutes the whole situation had changed.

After what seemed an eternity, the midwife came out and told them the baby was stillborn but the mother was doing well. There was partial relief for the family. At least God spared Sushila's life and as for the child, it was not destined to live. It was their fate, or karma, and one had to accept all events — good or bad — as part of Lord *Krishna's Leela*, his cosmic game. Nothing was in their hands; everything was ultimately God's will. Siva was despondent but he knew he would have to be strong for Sushila's sake. Young Balu was sure to have other siblings. Right now, he needed to be composed and take charge. After all, he was the oldest son, and this was expected of him. He sighed deeply and went into the room to console Sushila.

# Part II
# Dharmu

# CHAPTER 4 – MAHADEVAN NILAKANTAN AYYAR (KANDU)
## DINDIGUL – OCTOBER 8TH, 1929

The room was hot. Suffocating and hot. It was the 8th of October, and the rains had come and gone but the heat was unbearable. Gayatri filled the room with incense, knowing that the sulphur in it was healing, but Dharmu could not breathe. The pains in her belly and back were intolerable. She had been in labor for two days but the baby was not yet ready to face the world. The midwife looked worried. Dharmu was young but she had been in pain for a long time and pushing for three hours. The midwife noticed Dharmu was tired, not having eaten the whole day. The baby should come soon but this was going to be difficult labor.

They were in the town of Porambur near Dindigul, on a plantation called the *Ponni Malai Jameen*. Dharmu's father, Visvanathan Iyer, worked as the plantation manager for the local *Jameendar*, a landowner whose prosperity and generosity was legendary in these parts. Dharmu was here in the care of her mother, Gayatri, for the last month of her confinement. Her husband, Mahadevan, could not get away from work but was expected soon. It was customary for women to go home to their mothers' to deliver babies and this was the third time Dharmu had come here for that very purpose. There were no doctors nearby and Visvanathan was worried. He sat outside swatting mosquitoes, asking every five minutes if Dharmu was all right. She was his only daughter; or rather his only legal daughter, and he knew that here in the countryside women died from childbirth all the time. The midwife was experienced and had delivered hundreds of babies. She was also the wife of the local Vaidhyar, the doctor who specialized in ancient herbal remedies. Maybe she would not need any of her

34

husband's medication and this would be over soon. It was strange. Dharmu had already safely delivered two baby girls, Vani and Rukmini. So why was her third taking so long?

He could hear Dharmu's pain-filled wail as she pushed through another contraction. The midwife came out of the hot, smoky room for some fresh air, while Gayatri crouched down next to Dharmu, wiping her face with a wet towel in between giving her sips of water. Another contraction. Gayatri sat her up and massaged her back gently, yelling at the same time for the midwife. The head had crowned. She could feel it. The baby's head was very large and covered with slime and hair. Lots of hair. With a head this size, he would probably be good at Mathematics like his father, Mahadevan. One more contraction and Dharmu screamed as her perineum tore, allowing the baby's heads to slip out. The bed was covered in blood.

"Mama, we are almost there, the baby's head is out. And it's a fair baby."

All the time Visvanathan kept breathing heavily, asking, "*Aacha? Aacha? Yenna kuzhandai? Aanaa penna?* Is it over? Is it a boy or girl?" But the ladies inside were too busy to answer. In a few moments he had his answer partly, when he heard the wailing of the newborn. In relief, his body slumped into the chair but he wanted to know if it was a boy, and he yelled once again, "*Aanaa penna?*"

The midwife held the baby in her arms. Ten fingers, ten toes, and yes, a generous bundle between the legs.

"*Mama aan kuzhandai* It's a boy!" Dharmu smiled weakly and held the suckling neonate to her breast. But the bleeding would not stop. Ten saris were soaked up with blood and if this continued, Dharmu might die. The midwife went to the corner and gathered some herbs from her *potlam*. Then she ground them using a mortar and pestle and put them into a pot of water to boil. After filtering the mixture, she poured the liquid into a tumbler and brought it to Dharmu.

"Drink, this will stop the bleeding." But Dharmu couldn't open her eyes. She had lost a lot of blood and her pulse was very weak. The midwife forced the liquid in, between her dry chapped lips. It was crucial to drink this kashaayam, this potion of herbs, if she were to heal. No one was thinking about the baby yet. The little boy was swathed in old clothes and kept on the floor while the ladies attended to the mother. Finally, after Visvanathan asked for the baby several times, his wife, Gayatri brought out the newborn and placed him in the strong, caring hands of his grandfather.

His eyes that had been tightly closed, now opened, and Mahadevan Nilakantan Ayyar, or Kandu, as he would affectionately come to be called, got the very first look at the world he had just entered.

# CHAPTER 5 – DHARMU
## RANGPUR, EAST BENGAL – 1934
## FIVE YEARS LATER

Dharmu came out of her bath wearing her *jacket* (blouse) and petticoat, her wet hair wrapped in a thin towel. She sat in front of her dressing table, the first part of her routine. Routine meant everything to her — when she bathed, how she bathed, what was soaped first and what came next. Everything had to be just so. Organizing gave some order to her life, making her feel she had control over something at least. She opened the first drawer and took out a small box in which she placed her jewels just before bathing. She picked up a soft piece of white muslin, remnants from her husband's old veshti, which had been cut into even squares. One by one, she took out her jewelry — diamond earrings, and the eight stone diamond *besari* and *mookuthi*. She painstakingly wiped the stem of the earrings and noserings and then polished the stones. When she felt they were clean enough, she proceeded to wear them.

It was hot in Rangpur. Even with the river nearby, the air was still, the climate always muggy. And when it rained, which was always but more so during the monsoon when the rain was incessant, the heat became unbearable.

"Meera, *dhuno laao.*" Dharmu was still grappling with Bengali. Although all the servants mainly spoke Bengali, they also spoke a Bengali version of Hindi, which Dharmu didn't understand. She could give basic instructions to the servants in Hindi but was fluent only in her mother tongue, Tamil. She ended up speaking a garbled mix of Hindi, English, with a few Bengali words thrown in.

Her husband, Mahadevan, on the other hand was a linguist. He could read and write in five languages. He learned Tamil and English early in life, and when he graduated from Presidency College in Madras, his command over the English language was perfected. It was here he developed a love for English poetry and could quote eloquently from Shakespeare and Byron. In his free time, he read voraciously and mastered all the Greek and English classics. It was essential to have complete mastery over English, the language of the rulers, especially since he planned to join the Indian Civil Service. Even more admirable, as a child he studied the *Vedas* and could chant passages from both the *Rig* and the *Sama Vedas*. This initial training sharpened his ability to read and memorize. After spending a year in Cambridge, on passing his Civil Service exams, he was assigned to the Bengal cadre. In a short period of time, he became fluent in both Hindi and Bengali. Exceptional intelligence combined with a natural flair made languages come easily to him.

Mahadevan was certainly a scholar with a gift of memory, a complete contrast to Dharmu, who was uneducated except for a few years of private tutoring before marriage. She was the antithesis of whatever he stood for. Her knowledge of written Tamil was rudimentary, just enough to write letters to her family. She was definitely not ready to be presented to his British peers and certainly not to his superiors. Mahadevan had decided he would have to train her to speak in Hindi, to at least be able to communicate with the servants and run the household. Now that her Hindi was better, she was learning English.

Poor Dharmu. She could just not roll her tongue around those alien words. Every time a new phrase came up, she wrote it down in Tamil and practiced phonetically all day.

*"Meera paani laao."* "Bring the water."

*"Khaana garam karo."* "Heat the food."

Just when she had built a reasonable repertoire of Hindi phrases, Mahadevan got transferred to Rangpur in East Bengal as the Assistant Collector. Now she had to deal with Bengali. She could not help thinking it would have been so much nicer if she had married someone with a comfortable job as a clerk in her native south, where she could speak Tamil. Life was not fair. You never got what you wanted, just what you deserved, which was not always what you needed.

Dharmu was in fact blessed. Very few Indians had the opportunities she did, or the lifestyle. She lived in a huge house with a battalion of servants, where she did not even have to lift a spoon;

38

someone always offered to do it for her. Most women would give anything to be in her place but for Dharmu this lifestyle was totally alien. She was brought up in a conservative Brahmin home and her formal education consisted of rudimentary reading and writing skills. Other than that, all she knew were basic household chores, skills redundant here in her new home, where there were servants who did it all. She married Mahadevan at the age of twelve and continued to live with her parents until she matured. In the meantime, Mahadevan went to England, absorbed in the grand task of preparing for the Civil Service exams.

When Dharmu got her first menstrual period, her parents took her to Nagarcoil, where the nuptials were arranged on Mahadevan's return from the U.K. Almost immediately after Mahadevan's return, she became pregnant. She delivered her first daughter, Vani, when she was only fifteen years old and her whole life then centered on raising her daughter. She was taught from infancy that she should spend her life devoted to her husband; his word was law and his wish her command. When she spoke to him it was only in monosyllables and the thought of crossing or challenging him never entered her mind. She was totally in awe of him. Though he was short and a little on the plump side, he exuded an air of confidence without ever being arrogant. His requests, though at times seemingly unreasonable, were made after careful consideration and always purposeful and directed, with a higher intent in mind. Dharmu was scared of him in some ways, and for the first few years of their marriage, never raised her eyes to meet his. It helped in the initial stage of her marriage; she was either with her in-laws or at her parents' for her confinement, limiting her interaction with him. Only after the birth of her second daughter Rukmini, did she move from Nagarcoil to live with Mahadevan in Bengal.

As instructed, Meera walked in moments later with the dhuno. She had just given Kandu a bath and left him in the care of the *bearer* while she heated coals on the stove. Meera brought the red-hot coals in an ornate brass container and sprinkled powdered incense over it, allowing fragrant smoke to emerge, filling the air with the pungent smell of sulphur. Every morning and evening it was Meera's job to prepare the dhuno and allow the smoke to fill the rooms. The sulphur in the incense acted as a disinfectant and its strong smell prevented mosquitoes from taking over the house. Rangpur was overrun with mosquitoes. At dusk, they rose from the stagnant marshes in droves, to feed on the helpless flesh of unsuspecting victims, at times, resulting in huge and fatal outbreaks of malaria. The dhuno was the only way to keep the mosquitoes at bay.

Twice a week, on Tuesdays and Fridays, Dharmu washed her hair using imported Yardley shampoo and Meera dried it and combed it into place. This was quite a job because Dharmu was blessed with an abundant head of hair. Without oil to flatten it down, her wavy tresses would swell outward reaching alarming proportions, rising to float almost parallel to the ground. Meera gently wiped her hair with the towel, squeezing out all the excess water. Covering the brass container with a coir basket, she helped Dharmu lie down, allowing the fumes to permeate her thick curtain of curls. Dharmu sighed and relaxed her tense shoulders, luxuriating in the heat emanating from the coals and the fragrance of incense.

Taking advantage of Dharmu's good mood, Meera began,

"*Memsahib?* Can I bring my daughter, Kamala, to stay here for ten days?"

"Why? Isn't your mother-in-law there?"

"No, Memsahib, she has gone on a pilgrimage. Kamala is only sixteen and I don't like her to be all by herself."

"What about your husband. Can't he take care of her?"

"No, Memsahib; he is away and Kamala has to be alone. Many men hover around with bad intentions. I don't want anything to happen to her." Dharmu coughed as the fumes became thick and Meera was quick to disperse the smoke with a palm hand fan. Dharmu was in a benevolent mood.

"Okay, go next week and bring her back. But make sure the cook's wife comes and helps when you are gone."

"Thank you, Memsahib. Kamala won't be any trouble. She is a good girl. She'll sleep with me and play with Kandu baba. Thank you, Memsahib."

Meera felt much lighter knowing that her daughter was going to be with her soon and she waved the fan energetically. In a few minutes, Dharmu's hair was bone dry and Meera took the brass container of incense to all the rooms, filling the air with its smoldering scent.

Dharmu went to her closet, her wooden *almirah*, to choose her sari. Her almirah was organization personified. Saris arranged in neat piles, each folded edge to edge in even rectangles, sorted by color, texture and design, and it was sacrilege to keep the blues with the reds. On the top shelf were Kanjeevaram saris with heavy gold embroidery, one pile for weddings and another with slightly less ornate work for less important occasions. On the next shelf were silk saris with checks and gold work. Next was the shelf for crepe saris, which had recently become very fashionable. Then, those for daily wear in plain colored silk with simple gold borders. Another shelf had satin petticoats in every conceivable color next to which were jackets arranged in two neat piles: velvet jackets for evening wear and white ones in fine cotton for daily wear. On the lowest shelf were shoes lined in order: slippers for the house, slippers for the bathroom, closed pointed satin topped shoes for evening wear, some with stone buckles, others ornately embroidered in gold and colored silken thread. Covered in muslin at the back of this massive almirah were colorful evening bags, each opulently decorated with colored stones and beads.

Since Dharmu was going to be in the house for the rest of the day, she chose a simple peacock blue sari with a magenta border. By the time Meera returned to make her hair, she had draped the sari in the more contemporary six-yard style, with the pleats in front and the *thalapu* or free end draped over the left shoulder. She had a few traditional nine-yard saris for religious occasions, preferring the convenience of the six-yard style for everyday wear.

Meera walked in just as Dharmu put a huge kumkumam *pottu* on her large forehead. Taming Dharmu's unruly hair was a complicated task. First she oiled it with fragrant, jasmine-scented coconut oil, pouring out just the right amount from the bottle. Carefully wiping it with a piece of paper, she placed the bottle back in its spot on the upper right hand corner of the dressing table. Next, she took out the comb from a box which had six hairpins, one hairnet and one round ring, each in individually wrapped muslin bundles. Combing was the most difficult task because the shampoo created tangles in her already wild head of hair. It had to be done in sections, with each lock of hair wrapped around her fingers so it would not pull on the scalp.

"Memsahib, the *maali* says that two men were attacked in his village. There's a tiger that has got the taste for humans. Maali says it is an old animal that has lost some of its teeth."

"I know. Sahib says there have been many attacks. He has asked for help from the government. They will send someone to take care of it. Don't worry, nothing will happen."

"I am not worried, Memsahib. The maali's village is ten kilometers away from mine. His village is surrounded by thick jungle. Last year, the maali's son was attacked by a tiger while he was grazing cattle. He tried to shoo the tiger away with a stick to save the cows. Imagine that! Very brave boy. The tiger bit him on his leg and he got a very high fever. They had to cut off his leg to stop the fever. Be thankful, at least he is alive, I told maali."

"I hope the tiger doesn't come near this house Meera. Make sure baba doesn't step outside the compound walls."

Kandu came prancing in just in time to overhear the last bit of the conversation.

"What tiger? Is there a tiger here? Can I see it?"

"No Kandu, no tiger here and no, you cannot see it."

When Meera inadvertently pulled a hair on Dharmu's scalp, she cried out angrily. "Be careful, Meera. You know how I hate it when you do that."

"Sorry, Memsahib," said a contrite Meera, not wanting to spoil Dharmu's mood.

Dharmu was not terribly patient and if by chance she felt the sharp pain from the comb pulling at the tangle, she would not hesitate to lash out at Meera, both verbally and physically. Once the knots were removed, Meera passed the hair through the round coil and twisted it in sections, pinning it in place with exactly six hairpins. She washed the comb with soap and water, wiping it thoroughly. Then she wrapped it in muslin and placed it in the same spot inside the box. After six months of scolding and training, Meera had perfected the routine and the whole process was completed without any untoward incident. She took the home slippers from the coat stand and placed them on the floor helping Dharmu to ease her feet into them.

The 'Queen of Rangpur' was now dressed and ready.

# CHAPTER 6 – DHARMU
## SOMETIME LATER

Dharmu walked out onto the verandah where breakfast was served. The verandah ran all around the house; every room had access to it. The breakfast table was in the front of the house, from where one could see the rising sun and admire the brilliant green foliage of the nearby forest.

She sat down on the cushioned, white wicker chair and surveyed the spread. There was oatmeal porridge, toast with yellow butter and marmalade and plenty of fruits – melon, golden yellow papaya, apples and grapes. Everything had been laid out perfectly: the porcelain plates and side plates, crystal glasses and pitchers and silverware. How life had changed. She was no longer the village bumpkin squatting on the floor eating off a banana leaf with her fingers and licking the back of her hands. No, now she had almost become a British Memsahib.

As she spooned the warm porridge into her mouth, Dharmu smiled, thinking of the first time she had used a fork and knife, clamping her hands around them like a fist, trying to attack the food, flinging it in the general direction of her mouth. She didn't get to eat much back then because Mahadevan's instructions were she could only eat the food that went into her mouth using the fork. How strange these foreign implements were! Wouldn't it be easier simply to use your fingers and put the food directly into your mouth than to try and juggle these strange tools, which were thoroughly useless to begin with? You could only stick the fork into a small morsel of food and by the time you got that fork to travel the distance to your mouth, the chunk would fall off. It was frustrating! Initially, she kept her face about an inch away from the plate, shoveling the meal into her waiting mouth to make sure the maximum amount entered her open and hungry orifice, but now she had learned to sit upright like a true English *Mem* and slide in delicate morsels through partly open lips. What an achievement! Finally, she could get up from the breakfast table with a full stomach.

She sat and watched Kandu play in the garden. He had put on a tiger mask made of real tiger skin, which Meera had brought for him from her village. There he was, prancing around on all fours, growling and purring, pretending to be a tiger, much to the excitement of their dog, Raja, who was yelping, barking and cavorting around Kandu. Dharmu smiled, marveling at Kandu's ability to amuse himself. She sighed and took a deep breath, taking a moment to admire her home.

The house sat on the outskirts of town close to the forest. It was situated within a huge compound enclosed by a high wall, with glass shards embedded on top to prevent thieves from climbing over. In the front was a small room where the *chowkidars* sat, as they guarded the house. There were always two of them at any time, changing shifts every eight hours, all Kandu's playmates. With no neighbors nearby, Kandu had no friends his age, so he was forced to make the battalion of servants at home his friends. He loved playing 'soldier,' his favorite game, with the chowkidars, although it peeved him that they would never lend him their guns. Kandu never stopped asking for it in case one of them relented under pressure.

Rangpur weather converted the garden into a verdant Shangri-La, with plenty of fruit and flowering trees. Of course, having a head *maali* with four assistant gardeners certainly helped. There were lime and tamarind trees, mango and pineapple trees, tropical frangipani, hibiscus and colorful bougainvillea, roses in every color imaginable and about fifteen varieties of jasmine. In one corner of the garden, vegetables grew seasonally: tomatoes and basil, curry leaves, snake gourd and all kinds of squash. The green, evenly mowed lawn was large enough to play golf on, though the family used it to play croquet. The maalis worked very hard; they understood and loved the garden, nurturing every plant as they transitioned from seed to flower. The rains made the colors even more vibrant but often it rained too much and then as the rivers broke their banks, the gushing waters would destroy the garden, reducing it to a soggy marshland. Then, when the waters receded, the maalis would begin afresh with renewed vigor, never despairing but instead simply working with nature, accepting her bounty and her wrath.

For this very reason, the main house stood on a raised platform. A flight of stairs went up along the front and the back of the house. The house was painted white, with green windows and doors. White wicker sofas and easy chairs, as well as wicker breakfast table and chairs, lined the front of the verandah. A spacious living room greeted guests as they entered through the front door. The red granite floor was covered in Kashmir silk carpets on which were placed European style, heavy, rosewood furniture. Dharmu had no real decorating sense, so the room remained simple with very little adornment. Leading out of the living room, the dining room held a magnificent teak table for twelve. One end of the room near the kitchen contained a pantry that the bearer used as he brought food from the kitchen to serve the family.

At the other end was a large powder room, with two doors for easy access from the living area as well. It had a washstand with a porcelain jug and basin as well as a thunder box. There was no running water in the house and the bearer made sure that the jug was filled periodically and ready for use.

Three large bedrooms occupied the right side of the house, all equipped with mahogany four-poster beds and mosquito netting. Each bedroom had its own bath area with a door to the verandah for the cleaners to access it without entering the main house. On the left of the house was Mahadevan's study with his large collection of books and a sturdy mahogany desk. Sometimes, when it rained too much, government work would be conducted from here. Since all the rooms had access to the verandah, the coming and going of people didn't disturb the family. Another bedroom for guests and a capacious storeroom flanked the study. The dark, cool storeroom contained several large meat safes — wooden cupboards with netting in front, perfect for storing meat, food grains and perishables. Dharmu did not go in here very often but she unlocked the room once a day so the cook could take out supplies. On bazaar day, she sat outside the room on a chair, keeping a close watch on everything that was taken in or out. Nothing could get past her eagle eyes. One couldn't be too careful. These servants were thieves.

The house lacked a *pooja* room, a prayer room, common in every Indian household. Nevertheless, in spite of being extremely westernized, Mahadevan was a devout Hindu. In his study he had a small altar with a silver lamp and vibuthi. He never failed to pray each day after his bath.

Kandu walked into the verandah wailing, "Mummyyyy... Rukku pinched me." He held out his arm, red and swollen where his sister Rukmini, or Rukku, as she was called at home, had pinched him. Dharmu lifted Kandu onto her lap and kissed his wound. Just a moment ago he was a brave tiger and now he was reduced to tears because Rukku had pinched him.

"What did you do?"

"Nothing. By mistake I tore her homework," he said, staring up at her with large tear-filled eyes. Dharmu smiled.

She knew there was no mistake here. Kandu was mischievous and always took advantage of Mummy and Daddy's adoration. He got away with anything he did, even if it was 'by mistake.' She thought of the many mistakes she had forgiven. By 'mistake' I punched her stomach, by 'mistake' I put a cockroach in her food and by 'mistake' I cut up her favorite dress. All was forgiven but then, Kandu was special. He was a male child, born to do great things like his father. The girls . . . well, they just needed to be cared for until suitable husbands were chosen for them.

Both Vani and Rukku knew this, although it was never openly discussed. Dharmu simply never had time for them. It was always 'Go find Meera. Go find the ayah. Go find someone else.' Meera did everything for them. She bathed them, told them stories, combed their hair and even put them to bed. They met Dharmu and Mahadevan only at mealtime and it was not polite for girls to talk with food in their mouths. Kandu however, could not only talk with food in his mouth but could also spit the food or feed it to the dog and Dharmu would laugh and say, "How sweet."

Sweet indeed! Vani always complained this was pure and simple favoritism. Since Kandu was never punished, periodically the girls would slyly pinch him. But his skin was so fair it would swell and create a telltale welt and they would be punished anyway. A lose-lose situation.

The chowkidar called out, *"Bhola Memsahib aa gaye."*

He was announcing the arrival of the English tutor, Mrs. Elizabeth Bowler. She had arrived at the gate by *tonga*, a horse-drawn carriage and the main means of public transport in Rangpur. It was not as classy as the phaeton, the covered carriage that Mahadevan used to go to work. The tonga had a tin cover and one had to climb in from the back and sit on the edge, letting the legs dangle, or simply sitting with them curled up under. Either way, the ride was bumpy but it was the fastest mode of transport in these parts for those who did not own a bicycle. Mrs. Bowler got out as elegantly as possible after a bouncy tonga ride, paid the driver and waved to Dharmu. She was out of breath as she carried her portly self up the stairs.

Mrs. Bowler was Anglo-Indian. On seeing her, Dharmu was immediately reminded of the nasty comments people in Calcutta passed about Anglo-Indians, calling them misfits, born as a consequence of a roll in the hay with a tea picker, or the result of spilled seed by some Englishman in an uncaring, drunken stupor. They rejected them as half-breeds but Mahadevan said that Anglo-Indians actually considered themselves superior to Indians, whom they called 'darkies.' Dharmu grew up in a community where caste purity was esteemed more than anything else and she felt sorry for them. An accident of birth left them hanging in the middle, unable to hobnob with Europeans and not caring to associate with Indians. Mrs. Bowler was fair skinned and Dharmu wondered if there was a Mr. Bowler. She could easily pass off as being white. Mahadevan knew many Englishmen, soldiers in the army who had Anglo-Indian wives. Dharmu wondered if they had gotten duped into marriage, thinking their wives were English ladies with impeccable genealogy. Thank heavens Mrs. Bowler was fair skinned. If she had been darker, the poor soul might have spent the rest of her life as a white person in brown skin, hating her color, her situation, her destiny but most of all hating the society she had the misfortune of being born into. Ironically enough, Dharmu envied Mrs. Bowler. She spoke English like an English Memsahib and made Dharmu feel like the misfit.

There were no schools in Rangpur and Mahadevan was hell bent on getting a decent education for the children. He knew it would only be for a short time, as ICS officers were transferred every few years. It was only a matter of time before they moved to Delhi or Calcutta, where there would be many schools to choose from. He was grateful to find Mrs. Bowler, who had moved to the Rangpur district to teach the Collector's children. When Mahadevan replaced the previous Collector, she was actually thankful for the job, even though it meant working for a 'darkie' family. Mrs. Bowler usually arrived at their home mid-morning, a little before noon. She first taught Kandu for an hour and then it was Dharmu's turn. Finally, the girls were taught English, Math and the Sciences until four in the afternoon.

"Awful weather isn't it?" she said to Dharmu. Then she turned to Kandu who did not look too happy. "Come on Kandu, time for school," Mrs. Bowler said cheerfully. Kandu ran in ahead of her into the dining room, where he normally spent the better part of the hour either under the table or behind the chair. Meera had to be around to periodically plonk him back into the chair. Of course, there were at least a couple of urgent toilet breaks.

"Come on Kandu; get out from under the table. That's a good boy."

"Mrs. Bowler, there's a spider under the table."

Then all hell broke loose, with Mrs. Bowler shrieking and flapping her dress around, with Kandu laughing in glee watching Mrs. Bowler's thighs jiggle. That took care of at least five or ten minutes. It was amazing how Kandu thought of different ways to avoid sitting down to study. The only time he sat for any length of time was when they did Math. Then he would stick his tongue out of the corner of his mouth and finish all the assignments in minutes. He always complained that Mrs. Bowler spoke too slowly. Actually, Kandu's mind worked too fast. At five, he could read sentences and do addition and subtraction problems and Mrs. Bowler just could not keep up with him.

When Dharmu finished her lesson, she stood up and aimlessly wandered around the house. She found herself sitting at her husband's desk staring vacantly out of the window. The boring sentences she had just read kept repeating themselves in her head like a broken record: "Peter and Kate, Peter sees Kate, Kate sees Peter Good morning. How do you do? Very well, thank you." *Why do I need to know this?* She was mentally exhausted spiritually drained. She looked at the sky — the same sky that perhaps her mother was looking at right now. Then her hand reached for a pen and she began writing.

*Dear Amma*

*Aneganamaskaaram. (my greetings to you)*

*I am well; at least my body is functioning the way it should. The girls are growing. Vani will turn twelve and Rukku is nine. But you know that. I am trying my best to be a good wife to Mahadevan but it is so hard. Life is good here. I have a dozen servants in the house but I feel so alone. I wish I could just lay my head in your lap and forget my problems. I try to be obedient and change my ways to please my husband but how can I wipe out five thousand years of culture, the rules you taught me, the values you gave me, in just a few years? I eat meat and I have tasted alcohol. I am so ashamed of myself I can't face God. I have stopped praying. What is the point? I feel so unclean eating the flesh of dead animals; I cannot go in front of his altar. I haven't been to a temple in three years. My children are growing up without any religion. What can I teach them? I don't understand anything anymore. How can I tell them to do all the things that I do, when it doesn't feel right? I don't know what is right anymore — to follow what you and Appa taught me? Or to listen to my husband? He isn't a bad man. He doesn't beat me like Meera's husband. She sometimes comes to work with a swollen eye and prefers to stay here, where she feels safe, hardly ever taking leave to go home. At least I don't get physically abused. But who will I tell about the turmoil in my mind. I can't tell Mahadevan. He would not understand. At least he lets me wear a sari and a pottu. Some of the ICS wives wear dresses and look foolish. I can't deal with the change. It is too much too soon.*

*My brain is full of new rules: how to eat, how to talk, how to sit. I can't sit on the floor and I can't talk at the dining table. I am always so tense, wondering if I am doing things right. At times I get so unhappy. I used to cry a lot but never after Mahadevan came home. I could not let him know how I felt. He would not understand. He works from his intellect, not his heart. He does what has to be done irrespective of how he feels about it. But I function from my heart, my emotions. I have cried so much, emptying my eyes of all their tears. Mahadevan is too busy at work. When he comes home, he eats and sleeps. He sleeps next to me but we hardly ever share any intimacy. I think I repel him. I am too dumb to be attractive to him. But I am trying. I am trying so hard. I long for someone to hold me, love me, or care for me. Only Mrs. Bowler visits me. All the other people here speak Bengali and English. I think I will slowly even forget Tamil. No one in these parts speak Tamil. My life has really changed. I am tired of eating soup and cutlets, chicken and fish curry. I long to sit on the floor in your kitchen and eat rasam and rice with my bare hands. The monsoons will be here soon. Maybe Mahadevan will send me to Dindigul. I don't even know why I am here. The servants can take care of everything. They don't really need me. Maybe if I learn English quickly Mahadevan will talk to me more. I am not a fit companion for him. He is so clever and I am so ordinary. Only Kandu lifts up my spirits. He is always full of mischief. He makes me laugh and forget all the things I have to do, all the things I have to learn. I have to become someone else. I cannot hold on to the old Dharmu. Maybe then I will be happy. But first I have to stop feeling sorry for myself. Amma, I can't send you this letter because it would break your heart to know that your darling daughter ate meat. But I feel better after writing this.*

Dharmu tore the letter into shreds and threw it in the waste bin. She picked up Kandu and carried him to the bed. Then softly, she sang to him a little ditty that she always sang to the children when she put them to bed.

*"Nini baba nini, makhan roti cheeni, so baba so ja, nini baba soja."*

"Sleep baby sleep, butter, bread and sugar, sleep baby sleep, sleep baby sleep."

# Part III
# Rajam

# CHAPTER 7 – RAJAM
## VIZHUPURAM – 1934

Rajam truly missed her sister-in-law, Sushila. Ever since her marriage into this family, Sushila had been her confidante and friend, always helping her, giving her tips and just being her companion and ally. She was the only one other than Partha who really understood her. The two women shared their moments of woe and happiness and Rajam was absolutely devastated by Sushila's miscarriage. Conceiving a child was difficult enough but to lose a growing baby in the seventh month was appalling. Poor Sushila. She was so looking forward to having her own children. Perhaps all the housework had been too much for her, although the elders said exercise was supposed to be good for a pregnant woman. Maybe the additional strain caused by Nagamma's mere presence made her miscarry. Even as she thought the worst of Nagamma, she knew in her heart it was not possible. Nagamma may be domineering and a wretch but she was not a sorceress and would never wish harm to befall her own grandchild. Perhaps this was just Sushila's fate and maybe next time she would be luckier.

Sushila was at her mother's home convalescing and the entire burden of the household fell on Rajam. The days seemed never ending and at night she collapsed in sheer fatigue into deep sleep. She barely had time to sit down and rest and by evening her feet were always swollen from exertion. She was tired of her name being called out and for a change, couldn't wait to get her periods. At least that way she would get a break, leaving Nagamma to deal with all the housework. Rajam chuckled at the thought.

She wiped the last of the vessels and rushed to change into a fresh sari. Partha had told her to be ready, as he was taking her to the market. Rajam enjoyed going there and browsing through the stores. Most of all she loved the bangle store. Sometimes the bangle seller brought special gold inlaid bangles from the north, which Rajam couldn't wait to add to her collection.

When she heard Partha coming in, she rushed out to the thinnai and looked apprehensively at Nagamma for permission to leave the house. Partha had already told his mother he was taking Rajam out, so she was thunderously silent. As they walked down the street they passed by their neighbor Muthu Mami's house. Rajam could see her daughter-in-law sitting in the thinnai weaving jasmines into a garland. Rajam had tried to make friends with her at the temple but she wasn't particularly friendly. As they reached the marketplace, Rajam saw the new priest from the temple with his wife and son. Rajam had not met her yet but she seemed nice. Somehow, with the burden of housework, there never seemed to be any time to go out and make friends. The only people Rajam met were those who came to their house. She made up her mind to change that. She could begin by befriending Muthu Mami's daughter-in-law and the priest's wife.

The marketplace was buzzing with activity and shopping was a pleasure, especially since she was with Partha. After finishing their purchases, they were walking home, when they heard the drone of a vehicle behind them, a sound not so common in these parts. Rajam covered her nose to prevent the dust that it raised from entering her nose, when to her surprise the van came to a halt right by her. She turned to see her father getting down from the police van. "Appa!" she screamed in delight and ran to him, hugging him tight.

"Hey Rajam, my *chella kutti*," said Swaminathan, rubbing his hand over her head gently and holding her close.

"This is a surprise. You should have told us you were coming," Partha added, beaming from ear to ear. He enjoyed his father-in-law's company. He was friendly and full of anecdotes and always excellent company. Recently, Inspector Swaminathan's visits were drastically reduced ever since the family shifted to the nearby town of Chidambaram.

"Well, I had some official work in the next village and thought I would stop by and see my chella kutti, whom I haven't seen for a month now."

"I'm glad you did, Appa. We were just going home for dinner. Will you join us?" Rajam survived the first few years after her marriage because of her father's regular visits to their home. Living in the same town, she was also able to see her mother frequently and share her problems with her and take her advice. The unconditional love showered on her by her parents relieved her burden and made Nagamma's nagging much more tolerable. Now their meetings needed to be planned and since Nagamma did not approve of her spending too much time with her parents, she only went for a week at a time. Seeing her father was such a treat, she couldn't stop smiling.

"Why not, Rajam, I would love to join you for dinner if it isn't a problem — In fact, why don't you both get in? I can give you a ride home." Rajam got into the back of the van, excited to ride in an automobile, something she hadn't done in a long time. Here in the village no one possessed cars. The *vilvandi* or bicycle was much more useful on the bumpy roads. The van took the corner and turned onto the street where Rajam had grown up.

"*Appa*, can we stop here?" Rajam asked excitedly. "I haven't seen this place in so long." The house was unoccupied and looked rundown. Rajam opened the rickety green gate, which creaked just like she remembered. "Appa, do you remember how Mani and I would swing back and forth endlessly on this gate?"

"Yes I do. And you trained Baby to do the same," he said, referring to his grandchild — his older daughter Kunju's first born.

Rajam looked at the bare thinnai. It was filled with so many colorful memories. She remembered a time when the thinnai was adorned with one wood and rattan easy chair, Appa's favorite, where he would spend hours just sitting and talking to visitors, fanning himself with a coir hand fan. The thinnai belonged to Appa. It was his regal durbar where he reigned. This was where he met his friends, listened to local gossip and entertained them, while Rajam and Mani sat behind the door to eavesdrop. "You know, as a child I always wondered why Amma never sat outside with you when you had visitors. Even when she came out to serve coffee, she always had the end of her sari covering her arms and never sat down to talk to anyone, merely handed the coffee over the threshold for you to serve your friends."

"Her upbringing is different. It was not polite to talk with men. I know you have modern rules and you speak with Partha's male friends but our generation cannot give up some things."

Swaminathan sighed as he nostalgically recalled happy memories in the house which was their home for several years. Turning to Partha he said, "Every day I returned from work, parked my bicycle in the compound and removed my dusty shoes and socks. Right here, Mangalam always kept a huge brass pot filled with water, where I washed my hands and face. I remember thinking that along with cleaning of dust and dirt, I cleansed my spirit and washed away the weariness of the day's work. Then I kept my shoes on a rack and my constable collected them later in the evening to polish and shine. Mangalam always waited for me with a tumbler of hot filter coffee in her hands. I would hand over the string of jasmine I bought for her and then sink into the easy chair." His eyes were wistful, in spite of thinking about something as mundane as cooling his coffee and pouring it from tumbler to *davara*, two containers of shining silver. The further apart his hands went, the more the coffee would froth.

Just then, the old caretaker ran up to them and on recognizing the Inspector, was all smiles and salutes. As he unlocked the main door, Rajam ran towards the *mutram*, the open rectangular courtyard. The central *tulasi madham* was still there, though the plant had wilted a while back. She smiled as she thought about how her brother, Mani, and she ran around the cement pot for hours, pretending to reach out but still ensuring they didn't touch any part of the basil shrub. Amma said it was sacred and you could only touch the leaves after a bath. Even though Kunju was several years older, she would play hopscotch in the mutram with Rajam and Baby. The images flashed by her in vivid colors almost as if no time had lapsed. Such simple yet pleasant memories of them pottering around in the mutram, their bright clothes, pavadais and *chattais*, contrasting sharply with the dull grey slate floor. Partha walked in just then. "*Yenna* Rajam? Lost in memories?"

Rajam walked towards the raised parapet which bounded the mutram on all sides. She stood by the spot where there used to be an antique swing, recalling how Mani and she routinely launched themselves onto it much to their mother's horror. It was a wonder it lasted so long. "You remember the swing, the Tanjore *oonjal* that was

55

kept on this side? Of course you do. We sat here silently every time you came to visit," Rajam said with a naughty smile. Partha raised his eyebrows and rolled his eyes not wanting to remember that unsettling period of their marriage. That was before Rajam got her period, when she continued to live with her parents and he visited her daily. Rajam continued, "Somehow this place looks so empty. The mutram was the center of activity in this house. This was where Amma dried the chillies and aired the bedrolls. Every week something else was out, roasting in the bright sunlight. I loved to help make the *appalaam* and *vadaam*. Amma kneaded the dough, rolled and flattened it till it was paper-thin. Then we arranged them in straight lines on white sheets. Every five minutes I would be back to see if they were dry." Rajam's eyes were glistening with tears as she thought about her happy childhood.

Noticing she was sad, Partha herded her towards the entrance. "Enough walking down memory lane for one day. It's getting late for dinner. We should leave."

# CHAPTER 8 – SWAMINATHAN
## A SHORT WHILE LATER

Nagamma saw Rajam and Partha walk in and she launched into a tirade, "About time you love birds…" when she saw the Inspector entering the house as well. Immediately her demeanor transformed and she welcomed him in. *"Vango vango Sammandhi ..."* Rajam escaped into the kitchen, thankful that her father had saved her from listening to an hour-long lecture.

While waiting for dinner, Swaminathan picked up a newspaper to browse through. It was last week's edition of Swadeshimitran, a newspaper conceived in Madras which was gaining popularity in many parts of south India. It was the first patriotic newspaper to be printed in Tamil and one of the most powerful tools in the spread of Nationalism in the south. He looked up as Rajam walked in to tell him dinner was served. "There's going to be a *morcha* this week. Did you know that?"

"Hopefully it will be a peaceful one. Remember the one Velu organized ten years ago?"

Swaminathan remembered it only too well. "That is not a memory I want to hold onto," he replied somberly.

"I know how you suffered. I was only a child but I recall that monsoon night so clearly. The windows were open and I remember listening to the steady drumming of rain." As Rajam said this, she recalled the scent of jasmine from her mother's hair and of fresh earth that came with the first rains. Amma was with them, putting them to sleep with another story about Lord Krishna. She loved Krishna stories. He was so human, so naughty, the stories made her giggle. She must have heard them a million times but never tired of listening.

They were still under the spell of Krishna when someone came to see Appa. It sounded like Velu. Rajam heard the creak of the front door opening. And then voices. Amma paused to listen but it was hard to hear anything. She looked worried.

"Don't make me do this. Cancel your morcha!" Swaminathan yelled. Then more voices, followed by the sound of thunder and rain. Amma walked to the entrance where she stood behind the door quietly. Her hand went to her heart and she sighed deeply. Rajam knew something was amiss. She called out to her mother to finish the story but Amma wouldn't speak. She left without revealing how Krishna finally killed Pootani[1]

"I remember you locking yourself into the prayer room all of the next evening and into the following week. I knew something was wrong but you never told me what it was."

"No, I didn't," Swaminathan said with a finality which told Rajam she would not hear the rest of the story.

After dinner, Swaminathan climbed into the van, ready for the long drive back home. In his hand was the copy of the newspaper, crushed in a vice grip. He didn't want to think about that evening but no matter how hard he tried, the memories kept flooding in.

He had been on his way home from work and as usual had gone by the temple to buy a garland of jasmine for his wife, Mangalam. Navigating the narrow streets of Vizhupuram on his bicycle, he stopped at the temple crossing. The flower vendor measured one *mozham* from the elbow to the tip of her fingers, while Swaminathan leaned his bike against a tree. The flower vendor was everyone's source for village gossip. No sooner had he paid her than she delved into,

"Did you hear Ramanathan Saar has fixed up the marriage of his third daughter? They got an excellent alliance from Mayavaram. The family has lots of land there."

Swaminathan wasn't really interested, so he nodded perfunctorily and turned to leave, when more friends greeted him. "Inspector Saaaar.

---

[1] Pootani, a demon sent by King Kamsa to kill her nephew Krishna, met her destiny instead at the hands of baby Krishna

Wait for me." Srini, the local fruit vendor came puffing up to Swaminathan.

"Are you aware that Velu has joined the Indian National Congress, and is planning a morcha next week?" Now this was pertinent news. In the last few years the freedom movement had percolated into the south of India and piqued the interest of youth in the area. People talked about Gandhi and Patel in hushed whispers in case any police informants were lurking around. The INC had just opened a small office in Vizhupuram, with membership of around twenty people, mainly unemployed youth. Even though the British banned public meetings and demonstrations, they took place nevertheless in almost every village in India. Fiery speeches made at street corners and village plazas exhorted people to rise against the foreigners and demand freedom from the British. Many spectators responded to their emotional pleas for support by joining the movement.

Swaminathan wanted freedom for his country but he was in a delicate position. He worked as a British servant and his job provided his family with housing and food and possibly a pension when he retired. A morcha, a demonstration, meant he would have to be there and maybe even order a 'Lathi Charge' to dispel the crowd, though it pained him to do this. Every time the constables lashed out with their heavy wooden batons or lathis, he felt the pain in his soul. But what use was that? He had a job, this was part of his duty and he had to do it or else his family would suffer.

"Do you know this as factual?" asked Swaminathan.

"Yes," said Srinivasan. "I heard it from Velu himself, right from the horse's mouth. Tell me, what are you planning to do?" Swaminathan's mood became gloomy. He wished he did not have to take sides.

"I guess we'll deal with next week, next week. Let's see what happens," Swaminathan replied and proceeded to pedal furiously down the street, dexterously avoiding large stones and pebbles. Every so often he greeted and was greeted by friends and vendors as he made his way home. The sun had not yet set and there was a soft westerly breeze, carrying towards him the sound of his two daughters singing. His older daughter, Kunju, was visiting with her infant daughter. A few months after Rajam's birth, Kunju had got married. Now her daughter, whom they affectionately called Baby, was Rajam's playmate. She was just a toddler but wanted to do anything Rajam did.

"*Saa ni da niii da pa Daa pa ma Pa pa.*" The girls were going at full gusto, practicing voice exercises at the top of their lungs. As Swaminathan sat in the thinnai enjoying his coffee, the girls ran out to greet him. "Appa Appa, did you bring chocolates for us as you promised?" Swaminathan enjoyed the girls' chatter, their tinkling laughter and exclamations of amazement as he recounted anecdotes from his day at work. Kunju, now a married woman, could not climb onto her father's lap like her younger sister was doing. Instead her baby daughter clambered onto *Thatha's* lap. After a lot of cajoling, he took out two half melted chocolate pieces from his shirt pocket and gave one to each child, popping the imported Cadbury's chocolates into their mouths. The two girls ran off into the mutram. Rajam, being older, was the first to reach it, followed by Baby yelling, "Wait for me!"

"Kunju, I have a chocolate for you as well. I hope you are not too old to enjoy this treat."

Kunju smiled. "No, Appa, I will always be your child no matter how old I grow."

The conversation was lighthearted but Swaminathan felt weighed down by the events which threatened to unfold the following week. That evening Velu, the organizer of the morcha, came to meet him and no matter how much Swaminathan tried, Velu would not back down. The younger man had a vision, a passion, a dream of freedom and nothing could make him change his mind.

The following week, Swaminathan wished he could call in sick but he had to report to work. Superintendent Gilbert, expecting trouble, sent reinforcements from Madras. People were traveling from villages all around the district to attend the morcha and show solidarity. Velu promised it would be a peaceful march but would he be able to control all those hot headed freedom fighters? Swaminathan shuddered. He looked at the sky as he wheeled his bicycle to the gate. The clouds were dark and heavy with moisture, as if warning him of gloomy events that would unfold that day. The gate creaked loudly, the sound reaching an alarming crescendo. Swaminathan didn't like the omens. As he climbed onto his bike, a Brahmin priest crossed his path. This was not good. He got off the bike and turned back, waited for a few minutes and then resumed his journey. *Otha brahmana*—a lone Brahmin was not an auspicious sign.

Swaminathan reached the *chowky* and spoke to the battalion constable, preparing him and warning them not to resort to violence. Then they began the march toward the *maidanam*. The grounds were decorated with festoons of saffron, white and green flags. A raised dais stood in one corner. People clustered in groups, eating their tiffin of steaming *idlis* smothered with *molahapodi*, chilly powder, which made their mouths burn, reinforcing their burning desire for freedom. Groups of men huddled together, talking and arguing, discussing and disagreeing. Velu gave a fiery speech in Tamil, using flowery language to rouse the crowd. With every rhetorical crescendo, the crowd nodded in assent. More speakers came to the podium, more speeches and more passion; followed by freedom cries of Vande Mataram and Vidudhalai.

The march began, led by Velu, Pandyan and other core leaders. The constables walked alongside, some unwilling, others unthinking, but all of them duty bound. The clouds looked ominous. An eerie flash of lightning lit up the scene, followed by the rumbling of thunder but no rain yet. The temple bells began pealing. The priests must have completed the *Abhishekham* — the washing and anointing of the deity with water, honey, turmeric paste, sandal paste and *panchamrutham*. They would have painstakingly decorated the deity with fragrant sandal paste, vibuthi, kumkumam, silks and scented flowers, following which the door to the inner sanctum was opened to the accompaniment of temple bells. The sound was deafening, reverberating in Swaminathan's ears, almost in rhythm with his pounding heart, which was also racing in anticipation. His gaze moved swiftly among the crowds looking for potential problems.

Then it happened. No one knew who started it. A stone hit a constable on the head and all hell broke loose. The lathis began flying. Stones, bottles and branches rained on the beleaguered constables. People hurled whatever they could lay their hands on and screamed at the police.

*"Traitors! Dung sucking pigs! Vande Mataram!"* Lathis were flying, limbs flailing, and utter chaos ensued. Bodies were strewn everywhere. Young men, blood flowing from their heads, searched wildly for rocks to hurl at the constables. Women wailed and children cried out but the batons descended unrelentingly on the crowd. They landed with disdain on men, women and even children. Swaminathan watched

aghast as this morbid scene unfolded. It was worse than his worst nightmare. The policemen were unyielding and the sound deafening. The screams of pain, passionate freedom cries, the sound of lathis breaking bones and of bodies hitting the floor. Swaminathan sensed each blow and winced as he watched his men fight with demonic possession. His stomach churned and heaved. He turned to one side and retched. There was blood everywhere. Never in his entire career had he seen anything like this. An abhishekham of batons, blows, curses, hatred, fury and venom, to the backdrop of temple bells, thunder and lightning. Nothing seemed to have meaning anymore. Everyone had lost the last shred of reason and the insanity was uncontrollable. The sound of the temple bells faded away.

Then, as if the gods had seen enough, the rain commenced. Torrents of large raindrops beat down on the angry mob, quenching their ire and diluting their passion. Enough of this madness. The heavenly Abhishekham took effect, calming the frenzy, drowning the cries and forcing the batons to rest. Only the moans of the injured and the wailing of the wounded were heard. It rained continually, the drops of rain washing off the blood, till they mingled with the red dust and flowed down the street in rivulets of anguish. Swaminathan wept in an uncontrolled outpouring of grief. He lifted his eyes to survey the damage. Velu was seated on the pavement with his head cradled in his hands. As if he sensed being observed, he raised his eyes and for a moment, they locked with Swaminathan's. That moment told him everything. The despondency, the anguish and the pain in his eyes were mirrored in Swaminathan's. Velu's face was glistening. Were those tears, blood, or raindrops? Perhaps all three.

Then there was no sound. Just bodies sprawled everywhere, supine with injuries, pain and grief. Everyone was reeling from the aftermath of this intense encounter and divine intervention. The rain cooled their passions and made them sharply aware of their pain and their wounds but more particularly, of their madness.

That evening, Swaminathan did not speak to anyone. He sat in front of the altar in the pooja room and prayed. Rajam was too scared to go near him. She knew something terrible had happened. She had never seen him this way. Till the early hours of the morning, he repeated the holy mantra, the Gayatri Japam. He prayed for forgiveness, for healing of bodies and spirits, for strength to carry on and find peace amidst the insanity.

"*Om Bhur bhuvasvaha*   *Tatsa vithuvarenyam*
*Bhargo devasya dheemahi*   *Dhiyoyona prachodayaath.*"

"Sir? Did you say something?" the constable asked.

Swaminathan looked up at the driver realizing that unwittingly he was reciting the Gayatri Japam just as he had that evening after the morcha. He smiled and replied, "No, just reciting my prayers. You can keep driving."

# CHAPTER 9 – RAJAM
## VIZHUPURAM – 1934

Two weeks passed since Sushila had miscarried. While recuperating at her mother's house in the next village, she left her stepson, Balu, in her husband Siva's care. Since Rajam was the youngest and the liveliest in the family, Balu liked to be around her. Rajam was a mere four feet ten inches tall, a dwarf compared to the rest of the family, all of whom were tall and well built, so Balu must have felt she was his peer of sorts. He was two years old and spoke in *Mazhalai*, baby talk that enchanted Rajam. Balu would scuttle along with her, climbing the stairs to hang clothes on the terrace, then helping her sweep the back thinnai with an oversized broom, all the while chitchatting non-stop with Rajam. She thoroughly enjoyed his company, which made her chores seem lighter.

That particular morning was hot as usual. Rajam had just finished washing clothes and with Balu's help was carrying them up to the terrace to dry in the sun. They had developed a good routine. Balu handed her a piece of clothing and she wrung it out to remove the excess water. Then, as she shook it vigorously, the cool water splashed all over half naked Balu, making him giggle in glee. Next, she draped it on the line with Balu handing her clothes pegs to keep them from falling to the dusty ground. They were half way done when she heard a call from the street that always chilled her to the bone.

*"Bhavati bhikshaan dehi"*

A *saamaiyaar* or mendicant was at the door, asking for alms. Rajam shivered in fear. She knew they were highly respected, having renounced material and sexual attachments, meditating all day in search of enlightenment. This mendicant was probably taking a break to eat a frugal meal and it was her responsibility to give him *bhiksha*. She knew only too well on hearing the familiar call of *Bhavati bhikshaan dehi* it was her duty to offer food to the saamiyaar, who would receive the alms and bless the family with prosperity and good health. She was already without child, so the last thing she needed was to be cursed. But she could not face him. Her terror was deeply rooted; all she could think of was trying to escape her predicament.

Rajam feared saamiyaars mainly because of their scary appearance. Shiva, the God of Destruction, reigned over the cremation ground through Yama the God of Death, and saamiyaars being Shiva worshippers, covered their bodies with ash and kept their hair in long matted locks.

*"Bhavati bhikshaan dehi."*

Rajam began trembling. Her back arched painfully and she could feel her muscles tightening into knots. Her heart was beating so loudly she was sure the saamiyaar outside could hear it. Sweat beads glistened on her upper lip and the palms of her hand became so moist she had to wipe them several times against her sari. Her face turned red and she found it hard to breathe. Nagamma knew Rajam was terrified of saamiyaars and in a few seconds would probably call out for her to give him food, a special torture designed to further break Rajam's spirit. She had to find a hiding place where no one could find her. Forgetting all about Balu, who was blissfully unaware of her predicament, she dropped the clothes in her hand and ran down the stairs, fleeing across the courtyard and into the cowshed. She was aware of Balu's voice following her as he gingerly made his way down the stairs in pursuit. He loved to play hide and seek. Where could Rajam be?

In spite of the strong stench, the darkness in the cowshed gave Rajam the refuge she was seeking. She ran to the far end of the shed and sat behind a haystack. From this vantage point, she could see the entrance and be forewarned in case Nagamma decided to come looking for her. The door creaked open and the little breath left in Rajam's body went out of her. It was Balu.

"Rajam Chithi, where are you? Are you hiding? Is it my turn to find you?"

Rajam breathed a sigh of relief and left her sanctuary to run and grab Balu. Keeping one hand over his mouth, she whispered, "We are playing a new game where we both have to hide and talk only in whispers." Balu was a bit confused. If both of them hid, then who would find them? But he went along with her and sat down just like her on his haunches. He watched her for a few seconds. Did he have to imitate her? He attempted mimicking Rajam, breathing hard and fast just like her. It took Rajam a few seconds to figure out what he was doing and when she saw him mimicking her, amidst all of the tension, she couldn't help smiling. Smiling and crying simultaneously. It seemed as though all her bodily functions had gone crazy. She didn't know how to calm herself.

Her fear of saamiyaars was planted when she was a child. Rajam was a bit of a tomboy and loved to run around outdoors and climb trees. Her mother, Mangalam, was exasperated with her. She worried that this wild nature would create disharmony in her married life. If she behaved like this in her mother-in-law's house, it would only reflect on her upbringing. Girls had to behave in a controlled and modest manner, especially if they were from Brahmin Iyer families. The advent of the British had changed many things in the country, especially for Brahmins. Since they were traditionally the educated class, they took to western education and broke out of traditional apprenticeships into priesthood. Rajam and Kunju belonged to the first generation of Brahmin women to attend an English school. Swaminathan was also educated in the western tradition and believed in equal opportunities for both men and women. Mangalam tried to oppose his decision but he was firm; the girls would go to school until they were married.

Mangalam worried that Rajam was such a free spirit. She always blamed Swaminathan for encouraging the girls to express themselves too freely. Rajam was active from sunrise to sunset. She explored, questioned and chatted all day long. As soon as she awoke in the morning, Rajam would slip out of the house to play in the mango groves and climb trees. Mangalam would have to call out for her for hours and then send someone to look for her before she finally reappeared. This was not acceptable behavior for a girl. In addition to escaping household chores, Mangalam also worried about her daughter's safety. Rajam always wore gold earrings and a gold chain around her neck. At the tender age of five, she would be easy prey for predators or thieves. Swaminathan always laughed it off, saying no one would dare touch the daughter of the Inspector of Police. But Rajam was beautiful and the village had many traveling peddlers and gypsies who did not know about her ancestry or genealogy. No matter how much Mangalam tried to reason with her, Rajam would not reform.

Finally, like all mothers, Mangalam decided she had to frighten her into obedience, and she did so by telling her that a saamiyaar would carry her away. This tactic also proved unsuccessful for a while, mainly because Rajam had never seen a saamiyaar and so was not scared of one. But that was soon to change.

Every Friday, Mangalam took her children to the neighborhood Kamakshiamman temple to offer prayers. This Friday, like every other, she bathed the two children very early and once they were all dressed, she got her pooja vessels ready. The silver flower basket was filled with a small garland of fragrant jasmine, which she had woven herself. To this, she added a coconut, betel nuts and betel leaves. Lastly, a few sticks of incense and two paise tucked into the recesses of her blouse to pay the shoe keeper and she was ready to go.

The temple was about a half mile away from the house and the stony pathway was quiet, except for the occasional bullock cart or wobbly bicycle trundling by. The road was a little busier as they approached the temple. Mangalam paused near the tall *gopuram* at the entrance to the temple admiring the diminishing tiers covered in stone sculpture. As Mangalam collected their slippers to be deposited with the shoe keeper, Rajam and Mani stared heavenward to see who could name a statue carved into the topmost tier of the gopuram, a game they played every Friday. They chose a different statue each week and took turns giving strange unpronounceable names to each carving.

The temple was bustling with activity. People collected at all the different altars around the central sanctum but the lines were particularly long at the sanctum sanctorum to catch a glimpse of the deity in all her finery. Mangalam lifted young Mani so that he could get a darshanam or sacred view of Goddess Kamakshiamman. The priest noticed her straining to get a look at the deity amidst a hundred oiled heads and signaled to her to come forward. He knew she was the Inspector's wife and to everyone's chagrin, she moved through the seething crowd to the front of the line, from where she got a clear *darshanam*. Mangalam gave her flower basket to the priest, who then performed a special prayer in her name.

The peace and calm came to an abrupt end when Mani loudly proclaimed he had to pee. Of course, this could not be done anywhere in the vicinity of the temple and Mangalam hurried to collect everyone and briskly walked towards home. In the meantime, Rajam hurtled down the street, intent on racing her brother. Mangalam screamed at her to stop, scaring her with the proverbial saamiyaar who was sure to kidnap her but Rajam yelled back, "There's no saamiyaar here. I'll see you at home. I can run faster than Mani." And she could. As she took the next corner she ran full tilt into someone and fell backwards, her fragile head hitting the muddy floor with a thwack.

As she came to in a few seconds, she looked up at her human obstacle. Feet, large and filthy, with long curved unkempt toenails. Long never ending legs, covered in dust and ash. Her eyes took in the orange sarong-like garment over a protruding hairy stomach and then moved up to see a surprisingly contrasted skeletal chest, over which hung hundreds of rosary beads made with the sacred *Rudraksha*, straight from the Himalayas. And then the beard: long, black and tangled, over which was an even longer curled moustache. Fierce red eyes below a bushy unibrow. And the hair — black tangled locks. The forehead was smeared with red, yellow and grey from the sacred vibuthi, kumkumam and chandanam

From her horizontal position, all she could see was this saamiyaar outlined against the sky; his body seemed to stretch to the heavens. His face looked like that of a demon sent by the gods to scare the life out of her. Rajam stared for a moment and then as the image got transfixed in her young mind, she opened her mouth and screamed a loud and prolonged shriek. It came from the recesses of her gut, resounding and increasing in volume as it passed through her heaving chest and when it escaped from her mouth, it traveled through the air in one interminable resonant wail that continued through the rest of the day and into the wee hours of the morning. She was unaware of her mother urgently picking her up and holding her in her gentle arms. She screamed interminably, only stopping momentarily to catch her breath and once her lungs were filled, she began again. She saw the fearful saamiyaar whether her eyes were open or shut. And every time the image reappeared in her mind, she screamed. Nothing could calm her down.

By evening, she had developed a high fever and with it came hallucinations of the saamiyaar, his face distorting, laughing like a madman, his ash-smeared arms, curved talons reaching out towards her. In her delirium she clawed the air, pushing it away, screaming and crying. Mangalam and Swaminathan were helpless. The night was long and stressful, spent holding their darling baby, comforting her, promising her she was safe and that they were there for her.

But the fear never left her. It remained in the deepest recesses of her mind and came back to haunt and taunt her. It would never go away. Firmly ensconced in her subconscious, when it surfaced, it bubbled through her entire being with a visceral volcanic force, engulfing her very existence in a scorching blaze. No loving arms could quench it, no calming mantra could extinguish it and no prayer could calm it. It was a phobia with an onset early in life, which had manifested itself with regularity over the years, making her timid and scared, a perfect victim for the likes of Nagamma.

"Rajam. Come on out. Your saamiyaar is waiting for you."
Did cruelty have no boundaries?
Rajam sat quaking, watching the door of the cowshed.

When the Lotus Blooms

# Part IV
# Dharmu

# CHAPTER 10 – KAMALA
## SONARPUR, EAST BENGAL – 1934

Kamala balanced three large brass pots on her head and set off down the narrow path. She was a little nervous. There had been many tiger sightings and only last week, there was a killing but that had taken place much farther upstream. Filling water for the kitchen from the river was a daily chore and nothing bad had happened so far. At the shrine of *Banobibi*, the village deity, she put down her pots and fell to her knees. With her eyes tightly shut, she prayed. '*Hey, glorious Banobibi, you are kind and giving. Protect me today; make me strong and brave. You, the bountiful slayer of the demon tiger, stay in my heart always.*'

Strengthened by her prayer, she confidently placed two pots on her head and the third one she cradled in the curve of her waist. It was only a short walk through the forest to the *ghat*. In any case, it was not dark yet and she had enough time to get water from the river for the next day's cooking and still reach home before dusk.

She increased her pace as she entered the thick jungle, constantly listening for any strange sounds. If she heard a cheetal shriek, or monkeys chattering too loudly, then she would be forewarned and could run back to the village, or at least scream for help. She stopped and turned around. She could see many of the villagers still working in the fields, all within earshot. Emboldened, she quickened her pace and in a few minutes was at the ghat.

'*Quick*' she told herself. '*I shouldn't wait here longer than necessary.*'

Her heart was pumping rapidly. She was nervous.

'*Don't be silly,*' she comforted herself. '*You are only five minutes from the village.*' The village headman told them tigers don't move away from their territory, so there was no fear. The last tiger kill took place several miles upstream. '*This village is too far and tigers are scared of humans. It cannot come here.'* Thus consoling herself, she lifted the brass pots and placed them on the steps of the ghat. The topmost pot tipped over and bounced down the stairs with a noisy clang a few times before falling into the water. Kamala felt uneasy. That had never happened before. Was it an omen of sorts? *'Don't be ridiculous,'* she chided herself. *'These things happen.'*

She leaned forward to reach for the pot, which was bobbing away from her. The jungle sounds of crickets and birds created a musical symphony, broken only by the gurgling of clear water filling the brass pot. Her fingers were numb with fear. She was tense and her body on high alert, listening closely for any strange sounds.

She heard the unmistakable crackle of movement against the undergrowth. Someone must be approaching the ghat. Kamala paused and sat up, her body rigid with apprehension. She felt the perspiration dampening the insides of her blouse. It was very hot and rivulets of sweat trickled down her back. A shiver went down her spine and the hair on the back of her neck stood on end. She regretted coming alone to fill water. Maybe she should have listened to the warnings and brought someone along with her. She pictured the image of Banobibi in her head and felt the fear ebb, if only for a moment.

*"Ke?"* She called. "Who is that?"

There was no sound except for crickets. She waited for a while, but was quite certain no one was approaching. There was no unfamiliar noise and she reproached herself for being so anxious. Picking up the second pot, she immersed it in water, when she heard the distinctive crackling sound again, this time much closer. She turned around and looked in the direction of the sound.

The sight was so shocking, she could not move. There, framed in the thick shrubbery, was the face of a fully grown Bengal Tiger. Her jaw dropped open, drying the saliva within. All her life she had heard stories of tiger encounters but nothing prepared her for this ferocious sight.

Fearlessly, the magnificent animal boldly stepped out of the foliage that had camouflaged it all this time. It was a gigantic cat, ten or twelve feet long, with striking auburn yellow and black stripes. Its coat was mangy in parts but its stance was regal. Its head slunk low, resting on powerful shoulders and its feline slanted eyes locked on its prey.

Kamala sat transfixed, unable to move. Her gaze was riveted on the slanted golden eyes of this large feline, playmate of the goddess Banobibi. Even though it dawned on her this vision was going to be her last, she couldn't move. She was mesmerized by the mystique of those yellow eyes and the majesty of its carriage. She opened her mouth to scream but no sound escaped her mouth.

The tiger roared, the sound echoing through the forest in vibrations that shook the leaves making them fall to the forest floor in ripples of fear. It was so close that Kamala could smell its fetid breath, the stench of putrefying flesh. The two canines that should have been on its upper jaw were missing. Kamala's heart sank and all her muscles went limp as she prepared for the inevitable. Her grip on the brass pots loosened. The tiger crouched on its hind paws, its muscles rippling under the striated flesh.

The last thing Kamala saw were those yellow mesmeric eyes.

The pots rolled over, the water emptying onto the damp forest floor, as they tumbled noisily down the steps and splashed into the turbulent water. Sinking beneath the tide, then slowly filling up, they rose to the surface once again to bob in the churning water.

Only this time the water was not clear; it was tinged with pink.

# CHAPTER 11 – DHARMAMBAL
## RANGPUR – 1934

The sound of the phaeton bell jerked Dharmu out of her afternoon nap. Mahadevan had already arrived from work. Was it that late? It seemed as though she just lay her head down on the pillow to sleep. Her thoughts went back to the letter and she hurriedly ran into the study and collected the pieces of paper from the dustbin, quickly transferring them to the one in the kitchen before rushing out. She reached the verandah just as the chowkidar opened the front gate to let the covered phaeton into the compound. Mahadevan stepped out of the carriage and right after him, someone else got down. Dharmu was puzzled. She was not aware of any visitors coming. To her dismay, she noticed the surprise visitor was an Englishman. Her heart sank and started beating rapidly. Every English phrase she knew ran through her head. *'Good evening, how do you do? Nice to meet you, lovely evening.'*

*'Oh Lord, tell me this is not happening to me,'* she thought, as the panic went out of control. Thankfully, Kandu ran past into his doting father's open arms and began chattering away, not waiting for a response.

Mahadevan climbed up the stairs with his visitor. *"Chowkidar, saaman andar laao,"* he called over his shoulder. Dharmu watched the chowkidar take two brown leather suitcases out of the phaeton and to her consternation, two guns!

"Wow," said Kandu excitedly. "Guns! Can I touch them? Can I play with them?"

"Oh no!" said Mahadevan quickly, knowing what might take place next. "These guns are real and you cannot go anywhere near them." Turning to his visitor, he added, "Mr. Corbin, may I introduce my wife, Dharmambal, and my energetic son, Kandu."

Dharmu stuck out a clammy hand, mumbling, "Pleased to make your acquaintance," under her breath.

"Mr. Corbin has been assigned here for the next few weeks to take care of the man-eating tiger that attacked again last week. He will stay with us. Please make arrangements for his stay." Dharmu scampered off, her mind in a whirl as she tried to think of what to do next. She ran towards the kitchen, barking instructions to the servants. "Change the sheets. Don't forget the mosquito net. Dust the windows." Then she ran into the kitchen where the cook, a *khansaama* from the neighboring state of Bihar, was marinating fish to be baked in the clay oven. Fresh Darjeeling tea was being brewed and the bearer prepared the tray, using fine English china and silverware. "The *Angrez Saab* will be with us for a while. Make sure you put an additional table setting. Is the fish fresh? Make a soup and salad as well and cut fresh fruit for dessert." There were a million things to attend to and even more instructions to be given.

The two men sat in the comfortable wicker chairs in the verandah as the orderlies removed their dirty mud-splattered shoes, replacing them with home slippers. Though Mahadevan adopted many British ways, he was very finicky about not wearing outdoor shoes inside the house, an ancient Indian custom designed to keep the house free from outside contaminants. In a few moments, the bearer brought out the tea and biscuits and the two men continued to talk. Dharmu took a breather and made her way to the verandah to join them. She stood just inside the hallway, listening to their conversation as she gathered courage, wondering whether to sit with the men or not.

"Your wife looks very young to have had a child."

"Not so young," replied Mahadevan, "This is our third child. She was twelve when we married."

"Twelve! Quite the cradle snatcher, aren't you! Did you love her before you married her, or was it an arranged match? I don't know how you natives do this — marry a stranger, with no love in the equation."

"Mr. Corbin, you have a lot to learn about the way things work here. In Indian marriages, love comes afterward. Marriage is not between individuals but between families." Dharmu listened silently, fading out of the conversation and retreating to the comfort of her own memories. Love and marriage; she remembered her marriage like it was yesterday. Only, at that time, she had no idea how it was going to change her life. Her mind wandered back to the time when the marriage proposal to Mahadevan was the topic of excitement for her family.

# CHAPTER 12 – DHARMAMBAL
## DINDIGUL – 1920

Dharmu wailed loudly as her mother, Gayatri, attempted to tame her hair. She washed it with shikakai and her curly hair, which was unmanageable to begin with, was now completely out of control. Gayatri oiled it with warm coconut oil and was in the process of untangling the knots with a thick comb. The third one this month. Two others had succumbed to the battle of tangles. Although she wrapped a thick strand of hair around her fingers, she was in the midst of a raging encounter with the lower half of the coil of hair. Dharmu felt as though her brains were being pulled out and screamed continually, begging for the ordeal to be finished. After almost a half hour of torment, Gayatri was satisfied with her handiwork and braided her hair into two thick plaits.

"Gayatri…Gayatri, where are you?" Visvanathan Iyer rushed in excitedly, waving a letter furiously in the air. His face was flushed with excitement.

"Gayatri, the letter is here from Nilakantan Ayyar." He spotted his daughter slouching on the floor, exhausted by the hair braiding ordeal and pinched both her cheeks.

"Dharmu, you lucky girl I have got the best *varan* for you. Gayatri, this letter is from Nilakantan Ayyar from Nagarcoil. Remember, I told you I sent Dharmu's horoscope to him three months ago? Well, he replied saying he will arrive next week to see her. We have to go to Mayavaram station and receive him. Can you get better news on a Friday morning?" beamed a hyperventilating Visvanathan.

Gayatri smiled, "Slow down. Is this the boy who is going to study in England? Is it all right to proceed with this varan? You know how we feel about crossing the seas. My mother will never agree to it.

Nobody in our family has ever married someone who has crossed the oceans."

"Then we just must not tell your mother. Gayatri, we must have gained good karma for seven generations to receive an alliance from such an illustrious family. I will not let any of our traditions or taboos spoil Dharmu's future. If he crosses the seas, then we will do some prayers to avert any misfortune. Don't you cross me now. Come on, there's lots to be done. The house has to be ready in six days. Don't sit, get up and let's get things ready." So saying, an exhilarated Visvanathan Iyer ran out, leaving everyone puzzled and confused.

Gayatri looked at her daughter with mixed emotions. Only eleven years old and blissfully unaware of what was happening around her. She put her hands around Dharmu's face and then cracked her knuckles against the sides of her own forehead, a gesture designed to remove any bad luck that may prevent this alliance from resulting in marriage. Yes, Dharmu was truly lucky to be considered for the position of the first daughter-in-law for this illustrious family. The alliance was brought to their notice by Jameen Amma, the Jameendar's wife, who loved Dharmu like her own daughter. Visvanathan had sent Dharmu's horoscope to the Ayyar home months earlier and every day they waited for a response. The first step in the marriage preparation was to check and see if the horoscopes matched. They waited for the family astrologer to look at both horoscopes and make predictions about the couple and their lives together, and only if he agreed the match was good would matters be taken further. Visvanathan Iyer already got an okay from their family astrologer, who called it an excellent match but according to protocol, they had to wait until the boy's party consented.

Nilakantan Ayyar and his wife, Sitalakshmi, lived in Nagarcoil deep in the south close to Cape Comorin. He had a lot of land, some awarded by the Raja of Travancore, and the rest which he purchased. Highly educated, Nilakantan was the Chief Engineer for the princely State of Travancore and received the title of Rao Bahadur from the British. Rao Bahadur Nilakantan Ayyar. A title meaning 'the most honorable prince,' in recognition for his outstanding service to the British Empire. His son Mahadevan was studying at Presidency College in Madras, finishing his M.A. at the young age of twenty. Dharmu was truly fortunate to be even considered as the first daughter-in-law for this family. She would soon be twelve years old, the perfect age for a

Brahmin girl to be married. In any case she would remain home until she got her period and only after that, move in with her in-laws, which could mean an extra couple of years at home for Gayatri to pamper her.

Dharmu stared vacantly at her mother. She was too young to comprehend what her parents were talking about. She picked up her *Gilli Danda* stick and ran out of the house to play when she bumped full tilt into Jameen Amma, who was just stepping into the house.

"Dharmu, love of my life, where are you running off to? Are you so eager to embrace me you can't wait till I enter your home? Come on, give me another hug without knocking me over."

Dharmu snaked her arms around Jameen Amma's ample waist, her head nestled in the cushiony comfort of Jameen Amma's generous belly. Dharmu had a special soft spot in Jameen Amma's heart. She would run over to the big bungalow, 'the Bangla,' every time she had a chance. The Bangla was exciting with so much to do. She loved to lie on the branches of the old knotted trees around the house and spend hours gazing through the leafy foliage at the sky above. Jameen Amma always took her around the garden to pick flowers for the pooja, telling her stories about the gods, or just chatting about nothing in particular. No matter when Dharmu went over, Jameen Amma welcomed her with a smile, a warm embrace and a smacking kiss on her forehead. Jameen Amma played games with her for hours on end. Dharmu's favorite was *Palaangozhi,* mainly because she loved the sound of the shells hitting against one another as she gingerly dropped them into the carved cups on the ornate wooden board. But Jameen Amma drew the line at playing *Pandi*. She was too fat, she said, to hop on one leg, so hopscotch was totally out.

Jameen Amma always dressed perfectly. She wore beautiful colored Kanjeevaram saris, always with a red velvet jacket. On her nose, she had the double *mookuthi*, her oversized nosering set with pigeon-egg sized diamonds. At least four gold chains coiled round her neck, including her *thaali*. What was more striking was the huge coin-size pottu she wore in the center of her forehead in bright red kumkumam. That her husband was the Jameendar and Visvanathan worked for him did not stop the two women, Jameen Amma and Gayatri, from being close friends. And it certainly didn't stop Dharmu from being a constant visitor at the Bangla. Jameen Amma loved

Dharmu's visits because it added a spark of excitement to her otherwise boring day. Her sons were studying in Thanjavur and her older daughter had married. It was always enjoyable when the grandchildren came to visit but that was only for a few weeks in the year. Her younger daughter, Sita, was of marriageable age but was not given much to conversation. In fact, Dharmu initially tried to engage her in dialogue and gave up after Sita replied in monosyllables. Being with Dharmu made Jameen Amma feel young again. She would miss Dharmu's visits when she got married.

Gayatri welcomed Jameen Amma, talking excitedly about the alliance. Visvanathan joined in, adding to his wife's narrative and soon Jameen Amma's head swiveled from side to side as she attempted to understand what both of them were saying. Gayatri began talking about Dharmu and then Visvanathan interjected with something about the boy's family. Jameen Amma was only getting snatches of each conversation but realized they were very excited and she didn't want to spoil their moment. After all, this was going to be the first wedding in the family. Finally, she smiled and asked a very potent question, "What does Dharmu have to say about all this?"

"Dharmu? Why, we haven't asked her opinion on the matter. She should consider herself blessed to have this opportunity," Visvanathan insisted. Jameen Amma realized in the midst of all this excitement that no one had paused to explain to Dharmu what was happening and what it meant for her. The young girl had no idea that in a few months she was to leave the security of her home and become part of another family. No more Amma, Appa and Jameen Amma. In a few months Dharmu's entire life would change. In a few months she would dramatically metamorphose into a woman. No more Pandi and Palaangozhi. No more idling around playing with her kitchen *choppus*, tiny replicas of kitchen utensils. Now she would be in charge of her own kitchen and the pots and pans would become magnified and real, leaving her play choppus behind as a distant memory. No one was going to explain anything to the poor child. Her thoughts and feelings were never going to be considered. She was a child after all and it was her duty to do what her parents told her to.

Jameen Amma walked out into the yard. In one corner Dharmu was intently playing Gilli Danda. She placed one small stick on top of the other. When she hit the bottom stick, the top one popped up, allowing her to catch it in midair; then with a swipe she hit it into the distance. Her brother Venkat was an expert at the game and could hit it much farther than Dharmu. Jameen Amma watched as Dharmu concentrated, the end of her tongue sticking out from the side of her mouth. Plop! Whack! The stick flew up into the air landing almost in the same spot. Patiently, Dharmu retrieved the stick, gingerly placing it on the ground to make another attempt. Jameen Amma called out to her.

"Dharmu, come here. I want to talk to you."

"*Varen*," Dharmu cried out, making one last futile attempt at whacking the stick, before running across the yard to Jameen Amma. They walked together and sat on the shaded parapet under the enormous banyan tree. The sun was high in the sky and it was difficult to be in the open sunlight for a long time.

"Dharmu," Jameen Amma suggested softly. "You are going to get married. Do you know what that means?"

"I know," said Dharmu cheerfully.

"You will have to leave this house. Do you know that too?"

"Leave this house? Why? I want to stay here with Amma and Appa."

"I know. That would be nice but this is the destiny of all girls. We are guests at our parent's house till the time we get married. Your Amma and Appa found a very nice boy and he and his parents will be coming next week to see you. At the *Ponpaakal*, if they like you, then a date will be fixed for the marriage."

"Will the boy come?"

"Of course."

"And if I don't like him?"

Jameen Amma squirmed as she thought carefully about her reply. "You will. Eventually. It is possible that you don't like him immediately but you will learn to like him, even love him. But first, you must respect him and his family."

"What if he's ugly with marks on his face?"

Jameen Amma laughed. "Don't worry; I heard he looks like a prince. You will like him," she said aloud, thinking inwardly it didn't really matter what Dharmu thought. No one asked for her opinion when her own marriage was fixed. In fact she did not even meet the groom's family till the day of the wedding. But she kept her thoughts to herself.

"Let's make a deal. If he has pock marks on his face, then I will stop the wedding proceedings. I will make sure of that but otherwise, you have to marry him."

"And then? Do I have to go with this man to his house?"

"Not immediately," said Jameen Amma. "You have to wait until you mature and then they will perform another ceremony called the Shanthi Kalyanam. After that, you will have to leave this house and go to live with your in-laws."

"Mature? What is that?"

"You know how Amma stays in the back room for a few days every month?" Dharmu nodded. "That is because all women get their period. They bleed for three or four days, so they have to rest."

"Bleed?" Dharmu looked horrified as the intricacies of womanhood unfolded for her in a single five-minute lesson.

"Don't worry. It doesn't hurt, at least not initially. Every woman must get her period; otherwise they can't have babies. As a wife, it is your duty to have children so the family line can continue."

Dharmu stared at her toes, now curling them, now uncurling them. She didn't really understand any of this: boy, period, bleeding, children. What was worse, the less she understood, the more frightened she became. Suddenly, apprehension gripped her as she struggled with the unknown. She realized one thing and one thing only: she would have to leave home and the future became a dark scary abyss waiting to engulf her.

"I don't want to… l…l… leave," she stuttered, and the tears began rolling down her cheeks. "I don't know those people. How can Amma send me away forever to their house?" Jameen Amma held Dharmu close, gently calming her quivering body. She understood Dharmu's fears. She had experienced them herself and knowing how painful it was, she had willfully imposed the same condition on her own daughter. And now, she was watching the same heart-wrenching event play out with Dharmu. This was every woman's lot; there was nothing to be done. It was this which eventually made every woman strong, giving her the ability to face unknown challenges.

"Don't worry Dharmu. You won't have to leave for a while, so don't fret about it now. We'll cross the bridge when we come to it. Think of this — you are going to get many new clothes, beautiful silk pavadais in any color you like."

"Can I get one in blue? With matching ribbons for my hair?"

"Of course you can, my sweetness. What kind of blue?"

"This kind," said Dharmu pointing to the blue cloudless sky. "I want the blue of the sky."

Dharmu stared out through the window at the evening Rangpur sky.

It was not blue. It was an ominous grey and orange.

# CHAPTER 13 – DHARMAMBAL
## RANGPUR –1934

Dinner was served and the evening proceeded without a hitch. While the men retired to the living room to enjoy some port and cigars, Dharmu returned to her room thoroughly exhausted. She sat down on her bed and listened to the conversation wafting in from the living room. Kandu, who should have been asleep, was obviously with the men.

"Are you a real Englishman?" asked Kandu, a bit too frank and curious. From the awkward silence that followed, Dharmu could sense Mahadevan's embarrassment but there was no controlling children.

"From England?" continued Kandu, oblivious to his father's discomfiture.

"Yes. Absolutely, son. Maybe one day you will visit England."

Dharmu couldn't hear much more as the conversation began fading out.

Her memories of childhood gave her solace in this alien world. She missed home terribly. Maybe in the winter she would make that arduous journey back to the south. Amma and Appa lived alone now that her brother Venkat had married and moved to Madras.

Dharmu thought to herself, *Jameen Amma's life had probably become routine since her sons had all married and were living in cities all over India. She must be so relieved that her younger daughter, Sita, also got a fine alliance. That poor unfortunate child had suffered a lot. And Jameen Amma did not deserve this grief.*

◆ ❖ ◆ ❖ ◆

Dharmu had been very young when Jameen Amma's daughter was raped at the tender age of five. When Dharmu learned about this after she had grown up, it made a lot of things clear. Why Sita never spoke. Why Jameen Amma never let her out of the house. Why, in spite of laughing and cheerfully tackling her chores, Jameen Amma would turn suddenly gloomy, her eyes wearing a faraway look and her face sad for no obvious reason. Being the mother of three, Dharmu now understood that pain. Thinking she had let her child down, Jameen Amma must have felt an overwhelming sense of failure, unable to protect her. She probably felt terrible wondering how this would affect the child physically and mentally in the future. The gardener, like many men afflicted with syphilis, had raped the child because of the belief that you could get rid of the disease if you slept with a virgin.

But how was it possible to rape a five year old? Apparently he had sliced open the child's vagina with a knife. Just thinking about it made Dharmu weak. She felt a sympathetic pain in her genitals and moaned. Bending over, she placed her fists between her legs to ease the sensation. The gardener ran away but was caught and beaten up by the servants at the Jameen. They could not report the crime because that would bring untold shame on the family. No one from a decent family ever reported a rape. Death was preferable to dishonor, and rape brought dishonor to the family. Three other children needed to get married and the smear of rape would disgrace the family. They would have no face to talk to their neighbors, let alone arrange a marriage for any of their children. Nobody ever reported rapes. They would deal with the situation with as much secrecy as possible and all family members kept their secrets well. The servants talked in hushed whispers but they knew the harsh consequences of leaking this information to outsiders. Jameen Amma wondered if she should involve the English doctor or rely on the local Vaidhyar. Would his herbs and salves have good results, or would it make her worse? And then what if she died? Many did, and with their merciful release their families were actually relieved.

A maidservant found Sita in the early evening under a tree, a small crumpled heap in the corner of the garden, resting on a pool of oozing blood. She was unconscious for a long time and for the next few years not a word escaped her traumatized lips. The Jameen was such a safe haven. All the servants who worked there had been with the family for generations and their loyalty was unquestionable. The possibility of a vagrant out-of-work gardener on the prowl for a young virgin never crossed their minds. But bad things happen when you least expect it, to people who least deserve it, for reasons nobody understands. Karma catches up with you sooner or later in life and even makes you pay for misdeeds in past lives. What else could cause such untold suffering on an innocent child and a God-fearing family?

Jameen Amma never really forgave herself. She had been on the thinnai watching her daughter play in the garden when the cook summoned her inside. She was inside for a short while and was about to return to the thinnai when the pleats of her sari got caught in a stray nail and ripped. She went into her room to change and got distracted by the state of her closet, so she busied herself reorganizing her almirah. Perhaps an hour had passed when she heard the piecing shriek of the *ayah* calling out to her. Running out, she saw the distressed ayah setting Sita down on the sofa, screaming, "Jameen Amma *ayayyo* Jameen Amma *ayayyo*!!"

Perhaps it was this scene that Jameen Amma's mind reverted to when her eyes wore that distant look. The servants gathered and Visvanathan was summoned to deal with the crisis. Besides being the estate manager, he was a close confidante of the family. In a few hours, the assailant was captured and brought before the Jameendar. The servants beat the ingrate with sticks and bare fists, till his face and body were a bloody mess. But they did not kill him. The disease would take care of that.

The Vaidhyar arrived and began the treatment. But the herbs and salves could not soothe the child. By morning, she had a high fever combined with convulsions. Jameen Amma was like a ghost of herself. She was unable to think clearly but she kept praying to Kamakshiamman. Her faith in the goddess was firm and she made it a point to visit the temple in the village every Friday. She promised that if her daughter improved, she would offer flowers, fruit and one hundred coconuts to her family deity. If Sita recovered, she would give twenty-one silver coins every full moon day to worshippers at the temple for the rest of her life. She knew in her heart that her *bhakti*, her devotion, was sincere and the Goddess would never let her down. And she didn't.

The family gathered together and jointly made the wise decision to call in the English Doctor, who stitched her badly torn genitals and gave her some pills and a host of pink lotions and concoctions. Over the next few days, sores emerged in her genitalia but slowly they

86

subsided. The fever that racked her weak body also abated. But the psychological scar took a long time to heal. Sita never talked about what happened and neither did the rest of the family. Getting her back alive was the best gift and Jameen Amma never forgot that. She treated her with gentle care and tenderness, constantly by her side, attending to her every need and just loving her unconditionally. Sita did eventually talk but became a little reticent. She was never ever allowed to play with Dharmu in the garden. Recently, she married into a wealthy family from Thirunelveli, and this unpleasant incident was forever buried, consigned permanently to stray discomforting thoughts and unspoken words.

To Jameen Amma's credit, she did not let the incident affect her outward disposition. She continued to love everyone around her and was a source of positive energy for everyone. Most of all, she was Dharmu's best friend.

Dharmu smiled as her mind came back to the present. "Aahh, Jameen Amma, I miss you," she said aloud as she lay down ready to sleep. "What a joy it has been to know you."

Then, suddenly, she sat up and rushed across the hall to her daughters' bedroom. They were both safe and sound, fast asleep under the mosquito net. She kissed them both, allowing herself a rare moment of tenderness.

The next morning Dharmu woke up later than usual. She looked outside and to her consternation, Corbin, the English Saab, was seated in the verandah polishing his gun, and right next to him crouching on the floor, was 'a-million-questions-Kandu.' Their guest patiently answered all of Kandu's probing queries and explained to him how he would catch the tiger. Kandu listened with rapt attention, his eyes unwavering, absorbing everything about the *machaan*, the bait and the kill.

A short while later, Dharmu rushed out to the verandah after hearing Corbin's hearty laughter. He was standing at the side of the house watching the pantomime unfold under the direction of Kandu, the Great Tiger Killer.

Kandu had rounded up all the servants to help him. He put a large piece of cardboard on a broad low limb of a tree to resemble a *machaan* and was seated cross legged, dressed for the part, in khakis, a bowler hat and a toy gun. Right underneath him, barking and yelping away, the family Labrador, Raja, was tied securely with a long leash to the grand trunk of the tree. The cook wore a tiger mask and all the others banged pots and pans, to scare the 'tiger' towards the bait. In between Raja's vociferous growls, Kandu directed everyone's actions, barking out commands, "*Aur Chillao! Bhago! Idhar Aao!* Down Raja down!"

The pantomime became even more hilarious. Every time the cook approached Raja, who was supposed to be a goat tied up as bait for the tiger, the dog leaped up on his hind legs barking ferociously, straining at the leash, making the poor 'tiger cook' jump back to a safe distance. The dog was excited by all the noise and confused because he was tied up and of course terrorized by the mask.

"Maybe the dog should have worn the mask instead," said Corbin, laughing helplessly, as he watched the cook dancing around the excited dog.

"Hope it doesn't turn out this way at the machaan this week," he added as he picked up his guns and went into the house, much to Dharmu's relief. Knowing Kandu's inquisitive nature, she was not happy at all about guns lying around. Those weapons were much safer in Corbin's room, off limits to Kandu.

A heart wrenching wail suddenly emanated from the servant's quarters.

"*Maago...Naa...Maago...naa...Amaar Kamala...Maago!!*"

No, Mother Goddess, no, not my Kamala!!

It was Meera. They had found Kamala's remains and Meera's worst nightmare was realized. It was almost as if she had a premonition about the foreboding event when she asked for permission to bring her daughter to the big house. Why did Kamala go alone to fetch water? She knew the rules. She knew one must never go into the jungle alone, aware fully of safety in numbers. But she had disobeyed the cardinal rule and paid for it with her young life.

Dharmu walked round the back of the house to the servants' quarters where the inconsolable Meera was crying and lamenting. She banged her chest and swayed from side to side, all the while repeating,

"*Maago…Maago…Kamala.*" In the span of a few minutes, the comic scene in the garden had converted into one of desolate, desperate grief. Talking in loud whispers, the servants huddled around Meera's room, their faces mirroring the deep angst consuming Meera.

News had come from the village. When Kamala did not return to the hut at sundown, the neighbors realized something was wrong but they could not begin the search till the following morning. It was too dark and they did not know where to begin. The farmers had seen her walking towards the jungle but she could have gone anywhere. There were several ghats along the river bank and Kamala could be near any one of them. The next morning, the men set out in parties of five. In an hour, one unfortunate party arrived at the ill-fated ghat and confronted a horrific sight.

Two brass pots were bobbing on the edge of the river and in the wet, bloody mud, they saw fresh pug marks. Kamala definitely had been attacked by the tiger but there was no sign of her body. They noticed the surrounding area had blood smears in the mud, where the tiger probably dragged the body into the shade of the trees to complete his meal in solitude. The bushes were covered with long strands of black hair. Then, they found in the undergrowth one nubile leg still awash in its own gore, torn above the knee but intact otherwise. On the slender ankle gleamed the anklet Meera had bought for Kamala the previous year. There was no doubt Kamala was the tiger's latest victim.

They brought the leg back to the village and immediately set out to inform Meera, as her husband was away and someone needed to arrange to cremate her remains. Corbin joined them soon after, questioning and commiserating, trying to understand what happened. The cook, who spoke a smattering of English, translated. In the midst of this grief, Dharmu suddenly felt a giggle bubbling up to her lips at the cook's comic attempt at English, which was worse than her own. Dharmu went in to see Meera, who was rocking from side to side banging her head on the edge of the bed. No matter what anyone said, she could not be consoled, so intense was her anguish.

Once again, Dharmu watched karma unfold right before her eyes. Death struck unexpectedly, completely disrupting her life. Meera was a good woman. She did nothing to deserve this.

Meera's whole life was one of sacrifice and hardship. Born into a poor farming family, she struggled to keep them fed. Sometimes, when there was no food, she slept after drinking just a cup of water. The pangs of hunger kept her awake all night but she comforted herself with the thought that her husband needed food to work in the fields under the grueling sun and her child needed nourishment, so one more day of hunger would not kill her. These last few years the position as an ayah in Rangpur had improved her quality of life. At least she received two full meals a day. She felt guilty about her own good fortune and often spoke of how people in her village were so poor; sometimes when the crop was bad, they ate mud cakes to keep hunger at bay. But she consoled herself, saying she was in Rangpur for her family's sake.

Meera's saw her child for only twelve precious days a year; all her actions were done so that her daughter could be fed and clothed. Now what did she have to live for? There seemed to be no purpose. God was testing her in ways incomprehensible to mortal minds. And Kamala? What did she do to deserve such a death? All that was left of her was one leg. She had so much to live for. Like other young girls, Kamala should have married and had children of her own. But that was not how things turned out. Nothing made any sense. They must have committed terrible acts in their past lives to deserve such a fate in this one.

What words could heal her tormented soul? What could Dharmu do to calm her mental anguish? How was she going to go on? There were no answers.

She knew Meera had to return home to cremate the remains of her daughter. She needed to be with her family and friends at this time. She never got a chance to say goodbye to Kamala and required some time to grieve and find some peace after this terrible ordeal. The ritual death ceremonies and company of her close family would give her some comfort. But she would probably never get over Kamala's violent death.

Just then Corbin walked into the room and informed them of his intention to accompany Meera to her village. If he saw Kamala's remains and the accident site, he would get vital clues to track down the Man-Eater. He also needed help from the villagers to track and kill the tiger. Meera would get closure with the death of the tiger, and Corbin would be instrumental in bringing her some justice. But the death of a tiger was poor compensation for the life of a young girl.

## CHAPTER 14 – CORBIN
### SONARPUR, EAST BENGAL

Jeff Corbin reached Sonarpur at midday. The grueling sun combined with the humidity made it almost impossible for him to breathe. His clothing didn't help. Thick khaki pants and a full-sleeved shirt made the sweltering heat even more unbearable. Corbin preferred to be fully covered, so he would not be prey to the swarms of mosquitoes that inhabited this scorching delta. The local people were immune to insect bites and men were clothed in mere loin cloths, never bothering to use upper garments. For the local populace, death from disease was commonplace and with poor access to medical care, life expectancy was low. Corbin always wondered why anyone chose to live in such harsh surroundings. But to the locals, this was home, this was their entire universe.

Corbin and Meera got down from the horse cart about a mile away from the village. From here, they had to trek through the thick forest on foot, as there were no accessible pathways, just a dirt track carved out of the jungle. Meera became his guide, navigating through the thick foliage with an uncanny familiarity. She had not spoken at all. For one, she did not know English and added to that, her mind was singularly focused on reaching her home in Sonarpur. In the village, only one man knew English, who officiated as the guide for all the Forest Officers and visiting Englishmen. He was to be Corbin's companion for the next few weeks, or however long it took to kill the man-eater.

Corbin clutched the butt of the rifle, his senses on high alert for sharp birdcalls or the shrill cry of the cheetal that would signal danger. His eyes scanned the surrounding area for any sudden movement. It took about a half hour before they reached a clearing. From the edge of a copse of mangrove trees, he could see about two dozen huts. A huge fire was burning and he could spot more fires around the perimeter of the village of Sonarpur. This was typical after a tiger kill. For a while villagers became vigilant, trying to protect themselves from further attacks, leading to a frenzied tiger hunt. Once the animal was killed, they slipped back into their old ways, letting caution drop away. Meera broke into a run and Corbin watched as people emerged from their huts and on spotting her, ran out to greet her. Corbin slowed down, not wanting to interrupt Meera's reunion with her family.

He could see the entire village of Sonarpur in front of him. On either side of the community were fields of paddy, beautiful velvet green rice fields stretching out from the tree line. The huts were very rudimentary, built out of dried mud with thatched fronds for roofs. Most of the people who lived in this area were subsistence farmers. The soil was very rich and every year the summer brought with it torrential rain and floods. The Ganga and the Brahmaputra rivers met at the Sunderbans delta and floods could sometimes be sudden and devastating, killing hundreds of people. Hungry tigers probably got their first taste of human flesh feasting on bodies brought in by the tides. But when the flood subsided, the rich alluvial soil remained, replenishing the land. Cut off from the rest of the world, these farmers grew the rice, pulses and vegetables needed for survival. The river was nearby and farmers complemented their meal with fresh-water fish. Their favorite meal was fried *Bhetki* soaked in spices with boiled rice. As the community grew, more land was needed and farmers began encroaching on the surrounding forests, cutting down and burning trees in their quest for more arable land. The only way growing communities could survive was by going deeper into the forests to collect food like honey, fish, shrimp and crabs by the water's edge and wood for their boats and homes and this brought them in closer proximity to the tiger. Fishing expeditions took the men away from their villages for many hours at a time, leaving them vulnerable to tiger attacks.

Territorial in nature, tigers found their hunting grounds were smaller with the depletion of forests and switched to targeting humans, becoming the biggest threat to these isolated villagers. Every village had a local deity they prayed to for protection against this fearsome predator, like Banobibi in Sonarpur. Before venturing out into the forests, the villagers always prayed for her protection. Kamala did too, but her destiny was overriding. Knowing there was a man-eating tiger on the prowl, she should not have tempted fate by venturing out to the ghats alone.

The rivalry between the region's top two predators was based on equal amounts of fear and respect. Old and wounded tigers discovered long ago that humans were easy prey. Many villages domesticated cattle and goats and tigers showed their displeasure at the encroachment by carrying off a cow or a goat. The Sunderbans' maze of swamp, islands, and mangrove forests was one of the very few places left in the world where man was not on top of the food chain, and it was just a matter of time before an emboldened tiger wandered into the village to carry away a child or woman, even as they slept inside their huts. The chase was less exhausting and the kill was easy. Locals believed once a tiger tasted human blood, its thirst for more would become an addiction that could only end with the death of the tiger. Villagers stood in groups at night with fires burning, so at any moment a burning log could be used to fend off a tiger attack. They beat drums and screamed together to alert fellow villagers on sighting a tiger, even on sensing any suspicious sound or movement. One cardinal rule they always followed was going out in groups, never alone, no matter what the urgency. Sometimes people going into the forest wore tiger masks with the face on the back of their heads in the belief that tigers always attack from behind. Meera had given one of these masks to Kandu.

Bantu, the official translator, ran out to meet Corbin. "Come Saar, leg of Kamala here. Come."

Corbin followed him to the back of the village near the small Banobibi temple. What he saw affected him deeply; he would remember it for the rest of his life. A comely leg, bitten off cleanly a little above the knee, as if it had been severed by an axe. On the ankle was a silver anklet, round and tubular, filled with shells. Looking at the clean bite of the tiger, Corbin knew that Kamala's death would have been very quick. This was a hungry, devious and efficient killing machine. More than half a dozen deaths were attributed to this killer, whom Corbin named the Sonarpur tiger.

"Don't let Meera see this. Spare her the agony," he said to a bewildered Bantu, whose English was not that advanced. It was clear from the lack of expression on Bantu's face he did not understand a word. So Corbin mimed it. "Cover the leg. No show Meera."

Bantu shook his head from side to side. "Understand," he said. "Sad, very sad. Meera only child now dead."

'Yes,' thought Corbin, 'for Meera's sake I need to end this story.'

93

The next morning news arrived from a neighboring village that the tiger had been spotted five kilometers downstream. People working in the fields said it was huge, maybe ten or fifteen feet long. Corbin knew he had to discount the accuracy of the information he received. To terrified villagers, the tiger was always larger than its actual size. He asked Bantu to accompany him to the site of the killing from where he would begin the tracking process. After a hot cup of tea and a breakfast of steaming rice balls and spinach, Corbin and Bantu set out. Corbin's back was sore from sleeping on the floor but he would get used to it. Bantu shared his hut with Corbin, and all the villagers were so hospitable that Corbin did not have the heart to complain. Although he had his own supply of dry packaged food and water, over time he had developed a taste for Indian food. Over the years the spices that initially burned his mouth and inflamed his intestines had become more palatable, and soon he could tell the difference between the cooking in the northern Himalayas, where he was normally stationed and here in Bengal. A lot of mustard and green chilly was used here, whereas in the North, they were partial to cumin and red chillies.

The walk to the ghats was not very long but Corbin imagined himself as a frightened child, walking alone in these parts. He felt Kamala's presence guiding his movements and it made his resolve to find the tiger even stronger. The edge of the ghat was full of footprints and several pug marks. Corbin bent down and examined them closely. A pad was missing in the hind paw, which would help in identifying and tracking the tiger. The attack must have taken place on the edge of the ghat. The tiger would have killed her with one powerful bite to the neck perhaps and then dragged her body into the trees. The thick bracken bushes were spotted with blood and long strands of raven black hair draped over its prickly branches. There were no more remains of the body. Either the tiger ate all the flesh or carried the remains someplace else to eat at a later time. This was very common. Tigers ate voraciously initially because the gnawing hunger would be unbearable and once they were satisfied, they returned to the carcass to feed on it at a later time.

From there, they walked to the spot where the Tiger was last seen. Corbin examined the pug marks. Yes, it was definitely the same tiger. The pug marks had the tell-tale missing pad on the hind leg. The wound caused by the missing pad was probably painful, slowing down

94

the tiger's customary lightning speed. Corbin knew he would not need to travel too far, as tigers hunted only within a marked territory, which sometimes extended more than two hundred kilometers. But this tiger was wounded which could possibly hamper its movement, keeping it within a small area. They would spend the night at a nearby village and keep on tracking the movements of the tiger till they found the right spot for a machaan.

Both men were exhausted by the time they reached the village and grateful to rest their aching feet. Like all Indian villages, this one was extremely hospitable. Corbin was overwhelmed by the welcome he received, no matter where he went. However poor they were, they happily shared their meager meals and space, especially here in the wilderness, where they were excited to have visitors — particularly a white-skinned one. Most of them had never seen a white man before and stared unabashedly without blinking. Slowly, the children plucked up their courage and came up to him and attempted touching and rubbing his skin to see if his color was painted on. Corbin was used to this reaction and was gentle with them, allowing them to familiarize themselves with him. After all, he was going to live there for a few days at least. This village was called Gopalgunj, and the headman let them sleep in his hut. As the sun set over the trees in the distance, the two men sat down to a delicious meal of fish curry and soft, fluffy rice. The meal was served in a plate made out of dried *shaal* leaves, commonly found in this area and of course they ate with their hands, smacking and licking and swallowing every tasty morsel, unmindful of the liquid dribbling down their chins and fingers. After eight hours with no food, they considered this the most delicious meal they had ever eaten.

Over the next few days, Corbin and Bantu followed various leads they had received. The villages were well connected and they gathered a group of eight men, all very familiar with the jungle. Two of the men boasted of actual encounters with tigers and proudly showed off their scars. Corbin admired their courage, not realizing it was his guns that inspired them to follow the tracks of this feline predator along with him — that, combined with the adrenalin of the chase. Finally, they had a map of sorts, which showed that the animal was moving in an area within a three-mile radius. Corbin selected an opening in the forest not far from the river as the best place to build the machaan and lure the tiger. He chose a banyan tree with low limbs so a machaan could be comfortably built. He did not want to be too far away in case he missed his shot. But at the same time, the tree limb needed to be far enough from the ground, out of reach of the tiger. The men were busy that day, cutting wood and making a platform by tying planks of wood together with thick rope. Finally, it was lined with grass and leaves for some degree of comfort. The villagers brought a goat as bait and tied it to the bottom of the tree. At dusk, the beaters would begin their job, using loud drums and screaming in unison, walking around the perimeter they had set to chase the cat in the direction of the bait.

More than one week had passed since the last kill. The tiger was sure to be hungry. Corbin hoped it had not wandered too far away. Two nights went by with them sitting on the machaan but there was no sign of the tiger. The next morning, they discovered pugmarks by the river, just a few hundred feet away from where the machaan was. The tiger was definitely nearby and it was just a matter of waiting patiently. At sundown, Corbin took his position in the machaan. Bantu was with him, quiet and watchful. A few minutes later, he heard the rustling of leaves. The goat, sensing danger, started bleating pitifully. Corbin picked up his .275 Rigsby rifle and cocked it, ready for any sudden movement.

The tiger stepped out into the open, his eyes locked on the bleating bait. Then in a flash it pounced on the goat, biting at the neck and slicing it almost completely. Corbin discharged his rifle at the same time and got a clean shot just blow the ferocious tiger's muscular neck. The tiger reared up growling in pain and to Corbin's consternation and utter surprise, began climbing the tree. Corbin was an experienced hunter but he had never been in this predicament before and was not mentally ready for this eventuality. It took him a few seconds to pick up his second rifle and cock it. This time he was taking no chances. At a distance of five feet, he fired the second shot. As the shell entered the tiger's brain, the magnificent creature reeled back and with an earthshaking roar fell to the ground. Corbin was out of breath and wet with perspiration, the adrenalin pumping inside him, his body reeling from the after effects of such a close encounter. When he sensed all movement had stopped, he ventured to climb down. Bantu was transfixed, his loincloth wet, showing tell-tale signs of his fear. He climbed down after Corbin and stared for a few minutes at the vanquished cat. It was unbelievable that the animal which had caused so much anxiety and misery for the locals was actually dead. The sound of the dying tiger had alerted the rest of the team who joined them. They all just stood for a while silently, taking in the enormity of the event. It was too late to carry the tiger back and arrangements would have to be made the next day.

The following morning the tiger's body was strapped to a huge tree trunk and it took fifteen men to carry the heavy carcass. Bantu wanted to take the prize back to Sonarpur so that Meera could see it. It was a long and arduous journey, as they were weighed down by sheer mass of the tiger. However, they had many hands and made steady progress. Corbin always felt a little depressed after a tiger kill. He had been a hunter for many years now but over time, was consumed by a feeling of empathy for animals and a sense of oneness with nature. He saw that all things around him were interconnected, that killing animals in large numbers, especially predators, actually tipped the ecological balance. Living in the wilderness of the Himalayas developed in him a real understanding of the delicate relationship between humans and their environment. His fellow countrymen enjoyed the shikar but Corbin did not feel any thrill when he shot an animal. In fact after a hunt, he felt remorse for having killed one of God's creatures. Eventually, he stopped hunting for pleasure and only took his guns out when he was called to deal with a man-eating predator. He had mixed emotions as he watched the retinue make their way through the forest towards Sonarpur. This tiger was dead but it was just a matter of time before another man-eater emerged.

They reached Sonarpur at sundown and were spotted immediately by the children who ran up to them whooping and screaming in excitement. There was no tiger as good as a dead one. Meera was sitting on her haunches outside her hut and on hearing the ruckus she looked up but seemed to be in a trance. Slowly, she stood up. Her eyes were flashing with anger, hatred and remorse as she walked up to the dead tiger. Sinking to her knees, she pummeled the inert creature, screaming and crying uncontrollably. Everyone gathered around and watched this pitiful scene in silence. Finally, the despondent mother's blows weakened and stopped.

Yes, the tiger was dead but then so was Kamala, and nothing could change that.

# Part V
# Rajam

# CHAPTER 15 – RAJAM
## VIZHUPURAM

Rajam finished all of her morning chores and had a rare moment to sit and do nothing. She really missed her sister-in-law, Sushila, who was still at her mother's home convalescing after her miscarriage. This meant Nagamma focused all of her attention on Rajam, noticing and commenting on her every move, pre-empting her every thought and her every word. Thank heavens young Balu was around. His childish pranks made the day so much more bearable. Rajam waited for Nagamma to take a mid-morning snooze so she could get some respite from the constant harassment. Month after month she waited to miss her period, but it came like clockwork every twenty eight days like an unwanted guest, leaving her listless and anxious. Now she read disapproval even in Nagamma's casual glances. If only she would conceive. Rajam sighed deeply but her fatigue was more mental than physical.

Her father, Swaminathan, had moved to the nearby town of Chidambaram and Rajam missed his visits terribly. His constant support had kept her going, especially in the first year after she had moved here. Seeing him again and visiting the home where she grew up made her very nostalgic. She couldn't help thinking of the time before she moved into Partha's home, the period in her life after marriage and before she started menstruating. She was happy to continue living with her parents awaiting the onset of puberty. Only then would the nuptials ceremony, the Shanthi Kalyanam, be performed and she be permitted to live with Partha and share his bed; only now it seemed so long ago.

Rajam moved into her in-laws' home almost two years after her marriage. Although she was only twelve years old at her wedding, she did not have to stay with her in-laws until she was menstruating. That meant there was no sexual contact between Rajam and Partha at all during this time. In fact, almost no physical contact was permitted between them. Partha visited Rajam every day after school and then after college for the next two agonizing years. The waiting period was sheer misery for him and it took every ounce of latent patience and fortitude to wait out this time. They sat together in the mutram in her father's house, where Rajam focused intently on swinging back and forth on the oonjal, not paying any attention to Partha

All Rajam thought of was dressing up and playing with her dolls and toys. She was still a child and did not understand the significance of marriage — the difference between the world of a twelve year-old girl and that of a seventeen year-old boy. To her, Partha was this hefty boy who came to see her every day, which was so boring because she had to stop playing and come and sit with him. What's more, she had to talk to him, a tedious affair, because she had absolutely nothing to say to him. He didn't play hopscotch or house and he was always so shifty and edgy, always trying to touch her. Long periods of silence suspended languorously between them after her mother instructed her not to swing on the oonjal while Partha visited. She was supposed to show him utmost respect because he had a special place in her life as her husband. But to her, "husband" was just another word and had no real significance.

Slowly, Partha became a little bolder and periodically reached out to touch her hand but she would wriggle out of his grasp. She constantly threatened to complain to her mother, much to Partha's consternation. Her skin was so fair and ever so sensitive that even the slightest pressure caused it to redden and he did not put it past her to run off to her mother and complain that Partha had hurt her. That could cause problems for him, even result in stopping visitation rights!! It was terribly frustrating! What was the point of being married if you could not touch your wife? Partha could not wait for the official ceremony, the Shanthi Kalyanam, to be performed but that could only take place after Rajam began menstruating. How did you make a girl get her periods? Partha was exasperated beyond measure. All he could think of was the elusive Shanthi Kalyanam. Until then, Mangalam made sure they were chaperoned at all times and never alone for more than two minutes at a time. It was a game of wits. Partha would wait until Mangalam left them alone and then make a quick grab for Rajam but by the time the squiggling was over, it was time for Mangalam to return. This meant Partha had to quickly sit upright and pretend nothing had happened. Then he got a great idea: asking for coffee!! That sent Mangalam away for at least five minutes and gave Partha a few precious minutes alone with Rajam to wiggle and wriggle

Of course, protocol needed to be followed, which meant Partha had to make small talk with his future mother-in-law but as he was seeing her every day, the two of them had little to talk about. After "How are you? I am fine. And you? Fine. How are things at home? All right," an awkward silence fell between them.

Every morning on his way to school, Partha broke a coconut at the Ganesh temple, praying for Rajam to get her menses. Even as he did this, he immediately felt ashamed that he was so absorbed with carnal desire. But he told himself that, after all, he was a strapping young man and Rajam was legally his wife. Many times he was tempted to ask his friends if they thought of sex all the time but his courage failed him and he just assumed all young boys were the same and there was nothing wrong with him.

After his wedding, Nagamma sat him down, instructing him with the do's and don'ts of a married man. There were a hundred and one rules for men and that multiplied tenfold when it came to rules for women. Social etiquette was very important, especially in a Brahmin household, because it reflected one's culture and upbringing. It was no easy task to be a Brahmin, even though people envied their social advantage given their position at the pinnacle of the caste pyramid. It had been drilled into Partha's head that in ancient times you did not become a Brahmin by merely being born into a Brahmin family. You had to earn that title by rigorously studying the Vedas for several years and then impart that knowledge to other students. You had to perform poojas, rituals and *yagnas*, chanting the ancient mantras and perform these rituals for those who were yet uninitiated. In every home learned Brahmins were called to officiate as priests, performing ceremonies for birth, marriage, atonement and death. Partha knew in theory that to be called a Brahmin you had to give away your wealth and live only on the offerings from other people. This was given to the Brahmin as *dakshina*, "fees," for performing ceremonies. On days there was no food in the house, Brahmins would go door to door asking for alms and it was considered a privilege for housewives to fill their outstretched palms with food. More importantly, Brahmins ate only one meal a day and that too, in limited quantity; they were only permitted to eat the food that fitted in the palms of their hands. By all these measures, Partha was certainly not a Brahmin. He had not learned the scriptures, so he could not perform ceremonies for others, and he ate quantities of food that filled his large palms and those of every other person living on his street. His appetite was well known and Nagamma jokingly referred to him as Bheeman, the perennially hungry, mythical Pandava Prince. In his family, even though the concept of being a Brahmin had changed for several generations, the innumerable social rules of behavior were never given up. They were rigorously followed in the hope that at least this would make them worthy of their esteemed birth. Partha's mind reeled with the different rules to be kept in mind and practiced.

When you go there don't talk to Rajam first. Be patient. Converse with the elders first.

If any elders are present, you must bow down and do *namaskaram* to them as soon as you see them.

Be careful how you sit. Under no circumstances should you place one foot on top of the other knee. That is extremely disrespectful.

In case you are offered any food, accept it with both hands. Even by mistake, do not stick your left hand out.

And if you buy flowers for Rajam, do not smell them. Mangalam might offer the flowers to god in her pooja, so be aware.

You can talk to Rajam but there must be a distance of at least two feet between you and her. Do not attempt to touch her, and the list went on.

Partha of course was selective about following the rules. There were far too many and in any case, he thought he followed most of them.

When Rajam first noticed a smear of blood on her pavadai, she thought she had hurt herself but the bleeding continued, though it was sporadic. She knew everyone was waiting for this event eagerly but to fourteen year old Rajam, this meant she would have to leave her mother's house forever, so she wanted to hide it from them as long as possible. It wasn't until the third day that she decided to give her mother the news. Mangalam took her to the back of the house, the '*kollai pakkam,*' and gave her a long muslin sari, which she cut into four pieces. Then she showed her how to roll the muslin cloth into a pad and place it so that it would soak up the menstrual blood. She then helped her attach it on both sides of a piece of string that she tied around Rajam's waist. She had to wash the blood off this cloth every day and leave it to dry at the back of the house, where no male members of the house could see it. For Rajam, this was a repulsive act and she gagged violently every time she did it. However, Mangalam explained to her that in time she would get used to it and it would just become a routine task like any other.

Rajam was to sit in the back room and wait while Mangalam got busy making all the arrangements. She called for her sister, Parvathi, to come and help her. That evening all the ladies from the neighborhood had to be invited for a ceremony to celebrate Rajam's entry into womanhood, and Parvathi rushed out of the house to do just that. This was the first and last time Rajam was allowed to mingle with others during her period.

Rajam was dressed for the first time in a sari, a garment she was now allowed to wear, which would be her clothing of choice henceforth. She sat on a chair and all the women put *nalangu* on her feet and hands. Fresh turmeric was used for this purpose and lines were carefully drawn on the edge of her feet and across them in symmetric stripes. The women sang as they dressed her up, putting black *mai* in her eyes and strings of jasmine in her hair, anointing her with kumkumam and chandanam and praying for her long and happy married life. Everyone made lewd references to what was expected of her as a married woman but Rajam had no idea what they meant.

Mangalam was sad to send Rajam away and forced a smile on her face. The last of her daughters. She went through the day's ceremonies with a heavy heart. From now on, Rajam had to leave her childhood behind and face the harsh realities of womanhood. That evening, when Swaminathan came home, she shared the news with him. He was not allowed to see Rajam because she had three days of *theetu*, where she would have to live separately until she bathed on the fourth day and then re-entered her home. Swaminathan left immediately on his bicycle to inform Partha's family about the forthcoming Shanthi Kalyanam.

Mangalam spent the next day preparing for Rajam's departure. Tearfully, she packed Rajam's belongings, the saris, the jewelry and silver vessels that were part of her dowry. She was so busy she had no time to prepare Rajam for the events in the near future, about what it meant to be a wife. She had thought of doing this many times but always put it off each time, thinking she had time to get around to it. But that time had come and she had still not spoken to Rajam about anything.

The following morning the family departed in a beautiful vilvandi, a covered bullock cart specially decorated for the auspicious journey. Mangalam finally spoke to Rajam, giving her hurried advice that would prove crucial for her survival over the next few months.

"Rajam…," she began gingerly. "The next few days are going to be hard for you. You will have to get used to living in a new house. Remember all we have taught you and make us proud. From now on, your husband will be the most important person in your life. You must do whatever he says and always make him happy. Your mother-in-law will teach you all the rules of their household. Never raise your eyes when she speaks or sit in the presence of adults unless they specifically ask you to. You will have to awaken early to help with all the chores. Just listen to your mother-in-law. Don't do anything to make her angry. Ultimately, your happiness is in her hands. She can make your life bliss or a misery. It all depends on how you and she get along. Always be diplomatic and choose your words carefully. Never be the cause of discord in your family. Things in your new home are going to be very different. You cannot eat before others have eaten as you did all these years. From now on, you have to wait until your husband has eaten and then you may sit down to eat. You are now going to live the life of a married woman. A new phase in your life is going to begin. There will be many things you will have to do that you may not like but you will have to be strong and do them anyway. But don't worry; we are always here for you whenever you need us. Your father will come and see you as often as possible, just to make sure you are alright, so you will always have us."

Rajam listened but none of it was sinking in; she was so choked up with emotion. She did not want to leave the safe haven that had been her home. She did not want to go and live with her husband. Most of all, she did not want to leave her father.

Swaminathan looked at Rajam and knew her mind was in turmoil. A father's job was filled with tough choices. He had to make sure all

105

his children were married into good families but parting was like tearing away at his flesh.

It was strange that in life pleasure and pain always go together, although they are diametrically opposite. Pleasure could never be known or appreciated unless one felt the wrenching torment of pain. He knew this moment was inevitable but when it came, he could not prevent the rush of emotions flooding his being. Swaminathan was sad to part with his youngest daughter, but his sadness would have been much greater had she not married at all. He put down the melancholy and pain to the end of an era — the end of Rajam's childhood.

But there was happiness at the other end of the journey with Rajam beginning a new phase. Partha and his family were excited to welcome another addition to their family. Ever since Partha heard the news of her period, he could not sit still and the last two days were the longest of his life. He must have made a hundred trips to the front gate, squinting to catch the first glimpse of the vilvandi turning the corner. He was not sad at leaving behind *Brahmacharya*, his bachelorhood, but instead elated at the prospect of being a married man. Suddenly, he was the focus of all the attention in his house. His life was going to transform but this was change filled with promises of pleasure and happiness. Now he was a man, with new status and responsibilities.

The priest was waiting to perform the ceremony as Nagamma and Sushila did the *aarathi*, welcoming Rajam for the first time to their house. She caught a glimpse of Partha waving to her from the back, above the heads of all the other people; neighbors and relatives gathered here to welcome the new bride and attend the Shanthi Kalyanam. The rituals went by in a blur and the two were ushered into the bedroom for the first time as man and wife.

Mangalam told Rajam many things but omitted many others. Things that were extremely important. Like what happens between a man and woman on the night of their nuptials. Mangalam was too shy to broach the subject and assumed she would learn about it from her husband, just like millions of other girls who had gone through the same situation.

For Partha, the ceremony seemed to be taking forever. Finally, after an interminable wait, Partha was alone with Rajam in the bedroom. The bed was decorated with rose petals. A silver glass filled with crushed almonds in milk awaited the groom to give him the energy needed for his debut performance, and the aroma of incense sticks filled the room. Rajam sat on the bed not knowing what to expect. She remembered what her mother told her, that she had to do whatever her husband wanted and sat motionless, waiting for his next move. When he touched her, she tried to stay still and not wiggle and squirm. When he disrobed her, gently pulling off her sari and blouse, only her widened eyes betrayed her horror. And when the kneading and pinching of her nonexistent breasts began, she closed her eyes tight not knowing whether to laugh or cry. She felt completely befuddled when he spread her legs and tried to thrust what felt like a stick into her. She was sure she would never be able to urinate again. She could not imagine why anyone wanted to put a stick into your privates. After several unsuccessful attempts, Partha dropped off to sleep.

Rajam opened her eyes and sat up. Then slowly, she crept out of bed to look for the stick but she could not find it anywhere, not on the bed or under it. Maybe he was sleeping on it. She would look for it in the morning, when there was more light. She wrapped the sari around her several times, then lay down next to her supine husband and slept.

The next morning after Partha awoke, Rajam searched the bed once again for the elusive stick but it was nowhere to be found. She left the room and went to the back of the house to bathe. After her bath, she had the impossible task of draping the sari around her. She had no idea how to do this and wished she had paid more attention when her mother draped it for her. Finally, she wrapped it around herself several times and put the end around her shoulders. She could barely walk and had to take baby steps to move. Shuffling across the back porch, she reached the kitchen. Both Nagamma and Sushila were already in the midst of preparing the morning meal. There was a moment of silence when they saw her wrapped like a bandage and then Sushila burst into laughter. Even Nagamma could not stifle a smile.

"Go, Sushila, teach her how to tie a sari." Nagamma's older daughter-in-law put her arms around Rajam and led her into the bedroom.

"*Vaa maa* I'll show you how it's done. The only tricky part is in tying the pleats. And I'll tell you another trick: if you wear your sari high, just above your ankles, then you can walk freely." Sushila allowed her to practice wearing the sari several times and then the two of them returned to the kitchen. Nagamma did not want to haul her into household chores immediately, with her being a new bride, so she handed her a *morai* and asked her to clean the rice. Rajam had done that several times before, and she was happy her first task was an easy one. Soon, she would be in for another mild shock.

Amma told her that she would have to eat after her husband finished, but she omitted telling her that she would have to eat off her husband's *yecchal* banana leaf. From the time she was a young girl, yecchal and rules surrounding it were ingrained into her. Saliva or yecchal, was a source of contamination and you could not allow your spit to contaminate anyone else. It was sacrilege to drink out of another person's glass; even vessels from the kitchen were never kept in the dining area, lest some contaminating spit fell into them. The banana leaves they ate on were immediately cleared and the area wiped thoroughly before anyone else ate. So she was horrified when Nagamma instructed her to sit and eat off of Partha's yecchal banana leaf. She kept feeling her bile come up into her mouth and wanted to vomit. This was against everything she was taught. For several days after, she got up after meals eating close to nothing. Her mother in all probability did not warn her about this because they did not practice this custom. Swaminathan would not hear of it in his house, so Rajam had never seen it. Sushila ate heartily and Rajam wondered how she did that. It was the most revolting experience for her and all week she felt as if her stomach were aching. She was sure she was sick.

Partha spent the whole of the next day thinking about his unsuccessful 'first night.' He realized he would have to take the expert advice of friends and after a lot of thought, shamefacedly confided in his closest friend, Cheenu, who was the self-styled expert on the subject.

"Hmm, virgins are always a problem but nothing works better than a few drops of ghee." That evening before entering the room, Partha stole into the kitchen and took a spoonful of ghee, generously applying it to himself. That night was even more of a disaster, with his slithering member slipping around everywhere other than the intended aperture. Rajam was even more puzzled. First a stick and now this slippery, slithery, snakelike object. Her husband must be a *manthravadhi*, a magician.

The next day Partha confronted his friend, telling him his advice was useless.

"Partha, there must be some mistake, because ghee is an excellent lubricant. Where did you put it? On your wife or on yourself?"

He didn't need an answer. Partha's face told him all that he needed to know.

"Fool, you have to put it on the girl, not on yourself." Of course, Partha knew that!

The next day, a resolute Partha returned to the bedroom and much to Rajam's horror, wasted no time in applying the ghee to her genitals. Rajam was appalled Partha touched the part of her body that she urinated from. Dirty fellow! What in heaven was he doing? When he climbed on top of her, he had his magic stick once again, but this time she could feel the sustained pressure on her genitals. Then the wrenching pain as she was deflowered. She opened her mouth to scream but Partha realizing this, covered her mouth with his hand.

"Please don't scream; everyone will hear. Then it will be *avamaanam*, shame, for both of us. I'm so sorry, so sorry. I didn't want to hurt you. I promise I won't be so rough next time. Please don't cry."

Rajam was crying silently and as Partha rolled off her, she put both her hands in between her legs, rocking back and forth, weeping silently.

What was happening? Why did he want to hurt her? Is this what married people did? She did not understand anything. Partha put his arms around her, comforting her the best way he knew. The next morning was agony for Rajam, as the pain was incredible. She could not stand or sit and it burned when she urinated. She could not walk properly and kept both legs two feet apart to stop the chafing. Everyone was looking at her and smirking and she felt tears coming to her eyes. Sushila watched her for a while, shaking her head in sympathy. She too had gone through the same experience not so long ago and she remembered it clearly. Only she had no one to help her and had to process the whole experience on her own, but her heart went out to young Rajam. She knew she had to help her. She went to the kitchen and heated some coconut oil. Then she took Rajam to the back of the house, where she knew they would be alone.

"Here Rajam. I know how you feel. It hurts a lot, doesn't it? Apply this coconut oil. It will soothe the area."

"Akka, the pain is terrible. I can't walk or sit or do anything," said Rajam in between hiccupping and crying.

109

"Shh, don't cry now. Don't worry; the pain will go away. It will hurt initially but after a few months you will even enjoy it."

Rajam was crying copiously. "Akka I don't know what happened with you but my husband is a manthravadhi. One day he brings a stick to the bedroom and the next day a snake. Yesterday he had the stick again and he put it right inside me. The pain was so bad. But the funny thing is that I don't know where he puts the stick once he is done. I looked everywhere but I couldn't find it."

Sushila threw her head back, laughing uncontrollably. "Silly girl. Partha is no magician. That stick you are referring to is not something that magically appears. It is attached to his body."

"Attached to his body?" said Rajam, now more confused than ever.

"Siva Anna? Does he also have one attached to his body?"

"Yes. All men do."

"Then how come I never noticed it before? Doesn't it stick out of their veshtis? How do they hide it during the day?" This was getting more and more mysterious. Sushila knew there were plenty of questions on the tip of Rajam's tongue and did not want to go there. The conversation was getting too lurid for Sushila's comfort and she didn't want to expound on more graphic details about the male anatomy.

"You will have to discover that for yourself," she declared.

That day, all Rajam could think of was about this mysterious stick attached to men. All day she eyed the lower halves of all the men in the house, trying to see if she could see the silhouette of the stick.

In the evening, she went into the bedroom determined to investigate and get to the bottom of this mystery of the male stick.

Rajam giggled thinking about that time in her life. In hindsight it was funny, and she and Partha could laugh about it. Now her problems were different and much more complex. How life had changed.

She rubbed her belly gently and stared vacantly at her feet.

# CHAPTER 16 – RAJAM
## VIZHUPURAM

The following morning, the whistling from the *idli paanai* brought Rajam running into the kitchen. Idli was Partha's favorite dish and Rajam enjoyed making it for him. She just loved watching him eat, even though making idli was a long drawn out and tedious process. Two nights ago she soaked the rice and white lentils overnight, and spent all of the next morning grinding it. Finally, after an hour's work, the dough had the right soft and fine consistency. Rajam enjoyed the final task in the idli making process only because she knew that after this she could rest. She mixed the dough, salted it and left it in a large, covered, brass vessel out in the hot sun to ferment all day and overnight. By morning, the dough rose to the brim, ready for the preparation of idli.

She lifted the idli paanai off the fire and carefully pulled the cooked idlis off the thin muslin. Knowing how many idlis Partha himself could demolish, she knew she had to make some more. After filling some water into the pot, she poured a tablespoonful of fermented idli dough into the shallow mold over the thin muslin cloth. In about ten minutes, the idlis were steamed and ready to serve. Round, white, hot, rice and lentil cakes.

Making sure no one was watching, she dipped the idli into the green coconut chutney Nagamma had just ground, and popped it into her mouth. Idli tasted best when complemented with coconut chutney, sambar, molahapodi drenched in gingelly (sesame) oil.

Rajam took a while getting used to the daily routine. When she first came to live with her in-laws, the most difficult part was waking up at three in the morning to get the day's chores going. The first job was drawing water from the well. Drinking water was stored in earthenware pots after filtering it through muslin. Surprisingly, the water remained cool even though the kitchen was unbearably hot. Then the pots needed for washing and bathing were filled. The fire in the bathing area was stoked at the same time, over which a huge brass cauldron of water was placed. By the time the men awoke, there was hot water for bathing. The women always bathed early, before the men woke up, as that was the only time they had privacy in the open bathing area. The climate was so warm, on most days they bathed in cold water. On winter mornings, they woke up a little earlier to bathe in hot water. They could not begin any cooking until they had bathed and performed the morning prayers. Only after they lit the lamp in the pooja altar were they permitted to enter the kitchen to begin the day's cooking.

Following this, the women of the household washed the floor outside the main entrance. Luckily for Rajam, cow dung was spread over the floor weekly rather than every day. Once they washed the entrance, the women made designs or *kolam* on the floor out of rice flour. By the end of the day, the ants had eaten most of the kolam. By nine o' clock in the morning, the majority of the day's chores and the main meal for the day were over and the women could afford to relax and rest. This was the time they visited the temple, where offering prayers was just an excuse to meet and chat with their friends.

Later in the morning, when the sun was up, they washed the clothes. A granite washing-stone stood near the bathing area. The women rubbed soap on the clothes and then repeatedly slapped them against the inclined surface of the stone. Once they completed the washing, the women took a much-needed nap before arising to make the afternoon coffee and tiffin.

That evening all the family members gathered around the pooja as Nagamma did the *aarathi*, burning camphor and ringing the brass bell to ward off evil and bring in good fortune. Everyone briefly passed their hands over the flaming camphor, accepting the grace of God and then bent down in obeisance to do *namaskaram*, chanting their evening prayers at the same time. Partha followed Rajam out the front door and sat down on the thinnai watching her light the beautiful Kamakshi brass lamps, which anointed the entrance. "Are you happy?" he asked her tentatively.

"Why do you ask? You want to know now — after so many years?" Rajam raised one eyebrow quizzically.

"No, I just wonder if all this housework is too much for you with Sushila away."

"Every woman has to do it. The food will not appear like magic on the banana leaf."

"I know that. Do you want to go home for a few days? I know it has been difficult for you."

"Maybe we could spend *Deepavali* next month with my parents. Your mother will never send me home now."

"I tell you what. Let's go to the *chandhai* this Saturday after I bring Sushila home. It will be fun for the whole family. I'll buy you a new sari if you want. And shiny glass bangles."

Rajam always enjoyed going to the village fair. It was a time everyone in the village, irrespective of caste, congregated to buy and sell their wares. There were games, street theatre and lots of food. It was so much fun; the whole day would go by seemingly in a flash. Normally the fair was held close to festival time and there was always one before the major festivals, Deepavali and *Pongal*. Rajam had been so busy she had forgotten it was almost Deepavali.

"Is it already time for the chandhai? My God, I never realized it."

"Yes. And I am going to win the idli eating competition this year."

"Well, you can start practicing right now. Today's *palaharam* is idli."

"Aha! Idli! Just thinking about it is making me hungry," said Partha licking his lips.

"*Vango Naa.* Let me serve you dinner," Rajam said with an indulgent smile.

Partha put his arms around her miniscule form, hugging her close, and his warm embrace conveyed his feelings more than any words could ever express.

# CHAPTER 17 – PARTHA
## VIZHUPURAM – 1934

The scenery was unfolding slowly for Partha because his vision was blocked by Sushila and Siva on either side. In between their heads, Partha tried to get a glimpse of the paddy fields but the dust from the ambling *vilvandi* clouded his narrow vision. His body swayed to the rhythm of the moving vehicle, now to the left and then to the right. As he gazed into the dusty distance, he saw one side of the road and then the other, almost as if he were closing one eye and then the other. Sushila was tired. She had rested for over a month at her mother's house and now the brothers were bringing her home to Vizhupuram.

"How long has it been since you married, Partha?" Siva asked, breaking the silence.

"Almost five years."

Siva smiled and then convulsed into laughter.

Sushila stirred, "Did I miss something?"

"You certainly did. You should have been there when Partha was trying to arrange his own marriage. For two weeks he danced around me begging me to speak on his behalf. Hey Partha, *thadhinginathom aadiniyaa illiyaa?*"

"That was your fault. You didn't have the courage to confront Amma."

"And you did?"

"Eventually," Partha admitted.

Sushila was totally confused. "Stop speaking in riddles and tell me what happened."

"Ask Partha."

"I wanted to marry Rajam and Siva would not ask Amma, so then I had to do it myself."

Siva roared with laughter. "Yes you did, after drinking six glasses of buttermilk and umpteen cups of coffee."

"Laugh all you want to, Siva. Finally I asked her, didn't I?"

"You certainly did." Siva conceded.

By this time Sushila was totally lost and decided to sink back into slumber. But Partha could not stop smiling. In retrospect it was funny but thinking back, that period was the most stressful time of his life, when his whole future hung in balance.

Two weeks had passed since he approached Siva to broach the subject of him marrying Rajam with Nagamma. But Siva always had some excuse. Amma is asleep; she is in a bad mood; the sun is shining; I'm sleepy; it was always something or the other. Partha got tired of asking him and decided to take matters into his own hands. He would approach the daunting Nagamma and ask her; what was so difficult about that? He walked boldly into the kitchen where his mother was grinding chutney. "Amma," he started.

"What is it?" Nagamma paused and smiled indulgently at her favorite son. Just as he was about to speak, his sister, Pattu, walked into the kitchen, sending his thoughts into complete disarray. "Can I have some coffee?" was all he could say. Moments later, he walked out into the courtyard with his second cup of coffee. Siva was there. "What happened? Did she say anything?"

"I couldn't ask her; Pattu walked in, so instead I asked for coffee." Siva was on the floor doubled up laughing.

By the time he finished his sixth cup of coffee later that week, all the brothers were in on the joke and the laughter could be heard on the next street. Every time Partha had a glass of something — buttermilk, water or coffee in his hands — the brothers went, "Attempt number twelve, thirteen, fourteen. . ." By the end of two weeks, Partha had not slept, partly because he was hyper with all the coffee in his system, and partly because he had been up all night rehearsing his speech with his mother. All the while, his brothers teased him mercilessly.

Finally, the caffeine kicked in. Nagamma was sitting in the thinnai weaving jasmines into a garland, humming to herself and seemingly in good spirits. The backdrop was right, the timing perfect and the words just rushed out of his mouth in one long unending sentence.

"MotherIthinkthatIamoldenoughtobemarried.Ifyouarethinking

ofcontactingamatchmakerdon'tbotherbecauseIhaveseenagirlwhowould
suitourfamilywell.Ifyousawheryouwouldsurelyapproveso Ithinkmaybe
youshouldgoandseeherparentsandaskforherhand.Hernameis
RajalakshmiandsheisthedaughterofInspectorSwaminathan."

By the time he finished, his head was hammering and he was
completely out of breath. He turned red and could hear his heart
pumping at the tip of his ears. What followed was a stunned silence.
Even if Nagamma had spoken, Partha was in no condition to be
listening. Thankfully, Siva chose this moment to walk in and gratefully,
Partha rushed out into the backyard.

The next few weeks went by in a blur. Nagamma called the
matchmaker to take the alliance to Swaminathan's house and get the
girl's horoscope. The couple's horoscopes had to match if any alliance
were to be pursued. At birth every child had their horoscopes made
which included a diagram mapping the sky at the time of birth,
detailing the birth stars and planetary ascendancy. The astrologer was
expected to make predictions about their life together and the number
of children that could be expected. If by chance there was a *Manglik
Dosham* then all proceedings would halt as that would indicate that the
union was flawed. Nothing moved forward till they got a positive
response from the astrologer. For Partha, the tension was intolerable.
In between cycling past his future wife's home and pretending to
study, he constantly waited for the gate to creak open heralding the
arrival of the matchmaker. Never before did he welcome this portly
Brahmin as he did when the man finally arrived.

"*Namaskaram*, Ramachandran Saar," Partha said, cheerfully
greeting the visitor.

"*Namaskaram* Partha. Is Amma at home?"

"No, she has just stepped out to go to the temple but you can talk
with me."

To Partha's horror, the Matchmaker said, "Is that so? In that case,
I'll stop by another time."

"No no no," screamed a desperate Partha, dragging him in and
seating him in the easy chair. He ran into the kitchen and got a glass of
water for his esteemed visitor and in a flash was running down the
road to the temple, to hustle his mother back. In no time, they were on
the way home. Today she seemed to be walking slower than usual and
if he could, he would have carried her home. Once they entered the
house, he nonchalantly whistled as he pottered around the front room,

116

walking in and out, hoping to catch a bit of the conversation but still trying to appear disinterested. To his utter relief, his mother called him in and said the horoscopes matched and they could proceed to the next step, which was to fix a date for the "Ponpaakal," or the official viewing of the girl.

Partha smiled, inwardly mocking himself for his frenetic state of mind before his official engagement to Rajam. The days were too long, the nights longer still. Time hung heavily on his hands and it seemed as if no one was interested in fixing things fast enough. Although it was only two weeks between the time he approached his mother and the actual Ponpaakal, Partha felt he had aged considerably in the interim. His mind was centered on one thing and one thing only, and he could not focus on anything else. Every time he climbed onto his bike to run an errand, it would involuntarily take a detour past the Swaminathan residence. Sometimes he parked under the shade of a tree to watch unnoticed, hoping to catch a glimpse of Rajam again. His mother wondered how a ten-minute errand always ended up taking the better part of an hour, but Partha was always ready with some excuse.

Finally, the matchmaker returned with a date for the Ponpaakal. It was to take place the following Friday at 5 p.m. Partha was like a madman, unable to sleep or eat properly. He was nervous about getting married but then his brother was married at sixteen, so he calmed himself with the thought that he was almost seventeen years old, ready to take on the responsibility of a householder. Besides, he always had the financial support of his family and would continue to live at home. Nothing changed, except that Rajam would now enter his life.

Friday somehow arrived. Partha looked at himself several times in the mirror to make sure he looked all right. After taking another bath, he put on the silk *veshti* with a gold *jarigai* border and a matching *angavastram*. He wore a pure white terylene shirt and carefully applied the vibuthi and kumkumam on his forehead. Once more he checked himself in the mirror. He looked dashing!

The groom's party hired an extra bullock cart for the occasion, as theirs was not large enough to fit in the whole family — mother and father, Siva, Pattu, Thambu, Kannan and of course Partha; everyone dressed for this auspicious occasion. Finally, after what seemed an eternity, they arrived at the house. Banana leaves and flower garlands

117

decorated the front entrance. A group of people waited at the doorway; amongst them, right in front greeting them, was Inspector Swaminathan himself. Partha took one look at him and his heart sank. He recognized him instantly and judging by the twinkle in the Inspector's eyes, he too recognized Partha.

'*Oh no!*' thought Partha, '*All is lost. He will never agree to the match now that he has seen me and knows who I am and what I did.*'

His mind raced back to the chance meeting with the Inspector, which took place the previous year. Partha was at the temple when he felt the urgent need to relieve himself. His need was so pressing he could not wait a moment longer. So he went to the back wall of the temple and began gleefully emptying his bladder. Soon, both his friends followed suit, when two constables turned the corner. The three boys were so engrossed in what they were doing they did not notice the policemen. Before the boys had time to complete their task and make themselves decent, they felt rough hands on their shirts and were hauled off to the police station. Inspector Swaminathan looked up as the three culprits were brought into the station. "What happened?" he asked.

"Saar, urination and making public nuisance in the temple area," replied the constables.

The Inspector looked at them, asked their names and then delved into a ten-minute tirade on ethics and dignity, the sanctity of the temple area and upbringing. Partha was so ashamed he could not directly look at the Inspector's face even once. First, he was unable to control his urge, then of all places, he had to do it right there near the temple. Surely he could have waited until he was in a less public place. But to be caught in the act and get dragged off to the police station was the biggest shame. Now he would have a police record and even worse, he had to explain all of this to his mother. He did not even want to think about her reaction. He couldn't believe it when he heard the Inspector saying, "I'm letting you go with a warning. I don't ever want to see you here again." Partha was so relieved he wanted to pee, but this time he controlled himself until he reached home!

Partha looked once again in the direction of the Inspector. Had he recognized him? The Inspector was talking with his father and did not give him another look till they were seated inside. Partha looked around eagerly, his heart hammering in excitement but there was no sign of Rajam. Beautiful flowers decorated the *mutram* and colorful

118

Tanjore *jamakalams* were spread out on the floor for everyone to sit on. The polished silver pooja utensils gleamed in the evening sun. A single chair stood in the center of the room and Partha was directed to sit on it, as he was the *Maaplai,* the possible future son-in-law. Partha fidgeted in the chair, the *rexine* making him sweat. They had been exchanging pleasantries for a while now and still no sign of Rajam. Finally Mangalam, his prospective mother-in-law, left the room and returned with her daughter.

Partha stared unabashedly at this vision unfolding before his eyes. He was scared to blink in case this was a dream and he would wake up, alone, on his bedroll. Rajam was wearing a peacock blue *pavadai* and *chattai* with a magenta border adorned in gold *jarigai*. On her waist was a gold and ruby waist belt, the *odiyaanam*, a legacy from her grandmother. She had gold and ruby *jimikis* on her ears and wore two long gold chains. She was instructed to come and do namaskaram to her prospective groom. Partha could not believe the turn of events. Just yesterday he was cycling past her house to catch a glimpse of her and now she was bowing down at his feet. Close up, she was even lovelier. Pale ivory skin and light brown almond shaped eyes. The only decoration on her face was a *pottu* in maroon kumkumam in the center of her forehead. Her beauty was innate and seemed to be an effulgence of her wonderful nature. In the years to come Partha never tired of admiring her natural beauty and constantly thanked his good fortune.

Rajam sat cross-legged next to her mother and sister. Nagamma asked if she knew how to sing. Immediately the harmonium was brought out and the strains of "De...Viii ...Meenakshi..." filled the air. She sang beautifully and played the harmonium even better. Who could object to such a perfect daughter in law? The guests were then served hot *Sojji-Bajji* and coffee and then it was time for the groom's family to depart. Normally the groom's party informed the girl's family about their acceptance or rejection of the alliance on the following day. This way it wasn't embarrassing if they did not like the girl or the family. But in this case, it was the groom's family that asked for the alliance in the first place. As Partha reluctantly climbed into the bullock cart to leave, he heard his father say, "You know that we like the girl. My son also likes her. The rest is up to you. Please inform us through Ramachandran if we can proceed with the engagement."

The bullock cart went roughly over a large rock bumping Partha's head hard against the roof, quickly bringing him back from his world of dreams into present time. The journey had gone by fast. In the near horizon he could see the *gopuram* of the Vizhupuram Shiva temple, which meant they would be home in a few minutes. His thoughts were yanked back to his Ponpaakal, and he wondered if Rajam wanted him then as much as he wanted her. Somehow he never asked her. Sushila rose from her deep slumber as the cart trundled down the street approaching their house. As they came up to the front gate, Partha noticed a cycle parked outside and wondered who the visitor was.

The family rushed out to meet them, and Sushila waited till Nagamma and Rajam brought out the 'kumkumam aarathi' to welcome her back and prevent more bad luck. Three times with the plate one way and three times the other. Nagamma took the plate and poured the red liquid outside, thereby throwing away all the bad luck that had befallen poor Sushila, who stepped across the threshold with her right foot. As she entered the house the first one to embrace her was Rajam.

"Come, Sushila, I missed you. Are you feeling better?"

"Yes Rajam, just a little sleepy."

Partha walked past them into the front room where his father-in-law, Inspector Swaminathan, was seated. Rajam came in as well just as Partha finished touching his father-in-law's feet, getting his blessings. She said softly, "Appa has come to visit. He wants us to spend a week with him for Deepavali."

Swaminathan rose from the easy chair. "*Yenna Maaplai, Sowkyamaa*? Looks like I have come at a very busy time. I just wanted you both to come and spend Deepavali with us. Kunju is still there with our sixth grandson. It will be a very nice family reunion. What do you think? Would it be all right?"

Partha thought for a moment. He had a week off for Deepavali, so that would not be a problem. Besides Rajam loved going home, especially if he accompanied her. "Let's see, it should be no problem," he replied tentatively. Rajam was not very happy with his reply and knew she had to talk him into it. This week, Nagamma's barbs about her not conceiving were especially cruel. She wanted to tell Partha but then decided not to. Why burden him with household problems? It would only give him a lot of grief. He was Nagamma's favorite son and

Rajam did not want to be the reason for any bad blood in the family. Nagamma's comments hurt her but what could she do other than pray for a baby? A week away from her would definitely be welcome. Besides, she had not yet seen her sister Kunju's new baby. With Sushila away, things had been hectic running the household and there had been no time for a break.

Swaminathan had received his transfer orders a few months after Rajam's marriage. Leaving Vizhupuram was difficult, mainly because he was leaving behind his youngest daughter. Almost every other day he would stop by to visit Rajam, even if it was for a few minutes. And he missed that. Chidambaram was not very far away but still he felt heaviness in his heart whenever he thought of Rajam. Now his visits had to be planned and he could not see her on a whim. As Swaminathan climbed onto his borrowed bike, he said to Partha, "It would be nice if you could get some leave and come to Chidambaram to get Sankaracharya's blessings. I will be staying in Vizhupuram for a few days just to meet my friends. Hopefully, we'll see you at the chandhai this Saturday. Don't tell Rajam but her mother and brother will also be there."

Swaminathan had his work cut out for him when he returned to Chidambaram. He had to arrange police *bandobast* for the opening of the Sankara Madham. Paramacharya Chandrasekhara Saraswathi, the young head of the historical Sankara Madham, was coming from Kanchipuram to perform and supervise the ceremonies for the opening of a branch of the Sankara Madham in Chidambaram, and there would be visitors and devotees congregating from all over south India. It was the first time that the "order of the great Sankaracharyas" was opening a center in this area.

After seeing his father-in-law off, Partha walked back into the house with Rajam, sneaking an arm around her waist. It was so rare to be alone, just the two of them, that he took advantage of any opportunity. Rajam moved out of his reach as they walked into the house.

"*Yenna*, can we go to Chidambaram?"

"Your father has just left, Rajam. What is your hurry?"

"I was only wondering because we don't have any children yet. Maybe if we get Sankaracharya's blessings things could change."

"Why? Is he a magician?"

"Don't talk about holy men like that. *Thappu*, it's a sin," chided Rajam. Although Rajam was scared stiff of saamiyaars, Sankaracharya was somehow different. All her religious beliefs rose from fear of omission, and she didn't want any harm to befall them. Once her father mentioned getting his blessings, then not going was unthinkable.

Partha washed his feet in one corner of the backyard and said with a wry smile, "The only way we can have children is by sleeping together more often."

"Shhh… someone might be listening. *Yenna* you are so shameless."

"What is so shameless? Everyone does it, especially if they are married. If you can do it, why can't you talk about it?"

"*Pongo naa*, you always bring the topic back to that," said Rajam not being able to bring herself to talk about sex.

"Rajam, I always wanted to ask you. That day when I came to see you for the Ponpaakal, did you like me then?"

"No…I mean I can't really remember," said Rajam hesitantly, not wanting to hurt his feelings.

"Then why did you agree to see me?"

"Because Appa said he would buy me shiny glass bangles if I did."

"And when you saw me, what did you think?"

"That you were huge like an elephant."

"So then why did you agree to marry me?"

"I got my glass bangles," replied Rajam to an altogether puzzled Partha.

# Part VI
# Dharmu

## CHAPTER 18 – MAHADEVAN
### RANGPUR, EAST BENGAL – 1934

Mahadevan couldn't sleep. The rains were expected and the atmosphere was extremely humid and sticky. Once the monsoon set in, it rained incessantly for a few months but at least the weather was a little more bearable. The air was so heavy with moisture you could almost squeeze it out. The bedrooms, the study and the living room had *punkhas*, huge fans made out of palm leaves, suspended from the ceiling. Long ropes that worked on a pulley system went through the vents on top of the doors and hung outside the room. The *punkhawallah* sat and pulled on the ropes, moving the fan back and forth creating a draft of sorts. In most of the homes in Calcutta and Delhi, the electric fan had replaced this labor intensive punkha but here in the country, in remote Rangpur, the punkha had to suffice. There were two boys who worked round the clock, going from room to room, manning the punkhas. The night was terribly hot and sometime during the middle of the night, the punkhawallah fell asleep.

"Punkha," yelled Mahadevan, stirring from the heat, and the fan resumed movement again, though somewhat ineffectually. It was very early in the morning when Mahadevan woke up again, his body bathed in perspiration. His cotton *banyan*, the undershirt he wore to sleep, was soaked with sweat and sticking to his wet body like a second skin. The punkhawallah was asleep again. Poor boy; the child must be tired. Pulling on the ropes was tedious and monotonous work. Mahadevan didn't want to wake him again. He couldn't sleep anyway, so he thought he might as well get an early start to his day.

He glanced at Dharmu, who was fast asleep next to him in spite of the heat and felt sad for her. Things had been especially hard for her. Just then, almost as if she knew she was being watched, Dharmu

124

stirred. "Good day to you sir. How do you do?" she mumbled in her sleep.

*"Good heavens!"* thought Mahadevan, *"She practices English in her sleep."* He shook his head in disbelief as he sauntered out of the room, opening the doors to go and sit out in the verandah, where it was slightly cooler. It had not been easy for Dharmu. When Mahadevan married her, she was very young and did not move to their home in Nagarcoil until a couple of years later. Dharmu had been home tutored in Tamil. She was introverted to begin with and shy in front of her husband. As a result, they had very little to say to each other. Mahadevan was much more proficient in English than in his native Tamil and Dharmu spoke no English — the perfect foundation for an uncommunicative marriage. No one thought about all this when they arranged his wedding. His mind went back to his earlier conversation with Corbin about love and marriage. Corbin was right; it was an unfair system, being forced to spend the rest of your life with someone chosen by your parents. He did not see Dharmu until the day of their marriage. It was almost as if his parents were arranging a housekeeper or cook, or someone to take care of his primeval needs, and not thinking of a companion suited to his nature who matched his intellectual capability. He had a double Masters and could speak five languages fluently, but what use was that when you were lost for topics of conversation with your wife. She did not understand where he came from and very soon their conversations became rudimentary, always about mundane things. He could not partake in an intellectually stimulating conversation with her about world affairs because she knew nothing beyond her village and home. Sometimes he wished he had married someone of comparable upbringing and education. It was a shame that women were not educated beyond basic reading and writing. Hardly any women studied beyond high school and going to college was out of the question. The whole system undermined women's cerebral capabilities. If only Dharmu had the exposure, he was sure she would rise to the challenges. Right now, even though they had been married for several years, their relationship was stiff and strained, like that between a tutor and a student. He undertook to educate her in the ways of the west and to make her at least presentable before his British peers, even if it was for selfish reasons.

*'Maybe one day I will apologize to her for putting her through all this strain. But I have to do this. Once we move to Calcutta or Delhi, the society ladies there will eat her alive.'*

The Bengali women were much more fashionable and westernized, wearing sleeveless blouses and georgette saris with long dangling earrings, attending parties, often with a cigarette in one hand and a tall gin and tonic in the other. Those educated in English convent schools effortlessly spoke the language of the masters. Dharmu would look like a village idiot next to them. Mahadevan knew it was only a matter of time before he moved to Calcutta, where they would be thrown into a hectic social circle of balls and formal dinners, croquet parties and tennis mornings. He had to train Dharmu, enabling her to mingle with the crowd she would associate with in the near future. Already she had picked up many phrases in English and learned to use tableware but her education was far from complete. At least he overcame the biggest hurdle, introducing her to meat eating. He could still recall that momentous day with clarity.

He had ordered the morning meal that Sunday, chicken curry and rice and instructed the cook not to make any vegetables. The children had eaten earlier. It was past one o'clock in the afternoon when Mahadevan and Dharmu came to the dining room for dinner. The bearer served rice and then he put the chicken curry on Dharmu's plate.

*"Nahin nahin, sabji curry laao,"* she hurriedly told the bearer, who knew she was vegetarian.

"No Dharmu, no vegetables for you today." Mahadevan kept a poker face. This was going to be hard and he needed to do it with dispassion. He could not afford to exhibit any emotion.

"What do you mean? What shall I eat? I can't have this *maamsam!*" said Dharmu, pointing with disgust at the chicken on her plate. Mahadevan took a deep breath. He reached across, sliced the chicken off the bone, cut it into small pieces and mixed it with the rice.

"Eat," he said quietly.

"No I can't. I can't. It's a sin. *Thappu.* I can't eat this." Dharmu was horrified at the request but trying very hard to keep her tears in check. She knew Mahadevan thought of her as an uneducated child and she did not want to come across as a petulant youngster throwing a tantrum.

"Eat," Mahadevan repeated, his voice low, yet authoritative, and stern.

"Please, don't make me do this." Once Dharmu realized Mahadevan was serious, tears of fear streamed down her cheeks. Her face was flushed and her throat closed in repulsion and fear.

"I'll learn English, Bengali, whatever you want but I can't eat this," she pleaded to an unyielding Mahadevan.

"Dharmu, when you married me, you knew you had to make adjustments didn't you?"

"Yes, but you did not tell me about this. No one told me I would have to eat this horrible meat." Her voice was rising to a crescendo, echoing her emotions which had spiraled out of control.

"I didn't know back then that it would be so important for both of us to eat meat. If I had, I would have spoken to you about it right then."

"Why… why can't I be vegetarian?" Dharmu was now crying, her hot tears warming the cold chicken curry.

"Because I work for the British! They are our masters! We have to be like them, think like them and act like them if we want to succeed under them. Do you understand? You are my wife and you have to support me." He paused to control himself, when he realized he was almost shouting. This was a delicate but necessary task, one that needed tact and some coaxing. His voice mellowed to its customary smooth and placid tone.

"Very soon we will move to Calcutta, where you will be invited to the Viceroy's house and you can be certain, no vegetarian food will be served there."

"So then I won't eat for one day. It won't kill me. But eating this will." Dharmu could not think of eating the chicken. Just the thought of putting dead animal flesh into her mouth made her whole body revolt. She was not going to succumb to the pressure.

"It's more than just not eating Dharmu, please try and understand. My colleague's wives all eat meat and drink wine. They will laugh at me and make fun of you. They will call you names behind your back. Would you like that?" Mahadevan was trying a new tactic, trying to force her into complying. Anything to get the job done.

"What names?" asked an unfazed Dharmu.

"Village bumpkin, country girl, I don't know what else."

"Let them; I don't mind."

"But I do. And if you want to stay with me, then you have to eat meat."

"I have to?"

"Yes you do. Please don't make this harder for yourself than it already is. I went through the same experience several years ago that you are going through now. When you first eat the meat, it is chewy and repulsive but put mind over matter and you can overcome anything. You will get used to it."

"And if I don't?"

"Then you can go back to your father's home. I will keep a governess for the children."

Dharmu looked at his somber face and knew he was very serious and she could not talk her way out of this. She looked at the brown pieces of flesh on her plate. She pierced one piece of chicken with her fork and looked at it distastefully. She could hear the chicken squawking in pain, beseeching her not to eat it. As she brought the morsel up to her mouth, the chicken was getting bigger and bigger in her mind's eye, squawking in her face, begging to be allowed to live. She saw it grow in size until it completely dominated her vision.

"The chicken! It's alive!" Dharmu shrieked, horror imprinted on her face as she threw the fork back onto the plate.

"No it isn't. It was killed hours ago and you are in no way responsible for its death."

"How can I eat dead flesh?" Dharmu was not going to give in without a fight.

"Put it in your mouth! Now!" Mahadevan screamed, bringing his face close to hers.

Dharmu put the piece of chicken into her mouth, her ears throbbing with its deafening squawking, her mouth flooded with the bird's fear hormones released at the time of its death, adding to her own dread and aversion. The very act of chewing dead flesh was so repellant that her stomach heaved and she threw up all over her plate.

*Yes!* she thought gratefully, '*Now I don't have to eat this hateful chicken.*' Mahadevan was nonplussed. He called the bearer to clean up and bring another plate of chicken curry which he proceeded to patiently cut, as he had done before.

"Eat. And don't you dare throw up." His voice and eyes were deathly cold.

Dharmu shivered in fear as she put another piece of meat into her mouth and chewed and swallowed, all the time looking at Mahadevan with hate and revulsion.

She ate chicken that day but would not talk to him for the rest of the week.

Mahadevan sighed. He knew he had been harsh with her but it was just another step in her education. Unfortunately, he realized a long time ago, just being brilliant and doing a job well didn't bring in the promotions. He watched all his dumb colleagues supersede him because of their tennis or golf game and he knew with the British masters, when it came to job promotions, he couldn't rely on the prospect of equal treatment and fairness. Everything rested on your boss liking you and what he thought about your wife, whether she was up to hobnobbing with the Brits or able to host formal dinners. He realized the only way to succeed was by aping them, by learning to eat meat, drink wine, smoke cigars, play tennis or golf or whatever sport your boss played. It was all about reinforcing the superiority of British social niceties. There was no way he was going to remain a Collector all his life because of his Indianness. He would bend whatever values he could without compromising his integrity, without selling his soul. Then again, soul selling was a matter of personal definition and perspective. There were those who saw his so called 'Britishisms' as soul selling and complete mental slavery. But he knew how to keep these social refinements from affecting his core values, or so he thought. They were just things to be done and not pondered over.

Mahadevan wandered into his study and reviewed his latest case due for sentencing. As Collector and District Magistrate, he heard civil and criminal cases but this one was particularly complicated. A Muslim woman had been assaulted and raped and later succumbed to her injuries. The Muslim community was up in arms and wanted the case to be tried by their own Mullahs. Mahadevan knew the girl's family would get no justice under Muslim law, and so he tried the case in his court. After hearing the prosecution and defense, he had to decide about the severity of the sentence. It was going to be either life imprisonment or the gallows. Either way, the Muslim community was sure to be aroused and furious and he would have to ask for armed reinforcements before passing the sentence. He was always a little heavy handed when it came to cases against women. For too many years their pleas had gone unheard. They were always repressed, kept under close supervision and their cases hardly ever went to court, especially those involving rape.

His father, Nilakantan Ayyar, had ingrained in him ideas of equal opportunities for women. Nilakantan Ayyar was always partial to his daughters, much to the chagrin of his sons, and he educated them up to graduate level, something unheard of in those days. Even as a child, when there was a quarrel between the boys and girls, Nilakantan took the side of the girls regardless of blame, saying that women needed more support and boys could fend for themselves. Just growing up watching his father's treatment of women influenced Mahadevan in many ways. He wanted to make sure women would always be heard in his courtroom. As he sat deep in thought about the case, his eyes moved around the room and settled on his framed degrees from Presidency College and Cambridge.

Mahadevan completed high school when he was thirteen years old. He was way too young to attend college, so he spent the next two years helping his grandfather run the vast estates attached to their home in Nagarcoil. Sita Gardens was a massive, yet beautiful mansion. A civil engineer, his father had personally supervised its construction, naming it after his wife, Sitalakshmi. Mahadevan's favorite room was the library. Nilakantan Ayyar was a voracious reader. Every month, leather-and-gold bound books arrived from the Oxford Printing Press in England. He had books on every topic, including poetry, art, music and literature. Mahadevan spent hours just browsing through the books. To encourage his children to read, Nilakantan Ayyar made them check out two books every week, which they had to read. They couldn't cheat because the following week he questioned them on the content. Having read them himself, he knew when anyone deceived him. If he caught them, they would have to write up a critique or synopsis and read an extra book the following week. Mahadevan's younger brother, Kannan, was not very book minded in spite of his intelligence and would come to Mahadevan, begging him to write his critiques and bribing him with something or the other. No one needed to motivate Mahadevan to read. In fact Nilakantan Ayyar used his love for reading as a tool to punish him. All reading privileges would be taken away as punishment for errant behavior and Mahadevan would go crazy when that happened.

Mahadevan read Shakespeare, Byron, Shelley, Guy de Maupassant, Victor Hugo and many other authors, poring over the numerous volumes repeatedly until he was able to quote passages from memory. He spent two glorious years reading almost all the time. When he wasn't reading, he spent time with his beloved grandfather. It was wonderful to have so much time to be near the patriarch and learn from him. His grandfather or Appanshayal, as everyone called him, brought up all the grandchildren. Whenever anyone asked him the reason for something, he always replied it was God's doing, "Appan Shayal" — hence the name. Widowed early in life, the grand old man chose to live with his eldest son, Nilakantan and took on the responsibility of imbibing in his grandchildren a love for education. Although Appanshayal studied only up to high school, both his children had university degrees. Nilakantan became a civil engineer, and his younger son, became a veterinary surgeon. His daughter, attended up to high school, studying even after her marriage, an arrangement he made with her in-laws at the time of her wedding.

Appanshayal laid the foundation for a lineage dedicated to education and knowledge. Spending so much time in his company, Mahadevan learned from him the intricacies of accounting. Appanshayal worked in the treasury department for the Raja of Travancore. Even though the British controlled most of India, there were still many semi-autonomous princely states that traded with each other in gold. Every state had its own currency minted in gold and it was Appanshayal's job at the Raja's treasury to keep accounts. He managed Sita Gardens from the start, supervising construction from the time the first foundation stone was laid. Nilakantan was forced to be away from the house for extended periods of time, as he was a civil engineer and his work took him all over the state. Appanshayal brought up all his grandchildren and supervised their education in their father's absence. A learned man and a strict Brahmin, he did not live in the main house but constructed an outhouse with a room and an attached pooja room for his prayers. A devotee of Shiva, he spent almost two hours each with his morning and evening prayers. He had a strict regimen, practicing yoga and meditation and he ate only once a day. The food was served to him in a special room by his daughter-in-law and once she served him, she would have to leave, allowing him to eat in complete seclusion. Everyone in the house knew to respect his privacy and never dared disturb him whenever he ate or prayed. The rest of the day was devoted to the family and to the upkeep of the property.

As a great Shiva worshipper, Appanshayal took special care to teach all the male grandchildren to chant the *Rudram* and *Chamakam*, special prayers for Shiva. He supervised them as they chanted, alert for any mispronunciation or missed inflexion, making them repeat the hymns over and over until they could recite it perfectly, even in their sleep. Of course, when Nilakantan Ayyar returned, he would check that they had learned their lessons well in his absence.

At the age of fifteen, Mahadevan was admitted to Presidency College in Madras, where he completed his program in three years, graduating at the top of his class and receiving the Gold Medal for Math. His father was so focused on teaching his sons frugality that he sent Mahadevan to college every year with only two sets of clothes and one pair of shoes. Mahadevan washed his clothes daily and alternated between them. He still remembered his father's reaction to his graduation results.

The results arrived by mail and he went into the study where Nilakantan was sitting in his easy chair, reading. He peered at Mahadevan over his glasses. "Hmm." (Meaning what do you want?)

"Appa. Result *vandurku*. The results came by mail."

"Come closer. *Inge vaa da.* — Sit down."

Mahadevan came up to his father and sat cross legged at his feet. Nilakanta slapped him on the back of his head saying, "*Madaya, yenna result vaangine?* Fool, what results did you get?"

Mahadevan looked down at his feet and mumbled, "First class first. I have got the Gold Medal for the highest marks in the college."

"What did you get in Mathematics?"

"Hundred percent."

For a brief moment, Nilakantan let down his shield and Mahadevan caught a brief glimpse of pride in his eyes. That was enough for him. Right then, he knew he had made his father proud and that meant more to him than any medal.

"When do you go back for your M.A.?"

"In two months."

"Sita," he yelled for his wife. "*Payasam pannu.* Make sweet rice pudding. Your son has passed his B.A." He turned towards Mahadevan saying, "*Yenna paakare? Namaskaram pannu.*"

Mahadevan bent down and touched his revered father's feet, taking his blessings. He knew it was the blessings of elders that brought good fortune and like most Indian children, did namaskaram to them at every opportunity.

Mahadevan smiled as he thought about those happy times. He looked at his gold pocket watch, a solid gold Omega that Nilakantan presented to him on the night he left for London.

Only five o'clock. It will be a couple of hours before the children wake up. What shall I do till then?

## CHAPTER 19 – MAHADEVAN
### RANGPUR

Mahadevan glanced at his timepiece, a beautiful handmade pocket watch with a long gold chain. Perhaps this was the most expensive gift he had ever received from his father. His father had brought up all five brothers with a discipline that was almost regimental. The patriarch made most of the major decisions for them: what they would study and whom they would marry. All the boys were terrified of their father. He was quick tempered and harsh with his punishment. No one ever sat in his presence and they only spoke to him in low respectful tones. The thought of crossing him never entered their minds. Nilakantan Ayyar also planned his sons' careers: Mahadevan would sit for his civil service exams, Shankar would be a doctor, Dandapani a lawyer and Ganesh would join the Civil Financial Department. The prodigal son was Kannan, the youngest, who challenged his father at every turn. In his last letter, his father mentioned that Kannan wanted to join the Merchant Navy. Merchant Navy was for fools according to him. Mahadevan sighed. When he went home at the end of the monsoon, he would talk some sense into his brother and try to patch things up between his father and brother.

Mahadevan looked down at his watch and remembered when it was given to him in July, 1920, on a day just like this — hot and muggy. Mahadevan had been married for over a month now and his new bride came to stay with them, although they were not permitted to share the same bed. Mahadevan's mind was not on his wife. She was shy and reticent and spoke in monosyllables, replying only to questions directed at her. He couldn't blame her. Coming into an alien household was difficult, but still it gave her an opportunity to know the large family she had married into: six sisters-in-law and four brothers-in-law. His mother was soft spoken and kind and treated Dharmu like another daughter; Nilakantan made sure of that. Mahadevan felt odd and uncomfortable with his new bride, especially when the family discreetly left them alone to talk. He was never particularly interested in girls and married only because he was instructed to. When the engagement took place, he was busy with exams and it was conducted without him being present. He trusted his father's judgment and knew he would not deliberately choose someone who was wrong for him. Looking at his young wife, he wondered if this time around Nilakantan had made the right choice for him.

Mahadevan glanced at his wife, scarcely noticing her, his mind preoccupied with more pressing thoughts that day. He had applied a month ago to take the Indian Civil Service exams and was anxiously awaiting a reply. It was already the fifth of July and he had not heard from the ICS Board. The family was sitting in the back porch enjoying the early evening breeze. It was on the west side of the house, with an awning keeping out the evening sun and was the only part of the house that was cool. On hot summer days, everyone congregated there just to talk and relax. All the women sat cleaning rice, carefully removing any stones before storing it in the huge *kudhir*, a granary to store rice. Appanshayal rushed in, waving a paper in his hand, his wrinkled face alive, beaming from ear to ear.

"Good news. Very good news, Mahadevan. Your application for the ICS has been accepted. You have to leave for England within the week."

Mahadevan had been awaiting this news all week but was still taken aback for a moment. Although he was mentally and intellectually ready to take the exam any day, the thought of living in a foreign land made him uneasy. The examination for the ICS took place in London and was designed in such a way that no Indian, unless educated in England, had much chance of success. This was difficult, because few Indian families, if any, could afford to support them for their entire stay of almost two years duration. There was a strict age limit for taking the exam and a candidate could attempt the exam three times between the years of twenty-one and twenty-four. Mahadevan hoped he didn't need to take the exam more than once. The idea was to minimize the number of Indians in the civil service. In recent years, however, the Indian Congress party was demanding greater local participation in the Government to prepare for the eventual transfer of power, whenever that happened, from British to Indian hands. They were pressing for the exam to be given in India, so more Indians could take it. Right now the only way to attempt the ICS exam was by going to England.

The exam curriculum reflected a certain racial and cultural bias. The English section required a general understanding of English prose and poetry of greats like Chaucer, Byron, Milton and Macaulay. Mahadevan was extremely privileged to have the good fortune of spending two years virtually devouring English prose and poetry. He knew that even if he passed the exam and secured the necessary marks, he still had to go through a special test called the Viva Voce, which was an oral section designed to weed out potential troublemakers and misfits and select who got to stay and who left the program. If you were chosen and passed this rigorous exam, then you went through one year's probation in Cambridge or Oxford. The final test was horseback riding! Mahadevan was not looking forward to that, not being particularly comfortable with horses but he was already taking lessons at the Raja's stables. Getting his portly form onto the horse was the first hurdle, after which he underwent the torment of trotting around the *maidanam*, attempting to keep his balance on the wild creature. Even after he dismounted, his innards jiggled for hours.

A message had to be sent to his father, who was working as the Executive Engineer in Madurai. There was no way Mahadevan was going to leave without bidding farewell to him. In the meantime, he needed to mentally prepare himself for the journey ahead. He would be away from his home for the first time in his life, unable to see his family for the next two years. Dharmu was to leave for Dindigul to be with her parents until he returned. The whole house was buzzing with excitement. His mother came up and unexpectedly kissed him on both cheeks. Mahadevan looked down at her diminutive figure, her plump cheeks and generously proportioned form, her twin diamond nose rings sparkling and her sad eyes with tears welling up in them at the thought of being separated for such a long time from her oldest son.

"It's going to be difficult, Mahadevan. Never forget who you are and where you're from because that will ground you and allow you to

136

face any obstacle. When your father comes home, we must all go to the *Krishnan Kovil* and offer our prayers. I will give you plenty of spicy powders that you can mix with rice and eat. It will be very difficult to find food once you are in England; they say that the British only eat meat."

"No, Amma, they eat other food too. I know you are sad, Amma. I feel it too. I will be alone but I am excited about the new adventure. Let's see what happens. I will write to you every week, although the letters may take a while to get to you."

He turned to look at Dharmu, who was gazing at him with soulful eyes. He couldn't tell if she was affected in any way by the news. She was still a child and did not know what to do or say.

Three days later, his father arrived. He hugged Mahadevan, holding him close for several minutes, one of the few occasions when he exhibited any emotion. There was a lot to be done before he caught the steamer from Bombay. Tickets to be bought, clothes to be purchased and money to be arranged — and Nilakantan galvanized into action, getting things organized. He gave Mahadevan a brown leather suitcase into which his mother put a potlam of kumkumam wrapped in newspaper, for luck. After that he put in his frugal belongings: four shirts, four veshtis and a pair of slippers. He didn't have anything else other than his physics textbooks. As he was about to leave the house, his mother put in an assortment of snacks and powders for him to eat on the way just as she had promised. The whole family came to the Trivandrum train station to say goodbye. All his brothers returned from their respective colleges to wish him bon voyage. He stuck his head out of the window and waved till they were tiny dots on the horizon.

Nilakantan Ayyar accompanied him on the train and once they reached Madras, they left their luggage with a friend and began their shopping expedition. The first stop was Oxford Tailors on Mount Road, where a bespectacled tailor brought out bolts of imported woolen fabric, ideal for suits. They chose two, one in a dark grey and the other in black. They shopped all day, buying precisely six pairs of socks, six shirts for casual wear, six long sleeved white shirts and two pairs of imported oxfords, one in brown and the other in black. Since no woolen sweaters or coats were available in Madras, he would buy those when he reached England. It was only July and there was plenty of time to prepare for the harsh British winter. Nilakantan spoke to a friend in the treasury and purchased two hundred British pounds to give his son for board and lodging. It was a lot of money but education was essential and to Nilakantan, wasteful spending was unacceptable but he had no problem with expense on education. He placed paramount importance on learning and most of his savings went towards it.

Once he had picked up his suits, Mahadevan neatly arranged all his new clothes into the brown suitcase and packed his leather briefcase, which he would carry around with him at all times. It held the letter which had to be presented at the college in London, as well as his travel documents and passport. Nilakantan traveled with him all the way to Bombay, and they conversed with each other like never before. Mahadevan sensed in his father a new found respect for him. That was the most precious week for Mahadevan, which he cherished dearly; those memories would build up his strength and fortitude whenever he was down and depressed in cold, grey and foggy England. Finally they reached Bombay, alighting at the glorious Victoria Terminus station and made their way to the docks at Ballard Estate, where Mahadevan would catch the H.M.S Victoria to Southampton. Just as Mahadevan bent down to get his father's blessings, Nilakantan handed him a small leather case. Inside, cradled in blue velvet, was a gold Omega pocket watch.

"Appa, this is too much. I mean, you have already spent so much money."

"You will need it. Think of me whenever you look at it to check the time."

Unwillingly, Mahadevan walked towards the ship, waving for the last time as he followed the coolie who was carrying his luggage into the steamship. He went behind him down several flights of steep, almost vertical stairs to locate his cabin. To his dismay, the coolie climbed down deck after deck, till they had almost reached the bottom of the ship. This was the floor for the Indians. The room was tiny, with one porthole and two bunks. There were two toilets on each end of the deck, which he would have to share with everyone else. This was the first time Mahadevan realized what a privileged life he led so far. All his life he had enjoyed the comforts and benefits of belonging to the highest caste but here on this ship, his quarters were the same as those of the servants accompanying the white Sahibs and Memsahibs back home. The Whites had the best rooms on the starboard side of the ship, with windows that could be opened to let in the cool sea breeze. That is how they always traveled, Port Out Starboard Home. The combination of the first letter of these four words formed the word POSH, connoting the privileged, luxurious, upper class.

Mahadevan wondered whom he would be sharing the room with, hoping it was not with a servant. Thankfully, his roommate was also going to take the exams in London. His name was Shantinath Banerji and he was from Calcutta. The two became good friends and even stayed at the same boarding house in their first year in London. Later that day, he met many more Indian boys going to England to take the ICS exams.

The second shocker came when the Indian contingent went up to the top deck for dinner. Although they did not have to eat with the servants, who thankfully ate in a separate mess, they were all put together in two tables in one corner of the room. Mahadevan felt demeaned. All of this — sitting for the ICS, going to England — was in ardent pursuit for acceptance by the ruling class, to become part of the British elite. In reality, to the British he was nothing but another Indian, inferior to the British Brahmins. It was like climbing a steep slope and moving one step forward and three steps back. By dehumanizing the natives, the British rulers alienated large sections of the local population who fervently sought their expulsion from their land. Right now, Mahadevan was experiencing the very indignation and deep humiliation that gripped the patriotic. But he recognized he was no Gandhi; he did not have the moral courage to languish in jail for a cause. Instead, he chose the path of least resistance, one that entailed mental enslavement to British colonialism, just like many Indian intellectuals all over the nation. He would become as British as the British. He would get into their minds and find what made them tick; he would show them that he was as good as any of them by becoming part of the cerebral elite.

The food on the ship was terrible. Apart from bread, vegetarians could choose from four boiled vegetables: carrots, peas, potatoes and cauliflower. At home they were accustomed to eating spicy, flavored vegetables and their taste buds were offended by boiled, unsalted vegetables. They consoled one another by saying they actually had plenty of choice; they could either have peas and carrots, carrots and potatoes, peas and cauliflower, peas and potatoes, carrots and cauliflower or potatoes with carrots. There were lots of choices. As a pure vegetarian, Mahadevan faced this plight for the next few months. Shantinath ate meat, so his choices were staggering. Lucky for him!

To make matters worse, two young princes hailing from small kingdoms in the north of India embarrassed the rest of the Indians on board. Indignant at being seated on the same table as the commoners and peeved at not being invited to sit at the Captain's table, they made an appallingly ostentatious show of themselves. Dressed in their silk *achkans* and fancy turbans covered in pearls and gems, they looked ridiculous. They were on their way to London, probably on a stipend that was a small fraction of what they were worth, while their treasury filled the already overflowing imperial coffers of Britain. On reaching England, they would waste the rest of their days in a debauched, indulgent existence, paraded as exotic puppets, trophies to demonstrate the might and reach of the British Raj. They had no concept of their own dignity, nor regret about being stripped of their rich cultural heritage, nor an inkling about the size of their inheritance, the jewels and gold that their ancestors had painstakingly collected for generations, now pouring into the Royal British Treasury.

Of course, it was Mahadevan's deck that housed their retinue of servants. Kings or Brahmins, educated or ignorant, they were all clubbed together as Indians. Even the top observation deck had designated areas for Indians. With the room so stuffy and dark, Mahadevan and the others studied in groups on the top deck and by the end of the trip developed some strong friendships. Seventeen days later they spotted the white cliffs of Dover. They had arrived in England, ready to initiate a new chapter in their lives.

When the ship docked, Mahadevan lugged his suitcase up five flights of stairs to the arrival hall with no one to help him. He missed being able to call a coolie to do the heavy lifting, something he took for granted in India. While the Indians grappled with their luggage, the dock hands helped the white families. All the Indian boys gathered together on shore wondering what to do next, when an official told them they would have to walk down the street a couple of kilometers to take the bus to London. Mahadevan and Shanti were not excited about dragging their cases such a long distance. They noticed a dock hand at the end of the platform smoking a cigarette and decided to ask if he would do it for them. He was sitting on a bench, his sparse reddish brown hair uncombed, his clothes a shade between grey and brown, dotted with samples of all the food he had eaten in the last three months. He looked up as they approached and disdainfully informed them, "Sorry, I don't talk to Darkies."

The realization hit Mahadevan so hard he could not think clearly for several minutes. In this country it didn't matter that you were a Brahmin. It didn't matter that you hailed from generations of highly educated and spiritual people. It didn't matter that you were racially so pure that you could trace your ancestry back five thousand years. It didn't matter that you spoke the Queen's English better than most Englishmen. It didn't matter that you had your master's degree in Mathematics. To every Englishman you were just a darkie, an outcast.

This was Mahadevan's first lesson in humility and self-control. He was so angry he wanted to slap the sardonic grin off the dock hand's blotchy, pink face, but he did not do that. He merely stepped back, turned around and walked away. There were many other similar incidents that made him realize his place in society, but this incident affected him most profoundly because it occurred almost as soon as they landed on British soil, making him apprehensive about what was to follow. As he dragged his brown leather suitcase down the street, he remembered his mother's words.

"Never forget who you are and where you're from because that will ground you and allow you to face any obstacle." Nothing had ever sounded more true to him.

Examining his pocket watch, Mahadevan was amazed at how many memories one small watch could trigger.

# CHAPTER 20 – DHARMAMBAL
## RANGPUR – 1934

Dharmu awoke after seven o' clock. The sun was streaming in through the window and she closed her eyes, unable to stand the glare. She sat up on the edge of her bed, with her legs dangling over the side. Her eyes were still heavy with sleep and she had no desire to awaken and embark on the day's chores. She could hear Kandu's voice. He was sitting in the study with his father, praying. Walking to the doorway, she observed them silently. Father and son, sitting cross-legged on the floor with their eyes closed. Mahadevan was saying his morning prayers. *"Om Rajadhi rajaya prasahya. . ."* His voice was low and melodious. Kandu was sitting next to him, attempting to imitate his father. *"Omamnamanmanaman"* was the best he could do.

Dharmu felt guilty not teaching the children to recite any Sanskrit chants. She did not feel sacred verses should emerge from a mouth that ate the flesh of animals. She was too impure and could not face God because she had sinned. Mahadevan tried to explain to her that God was with you irrespective of what you ate. If He did not like meat eating, then more than three quarters of the world would be Godless. Many times Mahadevan asked her to at least light the lamp in the morning after she bathed but Dharmu was stubborn. She would not go anywhere near the altar, forcing Mahadevan to teach his son about God. At least that way Kandu got some spiritual training.

Dharmu went into the bathroom to bathe in cold water. During the summer months she bathed at least four times a day. There was no other way of cooling the body. She called this *'Kaka kuli,'* which was how a crow bathed, in and out of the water in a couple of minutes. When she emerged from her room, father and son were sitting outside.

142

Kandu was firmly ensconced in his Daddy's lap, drinking his milk out of a small silver glass. This was a ritual every morning. He would sit on his father's lap and either Dharmu or Mahadevan, and sometimes both, would pour milk into his small glass from a large one. Mahadevan looked up and saw Dharmu walking out towards them.

"Did you sleep well?" he asked her.

"Like a log. It was so hot, I couldn't open my eyes."

"It was just the opposite for me. It was so hot I couldn't close them."

Dharmu picked up the large silver glass and poured a little warm milk into Kandu's small one. Watching this whole cozy scene with a scowl on her face was Vani, who had just woken up. *'There they go, mollycoddling him. Why does he need to sit on Daddy's lap? He's almost six years old for God's sake; surely he can drink milk all by himself,'* she thought to herself. There was no point in voicing her thoughts when no one wanted to hear them. She walked across the open balcony and sat down next to her mother.

"Did you drink your milk? Go, ask Meera to heat some for you," said Dharmu turning her back to Vani while she continued fussing over Kandu.

*'What about you? Can you not tear yourself from your son to heat it for me?'* Vani thought, a scowl on her face. But she didn't say anything and no one said anything more to her. They were too busy coochie cooing with Kandu. Vani sat there for a few minutes waiting to be noticed, and when she realized no one had anything to say to her, she got up and walked away, dragging her feet, her eyes moist with tears. Neither Dharmu nor Mahadevan realized what had just happened. They had no inkling Vani felt slighted and unloved, no idea both their daughters were craving their parents' attention. Both of them were so happy to have a son at last and unintentionally ignored the girls. Kandu was much younger and naturally more interesting. His nature was so bright and lively, they just enjoyed being in his company. Deep in their hearts they believed having a male child was more important to carry on the family name, and daughters were temporary guests till they got married. Mahadevan was always so concerned about women having a voice in his courtroom but he forgot that here in his house, they needed to be heard too. Their error was not one of commission but of omission. Neither of them intentionally kept the daughters at arm's

length. It was just something that happened over the years and no one could be entirely blamed for it. Kandu saw Vani walk away and ran after her. "Want to play?" he asked, dancing around in front of her.

"No, not with you," said Vani angrily. Kandu was perplexed. He could not remember what he had done to annoy her.

"Why?" he asked with all honesty, his eyes open wide.

"Because I hate your face." She didn't mean to be spiteful but it felt good being mean to him. Kandu stuck out his tongue and crossed his eyes.

"What about now? Do you hate my face now? See? It looks just like you."

Then he made a monkey face. "Ha ha…that's your face. Monkey face, monkey face, you have a monkey face." Kandu was dancing in front of her singing this ditty and pretending to move like a monkey. He thought it was hilarious but Vani was not amused. Already she was on emotional overdrive and this was the last straw. She burst into tears and ran into the kitchen. Blissfully unaware of his sister's resentment at his being the focus of their parent's affection, Kandu skipped sideways to his room, where he busied himself playing with his toy cars.

Meera was in the kitchen helping with the morning chores. "What happened? Who said something to hurt my *sona moni's* feelings?" She affectionately put her arms around Vani.

"That stupid Kandu. I hate him," Vani said stamping her feet in frustration.

"Now now, don't call him names." Meera used the end of her sari to wipe Vani's tears.

"He made faces at me and called me monkey face." Deep in her heart she knew it wasn't Kandu who bothered her but was unable to voice her real resentment. Meera held her close trying to calm her down. After Kamala's death, Meera tried to show more affection to the children to compensate for her own loss.

"Boys will be boys. Just because he says it, does your face become like a monkey?"

"I guess not," replied Vani, a little calmer now and able to think rationally.

"Forget it. He is just a child. Kandu baba likes to play around with you. Don't mind him. Come, my *sona moni*. Let me warm your milk for you." Vani sat on the floor, watching Meera heat the milk on the stove. Meera was nice. She had lost her own daughter recently but

144

still she was so good to all of them. "Meera, will you put the milk in a small glass and give it to me a little at a time?"

"Like Kandu baba? Of course." Meera sat next to her and watched her drink, rubbing her hand over Vani's hair and smoothing it back.

Vani closed her eyes and just for a moment imagined it was her mother stroking her hair. But when she opened them, she saw Meera's kind face and scowled at her. Immediately, she felt ashamed. Poor Meera, she was so nice and didn't deserve being treated badly. Vani's face broke into a smile; she put her arms around her kind ayah and nestled her head against her welcoming bosom.

Kandu walked out into the verandah just as the bearer was in the process of serving breakfast. Porridge, toast, two eggs sunny side up, freshly squeezed sweet lime juice and black coffee, the kind of food that was unhealthy yet delicious. For Mahadevan, who always rose before dawn, the day was almost half over and he was famished. He dug into his meal, watching Kandu fly paper airplanes replete with sound effects, all of them crashing repeatedly and then magically rising up again.

"Dharmu, I am going to make arrangements for you and the children to leave this week. It's getting too hot and maybe all of you will enjoy being home. The kids need to know their grandparents."

"When will I have to leave? This week? It's too soon. I have to pack and do a million things." Even as the words left her mouth, she did not know why she was protesting. After all, the chance to go home to her mother's house was all she thought about and now that it was here, she felt a certain panic of sorts.

"It's better you leave early. We are expecting some trouble in this area and I don't want you to get stuck. The orderly will come with you and you can take Meera if you want.

"What about you?"

"I will come as far as Calcutta and see you off there. I have some work to attend to. Maybe at the end of the month I can get some time off and meet you in Nagarcoil. Spend the first six weeks in Dindigul, and then go to Nagarcoil. Does that sound all right? We can come back together around Deepavali."

Dharmu was thrilled. She hated the climate and surroundings in Rangpur and only put up with it for her husband's sake. The children

145

were isolated and had no friends here. It would be great for them to visit home and be with their cousins. Happily she jumped up and went into the house, humming as she picked up Kandu, giving him a smacking kiss on his cheek.

"We are going home. We are really going home."

Mahadevan raised one eyebrow, pleasantly surprised at his wife's sudden change in demeanor, noting her sprightly step and the complete mood switch, dull one moment to delirious the next. He sighed aloud. Yes, he needed this time to reflect. Their marriage was not living up to her expectations. She was bored, scared and lonely. He needed to make some serious changes and take steps to improve their relationship.

But right now he had to be centered and in control. Nothing could affect his equanimity at work. He had to be composed and deliberate. That was important above all. He would think about Dharmu later . . .

# Part VII
# Rajam

# CHAPTER 21 – NAGAMMA
## VIZHUPURAM

Nagamma was resting in an easy chair after a heavy meal. Through half closed eyes she could see Rajam and Sushila talking and their laughter wafted in through the open door. She couldn't help thinking how lucky they were to be young. Although Nagamma was only in her early forties, she felt much older. Her life had been very hard. She was the one who made all the bold decisions in the family. It had not been easy. Her father died when she was very young, leaving large estates in the capable hands of his wife. A few years after Nagamma married, she and her husband moved into her mother's house. In the beginning, her husband, Munuswamy Iyer, resisted the idea, as he was studying law and didn't want the disruption. But eventually he succumbed to the pressure and once they moved in, actually enjoyed the benefits of being just an *Aathu Maaplai*, a son-in-law, who lived at home with no major responsibilities.

Nagamma's mother, Orukai Rukminiammal, took complete charge of the estates and only occasionally asked for help from Munuswamy. From a very young age, Rukminiammal had established a routine and understood the minute intricacies of running a business and of dealing with men. Although it was very hard for men on the estate to take orders from a woman, everyone in Vizhupuram held Rukminiammal in high esteem. The women admired her for what they aspired to but could never be, and the men admired her for exactly the same reason. When the farm laborers came in her presence, they would remove their turbans or head cloths, bow their heads and fold their arms across their chest in a show of deference.

It was uncommon to find a Brahmin household run by a woman. While their brothers played outside with friends, Brahmin girls stayed in the kitchen, learning how to cook and run a household. They had only a few years to apprentice with their mother, perhaps the only time they would learn with kind, encouraging words. Once they left their home, they would be under the eagle eyes of their mother-in-law and their shortcomings and lack of experience would become huge issues in their new home. Fate had given Rukminiammal opportunities to explore areas strictly reserved for men, which developed hidden talents and a sense of fulfillment that only comes with focused purpose. Since Nagamma was her only child, Rukminiammal had to be the strong father figure that destiny had stolen away from the child, but there were times when she was the gentle, comforting mother as well. From a very young age the underlying message had been strong: '*You can do it yourself because that way it will be done better.*'

Orukai Rukminiammal could not abide sloppiness or wasteful emotion. She never tolerated anyone who sat around moping over problems or wallowed in self-pity. She never allowed Nagamma to think, '*Why me?*' It was always, '*Thank God I have the opportunity to face and solve this.*' Nagamma was trained to be bold, independent, involved and proactive. Theirs was a household where the women were empowered and as a result, much more dominant than was the custom of the time. Rukminiammal drew a clear line between control and tyranny but did not teach that particular lesson well to Nagamma. As a result, Nagamma became officious and often dictatorial. Her word was law and with everyone asking for her advice on everything, she enabled them. The children hardly ever went to their father for guidance. He was like a non-entity in his corner of the house, lost in his own thoughts, cut off from reality

All kinds of crops were grown on the land, including coconuts, pepper, sugarcane, rice, pulses and vegetables. Some of this was kept for personal use but most of it was sold in the *mandi*, the open market. As the income from the estates was much more lucrative, Munuswamy did not bother to complete his law degree. In the beginning he tried to get involved in the day-to-day working of the estate. He kept accounts, held meetings with the workers and went to market to buy seeds and sell produce. Most mornings he spent out in the fields, most often accompanied by Orukai Rukminiammal. Over time, he noticed in all his activities he was overshadowed by his mother-in-law. Slowly, even his wife became involved in the daily workings of the estate and always came up with the better, brighter and more acceptable ideas. As Nagamma became more dominant and overbearing, Munuswamy conceded his position as the male in the family and let her handle most of the problems on the estate. He spent the better part of the day reading the newspaper, chatting with neighbors, or just napping. Even though he was home all the time without any real work, he never helped out in the kitchen or in domestic affairs unless explicitly directed to do so by his wife. Every time he spoke or tried to offer a suggestion, Nagamma would shut him up or shout him down. Rather than undergo her scorn, he preferred to retire quietly to his comfort corner in the thinnai. Nagamma didn't really need him for anything anyway because she took care of everything and she did it well. He was just an appendage that she had no time for, useful to run errands, send messages and do odds and ends. As a result, Munuswamy became reticent and withdrawn. He felt as if his manhood had been taken away from him. Nagamma even decided the time and place for sex. They had five children and his only involvement with them was taking them to school and bringing them back; Nagamma took care of everything else. In the early days, there had been gentler moments, nights of intimacy and even passion but once the children were older, the equation between husband and wife changed and that part of their life became a distant memory.

Nagamma had endless energy. Waking an hour before dawn, she had the morning meal prepared even before the children woke up. After that, the women took care of business while a hapless Munuswamy watched, feeling virtually castrated, helplessly resigned to his fate.

After her mother died, all the property went to Nagamma. Soon, she realized that the children would need a better education. The one near the estates wouldn't do; it was two miles away, where children of all ages sat under a tree, learning the basics from an aged schoolmaster. The world around them was changing. With the British in control of everything, it became very important for the children to attend a proper school that was age appropriate, where they could learn English. They had no choice but to move closer to town.

The money still came from the plantation and for a few years, Munuswamy continued to stay at home. But things were not going very well in the estate. Once a month Munuswamy made a perfunctory visit but he was so out of touch with the peasants. They had no respect for him and began stealing from under his very nose. Nagamma was so busy with the house and children she became less involved in the land.

Money became tight as the sale from produce dwindled. They knew they were being cheated but packing up and returning to the farmland to oversee their employees was not an option. As a result, the erstwhile trusted tenants took full advantage of their absence. Either it was a drought, or floods, or rats that ate half the grain. Not being able to control both places at once, Nagamma had to accept the situation. Every year they sold a parcel of land to enable them to run the household and when the money ran out, Nagamma sold her silver vessels and jewelry. This continued for a while until finally Nagamma decided it was time for Munuswamy to awaken from his stupor and find a job. Munuswamy, after years of idling at home, was reluctant and unsure of himself. He did not know where to begin. What could he do? He had no experience of any kind. But their family was well connected and using the influence of an old family friend, he finally got lucky. He had not completed law school but was able to find a job as an Assistant Lawyer in a small law firm. The hours were decent and he brought enough money home to make ends meet, but the best perk was that he could be away from home all day. In fact, when he returned from work, Nagamma was actually happy to see him.

Times were extremely hard. All of Nagamma's training as a child came into good use. She could make a bag of rice last for three months. She scrimped and saved and devised a cooking system so there was not an ounce of wastage. Everything in the house was reused. The cows provided milk and the family still received some food grains and vegetables from the land. Each child had two pairs of pants and two shirts, one veshti to wear to the temple and two old ones to wear at home. Pattu had two long frocks for school and when she was older, two pavadais. Excesses were never tolerated. They lived simply but ate well. Things got a little better when Siva began working and now with Partha also teaching, there was enough money. Life stopped being a struggle but Nagamma could not halt the momentum she had created and ease up on the family's lifestyle. She was always in crisis mode and had no tolerance for unnecessary waste of time or energy.

Looking at Rajam through the doorway where she was sitting and talking to Sushila, a pang of resentment gripped her. Rajam's diamond nose ring was sparkling in the sunlight. With smoldering envy, Nagamma eyed the bright green and maroon sari, a gift from her mother for Deepavali. No one ever bought anything for Nagamma. Once a year on Deepavali she would buy herself one new sari. But Rajam, she was lucky. At her wedding her parents gave her several saris and almost six sets of jewelry. Nagamma nostalgically thought about the time when she too had saris and jewelry. But now, all Nagamma had was her *thaali* and her huge eight-stone diamond earrings. She used a twig from the *vepalai* tree in her nose so the piercing would not close. All the rest of her jewelry had been sold. She looked resentfully at Rajam's glimmering nose ring and couldn't control her thoughts. '*She has everything; beautiful white skin, not pock marked dark skin like myself. She is so attractive and petite, not large like me with a huge nose.*'

What irked Nagamma most was that Rajam had the love of her husband and shared an intimacy with him that Nagamma could never have with hers. It never occurred to her that this was her own doing. Her own dominant nature had transformed the relationship with her husband and now there was no time for regret. For the first time in her life, Nagamma faced this negative, mean, envious, side of her own nature that years of hardship had brought on.

Like many other women, Nagamma got her gratification from her sons, Partha in particular. She loved him more than any of her sons. Partha brought out the gentler side of her nature seemingly back from extinction. He looked just like her and that was something special for her. She took pride in everything he did, laughed at anything he said. His achievements were her pride and his disappointments her agony. When he wanted to marry Rajam, she was very quick to arrange the match because his happiness was so important to her, but she did not realize how much it would hurt her to see his abrupt shift of affection. Suddenly, it was Rajam he called for when he returned home from work. It was Rajam who was the recipient of a fragrant string of jasmine bought at the street corner. Even when he ate he would ask Rajam for the extra serving of rice. Every outward demonstration of his affection for Rajam jerked at her heartstrings. What really peeved her most was her favorite son's moon-eyed adoration for this chit of a girl. Every time Nagamma saw this, she would quickly send Rajam away on some unimportant errand. It was like a spontaneous reaction. She found the slightest excuse to point out a mistake and recently, Rajam was always making mistakes.

Somehow she could never get it right. The rasam was too salty or tasteless, the beans cut too long, or the kitchen not cleaned properly.

152

Nagamma made snide remarks about her clothes and jewelry and her demeanor or lack of respect. Every day, she remarked about the rich little girl who was too spoilt to face the real world, about the privileged girl who can't put up with living with an ordinary poor family — all without any provocation on Rajam's part. It was almost as if her entire focus in life was to find out what hurt Rajam the most and then make cutting barbs about it. Her abuse was completely verbal. She never touched a hair on Rajam's head; instead, she toyed with her emotions. As a result, Rajam became jumpy and nervous around her and inevitably spilled something or the other, inciting more caustic remarks from Nagamma.

Timid to begin with, Rajam found it difficult to handle her mother-in-law's spiteful comments. Her mother's home was filled with so much love, understanding and tolerance that it was impossible to deal with someone who constantly said hurtful things. As a natural consequence, Rajam's personality transformed. She was always on edge, never calm, never knowing what was coming next. From the time she woke up to the time she slept, she was at a heightened level of stress. Her moist palms made it easy for steel vessels to slip out of her grasp. Sometimes when Nagamma walked into the room, Rajam's neck got into a terrible spasm, the pain so intense, she would have to stop what she was doing until it passed.

Perhaps it was this underlying stress that prevented Rajam from getting pregnant. She was nervous about sharing her pain with another person. Even if she wanted to, whom could she confide in? And after that, could they possibly get rid of Nagamma? Because that was the only way the pain would go away. If she ever told her father, he would be horrified and indignant that his precious daughter was unhappy. It was quite possible for him to come and create a huge scene, maybe even take her away and she loved Partha too much to allow that to happen. Besides, that would only add to her stress and make things worse for her. Most of all, the scandal would make it impossible for them to live in Vizhupuram. Partha had two more brothers to be married and Rajam did not want to besmirch the name and respect of the family. Besides, she was sure this would lead to barbs about her father and she could never tolerate that. He was always above reproach and she could never allow anyone to say anything about him. She loved and respected him too much. If she told her husband, he probably would not believe her because Nagamma was all sugar and honey with him. In fact, she was sugar and honey with everyone else.

Rajam could not fathom why she had been singled out for this mental torture. She was always extremely polite. She did things before being asked to. She worked tirelessly all day. But nothing she did appeased her mother-in-law. The taunts and barbs continued relentlessly. Rajam had no one she could really talk to or confide in. Although she had married Partha, her entire life had become focused on Nagamma. She constantly devised ways of avoiding her mother-in-law to escape her ridicule. She saw that her closeness to Partha resulted in painful derision and this made her avoid contact with him, at least in front of Nagamma. She almost wept in self-pity over the irony of it. As a result, Rajam made a momentous decision to shut off her mind: she would not react to anything, no matter how provoking it was.

Not long after she made the pronouncement, an opportunity came to put her new strategy into practice. She had been happily chatting with Sushila when she heard Nagamma's booming voice summon her. She dropped the bucket and ran in.

Nagamma looked at her with half closed eyes. "Press my feet," she ordered.

Rajam crouched down and proceeded to meticulously massage her feet.

"So? You look very happy now that Partha is back."

"Yes," mumbled a fearful Rajam, apprehensive about what was coming next. In the ensuing uneasy silence Rajam pressed Nagamma's calloused toes even harder, doing it just the way she liked it, from the base of the toes to the tip and down again.

"What's this I hear about you going back home?"

'Oh no.' Rajam's heart began pumping harder. 'Now I won't be able to go home.' She grappled for the right response. If she asked for permission, she ran the risk of being denied the privilege. If she said she had decided to go, then she would be chided for being too bold and she did not want to be crossing Nagamma. Finally she said, "Your son wants to spend Deepavali with my parents in Chidambaram."

"Partha wants to go?" Nagamma asked in disbelief. She could not challenge that. For once Rajam chose her words correctly, putting the onus on Partha, making it impossible for Nagamma to retaliate. Rajam continued to diligently press her mother-in-law's insole. She kept telling herself that no matter what the provocation, she was not going to cry.

"You better make sure you clean the front and the backyard and apply cow dung before you go." Nagamma knew this was one job she hated doing but that would be her punishment for willfully abandoning the family. Rajam had just completed this distasteful task two days earlier but she did not want to mention that in case it forced Nagamma to change her mind about letting her go home. Nagamma continued relentlessly.

"At least be useful in the house, since you are otherwise good for nothing. At least Sushila has been pregnant once. Look at you; you are bringing shame to the family. *Theruvulai ellarum peshara.* Everyone is talking about my barren daughter-in-law and feeling sorry for us."

What that had to do with anything Rajam didn't understand but who was she to argue with Nagamma? She wanted a child just as badly but God was denying her that pleasure.

"Remember this: a woman has status only if she has a child; otherwise she is nothing. What is wrong with you? You and Partha are at it every night like a pair of street dogs. Why is nothing happening?"

*'Stop! Stop!'* Rajam screamed to herself, but no words escaped her mouth. What kind of woman was she to compare their union to the rutting of dogs? The only time Rajam was completely relaxed and actually happy was when she was alone with Partha at night, with no audience. They were so much in love their union took on a sacred form. It was ethereal, holy and private. Rajam's ears turned red at Nagamma's reference to this personal element of her life. What business was it of hers to even broach this topic? No one talked openly about this. Sex was between two people behind closed doors, not a casual topic of conversation. But no words emanated from Rajam's mouth. Hot tears instead began welling in her sad almond eyes.

Nagamma saw the reaction and unflinchingly went for the plunge.

"I would never have agreed to this alliance if I had known you were barren." She paused for dramatic effect, before plunging the knife a little deeper. Rajam still said nothing but the pressure on the toes eased.

"I have been very kind to you this far but if you don't get pregnant by next year, I will have to find a second wife for Partha."

155

Rajam stared up at Nagamma in disbelief. '*No! Never! Could she really do it?*' Rajam knew several men who had married twice if their first wife were unable to conceive. Partha would never agree to it. He loved her too much. But then again, he was scared of his mother. If she put enough pressure, could he actually succumb? Rajam just stared up speechless, the tears now streaming down her face.

"What are you crying for? Your own father married twice. Surely you know that. So why not Partha?"

That was it. Rajam fled from the room out into the courtyard past Sushila and into the corner of the cowshed. She had no idea how Nagamma knew about her father's second marriage. It had been conducted in secret and no one but her mother and sister knew about it. The very fact that Nagamma mentioned it debased her father's dignity. Yes, he had married twice but that was a supreme act of kindness, not because of some depraved need. Nagamma had done the unthinkable. She talked about Swaminathan Iyer as if he were some debauched wastrel. Coming from Nagamma's mouth, even the sacred Gayatri Mantram became profanity. Rajam's ears were ringing after hearing this blasphemy. What made her feel worse was she had said nothing in retaliation, knowing that her father's sacrifice had been demeaned. He was a man of such noble principle and so respected in the community that Rajam could not console herself. She would never forgive Nagamma.

'*Please, God, end my life; I can't go on, I just can't go on. Take me into your refuge, please,*' she prayed fervently. She sobbed uncontrollably for what seemed an eternity.

When she finally composed herself, she walked back into the house.

Nagamma was asleep, a smirk on her face like a satisfied lioness after a kill.

Rajam went back out to the cowshed, her only refuge, rocking back and forth in an attempt to calm herself. She had heard about her father's second marriage from her mother, Mangalam, and now the memories of her maternal grandparents flooded her being. Stories from the past flashed by in images so real and so sad, forcing the tears down her cheeks even faster.

# CHAPTER 22 – MANGALAM AND SARASWATHI
## PUDUKOTTAI – LATE 1800'S

Rajam's mother, Mangalam, grew up in the village of Pudukottai. Her father, Guruswamy Iyer, was a schoolteacher. Like all other Brahmin women, her mother, Rajalakshmi, stayed home to look after the children. Guruswamy was born into a family of priests and until he was twelve years old, attended a *Veda Pathashala*: a school attached to the temple, where young children were taught to chant Sanskrit shlokas. Guruswamy's father worked as the temple priest in the Shiva temple, where his ancestors had officiated for generations. He belonged to one of the highest sub-sects, the *Vadama Iyers*. Guruswamy learned the ancient Sanskrit texts but to his father's disappointment, did not follow in his footsteps and become a priest in the temple. Instead, he taught at the local school. The income from the school was minimal and as he was good with numbers, he supplemented it by keeping accounts for the local merchants. Some of them paid in kind; the bags of rice and lentils very welcome in the poor Brahmin household.

Like all Brahmin priests, Guruswamy wore his *veshti* in the traditional *panjakacham* style but instead of being bare bodied like his father, he wore a long black coat, something the local people adopted from their British masters. He wore his hair in a traditional *kudumi* or top knot; across his forehead were three lines of vibuthi ash, a symbol that he was a *Shaivaite*, and in the center of his forehead a perfectly round kumkumam pottu. Around his neck, he wore a Rudraksha *japamala*, which had belonged to his great-grandfather. The beads of this japamala were from the sacred Rudraksha tree native to the Himalayas, the abode of Shiva. Several times a day he used his japamala as a rosary to keep count as he chanted the sacred Gayatri Mantra a hundred and eight times, an auspicious number in the Hindu religion.

# When the Lotus Blooms

For several years Guruswamy was the Assistant Teacher in the local school, until the old school master retired leaving him in charge. Attendance in the school depended on the season. Girls were not allowed to attend school and the boys' attendance would be erratic, as most of them had to help out in the fields. He taught them whenever they came, knowing that a thirst for knowledge could not be forced on anyone. None of his students ever crossed the eighth grade. The elders from the village *Panchayat* paid Guruswamy a small stipend. As his needs were minimal, he was content and did not aspire for anything different. In fact, he was so involved in teaching that he did not marry till he was almost thirty years old, that too only under pressure from his family. His father was deeply saddened by his son's single status and wanted to see him married. Every Brahmin needed to experience *grahastha*, the life of a householder, in order to get *moksha*, release from the cycle of births and deaths. At every opportunity, he tried to persuade his son to try life as a householder and not continue his bachelorhood forever.

Finally, Guruswamy agreed to marry, officially ending his long sojourn as a Brahmachari. A match was arranged with a young girl from a neighboring village named Rajalakshmi, who was several years younger than he. He was amazed when he realized how wonderful married life could be and adored his young wife. Within the first year, Rajalakshmi gave birth to a girl, whom they named Mangalam after his mother. Five years later they had another daughter, who was named Parvathi after her mother. The two girls added the much needed chatter and laughter to the household, but it was every man's duty to have a son to carry on the family tradition. It was the son who performed the *Anthim Samskara*, the last rites for the father honoring the ancestors, releasing them from human bondage, and though Guruswamy loved his daughters, he longed for a son. Almost every year after that Rajalakshmi miscarried and with each pregnancy her health weakened.

Mangalam and Parvathi were very close, even though there was a five year gap between them. Growing up in Pudukottai, they seldom experienced any hardship. They played together, ate together, slept together, sharing their lives with complete abandon. They were cosseted by their grandparents and spoiled by their father. Life was idyllic and it seemed as if nothing could spoil that.

But life as they knew it suddenly changed. When Mangalam turned eight, her mother died at childbirth bearing a third daughter. The birth was extremely difficult and though her old grandmother was experienced at delivering babies, she knew there was trouble when labor continued for three days. When the baby's head finally emerged, the cord was wrapped around her neck three times. Paati had to cut the cord before the small, slithering, unfortunate child could enter the world, albeit for a short time. A day later, Rajalakshmi breathed her last tired breath, leaving the small infant in the care of her mother. Guruswamy was devastated by her death and felt responsible for it. He never remarried, although it would have been wise to do so, having three small children. Instead, his mother-in-law, Paati, took care of the three girls: Mangalam, Parvathi and Saraswathi.

Saraswathi had a hare lip and her limbs looked frail. An astrologer was called and his prediction was foreboding. Saraswathi would not live long but she would be happy, and yes, she would also get married! Paati did not know what to make of this prediction because nobody in their right mind would agree to marry a deformed, ugly child. But she hoped against hope that things would change. By the time Saraswathi was a year old, Paati's worst nightmares were realized. She was certain something was not right with the child. In addition to the hare lip, her eyes had malformed lids and one leg was shorter than the other. The baby cried constantly and had very limited movement. Paati knew this was not a normal child and looking after her would not be easy. It was not uncommon in those days to abandon such children in the temple or in the forest, because taking care of them required too much effort. It was just easier to have another normal child. Some even fed the unwanted child a potion made from juice from poisonous cactus, called *Kallipaal*, which they would brew and add to milk. After ingesting the poison, the child would die a quick and painless death. But Guruswamy was vigilant and let his mother-in-law know that no harm should come to the child. She was the last child born and as such, was the living memory of his late wife. Guruswamy devoted his life and energy to his motherless children, giving them the extra care they now needed. He knew he would have a lot of trouble raising this child but he happily took it on in the memory of his dead wife.

After Saraswathi's birth, Mangalam's childhood came to an abrupt end. She suddenly had to grow up and take care of her sisters. Paati

159

was not able to work as she used to and spent most of her time caring for the new baby. The atmosphere in the house had changed too and everyone smiled and spoke less often. It was as if a dark rain cloud had cast a shadow over the family and their fortunes. Mangalam virtually became the surrogate mother for her sisters. She dressed Parvathi and made sure she ate. She helped in the kitchen, learning to cook from Paati, who now worked with less efficiency. At other times, she played with baby Saraswathi, hardly aware of her abnormality. Guruswamy aged considerably over the next few years. His hair turned white and wrinkles appeared, etched deeply on his forehead, bearing testimony to his grief. He did not even notice that his oldest daughter had reached marriageable age.

Paati was the one who found an alliance for Mangalam. In the same village she heard of a boy from a decent Brahmin family, who attended school in the city and had a very promising career. Although he was not a priest, he belonged to the same sub-caste. It was better to arrange the match before people got wind of Saraswathi's deformity. Mangalam was only eleven years old when her marriage to Swaminathan Iyer took place. When she finally left her grandmother's home two years later, she felt miserable to separate from her sisters. Her whole life so far had been devoted to them and it felt as though someone were tearing away her limbs but she knew they would both get all the love and affection of their grandmother. Living in the same village, she would not be far away from them after all and she could visit them regularly.

Destiny, however, brought the three sisters together again very soon, when the situation in the Guruswamy house became grim. Paati died suddenly of a stroke the following year. To add to their troubles, Guruswamy developed debilitating arthritis and could not go to work. With no money coming in, things became extremely difficult. Parvathi was not old enough to take care of the home as well as her sister and father. For over a year Mangalam spent time at her father's home, cooking and caring for her family. Guruswamy was in constant pain, his joints mottled and gnarled, sucking out the desire to carry on. He never really got over the death of his wife; the mental and physical pain weakened him, taking a toll on his health and within the year he became bedridden.

At almost the same time, Swaminathan got a job as a constable in the Police department in Vizhupuram. Mangalam was torn between staying with her father and moving with her husband. Her sense of duty was very strong and she did not know which way to turn. As if the gods had answered her prayers, Guruswamy got a merciful release from his agonizing existence and passed away peacefully in his sleep. No one in the family was willing to take the responsibility of the girls and Mangalam was at her wits end until Swaminathan magnanimously suggested they come to live with them in Vizhupuram. He knew Mangalam was very attached to her sisters and having them live with her would make her happy. Vizhupuram was a new town for him and having company would keep Mangalam occupied, leaving him free to focus on his new job.

As it turned out, the sale of Guruswamy's Pudukottai property enabled Swaminathan to buy a small house in Vizhupuram in the Brahmin agrahaaram, not far from his place of work, with enough money remaining to provide some security for the girls, maybe even celebrate a marriage. In Vizhupuram, Parvathi began her life-long career as midwife when she assisted in the birth of Kunju, Mangalam and Swaminathan's first daughter. Parvathi was past marriageable age, but by now people knew about Saraswathi and her condition and it became impossible to find someone willing to marry her. Every month the astrologer who officiated as matchmaker brought new varans, alliances which would fizzle out as soon as they heard about Saraswathi. Mangalam enjoyed having Parvathi around to help, not only with Saraswathi but also with the new baby. It was customary in India at that time for women to go home to their mother's to give birth, where they stayed for two or three months till their babies were strong enough and they had recovered their strength and energy to return to their husband's home. But as Mangalam had no mother, she stayed in Vizhupuram for the baby and was grateful for the support of her sister.

Saraswathi was really little trouble to anyone. She could use the toilet by herself but she had very few fine motor skills and needed help with small things like dressing, making her hair and eating. She enjoyed herself thoroughly when allowed to play with her food and would have food all over her face and chin. Her muscles were very weak and once a day one of the sisters would rub Ayurvedic oil over her aching limbs, massaging her muscles, helping to bring fresh oxygenated blood into them, but her condition got progressively worse. Her speech was slurred but the sisters knew exactly what she said and what she wanted. She never asked for much and was very glad to sit on the swing all day and despite her constant pain, was blissfully happy and content. The poor child was blameless and innocent.

In the meantime, the astrologer was paying weekly visits to the house, but the alliances for Parvathi were getting more inappropriate and the age of the boys progressively increasing. After many months of searching, they finally found a family that agreed to a match with Parvathi. The boy was an orphan who lived with his paternal uncle in Thirunelveli district. He was well off and their family had been the headmen in the village Panchayat for a long time; as a result, he was well respected in the community. He had been married before but his wife had died of cholera a couple of years ago. The only other thing that bothered Mangalam was his age. He was almost thirty years old, much older than Parvathi. The astrologer advised them to conduct the marriage quickly in case the other party changed its mind. Following his advice, the family arranged a simple ceremony in their courtyard with very few invitees.

After Parvathi left for her new home, Saraswathi became very morose. She must have sensed that her sister was not around and her health went downhill. Every physical act became more and more taxing, leaving her gasping for breath. There was no point taking her to see a doctor, even though her vital functions were weakening. She spent long hours sleeping, exhausted by simple acts like eating and dressing. Mangalam knew it was just a matter of time before her end came.

The astrologer came by the house one time just as Mangalam finished feeding her. "She looks very sick. Does not seem that she will live for very long."

Mangalam shook her head sadly.

"You know if she dies as a *kanya*, a virgin, your family will have seven generations of bad luck. Your daughters will never get married because her spirit will hover around preventing it from happening," the astrologer added.

Mangalam looked at him quizzically. "What do we need to do to prevent this from happening?"

"You have to get her married before she passes on."

"But who will marry her? Look at her. She can barely get out of bed. It was hard enough finding someone for Parvathi, who was hale

162

and hearty. How could I possibly find anyone willing to make such a supreme sacrifice by marrying this disabled, sick girl?"

The astrologer paused. He certainly had no one he could recommend. Finally he said, "Ask your husband. All he has to do is put a *thaali* around her neck. After all, it is his family fortune at stake."

Mangalam was taken aback. A second marriage! Swaminathan had already put up with so much. Would he be willing to make this one last supreme act of kindness? It might result in a scandal if the neighbors got wind of it. Mangalam was terribly confused. All of the next day she thought about what the astrologer had said. Once the idea was put into her head, she had to follow directions. She did not want poor Saraswathi to be blamed for any misfortune in the family, but the bile rose up in her mouth at the thought of making such an unreasonable request of her husband.

That evening she told her husband what the astrologer said.

Swaminathan listened quietly. Then, without a moment's hesitation he said, "Call the priest. I will marry her tomorrow."

The marriage was conducted in secrecy and the priest was paid handsomely to keep the secret. Saraswathi was so sick the ceremony had to be performed in her room next to her bed. No one knew if she even understood what was happening, or if she realized she was getting married. After the ceremony, she touched the M-shaped pendant on her *thaali* and she smiled.

That night Saraswathi passed away in her sleep. The curse of seven generations would be avoided. The girls of the family would now find good husbands and happiness.

She was honored as a *sumangali*, a married woman and her *kriya* was performed with solemnity, celebrating the honor of dying as a married woman. She was dressed in a red wedding sari and had a peaceful smile on her face.

In her life she had been a burden to everyone around her, even as she brought out the noblest in them. In her death she brought peace and good karma to the entire family for successive generations.

When the Lotus Blooms

# Part VIII
# Dharmu

# CHAPTER 23 – KANDU
## CALCUTTA – 1934

The train rattled into Howrah station at the unearthly hour of four in the morning. The children were shaken out of their slumber and herded onto the bright, lively, bustling platform.

Kandu rubbed his half-closed eyes, shielding them from the bright platform lights. Mummy held his hand in a vice grip and Meera was holding the girls' hands. There were so many people here it was easy to lose your children — not a rare occurrence, especially in such crowded places — and Dharmu was extra vigilant. Kandu looked around at the incredible activity around him. *Chaiwallahs* touted their wares in loud, raucous voices and then stopped for customers to pour piping hot tea into little clay cups. With the river nearby, potters molded the red mud from the riverbank into small cups and dried them in the sun, perfect for drinking *chai*, the red clay enhancing the flavor of the strong Assam tea. Once used, they were thrown back into the river, to dissolve and replenish the source for more clay cups.

*Coolies* in red shirts and white *dhotis* walked around coercing passengers to hire them, literally picking up the luggage, ready to carry them to waiting tongas or cars. But the Bengali women would not allow them to touch the luggage without a raging fight to fix the cost of their fee. Coolies were notorious for charging exorbitant sums and would refuse to deposit the luggage till they were paid. It was amazing how much one man could carry. Kandu watched in awe as one coolie folded his turban into a round base and then with the help of an associate, placed two or three suitcases on his head. Then he slung a carry-on cloth bag on each shoulder and picked up two smaller bags in each hand. With the weight perfectly balanced on each side of his body, he began walking briskly down the platform. If he carried the entire luggage himself, he wouldn't need to share the fare with another coolie.

Coolies knew the locals always haggle and as the train lumbered into the station, would initially head for the first class compartment, some boarding the train even as it approached the platform. They preferred carrying luggage for the Angrezi sahibs, as Englishmen were better paymasters. The spillover trickled down to the rest of the Indian passengers, the slower coolies settling for third class passengers, who rarely paid more than two paise, having greater bargaining power, content in the knowledge that the coolie came to them only because they could not get a better fare elsewhere. Then they happily overloaded the man with a dozen overstuffed suitcases and packages, smugly walking ahead with a satisfied smile on their faces, pleased that they got the best bargain. It was a matter of pride to get *paisa vasul*– value for money. Mahadevan had no patience for haggling and left the dirty job to his orderly. Kandu watched awestruck as the price battle raged on. Finally, the much experienced orderly was happy with the price and two coolies with long waxed moustaches picked up the luggage but not before pinching Kandu's plump cheeks, much to his chagrin.

The rest of the world was asleep but Howrah station was alive and buzzing with activity. There were newsstands and makeshift carts stocked with all kinds of goods, from English newspapers to food and *bidis*.

*"Gopal Bhattacharjee's News Stand, Established 1910."* Kandu tried to decipher the names of the newspapers as well, but they were mostly Bengali publications and he had little success figuring out the letters. Besides, Dharmu was dragging him really fast across the platform to beat the crowds and it annoyed him when he couldn't read all the signs.

*"Number 1 bidis… Hamam soap soft on your…Yardley perfume fragrance for…"* Not one sign could he read completely. The platform was a melting pot of people from all walks of life. English Mems sweated profusely in their incongruous, full-sleeved, high-neck dresses, completely unsuitable for the hot Bengal summer. He noticed several *Marwari seths*, merchants who ruled the financial world, especially here in Calcutta, having moved here generations ago from their native Rajasthan. They could be distinguished by their typical embroidered

cap, similar in shape to the *Nehru topi*. Marwari women draped their saris differently, always with their faces covered in public, walked rapidly, to keep up with their pot-bellied husbands. Dharmu had to slow down, as the crowds were milling around the third class compartments and Kandu noticed one Marwari Seth pause by the central pillar. After quickly checking that no police constables were around, he blatantly spat his red betel nut juice onto the already red, *paan*-splattered pillar. Kandu's eyes widened in shock as he watched the offending red juice emanate from the man's mouth, sail through the air like a ruby red arc and then make a perfect landing against the pillar. The offending spitter must have seen Kandu's horror-struck eyes locked on his face and he cracked a smile, exposing his bucktoothed, blood red teeth.

"Ahh … Mummy…the man spat blood. Look, look his mouth is full of blood."

But Dharmu was too busy trying to keep up with the disappearing coolies, making sure she could spot their heads bobbing above the oceanic crowd, in case they made off with her trunk filled with silk saris, so she didn't answer him. Of course, this paan chewing Marwari was only the first in the army of his brethren, many of whom Kandu encountered in his short journey from the compartment to the end of the platform. In fact, he soon lost count of the many bloodstained mouths that passed by. Kandu's neck ached from all the swiveling it was doing. He shook his head in disbelief. Calcutta was filled with sick men, whose blood was oozing out of their mouths!

Never having been exposed to paan chewing or the sight of its red-mouthed consumers, Kandu didn't understand how common it was in India. Paan leaves grew from a creeper and in almost every street corner was a *paanwallah*, a vendor who specialized in making paans. This addictive leaf was famous in the city of Benares and even in the station was a sign saying, *"Lalloobhai phemus Banarsi Paan."*

Paan was rarely eaten by itself but was usually combined with varieties of areca nuts, some sweetened and others spiked to cater to different tastes. It was offered to guests after a heavy meal to ease digestion. The only problem with paan chewing was the large quantity of fluid filling your mouth, created by a combination of saliva and the lime applied on the paan leaf. Ordinarily, this juice could easily have been swallowed but people who ingested large quantities of betel juice all day were quite at ease spitting the liquid out when they could no longer hold it in their mouths. That was fine in their homes when a washbasin was around but with no spittoons on the street, they made the entire countryside their spittoon. The technique of spitting had been developed into a fine art of sorts and Kandu was quite astounded at how and where people spat. They spat when they were sitting, standing, crouching, sleeping, getting onto a tram, or off a train, at street corners, in the middle of the road, climbing up stairs, or through their car windows; some could spit five or six feet away, in straight lines and from all angles. In graceful arcs, this river of juice landed on pavements, street corners and streetlights, staining whatever it came in contact with, smearing the area with an indelible, blood red tarnish.

As the family finally reached the parking lot, Kandu's mind overflowed with images of sick, blood stained mouths. Two large, black American Buicks awaited to take them to their destination. Jameen Amma's son, who had lived in Calcutta for many years and was a leading businessman dealing in auto parts, had sent two of his cars with chauffeurs to meet the family at the station. It was incredibly silent in the car and they sank into the plush seats gratefully, their ears still reeling from the cacophony at the station. The sleek cars edged their way through the seething mass of humanity onto the floating pontoon bridge to cross the Hooghly River.

The sunrise on the river Hooghly was so spectacular that morning that Dharmu almost felt reaffirmed in the existence of God. The river at low tide was a shimmering blend of colors reflecting the golden resonance of dawn, its waters serene and calm, mirroring the same sentiments in all those that beheld her. This was perhaps the best time to admire the natural scenic beauty, before the day broke and people thronged to its banks. A few boats with solitary boatmen ferried passengers across to the other bank. All along the road leading to the Strand sat rows of handcarts with their owners still asleep inside.

Calcutta had all kinds of transportation, the tram and the *rickshaw* being the most significant. The rickshaw, a man-drawn handcart, was the main mode of transportation for the social elite, especially over short distances. Rickshaw pullers dragged the two wheelers, running all over the city, impervious to harsh weather conditions. Kandu watched an emaciated rickshaw-wallah struggling to move his cargo, which in this case were two extremely large ladies. Most of the rickshaw pullers in the city were refugees from the neighboring state of Bihar, who converged to the city to escape harsh famine. They rented rickshaws for exorbitant rates and then plied their vehicle tirelessly for sixteen to twenty hours a day, just to make enough money for one meal a day for themselves and their poverty-stricken families. Their plight was terrible but young Kandu knew nothing of this and he really wanted to ride in one, never having done so earlier. He had asked his mother several times at the station if they could go home in a rickshaw, but she had been deaf to his chattering until now that they were safely ensconced in the car. "Mummy can we ride in a rickshaw?" he reiterated for what seemed like the hundredth time.

"Why not? Let's reach Banu Mami's home and then after breakfast maybe we could visit the city and take a ride in a rickshaw."

Satisfied, Kandu spent the rest of the ride counting rickshaws and reached a hundred and eleven, as the car pulled into a large home in the neighborhood of Bada Bazaar. Jameen Amma's son, Ramji and his wife, Banu, were very hospitable and Dharmu stayed with them whenever they visited Calcutta.

The façade was narrow but as one entered, the house opened up. A huge courtyard opened to the sky, surrounded by many rooms. The ground floor had the kitchen and servants' area, as well as the living and dining rooms and the upper three floors held the bedrooms. The house had originally belonged to a family of muslin dealers from Murshidabad, who had fallen on hard times. The family had been in dire straits and sold the property to Ramji for a song, including the beautiful teak and mahogany furniture as part of the deal.

Every member of the family had a suite of rooms, which included a large bedroom equipped with a heavy mahogany four-poster bed, large almirahs to store clothing and an attached dressing room. Some even had a study as part of the suite. There was no dearth of rooms in the house and three were assigned to the Ayyar family. Kandu of course got his own room and clambered onto the bed, bouncing up and down till Meera hauled him away to wash and get dressed for breakfast.

Like most homes here, the house had two large kitchens, one for vegetarian cooking and the other for cooking meat. The family was largely vegetarian, though the children on occasion enjoyed a good fish or chicken curry which was made only if they had visitors. Banu had brought a South Indian cook back from the plantation in Dindigul, as she could not live without eating her native fare.

Dharmu was thrilled when she came to the breakfast table after her bath. There on the table was the most sumptuous spread she had ever seen. Not porridge and oats but instead, a real south Indian breakfast. Banu knew that Dharmu was starved for her home food and had gone the extra mile to make this meal memorable. Adorning the table were piping hot idlis, fried *vadais*, sambar and chutney, and if that wasn't enough, hot *adais*, or lentil pancakes, a delicacy that Dharmu had not eaten for ages. She embraced Banu in utter delight.

"Oh Banu Akka, just seeing this food is a treat. I don't know how to thank you."

"So don't. Just eat," replied Banu, a woman of few words.

And eat they did. No one spoke at all during the meal, a sign of how tasty the food was. After eating, Dharmu made up her mind this time she would definitely bring a cook back with her to Rangpur. The idlis were too delicious to sample only once a year. Half way through the meal, Kandu got up, intent on exploring, running up one staircase and sliding down another banister, with Meera chasing him, trying to sneak a piece of idli into his mouth when he wasn't otherwise occupied. The house was too exciting for him, with so many rooms, nooks and crannies to explore.

After breakfast, Mahadevan left in one of the cars for the office. Their train to Dindigul wasn't due to depart till nightfall, so they had the whole day to explore Calcutta. Ramji had a collection of cars, a passion of his, since he got into the auto industry. His garage sported a Vauxhall, two Buicks, a Bentley and a recently added Rolls Royce. The family piled into a Buick, much to Kandu's disappointment. He would have preferred riding in the new Rolls, but that didn't happen.

The children grew increasingly excited as they saw the sights of Calcutta. First it was Belvedere House, the Viceroys' old residence in Alipore. The Viceroys lived here until 1912, when the capital of the British Empire was moved to Delhi. After that, this stately home was converted into the National Library. As they drove through the imperial arch surrounded by the famed Botanical Gardens, they got a sense of the pageantry and pomp that was the hallmark of British rule here in Calcutta, when the city was the capital of the British Empire. After spending some time in the fabulously landscaped gardens, they drove to Chowringhee, stopping at the Grand Hotel for tea and scones. The highlight of the morning was walking up and down the

171

fashionable Park Street, with its fancy stores and restaurants. This was the best place to get western style clothing for the children and Dharmu shopped non-stop. Her need for order left little room for fashion, so it was six dresses each in the same style for the girls, six white shirts and four black shorts for Kandu, almost making their daily wear into a uniform. After a delicious lunch at Gangurams, of *Loochi* and *Alur Dom*, a Bengali delicacy, they headed for the beautiful Victoria Memorial. From a distance, the majestic view of the white marble building with a black bronze angel of victory crowning the central dome was just breathtaking. Meera stayed outside with Kandu, watching over him as he ran up and down the white marble stairs, while the rest of the family visited the museum inside.

For Kandu, the best part of the day was a rickshaw ride. All of them bundled into two rickshaws and then they rode along the race course, Kandu urging his driver to go faster and outrace the other rickshaw. He could not accept losing to women, especially when they were your sisters. The exhilarating ride lifted everyone's spirits. Everyone, except the rickshaw pullers, who looked ready to drop with the exertion, but no one really noticed them. No one but Rukku looked sad after the ride. She noticed the sweat pouring down the men's faces when they reached the Victoria Memorial and couldn't help thinking how these men were used like horses or other beasts of burden for a few moments of pleasure. She told no one and no one wanted to hear what she had to say anyway. Her only consolation was that they paid both men generously and that must mean something. If nothing else, it would at least mean a better meal for them and their families at the end of the day.

It was getting late and everyone was tired but they couldn't leave without eating *jhal muri*. The main ingredient, muri, was puffed rice, which the *muriwallah* kept hot by placing a container of hot coals on it. He had a stand with a number of tin containers containing various ingredients, like onions, tomatoes, coconut pieces, as well as a host of spices. He began vigorously mixing the ingredients in a tin with a spoon and the wonderful part was that each person could ask for a combination of different ingredients. The taste of the pungent mustard oil and the eye-watering chilly that made the muri *jhal* or spicy, combined to create a culinary experience that went beyond words. Finally, with aching feet and swollen bellies, the family set off home.

Dharmu spent the next few hours with Banu, wallowing in nostalgia before departing for the journey south. There was so much to talk about and so little time, but their meetings were always like that. Banu promised to visit Dharmu in Rangpur, which made Dharmu excited; visitors were what she looked forward to. Soon, they were in the car on their way to the train station.

Dharmu sighed and stared into the distant horizon, thinking about her lonely life in Rangpur. How slowly time passed when you were alone and how it flew when you didn't want it to. Dharmu took a deep breath, pulling herself together. This was no time to be gloomy, now the fun was just beginning. In two days she would be home again and she was determined not to spoil the present by dwelling on the past. After all the present moment was a gift from God, which was why it was called 'present.' She willed herself to be happy and experience everything to its fullest extent.

# CHAPTER 24 – KANDU
## TRAIN TO DINDIGUL

The rocking motion of the train lulled Kandu to sleep. They had a long journey ahead of them towards the south, changing two trains before they reached Dindigul but thankfully most of the time would be spent sleeping. Everyone was so tired from the hectic day spent in Calcutta that they slept soundly.

The first rays of sunlight poured in through the window, awakening Kandu. He peered out of the window and could see farmland pass by. The trees were still silhouettes in the sky, but farmers were already toiling in the fields trying to get as much as possible done before the sun's fierce rays made it impossible to work. Rukku joined him and the two of them pressed their faces against the window watching their breath fog up the glass and then writing their names on it. They passed by a village and suddenly there on the tracks were a row of men squatting with their backs turned to the train, performing their morning ablutions. Both Kandu and Rukku saw this incredible sight almost at the same time and turned towards each other simultaneously. Their incredulous, widened eyes were drenched in mirth and they covered their mouths in a futile attempt to stifle giggles. As the row of men continued unendingly, shamelessly exposing their rear ends for the entire world to view, or in this case for the occupants of the train to witness, it was too much for them to handle. They burst out laughing uncontrollably, trying their best to do this quietly as possible so as not to awaken their sleeping mother.

Kandu looked at Rukku and whispered '*kundi*', a Tamil word meaning 'rear end' which he knew was forbidden, and Rukku ruptured into giggles. Encouraged, he began repeating the prohibited word with childish glee, treading on forbidden territory. Profanity was not tolerated at home by his father, a rule upheld by his mother but as one was absent and the other asleep, the emboldened Kandu was not be contained. He repeated the word to a tune and rhythm repeatedly.

"Kundi kundi kundi kundi kundi…"

174

Rukku was doubled over with mirth, tears streaming down her cheeks. Like all children, bathroom humor thrilled her but additionally, here was a live scene in front of her meriting the use of the word.

Almost immediately, they encountered a long line of women who had their rear ends exposed, but their faces covered as the train went by. Bare butts and no faces! What were they thinking? Their rear ends could be seen but in shame they covered their faces so no one would recognize them, not that there was much chance of their friends being on the train. But this made the children laugh even more, their eyes gleaming in excitement.

"Hey Rukku, say DI KUN fast, many times."

Rukku tried it out.

"Di kun Di kun dikundidikundidikundi kundi kundi kundi kundi kundi kundi…" It was too funny! Now both of them were saying it in unison, the bare bums forgotten in the excitement of repeating a forbidden word.

Dharmu was stirring and Rukku stopped her recitation but Kandu was too excited and he went on, his voice progressively louder.

"Dikundi kundi kundi kundi kundi …"

His poetry was harshly interrupted as Dharmu realized what her son was saying and landed a hard smack on his back.

"Owwww…," yelped Kandu. "You hit me. How mean. I'm going to tell Daddy when I see him."

"Not before I tell him what bad words you are repeating. Do you think he will be happy when he hears that?"

"Slap Rukku also. She also said kundi."

So to be fair Dharmu slapped Rukku as well and the two simultaneously bawled, waking Vani up. Luckily Meera entered just then and took charge of the kids, dragging them to the washbasin to wash their faces. "What did you do?"

"We both said something. I can't tell you what, or I will get beaten again." Meera didn't press him for an answer and in a while, she herded the two now silent offenders back into the compartment.

The rest of the train journey was relatively uneventful, just spent doing the usual train things: playing cards, telling jokes, eating and sleeping. This was the time Dharmu spent talking about her childhood, getting the children into 'country mode,' where they would not have the conveniences they were used to in their own home. The toilet was something that bothered all of them because it was located at the back of the house. In order to reach it, they had to walk a short distance, which was fine during the day but scary at night. The children would be herded together to use the bathroom at dusk to avoid going at night, unless it was absolutely urgent. There would be other inconveniences too, but the love they got from their family more than made up for any discomfort. They rarely complained and just seamlessly slid into village mode once they were there.

The next morning they arrived at Mayavaram station and the children had their heads half out the window, competing to see who would be the first to spot their Thatha. Vani, being the tallest, saw his red turban way before the others could spot him. Visvanathan came to meet his daughter in two vilvandis. The family piled into one and the other was filled with their luggage, carefully guarded by Meera and the orderly. Everyone was talking at the same time and it was hard to follow the conversation. Their home was on the *jameen* in a village called Porambur, not far from the town of Dindigul. As the house came into view from a distance, Dharmu's heart swelled with nostalgia. It was such sweet reunion meeting her mother after all this time that Dharmu felt rejuvenated. She was animated, talking non-stop all through breakfast and well into the afternoon.

Kandu got tired of all the chattering. His Tamil was not up to par because he mainly spoke English and he couldn't understand half of what was going on. Bored, he went outside to play. The ground was dry and he crouched over writing words with a long dried up stick. Suddenly, he felt as though he was being watched. On the opposite side of the yard under the trees was a young boy, maybe six or eight years old, dark skinned with his hair neatly oiled and combed, staring unblinkingly at Kandu. Across his forehead were the traditional three lines of vibuthi, with a round chandanam pottu in the center. Kandu looked at him and the two stared at each other for a few minutes.

"Oy! Who are you?" Kandu called out, attempting to initiate a conversation.

"I am Sendhil. Who are you?"

"I am Kandu. This is my Grandfather's house. Where is your house?"

"It's down by the river," he responded

"So…why are you here?"

"I came to see my father," the young boy replied in a soft tone.

176

"Who is that?"

"Visvanathan Iyer." Kandu wrinkled his brow. As far as he knew he had only one uncle, his mother's brother Venkat Mama, and this boy certainly wasn't him.

"Visvanathan Iyer is not your father. He is my Grandfather and I don't know you," he declared emphatically

"Yes he is. He is my father," the boy persisted.

"No he isn't." Kandu was getting agitated but the boy would not relent. He kept insisting this was his father's house and that he wanted to see him. Kandu walked up to him and landed a square punch on his chin. Pretty soon the two were in the dirt, pulling each other's hair and landing random punches. Hearing the commotion, Dharmu and her mother, Gayatri, ran out and quickly attempted to separate the boys.

"What is this Kandu? Can't you behave civilly? It hasn't even been a few hours and you are already in a fight." Dharmu was visibly annoyed with Kandu.

"I hate him. He says Thatha is his father and he is lying. I hate him." Kandu shrieked, his angry eyes flashing.

Gayatri stopped in her tracks and stared at the boy. Her eyes hardened and she held him by his collar. Almost screaming she demanded, "Who are you?"

"I am Sendhil. My mother is Pankajam. Visvanathan Iyer is my father." Gayatri's breath was coming in shallow gasps. Dharmu couldn't understand it. Amma was always very composed and never given to anger but here she was shaking a small boy whom she barely knew.

"Get out." Gayatri screamed. "Don't you dare step on this property again, do you hear? Get out now!" The poor shivering boy retreated, his eyes filled with tears and he turned and ran into the distance. Gayatri covered her face with her thalapu and ran into the house. Dharmu was really perplexed. She didn't understand what was happening. Who was this boy and why was he saying that her father was his? Why was Amma so agitated? She ran in after her mother determined to get to the bottom of this.

Gayatri was on her bed, her body heaving, as she cried her heart out onto her pillow.

"Amma? *Yenna aachu*? Tell me please, what happened? What is the matter?"

"Nothing, nothing. I'm fine, just a little overwhelmed. Must be the heat." But Gayatri could not control her emotions. The tears just kept streaming out. Years of pent up emotions were finally finding some release.

"Amma, please don't get so upset. That boy is lying; don't worry about him."

"No Dharmu, that boy is telling the truth." Gayatri turned her head and buried it in the pillow, crying even more heartrendingly.

"What do you mean?" For a while Gayatri couldn't speak but when the tears lessened she reiterated the same in a broken, rasping voice.

"He is telling the truth. Your father is his father too. Your father has another wife."

It was as if she had been hit by a sledgehammer. Dharmu was so shocked she couldn't speak. She could not believe what she was hearing. Her father marrying twice! When had all this happened and why had no one told her about it?

"Appa… got married again?" She asked tentatively.

"Not married, he keeps a *Devadasi* in town. He has a *'chinna veedu,'* another house and another family."

"What!" Dharmu had heard of rich landowners keeping women from Devadasi families but not for a moment did she dream that her father would have the courage to do the same.

"Yes. He has another woman in his life," said Gayatri, breaking into a fresh bout of tears. Dharmu let her cry for a while. When her body stopped heaving she asked quietly, "Amma, when did all this happen?"

"I suspected something even before your marriage but I wasn't sure. Then I spoke to the overseer, who told me all about it. Many Mirazdars and Jameendars keep chinna veedus; it's very common, but I hoped that your father was different. He met this woman, Pankajam, in Thanjavur. She is a Devadasi and the women from her family are married to Kamakshiamman. Your father brought her back and set her up in a house in town."

"Why? Why did he do it?"

"Why? Because he can. Because he is a man and men do whatever they want."

"Didn't you confront him?"

"Confront him and do what? Was he going to leave her for me? What do I have? I have no education. I can't talk about anything, other than home, family and food. What do I have to hold him? Devadasis can dance and sing and are very knowledgeable about world affairs. They are masters of the Kama Sutra and know how to keep a man. I had no chance from the beginning." Momentarily, Dharmu was thankful for her marriage. Mahadevan was not interested in sexual contact with her or any other woman; at least she was grateful for that. Her heart was in turmoil. This news was too shocking and she had no idea how to react but she had to console her mother.

"No Amma, don't belittle yourself. You are the backbone of this family and the mistress of this house. Don't you ever forget that. No one can take that away from you. Legally, she has no rights over Appa. Take comfort in that."

"I did confront your father one day and told him I should never have to meet them anywhere. He promised, saying that he respected me and my position and I would never suffer in any way. Materially I may not suffer, but doesn't he see my torment when he rides away to spend the night with her? How many nights I have spent crying into my pillow, always hoping against hope that this week would be different and he would come home and tell me that he had broken off the relationship. I have prayed in so many temples, hoping God would instill some sense into him and deliver him back to me. But my prayers have never been answered. God alone knows what sins I must have committed in my previous births to deserve this." Gayatri stared into the distance. There were no more tears. She had dried out her reservoir of tears and now felt completely numb.

"Can I talk to him about it?" Dharmu asked.

"No Dharmu, don't even bother. It has been so many years now and I have come to terms with it. I am normally quite composed. I don't know what happened today. Just seeing that boy, a testimony to his unfaithfulness, triggered something in my brain. It won't happen again."

"Amma, how many children does he have from the other woman?"

"I think he has one daughter and two sons. This boy who came is the youngest. I am not sure. I never wanted to know but news like this somehow filters back to me."

Dharmu put her arms around her mother and the two of them sat silently on the bed for a while, just rocking back and forth in a comforting motion. Dharmu was consoling her mother but she couldn't help thinking how in a matter of a few minutes her opinion of her father had changed dramatically. She did not know how she was going to face him. She was so angry she wanted to spit on his face. All his display of affection suddenly meant nothing. He was a cheat, an adulterer. All these years he had another family and she had had no inkling. She could not imagine how difficult it must have been for her mother to keep this dark secret hidden for so many years. How could her father have the gall to return home each night and face his pure wife?

Dharmu was suddenly face to face with a reality that was true for many unfortunate women. Indian women had no chance to choose their own journey. They moved from the care of their father to the control of their husband and their destiny was inextricably linked to these important men in their lives. They were like mice in a maze, scurrying through narrow corridors within boundaries both physical and mental, set by the men in their lives, their journey often becoming a futile attempt to find an exit to happiness.

Tied to the home, the children, the kitchen, they had no escape from this prison that had no physical or overt signs of restraint. No chains, except those of maternal bondage, no bars, except invisible social dogmas, only a noose in the form of a *thaali* tied around their neck at the time of marriage.

Dharmu wiped the tears off her mother's face, her heart filled with renewed admiration. This small yet misleadingly reticent woman had developed an inner fortitude to face all those challenges in situations beyond change. For Dharmu, her mother was a symbol of womanhood, steeped in spirituality which supported her in an apparently crumbling world. She hugged her mother once again in an attempt to get a piece of that strength and energy, not knowing what the future held in store for her.

Dharmu sighed loudly. At this moment she could not tell what she despised more — men or womanhood.

# Part IX
# Rajam

# CHAPTER 25 – REVATHI
## VIZHUPURAM

Rajam went out to the front of the house to pluck some flowers to string together and decorate her hair. Looking up she saw her neighbor whom she wanted to meet for a while, walking swiftly towards her. Her face was covered and she was almost running, and from the expression on her face her urgency was apparent. She was probably going to the temple but it was strange she was by herself. Normally, women did not venture out of their home without either a female or male escort. Besides being socially correct, walking with company was also safer when you were out. One never knew what could happen. Rajam searched in her mind for the woman's name but she could not remember it. Sita, no it was Shanthi, or was it Revathi? That's right, it was Revathi. Nagamma was friends with Revathi's mother-in-law, and she had met them both several times at the temple but Revathi never talked much. She always answered in brief monosyllables and kept to herself, never volunteering any extra information. Then again, Rajam never met her alone. Revathi was always in the company of her mother-in-law and that could seriously hamper one's communication abilities. This time, however, Revathi was alone and Rajam decided to talk to her. "Hey Revathi? *Namaskaram.* Do you remember me? I am Rajam. I have met you and Muthu Mami many times at the temple."

Revathi looked up and she seemed to be upset. "Hello Rajam. How are you? I remember you well."

"Where are you off to?"

"I'm just going to the temple. Actually, I am in a hurry. I'll talk to you later. I must get back soon."

182

It was quite clear to Rajam that Revathi did not want to talk. Then Rajam noticed something strange. Revathi had put the loose end of her sari, her thalapu, over her head, covering part of her face. She was holding the tip of the sari in the corner of her mouth, almost as if she were hiding something. As Revathi turned her face away from Rajam, her thalapu slipped momentarily from her face, revealing a swollen purplish red bruise over her eye. Rajam was going to exclaim out loud but she swallowed her words, knowing intuitively it would be better if she stayed quiet. No married woman in the south of India covered her head and if Revathi was doing this, then she did not want anyone to see her face. What happened? How had she hurt herself? It seemed as if Revathi was accident prone. Last month she had a bandage around her hand. Muthu Mami said it was an accident in the kitchen but now looking back, it seemed to be a pattern and appeared very suspicious. Rajam was sure something odd was up with Revathi and her family and she went inside to see if Sushila knew more about them.

Sushila had just finished giving Balu a bath. She was holding his face with her left hand and using the comb with her right to part his hair and comb it down. Rajam came close to her, talking in a hushed whisper so no one overheard. "Sushila, I just saw something strange. You remember Revathi? Muthu Mami's daughter-in-law? Well she was rushing down the street all by herself. I tried to talk to her but she did not want to talk."

"Yes, she is a quiet type. She doesn't talk very much. What about her?"

"The odd thing is that her thalapu fell and her eye was purple, as if she had hurt herself very badly. She tried to cover it up but I noticed it."

"Her husband must have hit her."

"What? Hit her?" Rajam was astounded. "How can her husband hit her? What a cowardly thing to do."

"Come on, Rajam, it is quite common. Many men hit their wives. You and I are very lucky to be married to men who don't hit us. I have seen it a lot of this in my village."

"But why? Why do they do this?"

"Frustration I suppose. They get angry with someone else and take it out on their poor wives, most often when they are drunk."

"But can't we do something about it? How can we allow poor Revathi to be a victim of such abuse?"

"How do we know for certain that any abuse has taken place? We hardly know them. For all you know, she might have bumped her head against a door. We can hardly go up to their house and accuse them without any proof."

"I am sure it is abuse; otherwise she would not have covered her head like that. It was obvious she wanted to hide it from outsiders. If she had hit herself, there would be nothing to be ashamed about, nothing to hide. I am sure her husband is hitting her. Poor thing. She must be scared. Let's go and talk to her at least."

"Rajam, how can we interfere in their lives? After all, it is their private matter. It is none of our business. They are certain to be rude if we approach them and try to intervene."

"What if we at least try and talk to her and find out what happened? I don't see any harm in that."

"No, Rajam, we hardly know her and we can't interfere in domestic quarrels."

"What about the police? I can talk to Appa about it. I am sure he will help."

"Don't be silly Rajam. Unless Revathi herself reports it, they will not interfere and I am certain she will not have the courage to make an official report. Besides, the police are so busy catching revolutionaries, they won't bother with all this."

"Sushila, if her husband is beating her, then can't we do something? She's a woman just like us and I'm sure she has no one to help her. We have to try and talk to her."

"Rajam what is this sudden interest in Revathi? You have never met her. In my opinion you can try all you want but I am sure that if he is beating her, he won't let you talk to her."

"Then I'll have to go and meet her when her husband is not there, that's all."

Just then, Siva and Partha walked in. "And just who are you going to meet, Rajam? I hope for your sake it isn't some man."

"*Yenna*, you have to come with me to Revathi's house. Right now."

"Why? Who is Revathi anyway?" Partha was puzzled.

184

"That young girl from the Raman house down the street. I just saw her with a bruised eye. I think her husband is beating her but I want to talk to her to be sure. "

"Are you mad? We can't just barge into people's homes and ask them about their private lives."

"If you can't, I will. Come now. Come with me. Let's see if she is alone. Maybe she will talk to me." Rajam rushed out of the house purposefully, followed by a befuddled Partha.

Revathi rushed home, grateful that other than Rajam no one had seen her. She reached her house and ran into the mutram. Leaning against the pillar, she slid down onto her haunches, holding her head in her hands, hot tears streaming down her face. She was crying silently, not wanting to awaken her mother-in-law, who was asleep, nursing a migraine. The salty tears made her wounded eye smart, making her cry even more. Vaithee had been there for her right through this ordeal and now he was going to take her away from it all. Just when she thought everyone had forsaken her, here was a real chance for salvation. All this time she was sure she would die and there would not be one person willing to shed a tear in her memory, but Vaithee rekindled hope within her. Hope, which had abandoned her for a long time, all through these tortuous months of pain and mental torment. Just when she thought she was too tired and there was no more strength left in her to fight, God had given her a reason to battle, a reason to live, something to look forward to. Vaithee was going to take her away. Finally, she would be safe, free from pain, free from Raman.

Revathi had been married to Raman for over two years now. In the beginning, everything was fine and Raman was considerate to her. He worked as the accounts clerk for a Mirazdar, a landowner near Vizhupuram. He was the only son and his widowed mother, Muthulakshmi, lived with them. Muthu Mami, as she was called, lost her husband early in life and struggled to educate her only son. He was a very good son, a little hot headed at times but never given to rage or temper tantrums. She was overjoyed when she found a good alliance for him. Revathi was a quiet, obedient girl, always ready to work and never crossed anyone. She was a little too timid at times, never speaking unless spoken to, doing what she had to and happy to be left alone. Muthu was hopeful she would have a grandchild soon and kept asking Revathi about it, much to the latter's embarrassment. However, many changes that took place over the past year completely altered Raman's character. Changes, which would irreversibly transform the fortunes of their household.

A few months ago, Revathi was dozing in the mutram, waiting for her husband to return. She had lit the evening lamps hours ago and was exhausted with the wait. She was hungry but could not eat until her husband had eaten. It was late, past midnight, when she heard him enter the house. The Mirazdar had invited him to the plantation and Revathi assumed it was to discuss business, but when Raman stumbled into the mutram, unsteady and reeking of alcohol, she knew this had not been a business meeting.

"*Yennadi Revathi. Vaa, kittai vaadi,*" Raman said crudely, pulling her close. She could smell the alcohol on his breath. Repulsed, she struggled to get out of his grasp, when to her shock, he slapped her across her face. She looked at him in disbelief, begging him to let her go, struggling as she tried to free herself but he held her in an iron grip. That night he raped her.

Muthu heard everything. It was a small house and there wasn't much privacy but she did not have the courage to confront her son. She kept quiet, hoping this was an isolated incident that would not recur. The next morning, she noticed that Revathi's face was swollen and she walked with a limp but Muthu said nothing. Quietly, she heated a wet towel in the kitchen and handed it to Revathi so she could use it to ease the pain. Revathi understood her compassion and helplessness in this situation. The Mirazdar gave Raman his first taste of imported Scotch whiskey and unfortunately, Raman enjoyed it thoroughly. Over the next few months, Raman was out two or three nights a week. Sometimes, he was brought home in the Mirazdar's vilvandi, dragged in by the driver and thrown on the bed, where he would lie inert, not moving till the next morning. But if he was awake on his return and not completely wasted, Revathi was always at the receiving end of his ire, lust and frustration. The next morning, Raman would always be all contrite, apologizing for his wayward behavior, making Revathi feel he needed another chance to repair his errant ways.

Soon after, Raman got involved in gambling with the Mirazdar's rich friends. Unfortunately he was not in their league, having neither the money nor the ability to gamble. Slowly, he moved to selling things from the house to pay his arrears. First, it was furniture — the coat stand, the mahogany desk — and then he sold the cows. On days he could not go to the Mirazdar's house, he bought local toddy, a crude alcohol made from fermented coconut water, which smelt disgusting. Things got progressively worse and the raping and beating continued relentlessly.

Muthu was unable to see her daughter-in-law suffer and decided it was time to confront her son. She knew her whole life had been one of sacrifice, devoted to the wellbeing of her child and was sure he would listen to her. When she summoned up her courage to question Raman the following day, he slapped her in his drunken stupor. She reeled backward, lost her balance and fell, hitting her head on the edge of the *ammi kallu*. She lost consciousness and when she awoke, she looked helplessly into Revathi's eyes and the two of them exchanged a silent embrace of mute empathy.

Raman was beyond control. Alcohol had completely taken over his life and there was no point trying to reason with him. Revathi decided she would talk to her parents. Initially, when she broached the subject at home, her mother told her now that she was married she was an outsider and they couldn't interfere in her life. She belonged to her husband and she had to live with him at all costs.

"Be patient and have faith," her mother said. "It is probably only a passing phase and things will definitely improve. Do not do anything to anger him. You are a woman and are dependent on him for everything. You certainly cannot leave him and come home because he slaps you. We can't do anything to help you." Revathi was left with no choice other than returning to her abusive husband.

But things got progressively worse until it reached a head. Raman and Revathi were arguing in the kitchen because Revathi refused to give the brass cooking vessels for him to sell. In a fit of rage, he picked up the tongs, heated it on the fire and branded her on her shoulder. Sitting outside in the thinnai, Muthu Mami could smell the stench of smoldering, burning flesh. She closed her ears to shut out Revathi's screams of pain. She knew Raman was uncontainable and crazy, and Revathi's life was in danger. She had no one to confide in and beg for help without compromising their family honor. Only Revathi's parents could help her now. Revathi urgently needed to talk once again with her parents, asking them to intervene.

When Revathi showed her mother the burn on her shoulder, she was horrified; still her parents were reluctant to intervene. Revathi's maternal uncle, Vaithee, who was also present, witnessed the events with growing discomfort. In some families, it was common for a girl to marry her maternal uncle, her *Mama*, and Vaithee always thought that Revathi would marry him. When things turned out differently, he was a little disappointed. Nevertheless, his feelings for Revathi never really waned. Now seeing her burned shoulder, he was appalled and it was his vehemence that finally persuaded Revathi's father to talk to Raman. The meeting was a complete disaster. Raman, consumed by alcohol literally threw his father-in-law out of the house.

Vaithee continued to meet Revathi every week in secret, just to make sure she was all right and the two of them developed a bond dangerously bordering on love. For Revathi, Vaithee was the ray of sunshine breaking through the dark clouds that symbolized her life. She met him whenever she could in the mango grove, not far from where she lived. He waited there for her every Thursday morning, in the hope that she would make the rendezvous. It was not easy to escape from the house and she would have to wait until her mother-in-law was asleep to sneak out. She never used the front entrance but instead, would sneak out using the back door, knowing that no one except the *parayans* used this entrance. The two would sit and talk under a special mango tree.

One day, after she left, Vaithee carved a heart on the trunk, with both their initials R and V on it. Revathi was horrified when she saw it, frightened that someone might see it and get her into trouble but Vaithee calmed her down, saying that the symbol on the tree would mean nothing to others, but that it was special to Vaithee. Their meetings were brief and most of the time Revathi talked about the week's ordeal. Two months ago Vaithee declared his love to her. She was aghast at first. It was sacrilege for a married woman to even think of another man, let alone love him. All this time, she only thought of him as a friend or a relative but now their relationship had changed.

That morning, Raman had entered the kitchen and pulled her *thaali* off her neck. It was her only piece of jewelry left. He had sold all the rest, along with her silver vessels. She begged him to spare her

188

thaali, pleading that only widows remove it. Raman threw his head back and laughed at her cruelly, declaring, "*Nee sumangali illai, nee thevdiya* - you are not a married woman you prostitute. Be ready tomorrow night. You have to come with me. I lost money to this Mirazdar and he is willing to forego it if he can spend a night with you. So get ready to become my prostitute." Raman left the kitchen swinging the gold thaali in his hand, while Revathi looked at him incredulously.

Revathi could not believe what she was hearing. Marriage was a holy sacrament, where the husband was supposed to protect his wife from danger. Instead, this man was ready to pimp for her and degrade her into a common whore. She had reached the breaking point and she rushed at him with a brass pot but he twisted it out of her hands and hit her repeatedly in the face until her eye split open. She fell to the floor, where he continued kicking her until she stopped moving.

"Whore! Piece of dirt! How dare you cross me? Next time I will kill you." Raman walked out of the kitchen with her thaali triumphantly held high, a trophy to celebrate her subjugation. This time she knew he meant it. Raman would not rest till she was dead.

Revathi could not move for a long time. Slowly, she got up and crawled outside to wash her wounds. Her mother-in-law had stopped coming in to check on her. The beatings became so frequent that apathy had set in. Moreover, watching mutely as her household crumbled in front of her eyes and being completely helpless and incapable of salvaging the situation, made her ill. Muthu suffered from severe headaches, especially when Raman was around and she would lie down in a dark room for hours.

It was Thursday, and Revathi knew Vaithee was waiting for her. Without thinking, she covered her head and ran down the main street, which was when Rajam saw her. Revathi was so intent on reaching the mango groves she could not remember what had passed between them. Vaithee was there, waiting for her and she hurled herself into his open arms, crying uncontrollably. Vaithee held her quivering body for several minutes and then as she calmed down, she told him what happened.

"I can't live here anymore. You have to do something."

"Oh Revathi, my heart is bleeding but we can't run away just yet. I have to make some arrangements."

"But what will I do now? He is going to take me tomorrow evening to his friends. How will I endure the torment of strangers touching me, of…raping me?"

"Oh God, Revathi don't use those words, I can't bear it. Try to be brave for a few days more. He probably won't take you there looking like this. Your eye is swollen and he certainly will not want his friends to see you this way. I need a day to arrange for a vilvandi from another village. I can't take you anywhere if I use one from this village. On Saturday, the village will be empty and by then I would have made all arrangements. Make some excuse not to go to the chandhai on Saturday and meet me here at noon. We will take the vilvandi to the junction and then a train to Madras. He will never be able to find us once we reach Madras. You will be safe and both of us can be together always."

"I can't wait two more days."

"You have to, Revathi. If we go today, we will not have enough time to escape and then if you are caught and have to go back, things will be worse for you. It's only two more days. I promise, after that you and I will be together always. Now go home and use the back roads. I will see you on Saturday." Unwilling to leave the refuge of Vaithee's arms, Revathi despondently made her way back to her house. Just as she arrived, she heard a knock on the door.

"*Yaaru?* Who is it?"

"It's me Rajam."

'Oh no!' Thought Revathi not knowing what to do. "I can't come out. Can you come by later?" But Rajam was single-minded and determined to talk to Revathi.

"Revathi, please let me come in. I know you are in trouble and I want to help you." Rajam waited for a response but was greeted with a steely silence.

"Please let me help you. My father is a Police Inspector and he can arrest your husband. At least let me come in and talk." Finally giving in to Rajam's persistence, Revathi opened the door, putting her finger against her lips, indicating to Rajam that she needed to be quiet.

"We can talk at the back. That way there will be some warning if my husband returns."

Rajam ran to the gate and told Partha to wait for her at the back entrance.

"What?" said Partha indignantly. "Only parayans use that road."

"Please, you can bathe when we go home. I need to talk to her." The two women walked to the back of the house and sat in the empty cowshed.

"Why?" said Revathi. "Why did you want to help me? You barely know me."

"I don't know. When I saw that bruise on your face, I knew something was wrong. I just can't bear to see you suffering. I know I can help you if you only tell me what is happening."

Like undigested food, Revathi regurgitated the story of her life. Rajam sat silently listening to the horror unfold. When she told her about Raman's plans to use her to pay his debts, Rajam closed her ears. She could not believe any man would stoop to this level of debauchery.

"You can't stay here anymore. You have to file an official police complaint."

"No, I can't do that."

"Why?"

"The shame. Everyone will know what is happening in this household and I can't deal with that."

"Living with gossip is better than living with this sadistic man. Think about it. I will talk to my father on Saturday and he can come here and take you away."

"And where will I go? Who will take me in? My parents certainly won't. Shall I stay with you? Do you think your people would take me in?"

Rajam knew she could not make any offer because the decision was not hers to make. She would have to consult the family and she was not sure that Nagamma would be happy with this situation and cooperate. No one would be willing to give her refuge because then they would have to get involved with the problem, the police and maybe a court case. Rajam knew she had no answer and searched for the right response to give Revathi.

"I didn't think so," said Revathi, knowing that this was not a battle Rajam could help fight.

"No one can help me from this village. That is why I have made other plans." At this point, she told Rajam about Vaithee and her plans for fleeing with him on the day of the fair. She was careful not to allude to the romantic connection between them, mentioning only that he was her uncle.

Rajam felt terribly helpless. She knew Revathi had few choices. Even though Rajam was eager to help her, she knew there was very little that she could do. Running away with her uncle was her safest recourse.

"Okay, I will wait till Monday. Please, if anything else happens in the meantime, find some way of letting me know. My husband, Partha, is twice the size of Raman and can easily beat him to a pulp. Just say the word."

"No Rajam, the whole town will buzz with loose talk. My only option is to run away. Once I am gone, then Raman can deal with the scandal."

"If I don't see you at the temple on Monday morning, I will assume that you have left."

"Rajam, you have to remember you cannot tell anyone what you heard from me just now. If anything gets back to Raman, that will be it for me. He won't leave me alive. This is my only chance to escape. Promise me you will keep this secret."

"Revathi, not a word about you will escape my lips. I will be seeing my father on Saturday at the chandhai. Should I talk to him about you?"

"No, Rajam, there's no need for him to know anything. Even if he knew, he would not be able to help me. It's better this way."

Their conversation was interrupted by Muthu shouting "Revathi, where are you?"

"You'd better go. I don't want anyone to see you here." She led Rajam towards the back door and Rajam paused to hug Revathi.

"Thank you, Rajam. Just talking to you has made me feel strong. Now go quickly before anyone sees you." She pushed Rajam out the back door, where an impatient Partha was waiting for her.

"About time," he said angrily.

"*Yenna*, how can you talk like that? If you had only listened to the most horrific story of torture and abuse that I heard just now, you wouldn't be as concerned about something as trivial as your time?"

"What are you talking about?"

"I can't tell you anything more right now. Let's get back before your mother gets annoyed."

# CHAPTER 26 –RAJAM
## VIZHUPURAM

The chandhai was to start on Saturday morning and continue all day. In every household, women were struggling to finish their tasks so they would be free to spend a relaxing day outdoors. As usual, the morning chores had to be completed and everyone needed to eat before they left. Although plenty of food was available at the fair, sometimes it was not very fresh and could lead to weeks of indigestion and diarrhea. Eating out was totally forbidden for Brahmins unless it was in the home of another Brahmin family. Allowing Partha to participate in the idli eating competition was Nagamma's rare moment of indulgence. The rules however, were different for the rest of the family.

Nagamma would not even think of eating outside the house and definitely not at the fair, so all the women were busy packing a picnic lunch in two big tiffin carriers. Idlis and *dosai* smothered with oil and *molahapodi*. Those were food items that could be enjoyed cold. Tamarind rice and fried vadaams, *thayir shaadham* with delicious mango pickle and of course fresh fruit and water.

Rajam's mood was mixed. She was really excited about going to the fair but at the same time, was worried about Revathi. She wasn't sure if she should broach the subject with her father or not. Thankfully, Partha had not questioned her any more about Revathi. She had given her word that she would not tell anyone about it and was very successful at keeping it a secret so far, in spite of Sushila's probing.

Siva brought an extra vilvandi from town so that all of them could travel comfortably. At about ten in the morning, the family piled into the bullock carts and set off towards the maidanam outside town, where the fair was held. Rajam stuck her head out of the cart, hoping to catch a glimpse of Revathi to wish her the best of luck but she couldn't see anyone outside or in the thinnai. Perhaps Revathi was busy sending the family off. Nagamma was intent on ensuring all the food items were brought and Sushila patiently answered all of her queries. In a short while, they reached the maidanam. Rajam got down, eager to reach the fairgrounds, excited about meeting her father once again.

Even though it was early, the fairground was filled with people. Vendors from nearby villages had set up stalls to sell their wares. Some had traveled from far off towns like Thanjavur and Chidambaram to participate in the fair. This is what many artisans did for most of the year, traveling from village to village trying to sell what they had spent the rest of the year producing. All kinds of vendors were selling food, pots and pans, sweets, saris and a host of other things. As Rajam entered the fairgrounds, she saw food vendors on the right. A huge variety of fresh delicacies were for sale, like fruit with chilly powder and colored drinks. In one corner vendors were selling hot idlis and vadais. A few had set up makeshift stoves and were making hot dosas, serving them with sambar and molahapodi. A powerful aroma wafted from the sweet stalls stocked with every variety of delicious sweetmeats. Already, flies were gravitating towards this area and shopkeepers had young boys shooing them away with hand fans. Large groups of hungry revelers spontaneously crowded around the vendors, devouring the delicious food.

On the left, vegetable vendors had spread jute mats on the bare ground with neatly piled fresh produce. Symmetrical pyramids of purple brinjals, bright red tomatoes, potatoes of all kinds and leafy spinach tied in green and red bundles. All kinds of fruit were on display: apples, pears, pomegranates, guavas, melons, papayas and different varieties of bananas. All the vendors had metal weighing scales. Some had real weights but most of them used stones of different sizes to weigh the vegetables. It wasn't exactly accurate but nobody seemed to mind. The noise level was incredible, with all the shopkeepers shouting out to attract buyers.

*"Inge Vango maa, tomato rombo malivu.* Come here madam, I have cheap tomatoes."

"Amma, look at these rosy apples. Where are you going? Come here, Amma."

"Melons, just for you, I will give good price."

"Come maa, I haven't made my first sale. *Boni,* I will give you good price ma."

It was hard to decide where to go first. Everyone was trying to pull them in different directions. Rajam just stood, looking around wondering what to do next, when Partha walked up to her. "Want to eat some chilly guava?"

"Where is your mother? I don't mind as long as she doesn't see me." Nagamma would never approve of anyone eating at the fair, not when such elaborate meal plans had been made.

"She has gone to the other side. Come along before the flies attack the food."

They walked over to the guava vendor and bought two yellow guavas, neatly sliced and covered in salt and chilly powder. "Oww," said Rajam, hopping up and down after taking the first bite. "That is really spicy."

"Is it too hot? I'll get you some soda." Partha walked over to the soda vendor, who had stacks of colored drinks in uniform glass bottles, each sealed with a marble stopper. Rajam took one sip of the fluorescent yellow drink and gave it back to Partha.

"I don't want to drink too much. Men can go anywhere but women have to wait and hold it till the evening." The two of them walked past the food area, chomping merrily on the guava. Rajam was scanning the crowd to see if her father had arrived, when suddenly her head was jerked back, as someone yanked her pigtails.

"Ahh!" she screamed as she turned around and was shocked to see her brother Mani. Squealing in delight, she hugged him tight. "Is Amma also here?" Mani pointed to the potter's corner but then was distracted by the small Ferris wheel and ran off towards it, waiting in line again for his turn. He had already been on it five times but that was not enough.

Rajam ran towards the potters. She could see her mother bending over and examining the *kalchattis,* special stone vessels for cooking. Rajam ran up to her mother and covered her eyes from behind.

*"Yaaru?"* Mangalam asked, tentatively touching Rajam's hands. "Who is that?"

*"Rajama?* Is it Rajam?"

Then mother and daughter hugged and chattered away. Mangalam had not seen Rajam for a while now. As she held Rajam's hands in hers she noticed her hands, rough with calluses. "Looks like you have gotten used to the housework. Apply coconut oil at night before you sleep; it will keep them soft."

The whole atmosphere was very festive, with all the women dressed in their best saris and the girls in beautiful pavadais with brightly colored bangles and ribbons to match. In between visiting the various stalls, they greeted all their friends and relatives. Rajam searched all the time for Raman, Revathi's husband, but she had not seen him so far, although she spotted Muthu Mami buying saris earlier. She said a quick prayer to herself, hoping by now that Revathi had managed to escape. Suddenly, she noticed her father at the far end of the fairgrounds, where the cattle sales took place and she ran to meet him. Swaminathan was busy talking to his fellow constables when he saw Rajam rushing towards him. "Hello my *chella kutti*. You look beautiful as usual."

Rajam and her father spent a few minutes talking to each other until he was hailed by the constable to attend to something. As he turned to leave, Rajam asked, "Appa, if someone was beating his wife what could the police do?"

"What do you mean?" said an indignant Swaminathan. "If Partha touches one hair on your head, I will break every bone in his body."

"No Appa, Partha wouldn't dream of doing anything like that."

"Is it someone you know?" Rajam nodded, not wanting to say more than she needed to. Luckily for her Swaminathan was preoccupied with work.

"I am busy now but I will definitely come by your house tomorrow and then we can go together to your friend's house. One visit from me will scare him into an obedient puppy." Rajam was happy. At least she knew she had a backup plan for Revathi. It was almost midday, and a turbaned man with a large handlebar moustache called through a megaphone for everyone to come around for the 'idli competition.' Rajam quickly herded her mother towards the entrance where the competition would take place. Clean banana leaves lay in front of cotton *jamakalams* in preparation for the participants to sit and eat. Each place setting had a brass plate and a tumbler of water. All the competitors trickled in waiting for the contest to kick off. Partha and some of his friends joined the competition and he knew that last year's

196

winner, Muhammad Salih, would be a fierce opponent. A huge crowd gathered waiting for the event to commence.

The comical turbaned man began proceedings by reading the rules. Idlis would be served six at a time. As soon as volunteers noticed a competitor's idlis were over, they would serve six more. The last one sitting and naturally the one who ate the maximum number of idlis would be declared the winner of the competition. The prize was the princely sum of five rupees. The first lot of idlis was served; then someone blew a trumpet and the eating began. The noise was incredible, with everyone cheering on their favorite competitor. Twenty minutes passed and over two dozen idlis had been served to each participant. Many had given up already and the competition had narrowed to eight gormandizers. After the next round, four more participants hobbled off, holding their bellies. Partha continued downing the rice cakes with resolve, while the milling crowd cheered him on. Rajam screamed so much that her voice became hoarse. Partha and Muhammad Salih each had their following and the noise was deafening. A few more rounds and the two gargantuan idli eaters were still going strong. After the sixtieth idli, Muhammad Salih had eaten enough. He turned to the side and noisily vomited. Partha lifted his sixty first idli, held it up to a cheering crowd and then with slow deliberate movements, put little tidbits in his mouth, prolonging the moment, until he polished off the last morsel. The new 'Idli Subbu' had been crowned. All his friends were hugging him and Rajam could not even get near him.

After the crowd dispersed, the family walked towards the vilvandi to have lunch. They spread a blanket under the shade of a tree and opened the tiffin carriers. The first container Rajam opened had idlis and when Rajam held one up for Partha, he held his belly yelling, "Noo…No more idlis! No more idlis for the next month."

Everyone was in a good mood, laughing and joking. After lunch they left Partha snoring under the shade of the trees and returned to the fair to continue with the festivities. There was still no sign of Raman. By now, Rajam was sure that Revathi must have reached the train station, well on her way to Madras. She felt momentarily guilty, enjoying herself here at the fair while Revathi was in so much trouble, but then Rajam comforted herself with the thought that each person had their unique set of problems. At least that she had helped Revathi the only way she knew, by talking with her.

At five o' clock, the street drama began. Consisting only of men, the drama troupe, was going to perform scenes from the epic *Ramayana.* Rajam sat down with her mother. From the corner of her eye, she saw Nagamma sitting a little distance away. Using her eyes, Nagamma indicated to Rajam that she needed to come and sit next to her. Rajam quickly got up and sat behind her. Mangalam turned around just in time to see Rajam stick her tongue out at Nagamma behind her back. Mangalam's eyes opened wide in horror and she shook her head in disapproval. The audience was enthralled with the drama, laughing loudly, especially when the men spoke in high pitched voices as they played women's roles. It was funny and interesting for villagers, who had few other forms of entertainment. They saw the same episodes year after year but never seemed to tire, laughing at the same jokes and crying at the same tragic drama.

It was almost seven o'clock when Rajam's family left the fair. Everyone was quiet, tired from the day's excitement. The bullock cart turned the corner and came to a stop in front of their home. Rajam looked towards Revathi's house but it was too dark to see anything. She would have to wait for the morning to know what had happened. Until then, she needed to be patient and stop thinking. She was so exhausted she fell asleep as soon as her head touched the pillow.

# CHAPTER 27 –REVATHI
## VIZHUPURAM

It was around nine o'clock on Sunday morning and like most Sundays, everyone was moving slower than usual. The food was ready but nobody wanted to eat just yet. Rajam was anxiously waiting for the morning meal to be over, so she could check up on Revathi. She was uneasy and apprehensive and didn't want to wait until the following day to know if Revathi got away. There was no more work to be done just yet, so the women sat around the mutram enjoying the morning sunlight, waiting to serve the food, when Siva came running in.

"*Ayayyo*! Come on everyone. There has been a death in the neighbor's house. Someone committed suicide. Come quickly."

Rajam's heart sank. She knew then that her worst fears had been realized. Revathi had not made it. She jumped up, her heart beating wildly, her mind in a whirl with a million thoughts entering simultaneously and she joined the rest of the family, rushing to find out more about this calamity. When they reached Revathi's house, a big crowd had gathered outside. In one corner of the thinnai, Raman was seated, holding his head in his hands, rocking back and forth. At the other end sat Muthu Mami, her dazed eyes staring into the distance, almost as if she were in a trance. Rajam tried to push her way in but there were too many people. Standing on tiptoe, she peered in between people's heads but she couldn't see the body.

"What happened?" she asked a neighbor.

"It was Revathi. I believe she was depressed and committed suicide. *Thooku Potuta.* She hung herself. They found the body when they came home from the fair."

"But I don't see the body anywhere. Is it inside?"

"No, they performed the last rites at seven in the morning. She has already been cremated. We saw them leaving and came to find out what happened."

"What? Why did they perform the last rites so fast? Why didn't they wait for her parents to come?"

"I don't know why they did that. Apparently, it was not a pretty sight and Raman wanted to save his in-laws the agony of seeing their daughter like that."

'*How convenient!*' thought Rajam. He wanted to cremate her before anyone could see the results of his handiwork. There was nothing that could be done now. As the husband, Raman had complete rights over his wife and the last rites had to be performed by him. It was his prerogative to complete the ceremonies whenever he wanted. The neighbor was eager to give Rajam all the information she had. "It appears that the priest said between seven and eight in the morning was a good *muhurtham*, the most auspicious time to cremate her."

'*Priests will say whatever you want them to if you paid them enough,*' thought Rajam. It was always easy to find one poor Brahmin to conduct a ceremony in a hurry. Laymen knew nothing about the right muhurtham to do anything, so they would have to take the priest's word for it.

Rajam pulled Partha to one side and whispered in his ear. "He killed her. I know that with as much certainty as my name is Rajam. I want you to call my father. We need to tell him about it."

"Okay, I'll go. But first let me express my condolences to Raman."

"Murderer! Rapist!" Rajam was so angry, tears were streaming down her face and her chest was heaving with emotion. What had happened? What went wrong? Rajam would never know how Revathi's end came.

While Rajam and her family were enjoying their day at the fair, Revathi had embarked on a journey of her own, where she would meet her destiny. She had been feeling strange that morning. Her stomach was churning and her mental state was one of excitement and fear. Her mother-in-law was getting dressed to go to the fair. It was only nine in the morning. She would have to wait another three agonizing hours before she could escape forever into Vaithee's loving care. Time was standing still. No matter what she did, the hands on the clock in the big room would not move more than a few millimeters. As soon as her mother-in-law left, Revathi tied up three of her saris in a bundle and kept it near the back entrance, so she could grab it when she made her exit. As soon as Raman left the house for work, which would be a little before twelve, she would sneak out from the back. She went and lay down in a corner of the mutram. From her reclining position, she could see the clock in the big room as it inched along. *Tick tock tick tock.* She watched the pendulum sway back and forth. She couldn't sleep, although she was tired. Her eye was throbbing. Could that be a sign of some sort? If so, what did that mean?

When Raman woke up, he was in a bad mood as usual. His head was throbbing from a hangover. He had drunk too much the previous night and had been throwing up till the wee hours of the morning.

"Revathi," he screamed. "Bring my coffee."

Revathi hurried into the kitchen to make his coffee. She didn't want any more problems. In a few minutes, she was back, handing him the steaming coffee. He said nothing, silently taking the tumbler from her. It was past ten o'clock and it seemed as though Raman had no plans of going anywhere. He hadn't yet eaten his morning meal and was just lolling around in bed. Revathi was nervous. If he did not leave soon, then she would have to escape when he was in the house and the very thought made her jittery. What if he heard her going out the back entrance? She would have to move the creaking back door extra slowly so he would not hear her leave. Raman rolled out of the room and sauntered past her to use the bathroom. He was back in a short while.

"Hmm. Don't just sit around. Serve me my food."

Revathi ran into the kitchen to heat the morning meal. The rice was piping hot and she only had to heat the sambar and vegetables. She served him his food and watched him eat. Liquid dribbling down his unshaven chin, locks of hair overgrown and uncombed falling over his eyes. As he finished, he belched loudly. Disgusting man! Revathi was totally repulsed by him. What must she have done to deserve such an uncouth oaf as a husband! Only a few hours more, she said to herself, not speaking one word, merely cleaning up before she went back to the mutram to watch the clock. Raman took a swig of the liquor which was by his bedside and then lay down. The clock was ticking rhythmically to Raman's snoring. He had been asleep for the better part of an hour but it wasn't twelve noon yet, so Revathi could not leave. Vaithee had specifically told her to be at the grove at noon.

At last, after what seemed like a lifetime, she looked up at the clock one final time. It was five minutes to twelve. She went to the pooja altar, closed her eyes and prayed. Then she tiptoed to the back of the house and slowly opened the gate, moving it an inch at a time so it would not creak. Then once she was out, she slowly closed the gate in the same way. She had wasted too much time. Just as she turned around, a black cat crossed her path. Revathi took a deep breath. This was no time for superstition. She could not go back into the house and leave again. There was just too much risk. If she went back in, she may not get another chance to leave. She clutched her bundle to her chest and walked briskly down the road.

Raman woke up soon after and became annoyed when he could not find Revathi anywhere. Taking another swig from his bottle, he decided to walk down the street to get a *bidi* from the vendor behind the temple. Revathi had to pass the temple to reach the mango groves and as she turned the corner, to her utter shock, she ran into Raman. Her eyes opened wide and she shrank back in horror. How could this be? He was fast asleep when she left. The back roads were longer but how did he know where to go? This was it. She knew in her mind that this time he would not leave her alive. She had planned her escape so meticulously but freedom was not for her. God had other plans to end her suffering.

Raman's eyes narrowed down to a slit. What in heaven was Revathi doing here and what was she carrying in her hand? Was she planning to run away? Seeing Revathi with her bundle of clothing made his blood boil. Already in a drunken state and crazy with anger, he reached out to grab her by her hair.

"Where are you off to? What is that in your hand? Were you thinking of leaving me? *Mundam!* Whore!" He twisted and yanked her hair, pulling out a bunch from their roots. Revathi screamed in pain but no one was around to hear her. He caught hold of her unraveled hair and literally dragged her, half running, half sliding, all the way home. The streets were completely empty; the only witness to this horrific scene were two stray dogs, who didn't even bother to bark.

Raman was wild with anger. How dare she attempt to escape! *"Bitch! Whore!"* He dragged her in and threw her down in the center of the mutram. Though dazed, suddenly she was not afraid any more. She

202

stood up, walked over to Raman and spat on his face. The audacity of Revathi's action took him completely by surprise, but she had made a fatal mistake. Raman's fury erupted like a dormant volcano. He exploded with a volatile force and slapped her across the face so hard she went reeling backward. Momentarily stunned, she looked at him with an expression that said, *"hit me you coward, hit me."* Revathi felt no fear. She was ready for whatever was in store for her.

He reached for the first thing that came into his hand, a wooden stick and with eyes flaming with rage, he walked towards a swaying Revathi. The first blow broke her lower arm. The second caught her side and broke two of her ribs. Like a seasoned fighter, she stood up again and laughed in his face. The next swing got her on the temple and the blood spattered all over the pillar. She leaned against the bloodstained pillar for support and looked at him straight in the eye, not flinching, not reacting to the pain exploding inside her body. Raman then struck her on her broken arm; she twisted in agony and stumbled to the other side. Before she had a chance to recover, he hit her again. Revathi swayed from one side to the other like a whirling dervish, as he alternately swung from the left and the right. She smashed her head so many times against the pillar that she lost count, but still she would not cry out. The pain was so intense it had gone past human threshold. She felt nothing. In a way, she had already left her body and moved onward to the next leg of her journey. Her eyes were open as she danced her last cosmic *Thandava*, her final dance of death, offering her own blood, as sacrifice to the blood thirsty *Kali*. Her sari was damp with gore as she whirled from one end of the mutram to the other. When the stick broke, her husband switched to using his fists, slamming her face until it was a bloody pulp. At some point, her legs buckled and she fell down. Relentless, Raman sat on her stomach and continued pummeling her face with his fists. He had no idea that she died a while ago, not even when he rose and kicked her repeatedly on her stomach. Then he stopped, breathing hard from the exhaustion of the fight and looked down. He looked around him. There was blood everywhere. Revathi was motionless, a smile on her tranquil face.

Raman bent down and shook his wife. "Revathi, wake up, Revathi please wake up." All at once, the horror of his actions, committed in a moment of passion, hit him like a sledgehammer. He screamed hysterically, pulling at his hair, not knowing what to do. He did not mean to kill her. It just happened. Now what was he going to do? He sat down and nursed her bloody head against his heaving chest, rocking her, crying, repeating her name over and over again. That is how Muthu Mami found him.

"So finally you killed her. You could not leave her alone could you, not till she was dead? What did she ever do to harm you?" Raman just continued repeating Revathi's name. He was overcome with remorse and grief. Muthu was shocked at the gore around her. She could not bear to look at Revathi's face. In many ways, she felt responsible. She had been a mute witness to the abuse and should have stopped her son somehow. Now they were faced with the worst possible situation. Never in her wildest dreams did she imagine that her son would do this. Now he had lost his mind and she needed to take charge and make sure that their name didn't go down the drain. The neighbors must never know what happened. Muthu brought water and rags and cleaned the mutram for hours. Then she bathed Revathi's battered body for the last time, dressed her in her wedding sari and covered her body and face with a white sheet. She went into her room and from the recesses of her cupboard, brought out a gold coin that she had saved for a rainy day. She gave it to Raman, instructing him to bring a priest from a nearby village, to complete the ceremonies before the neighbors awoke. No one must see Revathi like this. They would tell her parents that she had been depressed and took her own life, that she hung herself when everyone left for the fair. That was the story that the neighbors heard.

◆❖◆❖◆

Rajam did not believe a word. She knew Raman had killed Revathi but she was helpless, because all the evidence was gone. Revathi was dead and with her went any chance of arresting Raman. She would tell her father Revathi's story but she knew with no evidence, her story was just hearsay and the police could do nothing about it. Just then, there was some noise from the entrance. The crowd was moving to allow Revathi's parents in. Her mother was inconsolable but no one was making any accusations. Did they not know of Revathi's predicament? Why weren't they questioning the husband? Raman had managed everything very well indeed. Behind them was a young man with curly hair and a neat moustache. He was wearing a white shirt and veshti and staring at Raman. The look in his eyes got Rajam's attention. She couldn't tell if he was sad, angry, vengeful, sardonic, or if the look had a mix of all these emotions. His expression was completely inscrutable. He had his hands folded across his chest and was intently looking at Raman with that determined stare but he did not approach him, almost as if he wanted to keep some space between them.

Rajam knew at once who this must be. Revathi's uncle Vaithee. "He must know what really transpired and feel powerless, unable to do anything about it, just like me," thought Rajam.

The crowd lingered for a while but then slowly people turned away to attend to their own unfinished business. Rajam, too, left with a heavy heart, still trying to come to terms with this tragic saga that began for her only three days ago and had already reached its sad climax.

Two weeks later someone discovered a body in a mango grove in Vizhupuram. It was dismembered and the head was completely severed from the body. On closer examination, it was evident almost every bone had been broken. The genitalia had been severed and stuffed into the mouth. On the trunk of the tree, under which the remnants of the body lay, was carved a heart, with the letters R and V. In the middle of the two letters hung a blood-stained aruvaal, its curved tip driven into the trunk. The blood from this curved knife covered the carved heart and dripped down the center. The police identified the body as being that of Raman Iyer. The perpetrator was never found. After three months, the police closed it as an unsolved murder.

When the Lotus Blooms

# Part X
# Dharmu

# CHAPTER 28 – MAHADEVAN
## RANGPUR – 1934

Monday morning. The *Dak* boy had just arrived with the mail, which had been sorted at the General Post Office in Calcutta and then sent to Dacca, in East Bengal, from where it was taken to Rangpur. The town was not large enough to have its own post office, so the dak boy left the mail in a house known locally as the *Dak Bungalow*, a Government guest house on the outskirts of town for people who stayed there when visiting the area on work. Mahadevan sat in the verandah and looked at the letters. Most of them were work related but he noticed one with a British stamp, which appeared to be from overseas. Looking at the various stamps on the envelope, he realized it had been sent almost three months ago and was forwarded to various locations until it reached Calcutta, from where the letter was redirected to Rangpur.

He slit open the envelope and a photograph slipped out. It was Madame Rose and another man, and miracle of miracles, Rose was actually smiling. His face broke into a smile when he read in the letter that Rose was finally getting married! She had frittered away her youth over a man who was long gone and never wanted to meet other men. Somehow someone had broken through her tough armor and got to her. That was nice. Her new beau was also a retired pilot, who lived just down the street from her. Imagine that! Talk about coincidences. They lived on the same street all their lives and did not meet until the moment was right. The marriage was in the spring and Rose wanted Mahadevan to attend the wedding.

Mahadevan put the letter down and stared into the distance. Mme. Rose Leblanc had been his savior and mentor during all those months that he lived in England. She helped him in so many ways to become an 'English gentleman,' to understand the subtleties of British public and private behavior that had bewildered him earlier. He realized over time that her stern exterior was just a front for her warm and generous nature. Life had treated her very harshly, and to survive as a single woman in a man's world, she had developed a no-nonsense manner of speaking as a protective shield. Mahadevan's thoughts went back to his first night in England.

That evening when they finally reached Cambridge, it was already dark. They had the address of a boarding house on King's Street and after taking numerous wrong turns they finally located it, only to be told that someone else had taken their rooms. Mahadevan and Shanti were exhausted after lugging their suitcases all over town and couldn't believe what they were hearing.

"I'm sorry, the reservation was until four o' clock, and we held it till six." Looking at their crestfallen, exhausted faces, the lady took pity on them and directed them to another house, where a French lady kept boarders.

"Try your luck there," she said cheerily. After another fifteen minute trudge, they finally located the house on the corner of Kings and Primrose. Hanging on a small painted gate was a bright yellow hand-painted sign which read 'Rose Cottage.' Colorful phlox framed a narrow path that led up to the main door. Shanti waited on the pavement outside with the luggage, while Mahadevan walked in and knocked tentatively on the front door. After a few minutes the door opened.

"Yes? How can I help you?" said a petite, pleasantly plump lady. She was wearing a gingham-checkered apron over a long printed dress. Her face looked stern, though its severity was not reflected in her soft brown eyes. Her brown hair flecked with grey, was coiled into a tight bun at the top of her head, and specks of flour covered her clothing. He had obviously caught her in the midst of her cooking and she did not look too happy.

"Mrs. Leblanc, I presume? Allow me to introduce myself. My name is Ayyar, and my friend, Banerji, and I were directed here from the Inn down the street. They told us that you keep boarders."

Her face stern, she eyed the two of them, her brown eyes crinkling at the corners as she tried to keep her spectacles on her pert nose. "Just the two of you?" she asked in a mellow voice, inflected with an unmistakable French accent.

"Yes, Ma'am, just the two of us. It is dark and we have traveled a great distance. I do hope you can accommodate us."

"I have one room available, which you will have to share until the end of the month, till my boarder leaves for his native Egypt. Then you can get an extra room. That will be ten bob a week to be paid in advance. No excuses. Ten days overdue and I'll send you packing."

After consulting with Shanti, they agreed to the price and gratefully stepped into her warm and cozy cottage. Situated on the ground floor just near the staircase, the room was extremely small. It had one queen sized bed, a small side table with a porcelain lamp and a chest of drawers but given their state of exhaustion, it felt like heaven. Besides, it faced east and was sure to be cheerful in the daytime with the morning sunlight streaming in.

"The bathroom is up the stairs to your right. Please remember you bathe inside the tub, not outside, and for heaven's sake, do not squat on the toilet seat. Your feet should be on the floor and you sit like you're on a chair and do your stuff inside the bowl. Do you understand?"

"Yes ma'am," said the two in unison, wondering why she was explaining this to them. Soon enough they had their answer.

"The last boarder I had from India, P.P.S. Aiyer I think his name was. Oh dear, what a time I had with him! He actually bathed outside the tub on the floor, and the water ran all the way down the stairs and ruined the carpet. He is still paying for the mess he caused."

"Don't worry, ma'am, you won't have any trouble with us." Mahadevan snickered to himself. He could imagine what the toilet must have looked like to an Indian who was used to squatting over a hole in the floor. And the bathtub? It must have appeared to be another English adornment. This poor soul probably had no idea that he actually had to get into it and bathe. Luckily, Mahadevan had used a western style toilet before and had seen enough English movies to know what a bathtub looked like.

"Breakfast is at seven and no later," continued Mrs. Leblanc, "and it's included in your rent. Don't expect a huge spread though."

After paying an advance on the rent, Shanti and Mahadevan sat down on the bed staring into nothingness for an eternity. The room was too small for two people and they would have to take turns sleeping on the bed for the next two months. But today they were so tired they slept on an empty stomach without even bothering to change into night clothes.

The next morning they arrived at the breakfast room a few minutes early, so Mahadevan stepped into the salon to wait. Two comfortable sofas covered in multicolored upholstery occupied the salon, along with some brightly printed but mismatched curtains. But everything looked fine to Mahadevan, who was no connoisseur of fashion. The room was filled with various adornments: vases with flowers, small figurines, ashtrays and lots of photographs, including one of a man and a woman. The woman's face revealed a slim version of Mme. Leblanc, wearing a long skirt up to her knees, a cap sleeved blouse and high heels. Her hair was fashionably coiffed in bouncing shiny curls and she was leaning on a smart young man in an RAF uniform. He was probably her husband but Mahadevan would hear her story later. Hearing some noise from the breakfast room, he hurried back.

Breakfast was a somber affair and no one spoke a word. The two other boarders had their faces buried behind newspapers and were not in the mood to initiate a conversation. One of them looked Middle Eastern and was dressed impeccably in a three piece suit and black oxfords. His unparted hair was slicked back and a pencil thin moustache ran right above his upper lip. He was probably Rose's Egyptian boarder, who was leaving soon. The other young man looked European and was quite the contrast. His shirt unbuttoned at the neck and his tousled hair demonstrated his nonchalance and lack of style. It seemed as though he tumbled out of bed onto the breakfast table. During the course of the year Mahadevan met several boarders from all over the globe, a floating group of young men in need of temporary housing.

The next few months went by uneventfully, except that both Shanti and Mahadevan took their ICS exams. Mahadevan continued to have a formal relationship with Mme. Leblanc and never exchanged more than pleasantries with her. By October that year he had his own room on the first floor, which was convenient because now he did not

211

have to climb stairs to use the solitary bathroom, which all the boarders shared. Mahadevan spent most of his money on rent and food and had very little left over for extras. In fact, other than an umbrella, he had bought nothing for himself. His needs were few and being vegetarian, he hardly ate anything other than bread and butter, which he covered with the spicy curry powders his mother had given him. He asked his father to send him some money but it had not yet arrived. In the meantime, he tutored students from Cambridge in math and the extra income helped cover his basic needs. The air was turning cool and Mahadevan shivered uncontrollably on his way back from school. Mme. Leblanc noticed this and asked him why he had no warm clothes. With his eyes on the floor, he explained his situation to her. He did not want her to think of him as some impoverished Indian and was careful how he phrased his words. She said nothing but returned a few minutes later with a warm overcoat.

"It belonged to my husband but you can borrow it for a while."

What a surprise! In all these months this was the first time she had reached out to him. "But Mme. Leblanc, I can't accept it. I have no money to pay for it."

"Did I ask for any?"

"No, you didn't mention anything but I couldn't accept favors."

"It's no favor. It's a need. If you don't wear warm clothing in this dreadful weather, you will end up with pneumonia. Just take it and be warm." In spite of the overcoat, the weather in December was so cold Mahadevan found himself wheezing. The frost and humidity seemed to enter his bones. In all his life he had never envisioned or experienced weather this bitter. No matter what he did, he just could not keep warm. His room had a coin heater but as he was careful about money, he did not put coins into it after midnight. By morning, the room was at subzero temperatures and very soon Mahadevan had a hacking cough. One could hear him cough as he turned the street corner. One day he was so ill he could not get out of bed, even to have breakfast. Hearing a knock on the door, Mahadevan responded with another long bout of coughing.

"Maddie," she began using her nickname for him. "You don't sound good. Can I come in?" Without waiting for a response, Mme. Leblanc walked into the room. "Good gracious!" she exclaimed. "This is like being in the Arctic." She dashed out of the room and returned a

212

few minutes later with some coins for the radiator. She left the room again and was back with a bowl of warm chicken broth.

"What is this?" Mahadevan wheezed.

"Chicken broth," said Mme. Leblanc, and she attempted to feed him a spoonful.

"No," said Mahadevan horrified at the prospect of ingesting meat. "I can't eat it."

"Young man, if you don't attempt eating meat, you won't last the winter and then what will your lovely wife do?" she enquired as she spooned the broth into his mouth. It didn't taste half bad and the ravenous Mahadevan polished it off in a few minutes. That whole week Mme. Leblanc nursed him back to health. She sat with him and talked for hours about her life in France and her husband and told him amusing anecdotes about former boarders. Their relationship completely changed, and for the rest of his stay she took him under her wing and cared for him like a mother hen.

Mme. Leblanc had been born and raised in a small fishing village in the south of France. During the war her future husband, a pilot from England named Ron Mathew, had been assigned to France on duty. During a routine mission his plane took a hit but he managed to eject into the ocean, where her father fished him out to safety. The cold Atlantic waters gave him pneumonia and Fleur (Mme. Leblanc) nursed him back to health. Their courtship lasted a month but proved to be the happiest time of her life. Ron called her his 'French Rose,' and soon she stopped using her maiden name. They married in a small French church and in a few months she crossed the English Channel to live with her husband. They bought this small cottage in Cambridge on the corner of Primrose and King Street, which they named Rose Cottage, commemorating Ron's pet name for her.

They led an exhilarating life and spent two glorious years together until Ron's untimely death in the course of duty. Having loyally served the British Crown, he was buried with full military honors. For a few years she managed on her pension and many times she thought about returning to her native France. But Rose Cottage was the setting for the fondest memories of her dear departed husband, and she could not bring herself to return home to France. Instead, she merely changed her last name back to Leblanc in memory of her native heritage and continued to live in Rose Cottage. There was no dearth of offers but she never remarried. No one could possibly be as wonderful as Ron and she considered it a sacrilege even to think of replacing him. To make ends meet she kept boarders, mainly from overseas, students who could not find room and board elsewhere. Caring for them gave her some extra money and kept her busy. Thus far, she had not developed a close bond with anyone else. Perhaps she kept people at bay for fear that they force her out of her misery and show her that life existed, waiting to be enjoyed.

She taught Mahadevan everything about British customs, from eating correctly to dressing appropriately and he never forgot that. As a special honor, she allowed him to read the books from Ron's extensive library. The day that Mahadevan and Shanti passed the ICS exams was so special that Rose prepared a huge banquet and they drank and dined till they fell asleep right there in Rose's parlor.

Even after returning to India, Mahadevan never forgot her. He kept in touch regularly, always remembering to send photographs of the children, and he looked forward to receiving her letters.

*'Rose Leblanc, I hope you found your Ron again and your happiness,'* thought Mahadevan as he gazed at the photograph with tears in his eyes.

# CHAPTER 29 – DHARMAMBAL
## DINDIGUL

Jameen Amma looked at the calendar and noted that today was a full moon day, *Paurnami*, which meant she needed to visit the Kamakshiamman temple to offer her prayers as she had done for years. She wished to honor her vow to distribute twenty-one silver coins to the poor after her daughter, Sita, had been raped as a child and survived the trauma. Sita had recovered remarkably and now was happily married and had two sons. Jameen Amma was so grateful she never forgot her vow to Kamakshiamman. Devi's grace had given her child back to her. Dharmu and her girls went along in the beautiful horse drawn carriage. Kandu had every intention to go with them but got distracted when he saw the Jameendar's stables. He decided to stay back and be with the horses, hoping that the stable boy might teach him how to ride a horse.

The carriage was big and comfortable with seating on either side. Rukku and Vani lay down on the soft velvet mattress and stared up at the sky, watching and naming shapes of the clouds as they passed by overhead. The temple was not too far away and they reached it in a very short time. Beggars had lined up outside the temple, hoping to be the lucky beneficiaries of the silver coins and their eyes lit up when they saw Jameen Amma. Everyone knew that on full moon days, Jameen Amma would be at the temple with her red velvet pouch full of coins. Jameen Amma paused and spoke to each person and then, as a special treat, she let the two girls hand out the coins for her. When they entered the temple, they noticed a group of people gathered near the shrine of *Karthikeya*. A woman on the floor was shaking vigorously, and a priest was chanting some mantras and beating her with a long stick.

Rukku was horrified. "Amma, Jameen Amma, look at what is happening!" she exclaimed loudly. "That priest is beating the girl."

215

# When the Lotus Blooms

Dharmu tried to herd the children into the main shrine but they wiggled out of her grasp and ran towards the commotion. They pushed their way through the small crowd and surveyed the scene in front of them in utter horror. The girl on the floor must have been in her early teens. Her eyes had rolled back in her head and her face was contorted. While her limbs were flailing in all directions, the men were attempting to hold her down and put an iron spear into her thrashing fists. Her head lolled to one side and yellow foam oozed from the corner of her mouth. The priest was chanting some mantras and hitting her repeatedly on her back and thighs with a long stick. Dharmu ran up and pulled the girls away.

"Amma, what is happening to her?"

"Nothing. Don't look. Just come away." She did not want to tell the girls anything, hoping that in time they would forget what they saw. Jameen Amma came close to her and whispered, "Tell the children what is happening; otherwise they won't understand and will get frightened."

"Rukku, Vani, don't get scared — this girl is getting fits," spoke Dharmu with trepidation.

"Fits? What is that?" asked Rukku much to Dharmu's annoyance. She did not want this conversation to go on any longer. Luckily Jameen Amma stepped in.

"I don't know exactly but when it happens they lose consciousness and control of their limbs." Of course this led to more question about the yellow stuff near her mouth and the spear and Jameen Amma answered them patiently. But their questions continued, much to Dharmu's annoyance.

"And the priest, why he is beating her?"

"He isn't beating her hard. In any case she can't feel anything. The villagers believe that an evil spirit has entered her and the priest is trying to get the evil spirit out." Naturally, this led to another tirade of questions about spirits and exorcism and modern medicine. Dharmu became agitated. She didn't see the need for the children to learn about this and was in a hurry to get them out of there.

"Come on. We have to go to Thatha's before lunch. Hurry up." The children hurried up; their memories being short, they forgot all about the incident as soon as they entered their grandfather's house.

The house sat in the middle of a large wooded estate. This was where Dharmu and Mahadevan got married. The garden looked a little bare, though the grass was green after the rains. Dharmu's grandparents were older now and no longer had the energy of youth. The upkeep of the house kept them occupied, so the garden was left to care for itself. The children were meeting her grandparents after almost a year and were happy to be in the house. Dharmu had wonderful memories of this house, filled with people going in and out, with something or other happening all the time. Her grandfather lived in the main town of Dindigul, and people in the country were known for their hospitality. No visitor ever left the house without eating or drinking something, which was the tradition in these parts. Dharmu had spent most of the summer here all those years that she grew up in Porambur. After a sumptuous lunch, the women cleared up and then retired to the mutram to sit and talk while Paati made *beeda* for them, using betel leaves, areca nuts and grated coconut.

Dharmu was lying face down on the swing, the same swing that was used for her marriage ceremony.

May 26, 1920. Almost fifteen years had passed since that day. The muhurtham, or auspicious time during which the wedding *thaali* had to be tied around the girl's neck, was set early that morning, from 7:00-8:30 a.m. The ceremonies were going on all week but that particular morning they woke up very early. The older ladies of the household gave Dharmu an oil massage and bathed her, after which her mother tied a beautiful magenta pink sari with a bottle green border — her oonjal sari. She was still painfully thin and the sari looked out of place on her. She wore a thick gold *odiyaanam* around her waist and her hair was braided into one long plait. On her head, she wore an uncut ruby and gold headset, which ran along the hairline framing her face, with a centerpiece along the parting of her hair. On either side of the centerpiece were ruby adornments in the shape of the sun and the moon. She had ruby and gold bangles on both wrists and on each of her upper arms were two identical armbands in the design of a serpent. Fresh jasmine and *Kanakambaram*, an orange flower native to the south, adorned her hair; and then of course the nose rings and jimiki on her ears completed the ensemble. The flowers on her hair were so heavy that she could barely lift her head.

# When the Lotus Blooms

"Good!" exclaimed her grandmother. "Girls must be shy."

Once she reached the wedding platform in the front of the house, three or four rose and jasmine garlands were put around her neck. The additional weight of the garlands bent her head forward until her chin almost touched her chest. The scent of the flowers was so strong she could barely breathe. She had not seen her prospective husband before this day. He had been busy with exams and had not come for the Ponpaakal or the engagement ceremony. He, too, had agreed to the match without seeing his bride. She looked at him for the first time as he came into the marriage hall and he was not bad looking: fair, a little short and maybe not exactly slim but he was acceptable.

Her grandfather had made elaborate arrangements for the wedding. A huge *pandhal* had been erected in front of the house where the actual wedding ceremony would take place. The central mutram was also covered with a pandhal to seat guests for lunch that followed the ceremony. Although the wedding guests from the groom's family were staying partly in Dharmu's house and partly in Jameen Amma's, the actual ceremony was held in Dindigul, and the whole family traveled the short distance back and forth for two days.

The garland exchange was about to begin and someone pushed Dharmu forward with a garland in her hand; and from the other side, Mahadevan was brought closer. She reached up, all the while looking at the floor, mainly because of the weight of the flowers around her neck and put the garland around Mahadevan's neck. The exchange went on for a while. The proceedings were now more lighthearted and the revelers tried to make it harder for them to trade garlands. Her uncle lifted Dharmu on his shoulders and Mahadevan reached up, unable to get the garland anywhere near her neck. Then two of his maternal uncles lifted him up to successfully complete the task. Everyone was laughing but Dharmu felt stupid and wondered why this ceremony existed. Perhaps in ancient times, children married much younger, at five or six, and this was one way of amusing them at their own wedding ceremony. She did not get the point of all these rituals. They went on for so long and besides, her neck hurt. After this, the couple sat together on the swing while ladies from both families performed a ceremony to lift the evil eye off the couple. They washed the groom's feet with milk and wiped it clean with a silken cloth; all the while the women sang wedding songs.

*"Paal aalai kaal alambi pattu aalai thudaithu ....Laaaaa....li..."*

Inadvertently Dharmu caught herself singing *"Laaali,"* letting slip to the family around what her thoughts were focused on.

Jameen Amma laughed, "Are you lost in your wedding thoughts, silly girl?"

"How did you know?" asked Dharmu sheepishly, realizing almost immediately that she had been singing a wedding song.

"Mummy?" said Rukku out of the blue. "Were you in love with Daddy when you married him?"

Dharmu looked annoyed. "Now who has been saying silly things to you?"

"Vani reads Women's World romances and she told me that English people only marry when they fall in love. So were you in love?"

"No, silly, I was only twelve. What did I know about love?"

"I will only marry when I fall madly in love," Rukku declared.

Dharmu shook her head in disbelief but she said nothing, not wanting to disillusion her young daughter.

"Mummy, you didn't answer Rukku. Do you love Daddy?"

"Yes." The word slipped out of her mouth before she knew it. But she wasn't sure.

*Love. What exactly was that? What were you supposed to feel when you were in love? How did you know if you were in love? Were you supposed to shiver in excitement and feel hot and confused? If so, then maybe I have been in love, but when I shivered and was hot and confused, I attributed it to my fear of the unknown. Then was fear Love? No it couldn't be. Love was not something to be feared; it was supposed to be something you longed for, something you relished, something that lifted your soul to melt with the divine. Am I too simpleminded, unable to recognize love even as I am embalmed in it? Is it locked in the deepest recesses of my soul, and if so, what is the mysterious key that I need to access and unleash it. What I feel for Mahadevan is so different from what I feel for Amma, the girls and Kandu. For them I feel affection, possession, ownership and even obligation. Is that love? Then I cannot love Mahadevan because he alienates me and keeps me at a distance. With*

219

# When the Lotus Blooms

*Mahadevan I feel a vacuum that longs to be filled, sensations of comfort and anger, often at the same time like sunshine during rain. Which of them is love and which is not? Maybe love between a man and woman has only to do with the physical act of union but if that were so, men would not treat their wives as callously as Appa treated Amma. Is love admiration of a person's qualities? If that is the case, then I love Mahadevan terribly because I admire him for so many things: his level headedness, his intelligence, his calm attitude. But then I admire so many other people and their qualities too. Am I in love with all of them?*

*Do I love Mahadevan?*

*I really don't know.*

# CHAPTER 30 – KANDU
## NAGARCOIL

"Have we reached?"

"No Kandu, not yet," replied Dharmu patiently for about the hundredth time.

"How much longer?"

"Soon, we will reach soon," Dharmu said inattentively. In reality, she had no idea when they would actually reach their destination. She watched Kandu bobbing up and down restlessly. The train should have reached Trivandrum station hours ago but was delayed. They just found out someone had committed suicide on the tracks, but there was no need for Dharmu to tell the children about that. The train had stopped in the middle of nowhere for almost three hours and was now inching along in the direction of Trivandrum, moving way too slowly for Kandu, who couldn't wait to see his grandfather.

In Trivandrum station, an impatient Nilakantan Ayyar was fed up with waiting and asking the station master when the train would arrive. He didn't need to look at his watch to know it was past his lunch time. He was ravenous. He sat on a bench and opened his tiffin ready to swallow its contents in one gulp. His annoyance and demeanor mirrored Kandu's and this similarity connected them in a tight bond. They had comparable natures: both were perfectionists, quick witted and quick tempered, strong yet kind, controlling but sensitive, both with the same sense of humor, able to laugh at the same jokes. And now both were restless and angry for the same reason — the train being delayed! Nilakantan peeped over his shoulder to make sure he could see his blue Baby Austin, his pride and joy, the only car in Nagarcoil and the envy of his neighbors. A man was bent over looking

221

at himself in the side mirror combing his oily locks into place. Nilakantan shook his head, huffing in disbelief. Keralites! Never miss a good opportunity.

Kandu spotted his grandfather almost as soon as the train pulled into the platform. *"Thatha... Thatha..."* he yelled, and like a streak of lightning, he was out the door racing towards the exit; he would have happily jumped off the moving train onto the platform if the agile orderly had not stopped him. Nilakantan waited for the train to come to a grinding halt. He made a handsome picture in his silk veshti, black coat and golden yellow turban, his large brawny arms crossed across his great barrel shaped chest. His pride and self-confidence were evident in the mere carriage of his head, which exuded an overwhelming sense of authority. No power could contain a wiggling Kandu once the train finally came to a halt and he ran across the platform, hurling himself into the arms of his beloved grandfather, only to be tossed into the air before Nilakantan held him close, nuzzling him roughly.

The car was a recent purchase and Kandu was delighted to ride in it. If Nilakantan could have seated him on his lap and driven simultaneously, he would have but Kandu had to be content to sit next to his grandfather, looking up and watching him adoringly as they made their way to Sita Gardens.

Driving into the compound, they could see a beaming Appanshayal framed between the central arches, which were covered with green 'Rangoon Creepers.' Kandu was special to him, too, as he was his first great-grandson. Kandu loved the smell of camphor and vibuthi that he always associated with Appanshayal. You could smell the fragrance even as Appanshayal entered the room. Everyone had their own characteristic aroma and Kandu was especially attuned to linking people with this. Camphor and vibuthi with his great-grandfather, sandal wood with his grandfather, lavender with his father and jasmine with his mother. Kandu, as usual, got the first hug from his grandmother, Sita Paati, who incidentally smelt of coconut oil.

Almost immediately Kandu ran out into the gardens behind the house. He loved being here. It had so many secrets, unidentified hiding places, undiscovered treasures and constant activity that was all-consuming and interminable. Gardeners and cowherds worked in the vast garden at all times. The house was always alive with people coming and going. The family itself comprised almost twenty people at any point of time and food was cooked and served on a grand scale in this house.

The clock struck four and almost like clockwork, 'Coffee Mami' emerged from the Coffee Room with a tray full of steaming, freshly brewed coffee in silver tumblers. Janaki—Coffee Mami was the original owner of the property where Sita Gardens stood. She had been widowed and left with no source of income. For a few years she sold produce from the land at the local market to make ends meet but over time, was unable to maintain the property. When Nilakantan Ayyar bought the land from her, he realized that she had nowhere to go and insisted she stay on in the house. Janaki Mami was a proud woman and did not like the idea of living on anyone's charity. But she had no children and no place to go, so she agreed to stay with the family on condition that she work to earn her living. Nilakantan Ayyar was unwilling to make this noble Brahmin woman work for him, but he knew she was too proud to accept charity, so he told her she could make coffee for the family. The coffee beans were stored in a special room near the kitchen and every morning and evening Janaki Mami made coffee, a technique that she had perfected over the years. With almost thirty family members and visitors coming at odd hours, she made coffee almost all day. Soon, everyone stopped using her real name and she became 'Coffee Mami' to one and all.

Kandu crouched down in the cowshed intently watching the cowherd as he washed the fat cow's udders before milking her. "*Splish splosh splish splosh,*" he went, mimicking the sound of milk as it filled the can, foaming at the top. Appanshayal always drank the first glass, frothing and still warm from the heat of the cow's udder. Then it would be Coffee Mami's job to boil and store the rest of the milk and set aside a large container with culture to make fresh yoghurt. The women collected thick cream from the yoghurt then churned it to make butter, which was then melted for fresh *ghee* to be used in the kitchen. As the milkman stood up to find a new container, Kandu bent under the cow and pulled on her teats, getting a warm mouthful of milk and savoring it for a few seconds before making a second attempt. His aim wasn't good enough and most of the milk went into his eyes and up his nose. His coughing alerted the horrified milkman, who rushed back and pulled Kandu out from under the cow.

# When the Lotus Blooms

"*Chinna Saar*, please don't drink directly. Your spit must not touch the cow or it will spoil the milk and I will get into trouble with *Periya Saar* (Appanshayal)."

In the early evening the men took a dip in the 'water tank,' a swimming pool that was behind the house close to the cowshed. Nilakantan had this tank specially built because he loved swimming. He liked to drive to Kanya Kumari, a town twenty miles away at the southern tip of the Indian subcontinent and swim in the ocean. Sitting at the edge of the waters, Nilakantan could identify three distinct colors in the sea around the cape on all three sides — the sands from the Arabian Sea, the Bay of Bengal and the Indian Ocean; a sight that he savored.

Nilakantan taught all his sons to swim, and today he was swimming with his father. Kandu saw them from a distance, gleefully taking off his clothes as he approached the tank, jumping in buck naked. He was almost six years and had not yet learned to swim but that did not deter him. His darling Thatha was there to catch him as he hit the water and he rode on his back up and down the tank. After an afternoon of frolicking in the water and a quick shower, the children were ready for the evening meal

Paati had planned *Nila Shaapaadu*, dinner for the children, under the open moonlit sky. All the children sat in a row in the back open verandah. In two huge bowls, Sita Paati had made *vatha kuzhambu shaadham* and *thayir shaadham*, the former being rice mixed with a spicy sauce and the latter, rice with yoghurt. Everyone had a small plate in front of them with roasted appalam, a dry vegetable and spicy lime pickle. Kandu was thrilled because Kannan Chithappa, his favorite uncle, was also here and he gleefully sat next to him before anyone else did. The youngest of the brothers, Kannan had a brilliant sense of humor, and laughter and horseplay dominated the proceedings whenever he was around. Paati narrated a story about Krishna and how he fought with the evil *King Kamsa* and defeated him. As she told the story, she put a ball of rice in each outstretched palm. Then the children added the vegetable and appalam and gobbled it up. Within minutes, the large bowl of mixed rice was finished; the children had eaten it all and were ready for the second course of curd and rice. Kannan frightened the children with ghost stories and Kandu was not too happy about it. Once the elders had eaten, they retired to their respective rooms. Kandu snuggled up to his grandfather under the mosquito net in the large four poster bed. Nilakantan and his wife slept in separate rooms and had separate prayer rooms, not because of any marital strain but for mere convenience and privacy. After all these years and thirteen children later, Sita felt gratified to have her own space.

"Thatha, I don't ever want to use the toilet," Kandu declared to his puzzled Grandfather.

"Why? If you don't use the toilet, then you will be in trouble."

"Kannan Chithappa says that a terrifying ghost lives under the tree outside the toilet. A woman with long curly hair and red eyes lives there and if you touch her tree or use the toilet for too long, she will eat you up." Kandu was really disturbed and his heavy lidded eyes had a hint of tears in them.

"Have you seen my hand?" Nilakantan held up his large hand and Kandu touched it, savoring its roughness.

"See how big it is. If any ghost dares come near you, I will smash it to pieces." Kandu had seen Thatha kill scorpions and break coconuts with his bare hands on many occasions. Yes, Thatha was strong. Kandu slept peacefully, knowing that as long as Thatha was around, no one could touch him. He snuggled close and took a long deep breath, soaking in the heavenly scent of sandalwood.

# When the Lotus Blooms

# Part XI
# Rajam

# CHAPTER 31– RAJAM AND PARTHA
## VIZHUPURAM TO CHIDAMBARAM

Partha walked to the vilvandi stand early that morning, where four carts were waiting. All the drivers lay asleep in the back of their carts while the bullocks chewed grain placed in a bin nearby. "Oy, someone get up. Hello! *Vilvandi kaaran!* Wake up!" After haggling with a half asleep driver, he arranged transportation to the train junction. Partha rode the cart back to the house to fetch Rajam and soon they were on their way. Partha sneaked his arm around Rajam's shoulders, taking advantage of a private moment.

"*Yenna?* Would you think of a second marriage?" asked Rajam.

"Why do you ask? Did anyone say anything to you?"

"No," said Rajam a little too quickly, not wanting Partha to suspect anything. "Sushila said someone in her village married a second time because his wife could not have a baby; that's why I'm asking you."

Partha looked at her amused. "Actually, come to think of it. It wouldn't be a bad idea to have another wife."

"What!" said Rajam her eyes opening wide.

"In fact I am planning one for every day of the week."

"*Pongo naa.* Stop joking. I am serious."

"Okay, so tell me, have you got anyone in mind I can consider?"

"*Yenna*, stop it. I am really serious. Suppose I could not have a child, would you consider remarrying? Answer me, yes or no."

"No."

"No? Just that?"

"What do you want me to say? You asked me to say yes or no, and I said no. I tell you what, you let me know what you would like me to say and I'll say it."

228

"I can't understand why you always treat me like a child. I'm not a child. In fact I am old enough to be the mother of your child, so treat me with some respect."

"Okay. Respectfully, I hereby declare I love you and you only, and that you will be the love of my life as long as I live. I vow here and now, that you, Rajam, will forever be my only wife. There, I said it. Happy?"

"Yes, happy," declared Rajam shaking her head vigorously from side to side. "But do you think I will have a child?"

"Not if you constantly doubt it."

"So then what should I do? I wait every month and nothing happens."

"I tell you what. Let's go away for a month and do it seven times a day," said Partha gleefully.

"*Pongo naa*, you always joke. And you know how I hate it when you talk about you-know-what."

Partha was enjoying this lighthearted banter but Rajam was embarrassed. "The Vandi driver is listening. Have you no shame?"

"Anyway, we are here now, so I suppose I have to take my arm off your shoulder."

They reached the train junction and after paying the driver, made their way to the platform to catch the train to Chidambaram. Not too far from Vizhupuram, after a short train ride, they reached their destination by early afternoon. Swaminathan Iyer met them, together with a couple of constables, who would bring the luggage home. They got into a beautiful vilvandi lined with red velvet with soft cushions. Being a Police Inspector had its perks, as many people wanted to keep the police happy. A family of businessmen, who lived on the same street, had loaned it to Swaminathan for the day. The vilvandi meandered through the main streets of town, making its way to Swaminathan's house, which was right behind the police station. Centrally located across from the Great Shiva Temple, the first few streets around the temple were part of the Brahmin agrahaaram, where no other caste members were permitted to live. Mangalam was very happy here because she could visit the temple every day and had made a lot of friends in the area.

The cart came to a scraping halt outside Swaminathan's house. Hearing the gate creak, Mangalam ran out and on seeing Rajam and

Partha, dropped the laundry clothes that were in her hand. She yelled for her sister, Parvathi, to bring the *aarathi* to perform a ritual designed to remove the evil eye and bring good fortune.

"Wait, wait, and don't come in. We have to take the aarathi. Maaplai has come to the house. Wait right there. Parvathiii…"

Parvathi came out and placed the aarathi plate on the floor. Parvathi Chithi was unfortunately widowed soon after her marriage and returned to live with her sister Mangalam. It seemed to be her destiny to live in the Swaminathan household, where she was a pillar of support to everyone around, content to nurture all the children and grandchildren. As she was a widow she could not perform the aarathi and it had to be done by Kunju and Mangalam. Kunju, who was right behind her, picked up the plate, and mother and daughter did a quick aarathi. The plate had a mixture of kumkumam and lime, which when added to water, turned into a bright red color.

Rajam hugged Kunju. "Where is the baby? I am dying to see him." The two of them ran inside laughing and chattering and soon Rajam was back with the baby, a little bundle wrapped in a white sheet. Around them were all the grandchildren, two boys and three girls: Venkatu, Visu, Sundari, Lalitha, Jayalakshmi and the latest addition, Natarajan. Parvathi stayed busy with Kunju coming home every year for her confinement.

"*Yenna* have you ever seen anything as beautiful as this? Come, would you like to hold him?" Without waiting for a response, she placed the baby in Partha's arms and joined the others in the kitchen. In a few minutes a yell emanated from the mutram.

"Mami, Kunju, Rajam come quickly, take the baby. Oh my God, he has urinated all over me! *Ayyo moothram penjurthu!* Heavens, it's all over my pants. Oh my God, my hands! Someone come here!"

Rajam scurried out. "*Yenna na moothram daane,* a baby's urine is not dirty. Why are you fussing so much?" She scooped up the baby and then looked up to see a horrified Partha with a wet stain in the front of his clothes. It looked as if Partha had peed in his pants and she burst out laughing. Mangalam, Kunju and the children also walked in, all of them doubling up with laughter. The kids were thrilled, chanting *"Chithappa moothram penjuta."* "Uncle peed in his pants," much to Partha's annoyance.

"Laugh all you want. I am totally outnumbered, so I won't say anything." Partha made a quick exit to wash up and change, while

Rajam took the baby inside and put the soiled blanket for washing. Once again, she wasn't sure what dry clothes she needed to wrap the baby and asked Kunju for instructions.

"Just cover him with another thin blanket; he is not ready to use underwear."

"Kunju how do you teach the child to use the toilet?" Rajam was curious, never having paid any attention when her nephews and nieces visited.

"Why? Isn't it a little early to learn all of this?" Rajam looked crestfallen. Kunju was at once ashamed she'd referred to what she knew affected Rajam so deeply. Recently Rajam had become hyper-sensitive about her failure to conceive, so Kunju immediately continued with her explanation to cover up the awkward pause in the conversation. "As the baby starts crawling, he pees all over the house till he is six or seven months. I do nothing to teach him anything then. When I step in a puddle I merely mop up."

"Not the most hygienic clean up, considering that we Brahmins have millions of rules about pollution." Rajam commented.

"Like you said, a baby's urine is not dirty, Rajam. Anyway, after that you have to take him to the toilet every time he wakes up from a nap, and in six months he will be fully trained."

Kunju looked at Rajam and her eyes glossed over. She knew that Rajam really wanted a baby of her own, and she closed her eyes saying a quick prayer for that to happen speedily.

"Rajam, next Deepavali when we meet, both of us will have children."

"I should put sugar in your mouth for those wonderful words, although you really don't need anymore. May they be true." Kunju put her arms around Rajam and the two of them stood in a close embrace for a long time. Mangalam watched from the open doorway, not wanting to spoil the moment but she was anxious to get going. "Come on girls," she interrupted. "Let us send Partha off with the men and begin all the Deepavali preparations."

Rajam loved Deepavali and the brightness it brought to the mood in the house. Preparations began in earnest for almost a month before the festival. Deepavali was treated like the new year, though the actual Tamil New Year was in April. Everyone got new clothes and sometimes jewelry if they could afford it. For Rajam, the best part of the festival was making different varieties of sweets and savories. Every year, Mangalam hired a Brahmin cook who came with his family and stayed with them for three days to prepare all these delicious sweets. The day of Deepavali was particularly festive; visiting friends and relatives to wish them a prosperous and happy year ahead. Everyone dressed in their finest, carrying with them gifts of homemade sweets.

Leaving the baby in Parvathi's care, Mangalam took the two girls to the goldsmith's house. The goldsmith was from Rajasthan but spoke perfect Tamil. His family had been the official jeweler for the Rajas of Thanjavur for generations. As many people bought jewelry around this time of year, his reception room was crowded with women. Customers chose patterns from brass replicas and then ordered the same to be made in gold or with precious stones. Designs tended to be traditional and there were not too many varieties to choose from. The previous week, Mangalam had placed an order for bangles for both girls and a small gold chain for the new baby, and today was merely stopping to collect it. All transactions were based on trust and the jeweler handed over the goods to her without asking for payment, saying he would receive it from Inspector Saar later.

The next stop was for saris. The shop had saris stocked from floor to ceiling and salesmen brought bundles of silk saris for different customers, who were comfortably reclining against soft velvet cushions making their choices. The best part was they were always offered a hot cup of decoction coffee, which somehow was tastier than the same coffee prepared at home. The choices were mind boggling. Rajam chose an Aarani silk sari in a shot deep purple with a pink border, and both Mangalam and Kunju chose Kanjeevaram silks in different shades of blue.

The last stop for the evening was the firecracker store. Firecrackers arrived a week earlier from Sivakasi, a village in South India, which specialized in making them. After their morning bath on Deepavali, family members would light fireworks to frighten away evil spirits. Mangalam never allowed the girls anything other than sparklers, so the loud bursting bombs were reserved for the men. Deepavali was two days away and Mangalam had completed most of the preparations for the event.

When Deepavali finally arrived, the entire household awoke at four o'clock in the morning. Everybody assembled in front of the family altar, where new clothes were laid out: Kunju and her husband

Panchu, Rajam and Partha, Mangalam and Swaminathan, and of course the brood of children, including the new baby. After they prayed together, Swaminathan as head of the family put a drop of warm oil on each person's head and blessed them by putting kumkumam on their forehead. After that, he handed them their new clothes. Rajam received her sari and her father hugged her tight. "May all your wishes come true," he said, his eyes glistening with tears. He knew how much she wanted a child and prayed fervently for that happy event to take place.

After the ceremony, the women gave the children a hot oil massage and then oiled their own bodies with warm gingelly oil. The children were all bathed together, something they looked forward to every year. Parvathi Chithi already had hot water boiling in a huge cauldron at the back of the house, and the children stood in an assembly line. First Kunju rubbed shikakai on their heads and bodies to remove excess oil and then the child went to Chithi, who washed the shikakai off. Then off to Rajam, who rubbed turmeric paste all over their bodies to soften and bleach the skin. Then back to Chithi for a final wash down. Finally they were all done and dressed in their new clothes with their heads toweled dry. After the women finished bathing, the men followed suit. By five in the morning, everyone had taken their Ganga Snaanam, the bath they had just taken, symbolic of a purifying dip in the holy river Ganga. Then it would be time to meet friends and relatives, and they would enquire of each other, *"Ganga Snaanam aacha?"* Only none of them had actually taken a holy bath in the river Ganga.

Once they bathed, the fireworks began. The sky was soon dotted with rockets and you could hear the sputter of firecrackers from all over the city. After breakfast, the family went to the temple to pray to the Lord for a happy and prosperous year. As they entered through the grand portal, Rajam looked up to see the towering *gopuram*. The outer courtyard was filled with people visiting the sanctums of other deities. This temple had been built during the Great Age of the Chola Dynasty. It is said that the King Rajaraja envisioned this temple in his dream and built the monument to match the massive dimensions of his vision. After passing the impressive sixteen feet high Nandi statue, they entered the main temple. Rajam closed her eyes and prayed, "Oh

Nandi the bull, holy vehicle of Lord Shiva, please allow the Lord to hear my prayers."

The inner sanctum sanctorum was crowded with people peering at the Shiva *lingam*, perhaps the biggest lingam in any temple in India. Rajam would have been appalled if she only knew what she was worshipping, considering her bashfulness about sex. Shiva was never worshipped in his true form and was usually represented by the phallic symbol, the lingam, glorifying his part in the creation of the Universe along with his consort Shakti. Rajam just prayed with tremendous faith, never bothering to enquire too much.

Something was causing a commotion and the crowd in the inner sanctum was pushed back. From a distance Rajam could tell they were making way for some important person to arrive. Being short, she could not see who it was. In a few minutes, she saw groups of Brahmins entering through the main gopuram behind her. These priests or Deekshathars were distinguishable by the unique way they combed their hair: the *kudumi* or bun on their head was tied in such a way that it fell across the forehead. The priests belonged to a particular clan and only officiated in special functions like openings of temples or large fire sacrifices-*yagnas*. Following them was a young man in saffron robes carrying a stick in his hand. On seeing him, the crowd abandoned the temple god and ran towards him.

This unassuming man was none other than the famous Sankaracharya, Chandrasekhara Saraswathi. He was the head of the Sankara Madham, the order established by the great saint, Adi Sankara, in the 6$^{th}$ century B.C. when the Kanchi Madham was established. Sankara revived Vedantha, the ancient Vedic religion which the British later renamed Hinduism. Chandrasekhara Saraswathi was the sixty-eighth in an unbroken line of Acharyas. He had come to Chidambaram to open a new Sankara Madham. In fact, Inspector Swaminathan had moved to Chidambaram because of the Sankaracharya's plans. The opening of the Madham would take place later that week, and this visit to the temple was unscheduled. Swaminathan had a battalion of constables accompanying the saint at all times to control the crowds that gathered to get his blessings or just a *darshanam*. But the crowds were never rowdy. Their reverence for His position and status was evident in the orderly manner in which they assembled on either side, creating a corridor for him to walk through to the sanctum sanctorum, everyone bowing down, prostrating themselves before him, elated to get to see him, to obtain a rare darshanam.

Sankaracharya was a *Sanyasi*, an order of monks who had renounced the material world. He ate one meal a day and carried a stick and a small pot with him at all times, symbols of his renunciation. His predecessor, who had recognized his evolved soul, inducted him into the order at the age of thirteen. Most of his time was spent in prayer and meditation. He resided close to the temple at Kanchipuram near Madras, where he spent his time devoted to the main Goddess in the temple, Kamakshi, the consort of Shiva; hence, the order was known as Kanchi Kamakoti Peetham.

Rajam was a little nervous when she saw his saffron robes and she partially hid behind Partha, peeping to get a glimpse of the great saint. Swaminathan knew Sankaracharya well, as they were distantly related, and had arranged for a private darshanam the following day for Rajam and Partha. The family went back into the temple, hoping to see the saint up close but there were too many people milling around him. Besides, the children had little interest in such matters and were getting restless.

Rajam was happy to return home, as were the children. She wanted to spend as much time with her family as possible. Since it was a holiday, Swaminathan was sitting outside on the thinnai talking with his sons-in-law, greeting and chatting with passersby from time to time.

Kunju needed to attend to her new born and Rajam was more than happy to take charge of the older children while her mother and Chithi finished cooking. Rajam took out a huge bag of dried red tamarind seeds her mother had saved and carried with her to Chidambaram. She still remembered collecting the seeds with Kunju as children from their garden in Vizhupuram. She took out a handful and sat the children down to play *'Othaya Rettaiya'* — ones or twos. The rules were simple. You grabbed a handful of seeds and then the others had to guess if they were odd or even numbers; the one who guessed correctly took the seeds. The one with the most seeds won. In a half hour, the boys got bored and ran away, so she had to think of something new to keep them occupied. They played tag and blind man's bluff, followed by *Palaangozhi* and *Dayakattam,* tirelessly until dinner time. Rajam was grateful for the reprieve, as she had exhausted her repertoire of games. The evening meal complete, they prepared for sleep.

As there were only two rooms with privacy, Kunju and Rajam and their respective husbands got them. Mangalam pulled out a large bedroll and spread it on one side of the thinnai in the covered corridor. On one end slept Swaminathan and on the other, Mangalam, and in the middle was Chithi with two children on either side of her.

Rajam was so exhausted with the excitement of the day, she fell asleep almost immediately. Partha came into the room and nudged her but she wouldn't move.

"Hey Rajam.... wake up. We are finally alone Rajam...Rajam..."

But no matter what he did, she would not stir. Partha shook his head resigning himself to it not happening tonight, turned over and fell asleep. The house was silent except for the sounds of varied snores emanating from different parts of the house. Everyone was asleep, preparing for the big day tomorrow.

# CHAPTER 32 – RAJAM
## CHIDAMBARAM

Swaminathan dressed hours earlier than everyone else and was doing his best to get them to leave. The prayers would begin shortly, and he didn't want to miss any of the proceedings. "Come on, I can't wait all day. If you are not ready in fifteen minutes, then I'm afraid I will have to leave without you. Come on." But his requests appeared to have fallen on deaf ears.

"Amma?" Rajam asked softly, when she was sure Chithi was out of earshot. "Why is Chithi not getting dressed?"

"She can't come with us. She is a widow. Sankaracharya won't meet widows."

"Why?" asked a perplexed Rajam.

"That's just how it is; I don't know why. We never question these things but I'm sure he must have a good reason."

"How can we leave her all by herself?"

"She is used to it; she doesn't care. This is not the first time she has stayed home alone."

Rajam was sad. It wasn't fair. After all, poor Parvathi Chithi had done nothing to deserve her fate. Why did she have to live such an isolated life? How could such a holy man follow customs so blindly and not question them? Mangalam saw Rajam looking upset, her brow furrowing as she agonized over this injustice.

"Rajam, you have to learn not to question everything. Sometimes you just have to accept things the way they are. You can't fight the whole system. You and I may think it's unfair but if we take her to the Madham, then he may refuse to see any of us, and that would be terrible. I promise you, Chithi is fine with it. She is used to it, so please don't fret."

"That may be so but I still think it's unfair," said Rajam, who wasn't happy with her mother's reasoning.

"Never mind now, hurry up. Your father is screaming."

By the time they reached their destination, the morning prayers were already under way. The Madham was in a beautiful building donated by the Raja's family, with intricate ornamentation all around the facade. It had three floors and all the rooms on the upper floors had small balconies, which overlooked the busy South Street. They left their slippers on a large rack outside the building and climbed up the marble staircase leading to the entrance of the mansion. They entered a huge hall, which during the Raja's time must have served as a reception area or living room. At the far end, Rajam could see Sankaracharya seated on an ornate mahogany chair. The silence was only broken by the melodious Vedic chants of the pundits as they conducted the morning prayer. On the left side of the room the men were seated on white rugs, and on the right were the women. All the men wore simple white veshtis and no upper garments, and the women were dressed in traditional *madisars*, the nine yard sari worn by Brahmin women. Everyone was seated cross-legged, listening to the calming drone of the mantras. Sankaracharya sat the whole time in meditation.

Rajam looked at him in total awe. How could he sit so still for such a long time and what was he thinking about? Rajam could not sit for more than a minute without moving. Of late, she had developed a nervous habit of constant movement and could not keep her hands still. Maybe five years of Nagamma's constant persecution had finally gotten to her. She was always anxious about being idle, afraid of Nagamma's censure. Nagamma had no time for dawdling and no tolerance for anyone else's idling. She always made a point of reminding Rajam that she was wasting time. As a result, Rajam felt terrible guilt when she had nothing to do. Moving her hands all the time made her feel as if she were doing something, though the action clearly demonstrated her innate anxiety. Mangalam noticed this constant movement and quietly took Rajam's hands and enveloped them in her own warm ones. She knew Rajam did not have it easy but she was better off compared to most other women; at least she had the love of her husband. If only she could conceive, she would be occupied and have no time to think about trivialities.

After the prayers, Sankaracharya spoke to the audience. His voice was low and melodious and the topic he chose was Karma Yoga —

the Yoga of Action. *"Karmanye vaadhikarasthe maaphaleshu kadaachana,"* Rajam recited along with the saint this familiar couplet from the Bhagavad Gita. "Perform your duty, immerse yourself in action," the saint continued. "Do not worry about the fruits of your actions..."

Rajam glanced sideways at Partha, who was nodding off. She tried to catch her father's eye to tell him to nudge Partha awake but he was too absorbed in the lecture. This was embarrassing! In a short while, the saint got up and the crowd made two lines, filing past him and prostrating themselves before him to get his blessings. Swaminathan went to the side and spoke to some official who was in charge of the Madham. He came back and signaled to Mangalam to move to the side, from where they would take the family for a special darshanam.

The official introduced the family to the saint. Rajam was overwhelmed and at the same time a little nervous to be so close to him. Swaminathan spoke to him and explained their familial connection. Immediately Sankaracharya broke into a smile and talked about their common relatives, asking how they were. Swaminathan pulled Rajam and Partha to the front of the devotees gathered there. *"Periyavar,"* he said using a respectful title, "this is my daughter, Rajalakshmi, and her husband, Parthasarathy. I have brought them here to seek your blessings. She has been married for five years and has no children. With your blessings and God's grace, we hope she will have a child soon."

Sankaracharya looked at Rajam for a few minutes and then got up and went to the statue of Kamakshi. He picked up a large piece of fragrant sandal paste and a few flowers and then in a low monotone recited some prayers. In a few moments he returned and placed this in Rajam's outstretched palms.

"This is *Kamakshi Meru*. Next year you will have a daughter. Name her Kamakshi."

That was all he said. Rajam was overwhelmed; tears of joy streamed down her cheeks. A million thoughts entered her head simultaneously. Is it true? Does he really know, or is he trying to placate me? Will I really have a child, and a daughter at that? How does he know? Oh dear God, please let this be true. If I have a child, I will pray to him for the rest of my life. Oh dear Kamakshiamman, enter my womb and make it flower. Please. I cannot think of anything I want more than a child. She held her palms to her face and smelt the deep fragrance of jasmine combined with sandal paste and camphor. Was this Meru really magical? Could it change my fate? Rajam's confusion and emotional turmoil kept her from holding onto a single thought for any length of time. Almost in a daze, she made her way outside and got onto the vilvandi. She looked at Partha. "Do you think what he said will come true?"

Partha shrugged his shoulders, "I don't know. I hope so."

Mangalam intervened quickly. "Rajam, don't doubt for a moment the clarity of vision that Yogis like Sankaracharya possess. Evolved souls can see beyond our normal material life. If they say something will happen, then you can rest assured that it will happen. Don't ever let doubt cloud your mind. Have faith and never doubt Periyavar's word."

When they reached home, Mangalam gave Rajam a small, round brass box in which to store the Meru. Then both of them went to the pooja altar and placed it at the feet of the picture of Goddess Kanchi Kamakshi. They closed their eyes and chanted the *Devi Stotra*.

*"Ya devi sarva bhootheshu..."*

Both of them were silent for a while. Then Mangalam took a little chandanam from the Meru and applied it to Rajam's forehead and put some on her belly.

"Believe him. You will have a child soon."

"Yes," said Rajam. "I will have a child soon. And I will call her Kamakshi."

# Part XII
# Dharmu

# CHAPTER 33 – KANDU
## NAGARCOIL

Dharmu sat in the corner of the mutram, hoping the entire six weeks of their holiday in Nagarcoil would pass without anyone noticing her. She walked along the side corridors admiring the beautiful Ravi Varma paintings of women. The pearls and rubies glimmered in the light, making it difficult to believe they were merely painted on. Only Ravi Varma knew how to bring the canvas to life. She stopped before a painting of a Kerala woman in a white *mundu* and green blouse, holding a child at her waist. The woman's eyes were sad, as if they held a deep, dark secret. Staring for a while at the painting, Dharmu felt a deep connection with the woman. Ever since she heard the news about her father's infidelity, she had slipped into depression. She felt so sorry for her mother and hated that now she knew the secret too. She would have to keep it locked in her heart, unable to tell a soul about it. Now random thoughts of hate, revenge and anger swirled in her brain, and she was unable to be around anyone for long.

Her sisters-in-law didn't like her. She knew that by the way the conversation came to an abrupt halt every time she walked into the room. They talked in hushed whispers and then broke into peals of laughter, glancing slyly in her direction. She was no fool. She knew they talked about her behind her back and she had little control over that. To be perfectly honest, she did not want their friendship, so she was happy to just pretend they didn't exist. She supposed that irked them even more and resulted in more talk and jokes behind her back but she just did not care. Her mother-in-law was nice enough and six weeks was a short time. Besides, Mahadevan would soon arrive, so hopefully the focus would change and maybe their demeanor would follow suit.

242

For Kandu on the other hand, time spent here was never enough. What he loved more than anything else was to shadow his grandfather around the house, doing whatever he did. He even tried standing tall and holding his head high with his hands on his hips, mimicking Nilakantan's proud stance. This morning he awoke minutes after his grandfather, and after taking a quick bath, Kandu followed him to the garden to collect flowers for the daily pooja.

Still very early in the morning, shortly after daybreak, they stayed close to the house, only choosing the flowers on the bushes immediately surrounding the house. Snakes and scorpions inhabited the garden and it was still too dark to go into the back garden, which had a greater variety to choose from. In the evening they would gather the leaves from the *Vilva* tree, which was especially auspicious for those who did Shiva pooja — special prayers to Lord Shiva. Once they picked the flowers, they visited the store room and brought out a coconut. Nilakantan smiled at his grandson. "How many times do you think I need to hit this coconut before it breaks?"

"Once?" answered Kandu confidently, and he was right. The coconut had been removed from its earlier green encasing but still had stray hairs covering it; Nilakantan deftly tore them away from the brown surface, exposing the central seam. Kandu gleefully watched as his grandfather balanced the coconut in the palm of his left hand with the central seam facing up. Closing his eyes, Nilakantan raised his right hand. In one powerful swoop, his hand struck the coconut exactly on the middle of the central seam, breaking it into two equal halves, deftly cupping the water in one of the coconut cups but not before a few drops splashed on the floor. "How do you do that, Thatha?" Kandu could never control his amazement, even though he watched this very act every single day.

"Kandu, one day I will teach you. It is not just strength, but focus and concentration on the weakest spot on the central seam of the coconut that does the trick. I have had years of practice."

Next, all the deities needed to be washed, which was Kandu's favorite job. He rubbed the silver idols until all traces of kumkumam and chandanam had been removed. His next task was to make fresh sandal paste. He sprinkled water onto the round stone disc and then using a stick of fragrant sandalwood, he began rubbing it against the stone disc, diligently moving it in a clockwise direction. Nilakantan glanced sideways, amused to see Kandu working with such fierce concentration, with his tongue characteristically sticking out of the corner of his mouth. Once all the preparations were finished, Kandu sat down and stared at the altar. Everything looked so beautiful. All the shrines had been anointed with chandanam and kumkumam and the room was filled with the fragrance of vibuthi, camphor, incense and the powerful aroma of jasmine. The sun streamed through the open window, its rays directly shining on the beautiful *Maragada Lingam*, the emerald green lingam in the center of the altar. To represent Shiva's third eye, Nilakantan had a large diamond inserted into the emerald, causing the lingam to appear on fire, flashing brilliant shades of red, green and white. The spectacle was dazzling. Kandu knew he mustn't talk once his grandfather was immersed in his pooja but somehow the words slipped out of his mouth. "Thatha, from where did you get this lingam?"

Nilakantan turned his head sharply, his eyes momentarily angry, and Kandu shrank back covering his errant mouth with his hands. Thatha was kind but his rules had to be followed, and one of them was that you could not speak unless spoken to during his pooja. Kandu slunk out of the pooja room as silently as he could. He was a little upset and didn't want to annoy his grandfather any more. He was playing in the front yard when the sound of the temple bell alerted him, and he ran back into the house towards the pooja room. Nilakantan did his pooja twice daily and after he finished he did an aarathi, for which all the family members had to be present. As soon as they heard the bell, they dropped whatever they were doing and congregated in the pooja room, Kandu the first to arrive. Nilakantan lit all twenty wicks on the oil lamp and began the aarathi. A quick glance told him which family members were absent and he noticed that the errant Kannan was missing. Chanting the Rudram, he did the aarathi with the lamp, moving it clockwise in front of the altar three times. Then on a large silver salver he put a few pieces of camphor and did the aarathi again. One by one, the family members passed their hands over the burning camphor and then touched their eyes, thereby getting the grace from the day's prayers.

Kannan had joined the queue by now, late as usual, and had to face the disapproval in his father's eyes. He deliberately kept his eyes down, not daring to look his father in the face. All of them did namaskaram, bowing down and touching their heads to the floor. The men prostrated themselves, placing their entire body full length on the floor, and the women knelt down, leaning forward as they touched their heads to the floor. Once this was over, everyone dispersed, continuing with their chores where they had left off. This was a ritual that bonded the family, one handed down over generations. Kandu was about to scamper off when Nilakantan called him. Kandu was nervous. Was Thatha angry?

"Kandu, you asked about the Maragada Lingam. Come sit with me and let me tell you how it came into this family."

Kandu breathed a sigh of relief and gleefully plonked himself on Nilakantan's lap.

"Appanshayal was a great devotee of Shiva and we learned to chant all the Shiva mantrams from the time we could talk. Do you know any of them?"

"No, Daddy never taught me." Kandu was truthful but this news disturbed his grandfather, who believed religion was an integral part of a person's character and laid the foundation for the right values and attitudes. He was annoyed Mahadevan had not taught his only son any chants or prayers. This needed to be addressed but Mahadevan was a grown man, who could only be advised, not coerced.

"Hmm... that should be remedied. I will speak to him about it when he comes here. But getting back to my story, I was studying engineering in Trivandrum. Every morning on my way to work I would stop at the Shiva temple to pray. The temple was small but it had a lingam that had been there for hundreds of years. The deity was called Gangadhara Swami because the river Ganga streams out of the locks in Shiva's head."

"Really? How come?" Kandu had not heard this story before, and he loved what he called 'God Stories.' Vacation time was full of God stories, anecdotes from Hindu mythology which got siphoned out of his memory through the year until his next visit to Nagarcoil.

"Ganga was a celestial river, which flowed in heaven. If she came directly from the heavens to earth, then her power and force would split the earth apart. That's why Shiva absorbed the energy of the river in his matted locks and released the water in a small trickle."

"Really? One trickle makes such a huge river?"

"Don't forget that this trickle has continued for thousands of years. Don't interrupt Kandu, or I will forget my story. Anyway, following the aarathi at the temple, the priest gave out flowers from the feet of the deity as a blessing after receiving the holy water. That day was a special day —*Shivarathri* — and that evening the temple was very crowded. The prayers were to go on all night and people stayed there until early morning. After the evening aarathi, a huge crowd moved past the deity. I received my small bundle and as I was leaving the temple, I opened the basket and in between the flowers was this beautiful emerald lingam: the Maragada lingam. I was stupefied. I was sure the priest had made a mistake and I did not want to be accused of stealing such a large emerald. I ran back in but as the pooja was over, the priests had gone into the sanctum sanctorum and shut the door. I didn't know what to do. I took the lingam home that night. The following morning I came back to the temple and looked for the priest. When I showed him the lingam, he smiled. He said the previous night he had a dream about the lingam, and in that dream he understood that this lingam had found a new owner. I was scared and didn't know what to make of it. I was a religious person but I didn't know how one was supposed to do the special prayers for this lingam. The priest looked at my worried eyes and told me, 'Many families have these special lingams. Whoever has the lingam has to perform special pooja every single day. Perhaps the previous owner of the lingam could no longer perform the pooja. Such people put the lingam at the feet of the Lord in a Shiva temple and Shiva chooses his next devotee.'

I was overwhelmed and tears were streaming down my cheeks. This was a special gift to me, a blessing from God, and for generations this lingam would protect and provide for my family. From that time on, I have had this Maragada Lingam, and when I pass on, I will give it to one of my sons who is as devout as I am, and who will unfailingly perform the special pooja every day."

"Can I get it?" Kandu was thrilled by this story. Although he had seen the lingam for so many years, he had no idea about its importance and its significance for his grandfather. He loved his grandfather and wanted to be like him, and maybe even inherit from him this priceless family heirloom.

"Maybe. If it is in your destiny, it might come to you. Now run along, I have things to attend to."

Kandu ran to the outhouse where his great-grandfather Appanshayal lived, a quaint little house which he loved visiting. The outhouse had two rooms. The back room had plenty of books and on one side was a bedroll where the old man slept, meditated and prayed. One wall was covered with images of different gods and goddesses, under which was the pooja altar with many silver idols. Appanshayal met his patients in the front room. A low platform covered with a thin mattress stood on one side of the room. On the other side were shelves filled with glass jars, each containing a different herb or root. Appanshayal was very interested in herbal remedies, a very important branch of Ayurveda, the ancient system of Vedic medicine, and had trained under a famous teacher for many years.

People had complete faith in Ayurveds and went to them for any and every ailment. Remedies existed for every conceivable disease, from snake and scorpion bites, to constipation and diabetes. Appanshayal got some of the herbs locally but every year, he made a trip to a hillock near Cape Comorin, where plenty of medicinal herbs are found, and spent many days physically collecting the herbs and roots he needed to make his medications.

Appanshayal ran a free clinic in his front room, and every evening for two hours he attended to numerous patients, mainly locals and villagers from nearby villages. He was especially known for his expertise in treating snake and scorpion bites.

When Kandu walked in, he saw his great-grandfather seated on the floor, his brown spectacles hanging on the edge of his nose, as he ground some herbs using a mortar and pestle.

"Hello, Appanshayal Thatha. What are you doing? Can I help you?"

"Who is that? Kandu? Come come. I was waiting for you. Do you want to help me? I find it hard to keep getting up, so maybe you can get me the jars I need."

For the next few hours Kandu assisted his great-grandfather, helping to make all sorts of potions and powders, some of which were brewed in a pot over a small outside stove. Around lunchtime a man came running in with a small child in his arms. He was out of breath and crying. The inert child's head lolled backward. Appanshayal knew immediately that it was a snake bite but the father had no idea how it occurred and exactly what type of snake had bitten the child. Very often the offending snake would be non-poisonous but the villagers, thinking they were bitten by a poisonous snake, would get all the symptoms and almost be near death, such was the power of the mind.

247

The young boy was already exhibiting many symptoms. He was warm and in a semi-conscious state. The wound was red and swollen and the fang marks were clearly visible.

"Do you know how long ago it happened?"

"Maybe ten minutes ago. I don't know. I picked him up and ran all the way. I live down the road, so it could not have been too long."

"Did you see the snake?" Every bit of information was important for clues to decide on the right treatment.

"I only saw it disappearing into the bushes. It was black and maybe three feet long."

"Probably a King Cobra," said Appanshayal, judging by the bite and the father's description. To Kandu's horror, he put his mouth against the wound and started sucking the blood and spitting it out. After several minutes of that, he placed the child on the bed, making sure that the boy's hand hung down at a lower level, so the poison would take longer to travel through the body. The poison was thick and slow moving but ten minutes had passed since the bite. Still Appanshayal knew if he slowed down the flow of blood to the rest of the body, the symptoms would become less severe.

Kandu sat down near the boy. "Is he alive or dead?" he asked, his voice low. He had never seen anyone so sick ever before.

"He is alive but the symptoms have manifested."

Appanshayal combined his herbs and soon returned with two remedies. He put the one with a thick consistency directly on the wound and then began forcing a liquid potion into the child's mouth.

After almost an hour, the child's eyes fluttered open. The father, who had been beating his chest and lamenting the impending loss of his only son, was instead crying afresh at the unbelievable miracle. He fell down on the floor at Appanshayal's feet, calling him a god, a savior, which embarrassed the old man. He handed the boy's father the liquid potion and told him to give it to his son along with fresh honey for the next few days.

It was past lunchtime and with so much happening, Kandu was ravenous. Running into the kitchen, he could smell the delightful aroma of the food, which made him even hungrier. He reached for the potato curry but his grandmother slapped his hand away.

"Go and wash up. I'll serve the food."

Unlike most south Indian families, the main meal in this household was taken at noon. According to Ayurved, Agni, the digestive fire, is most active when the sun is highest, making noon the best time of day for the largest meal. Food was served in the closed verandah behind the house, and the men arrived one at a time. Silver plates and silver glasses for water were arranged in a row on the floor, and steaming hot rice and sambar began the meal. Kandu mixed the rice and lentils just like Nilakantan did, making a big hole in the center of the rice like a well for the piping hot sambar. No one spoke at all during the meal. The women knew who needed what just by looking at the plates and the different food items miraculously emerged from the kitchen and onto their plates. After the meal, Nilakantan washed up and immediately lay down to sleep. All that rice made anyone sleepy. The heavy food coupled with the midday sun made taking a nap natural and inevitable.

Kandu followed his beloved grandfather and snuggled up to him, rubbing his soft hairless chest, enjoying the feel of his smooth skin, and smelling the fragrant sandalwood.

Life was wonderful. Just wonderful.

# CHAPTER 34 – MAHADEVAN
## CALCUTTA

Mahadevan tried to loosen his tie. The heat made him sweat so profusely his neck felt swollen and he found it hard to breathe. Being dressed in a three piece suit did not help but today, he had no choice. He was attending a meeting at the Bengal Gymkhana with the Assistant Secretary, and he had to show up in the required club attire, appropriately dressed at all costs. He longed to get out of his constricting clothing and into his comfortable veshti but that would have to wait.

Almost a month had gone by since the family had left for their vacation, and the house in Rangpur was deafeningly quiet. Mahadevan missed the welcome Kandu would give him when he returned home from work every day. At least with everyone away, he was able to catch up on his reading without guilt. The weather had been unbearable, and he was glad to leave Rangpur. What a good thing that Dharmu and the kids left when they did because soon after their departure, as he anticipated, violence had erupted in town. Expecting trouble, he had asked for reinforcements from Calcutta and as a result the increased police presence had reduced the number of casualties.

The Muslims had gone on a killing rampage but thankfully, in a few hours they had been contained and the ringleaders apprehended. For the last few years, many Muslim League activists were working the minds of the locals, fueling hatred and distrust where none existed previously. Ten years ago, his ruling on the case of the Muslim woman would never have been questioned but now it fanned the smoldering hatred, erupting in violence, looting and murder on a scale Rangpur had never witnessed before.

The Muslims did not want their people to be tried in regular courts under the British Penal Code, but were demanding that cases

250

should instead go to communal court to be tried under their version of Muslim Law — a ludicrous demand, motivated by the desire to preserve male superiority. Mahadevan knew that if the mullahs were given a free rein, Muslim women's rights in this country would be quashed forever. Encouraging such separatist ideas would lead to a divided India, something the British were well aware of and willing to use in order to control the growing Nationalist movement. Such tendencies had to be restrained, and he could never tolerate interference from religious fascists in his courtroom.

For so many years life here had been peaceful but communal unrest had disturbed the fabric of society, threatening to permanently disrupt the peace. East Bengal had a majority of Muslims and the British had been encouraging them to think of their own separate state. For so many years Muslims and Hindus lived in almost complete harmony but now with all this talk about Muslim Statehood, the peasants were getting fired up to action. Recently, Muhammad Ali Jinnah returned to Bombay from his sojourn in England and rejoined the Muslim League. The British for many years had been abetting the divide between the two communities by promoting the idea of separate electorates as a means of furthering their control over the ancient land. The idea of separate electorates was tolerable but separate statehood was not an acceptable solution. How strange that Jinnah was now leaning towards the idea of a separate state, considering his overwhelming support over the last decade for Hindu-Muslim unity. But in all fairness, Gandhi had become more absorbed in his personal culture and tradition and seemed to represent the Hindu majority. Even so, that was not sufficient reason to justify the need for a separate state. An editorial in the Calcutta Gazette discussed the dangers of Partition.

Mahadevan shook his head as he put the newspaper down. A few more articles along these lines would close down the newspaper forever. He looked out of the car to admire the beautiful Victoria Memorial. He had seen the building from the outside on several occasions but his trips to Calcutta were so short he never had an opportunity to enter the building. He picked up the Amrita Bazaar Patrika, a Bengali daily. Fortunately he read Bengali. The reporting in vernacular languages like Bengali was more vibrant, pulsating with

251

editorials enriched by the passion of the journalists. Once again, the article expounded on the dangers of Partition.

Pakistan. That was the name they were talking about for the new Muslim state. Choudhary Rahamat Ali had already sown the seeds for a separate Muslim state, using the word "Pakistan," which was composed of letters from the five northwestern provinces: Punjab Afghan Kashmir Sindh and Baluchistan. Mahadevan had read somewhere that the word "Pak-i-stan" meant "land of the pure" in Persian. Wherever the name came from, the whole idea seemed wrong to Mahadevan, a huge mistake with severe repercussions for the subcontinent. A new state based on religion was a recipe for disaster, bound to result in a bloodbath. When Mahadevan toured the riot affected areas in Rangpur, the viciousness of the attacks shocked him. Every stab of the knife generated hatred and venom, pitting neighbor against neighbor. It was tragic to see so many deaths, such bloodshed for no apparent reason. Hate and anger reigned supreme, while a peaceful community was torn apart. No, partition was certainly not a good idea but he could do nothing to change the course of history. Rumors suggested that the new state would be divided in two, and Rangpur and most of surrounding East Bengal would belong to Pakistan. It was ludicrous to even conceive of creating a country in two different geographical areas with completely different demographics. Trying to administer a dual government would be an even greater nightmare. What were they thinking? Bengalis and Punjabis in one country? The two peoples were so different, it would never last.

The car turned onto Chowringhee Avenue, and Mahadevan picked up his file from the seat. He was meeting the Assistant Secretary to discuss the communal problems and the subsequent riots in Rangpur and had to provide a bona fide justification for his ruling. After attending this meeting in Calcutta, he would be on leave for three glorious weeks. He had not taken any time off for the last two years and could not wait to see his father and Appanshayal.

The driver went past the main entrance to the club and Mahadevan shouted out, "*Roko*. Stop the car. The entrance is here. You already passed it."

"No Sahib, that entrance is only for the Angrez."

"What nonsense! Stop the car. Reverse right now."

The driver reversed back up the street, muttering to himself that that entrance was definitely only for white people but Mahadevan paid

252

no attention to him. He got out and walked up to the main entrance, where he was greeted by a sign.

## "INDIANS AND DOGS USE BACK ENTRANCE"

His ears started ringing. He had not been to any of the English country clubs before and had absolutely no idea there would be separate entrances for Indians. But here in front of him was a sign that clubbed him in the same category as dogs. He had half a mind to jump into the car and drive away but was caught in a situation where he had no choice. He had to attend that meeting, so he would swallow his injured pride and use the back entrance reserved for darkies and curs. Shamefacedly, he returned to the car, where the driver waited with a knowing smirk on his face.

"Sahib, the back entrance is down the street. I told you, Sahib, only Angrez can use this entrance." Mahadevan said nothing. He couldn't speak.

Thrusting himself out of the car, Mahadevan walked in through the back entrance and stepped into the Gentleman's cloak room to freshen up. He entered through the swinging door and stopped in his tracks, his jaw dropping in horror. The room was full of Englishmen, nude as the day they were born. He could not believe what he was seeing and he did not know where to look. It was appalling! Some were shaving and chatting with each other, oblivious that they had on not a stitch of clothing. There were uniformed valets helping the men out, some even powdering their genitals! Disgusting! One valet crouched on the floor massaging the feet of a portly Englishman, who in the meantime indulgently smoked a cigar. There were a couple of men sleeping on easy chairs, their family jewels exposed to all who cared to observe. Mahadevan ran into the cubicle, relieved to be alone, trying to figure out if this was hilarious and absurd or bizarre and shameful. Perhaps it was all of the above. As he stepped out, the cigar-smoking Englishman kicked the valet hard in the middle of his chest, sending him flying backward. "Bloody rascal, black dithering fool. Watch what you do. If you hurt me again, I'll have your balls cut off."

The valet got up, crawled back to his previous crouch and resumed massaging again. Considering whose balls were exposed, cutting off the offending appendage would have been easy and

253

pleasurable for the valet. But the poor man probably didn't understand a word of what was being said to him. Mahadevan felt inadequate and shamed. He could not go to the meeting in this frame of mind. Every time he tried to justify working for foreigners, some incident would cause him to question his misplaced loyalty. *So they gave us the English language, railways, Government and even cricket but what was all that worth when you had no dignity. How long were we going to watch and wait and swallow our pride and search for some semblance of self-respect?* He had to compose himself and move past the incidents of the last few minutes. His performance would be affected if he went to this meeting emotionally strung.

He sat down for a few minutes, and then went out into the verandah where the meeting had already begun. David Kline, the Assistant Secretary, was sitting with two lawyers, one of whom he instantly recognized as Hussein Suhrawardy, an active member of the Muslim League. This meeting was going to be difficult but his conscience was clear and his work ethic meticulous and above board. He had nothing to fear.

"Good day, Mahadevan. Sorry old chap about the back entrance. Not my handiwork. I just finished apologizing to Suhrawardy here but he insists this is why we Brits need to leave."

"Do you agree, Mahadevan, that we have had enough of back entrances?" asked Suhrawardy, putting Mahadevan in a spot. He did not like controversies and was grasping for an apt reply.

"It does not matter what I think or feel but how I respond that counts."

"Come on, Mahadevan, you know your pride is hurt. Why don't you admit it?" Suhrawardy enjoyed goading Mahadevan and was not going to let this go easily.

"Admitting it makes me the loser; it does not solve the problem."

"Exactly. That is why you need to say and do something about it. It is a question of dignity."

"Hussein, all of us know it is only a question of time before we are masters of our homeland. I am willing to momentarily compromise on dignity and pride but I will not give the power to anyone or anything to rob me of my peace of mind."

No one spoke for the next several minutes.

# CHAPTER 35 – KANDU
## NAGARCOIL

The days were going by too fast. Soon it would be time to say goodbye to Thatha and Appanshayal and board the train for Rangpur. Boring Rangpur. Boring, hot and silly Rangpur.

"Daddy, I don't want to go back to Rangpur."

"Why, Kandu? You can't stay here forever."

"Why not? Thatha and Appanshayal Thatha will take care of me."

"And what will I do all year without you? Who will hug me when I get home from work?"

Kandu thought for a while. His father had a valid point. He loved being with his parents but he also loved being with his grandparents. This was tough.

"How about six months here and six months there?"

"Kandu, it's only a question of spending a few more months there. Then we will move to Delhi or Calcutta and you will have a lot of fun. You can go to a regular school and have friends."

"Really? Are we going to go? Oh my God, I have to tell Rukku. Rukku . . ." and Kandu ran off to inform his mother and sisters about their impending move.

"Kandu, don't tell anyone. We aren't moving . . . yet." But Kandu was out of earshot.

Mahadevan looked up at the overcast sky, which meant the sun would not mercilessly beat down on them. It seemed to be the perfect day for an outing.

"Appa, what do you say we go to Cape Comorin? The weather looks good."

Nilakantan looked up at him over his eyeglasses. "I am ready. Get everyone together and let's go."

# When the Lotus Blooms

In a short while, Nilakantan, Mahadevan, Dharmu and the children were on their way to Cape Comorin in the blue Baby Austin. On the way they stopped at the Suchindram temple. Nilakantan always made it a point of stopping there whenever he passed through the area because of its uniqueness. It had a lingam representing the Hindu trinity: Shiva, Vishnu and Brahma, the only one of its kind. In the outer corridor was a huge statue of the Monkey God, Hanuman. After a short visit, they headed towards the beach.

When they reached the shoreline in Cape Comorin, the sun was still thankfully hidden behind a cloud cover. Mahadevan sat at the water's edge and watched his father swim along the shoreline. Nilakantan was a powerful swimmer and was fond of saying that one day he would swim across to the Vivekananda Rock, which lay a mile across the ocean. But today was not that day because the waves were high from the monsoons. The grey and frothy sea had a strong undercurrent and Dharmu clutched the children, not allowing them to venture too far into the water.

They sat on the water's edge and stared at the ocean. Paati had packed a delicious lunch, including tamarind rice and yoghurt rice, which they devoured as they watched the waves crashing against the shore. Kandu looked across at the rock in the middle of the sea.

"Daddy, what is that rock?"

"That is a special rock. They call it the Vivekananda Rock. Many years ago a young man came here to this very part of the shore from Bengal. He had wandered all over the country and reached the southernmost tip of the subcontinent. His mind was racing with a million unanswered questions, just like yours always is. To calm himself, he jumped into these waters and started swimming and didn't stop till he reached that rock. His name was Narendranath Dutta, and he was a religious man in search of truth. He sat on this rock and meditated for three days and three nights."

"How did he do it? *Ommm*..." said Kandu sitting cross legged with his eyes closed and his hands in the classic *gyanamudra* and the girls followed suit.

"Yes just like that. He meditated looking at the whole of India. At the end of three days he woke up and found enlightenment and a new vision for India."

"Daddy, you use too many big words. Kandu is only five," Vani interjected.

"I'm sorry. It means he realized what he had to do to make Indians awaken and become free."

"You mean he was a freedom fighter?"

"No, Kandu, not free as in free from British rule but free in their minds, knowing what the path to truth was." That was an even more complicated explanation. Kandu was smart but not that smart.

Kandu didn't understand most of it and busied himself making a sandcastle. He built a huge mound with a moat around it. After making his fiftieth visit to the sea and emptying the contents into the moat only to watch it disappear into the sand, he gave up.

"This is a stupid moat," he declared. The family was dozing on the sand when the rain came in from the sea. The droplets were large and painful, stinging their skin and they scrambled to get cover, making their way to the car. By the time they left town, all three children were asleep. It was their last evening there. Just before dinner, Appanshayal came to the house looking for his great- grandson. "Kandu, where are you? I have something for you. Hurry up Kandu, come here if you want a present."

From nowhere Kandu appeared. "Present? What present? English chocolates?"

"Nothing that sweet but something magical," said Appanshayal as he led the way to his outhouse. Kandu trotted behind him, following him as he went into the garden at the back of the house and squatted next to a plant.

"Appanshayal Thatha, where is my present?"

"Here, this is what I want to give you," was the reply as Appanshayal lifted out a pot containing a plant with strange droopy leaves.

"A plant? My present is a plant?" queried Kandu, with a crestfallen look as he gazed at the strange plant with thin floppy leaves.

"This plant is dying, Thatha; it has no flowers."

"No, Kandu. This is a very special plant that grows only in the hills of Mansarovar in the Himalayas. You don't get this plant anywhere else in the world."

"Really? So how did you get it?"

"I brought it back when I returned from my pilgrimage."

"It looks pretty sad."

"Its leaves are drooping with the heat of the midday sun, but notice how the leaves grow out of other leaves. Have you ever seen that before?"

"Oh my! That is so strange; the stem has no purpose. I mean the leaves are not sprouting from the stems."

"That's why I called it magical. This is a special plant called the *Brahmakamalam* — the Lotus of *Brahma*. Very few people have this plant, and you are going to be one of the few exclusive owners. The magic of this plant is that it only blooms once, sometimes twice a year and that too just for a few hours. If you miss that, then you have to wait for a long time before it blooms again. Not only that, this blooming will mean something special for you. It will tell your fortune."

Kandu looked at the plant with renewed interest. A fortune telling plant was much more exciting. "How will I know when it is going to bloom?"

"A pinkish colored bud will appear from the leaves. Watch it carefully when that happens. It will bloom only for a few hours in the late evening."

Kandu looked at the plant once again. A magic plant with leaves growing from leaves and flowers growing from leaves. This was incredible.

*Brahmakamalam, the exotic Himalayan beauty, is called by many names — the Fragrant Queen of the Night, the Golden Heart and the Star of Bethlehem. A plant, which by a whim of nature grows only in the Himalayas, the abode of the God Shiva, around Mount Kailash and in the verdant valleys of Mansarovar. Ancient Hindu texts refer to this flower as being special to Shiva, although the word Brahmakamalam translates to the Lotus of Brahma. Perhaps this was the golden lotus on which Brahma was seated as he emerged from the navel of Vishnu to create the universe. So incomparable is this flower that it symbolizes every aspect of creation, expressing itself in the world we live in as a tribute to the creator. It creates from within itself in a design so complete that it overloads the beholder with emotion, sensation and passion — a lotus that includes aspects of Brahma, Vishnu and Shiva within its physical form. A unique plant, the likes of which is not found in any other part of the world, a flower which some say, belongs to the sunflower family, while others swear is an epiphyte, a cactus, or a lotus.*

*The first impression is deceptive, as its long drooping leaves look like any common foliage. But its magic lies in the leaves and flowers growing out of the leaves themselves and not from the stem. It has been seen in full bloom in spring and winter, and those who have the honor of seeing the Brahmakamalam flower, never forget the experience. At first a limp pinkish bud appears and for a while nothing happens, then all of a sudden, mirroring the miracle of life, it unravels in white splendor. The outer petals are thin and pointed, revealing within its folds a round petalled mound that uncannily resembles a Shiva lingam. Over this mound are white stamens tipped with yellow, resembling the hood of a cobra suggesting Adishesha, the hooded serpent associated with Vishnu.*

*Once a year it spreads elation and joy as it opens its face in the delicate moonlight for humans to admire. It blossoms only once and on occasions, twice a year, only for three or four hours, after which the petals wilt and fall to the ground. While the plant is in full bloom, its consummate fragrance is unparalleled, defying description, leaving the privileged gasping at its magnificence.*

Now, Kandu was the proud owner of this rare bloom, a magical flower that would bring tidings of fortune and happiness, of the birth of joy and hope that would give meaning to his life, rejuvenation that would fill his cup of happiness to the brim.

But he knew nothing about that. Not yet, anyway.

When the Lotus Blooms

# Part XIII
# Rajam

# CHAPTER 36 – RAJAM
## VIZHUPURAM – DECEMBER, 1934

For two days she cried. No matter what anyone said, the sadness was so overwhelming, it flowed through her veins and out of every cell and every pore till it reached her tear ducts, where with an uncontrollable outpouring of gloom and despondency, it finally left her grief stricken body. She wept so much that her eyes felt sore and it hurt even to blink. She had not eaten all day and could barely sleep. When she did, her dreams were filled with visions, bright and colorful, which then merged into nondescript shapes of grey, rolling over the earth till they fell off a steep precipice, jerking her into wakeful consciousness. So deep rooted was this melancholy, it seeped into her subconscious, presenting itself in images so disturbing that reality was preferable, no matter how painful.

It did not matter that it was the month of *Maargazhi*, special to lovers, when the air had a sprightly, fresh nip to it. Rajam was alone, forced to be apart from her own love, left to disseminate all these distorted images that merged from semi-sleep into awareness, making it difficult for her to tell dreams from reality. She could not accept that after so much prayer and so much faith, God had forsaken her. The cramps in her belly intensified and she cried aloud in a mournful wail, piercing the silence of the cool December air and alarming Partha, who was sitting on the terrace enjoying the moonlight. He ran down the stairs to the back room where Rajam had been confined for the past two days. Outside her room, her breakfast, lunch and dinner lay untouched.

"Rajam, please don't cry. I know you are sad. So am I but crying will make things worse." Partha understood her torment. He knew how she longed to have a child and how much faith she had put into that last meeting with the saint. She was making herself ill and it hurt him deeply to watch her suffering and be unable to alleviate it.

"Go away. I don't want to talk to anyone, not even you."

"Please Rajam, why are you angry with me? What did I do?"

"You did not fill my belly."

Partha eyed the untouched food. "Here, eat," he said with a smile on his face, handing the plate to her through the open door. "At least fill your belly with food."

But Rajam was in no mood for jokes. "Nooooo…" she screamed. "Go away. I never want to talk to you."

"Rajam, please don't behave like this. Everyone is concerned you haven't eaten. If you don't eat, then I will have to come in and feed you."

"No, don't lie to me. Everyone is only concerned that once again I have no child in my belly," and the wailing began afresh. Her self-pity was dragging her into despair. Partha knew somehow he had to make her eat and smile again. But he did not know where to begin.

"That too, but you have to keep your strength up. If you don't eat, then you will fall sick and then even if God willed it, you would not have the strength to hold a baby in your belly."

"Then your mother will be happy. She can tell everyone how she has a sickly daughter-in-law with a withered womb." In between a fresh bout of tears she declared, "That's all I am. A sick, barren, useless daughter-in-law."

"No, Rajam, you are not useless or barren and if you eat you won't be sick either." Even though it was taboo, Partha picked up the plate and walked into the forbidden room, much to Rajam's horror.

"Noo… Don't touch me; you will be polluted." Rajam truly believed when you were menstruating, you emitted negative energy, which spoiled food, turned milk sour and certainly resulted in indelible, unpardonable, pollution on humans.

"Polluted my foot! I don't care." Partha came up to her and held her close, her cheek against his chest and they stayed linked together for a while. Partha gently wiped the tears from her eyes and ran his hand over her hair till her body was quiet and the shivering stopped.

After meeting Sankaracharya in Chidambaram, Rajam was sure the miracle of pregnancy would take place. She watered the sacred sandalwood, the holy Meru he gave her every single day, resting

263

assured she would not get her next period. But now her faith was shattered. In spite of everything, she was not pregnant. When the cramps woke her two days ago, she was numb in disbelief. Getting her period did not merely shake her devotion but planted seeds of despondency. The tears were already in her eyes as she walked dejectedly to the back room. Nagamma saw her entering and was quick with a gibe about her empty bleeding womb; and that set Rajam off. She could not stop crying. For two whole days she sobbed till she was empty and frozen. She had not eaten any food or drunk any water but the tears had their own secret reservoir of fluid that needed no replenishment. Other than that one sarcastic innuendo, no one had said anything to her, yet she felt victimized and was punishing herself for a crime she was not responsible for.

Partha mixed the cold rice, sambar and vegetables into a little ball and put it into her mouth, opening his own involuntarily as he did this. He wanted to heat the food for her but didn't know how and certainly did not want anyone to know where he was. Men were not supposed to involve themselves in any matters pertaining to the kitchen.

As she chewed down on the food, the saliva came painfully streaming into Rajam's mouth, a reaction caused by her body's aching need for nourishment. She swallowed three more mouthfuls, all the time playing with her toes, not looking at Partha in the face. "I feel better," she said, turning towards him, opening her mouth for the next mouthful and when she noticed Partha opening his mouth at the same time, burst out laughing.

"What?" Partha said, surprised at the sudden turn of emotions.

"You opened your mouth."

"I did? Well, it's a good thing. At least it made you laugh."

When Partha left, she was definitely feeling better with food in her stomach and no more sounds of crying emanated from the room.

At night, just before they retired, Sushila came to her with the evening meal. "Rajam," she said softly, "come, eat. I have two dosas for you and a glass of buttermilk." She slid the plate in but was not so adept with the glass and a little buttermilk spilled on the floor. "Have you stopped crying? I'm so glad. Even Nagamma was looking worried. Can you believe that?"

Rajam certainly couldn't. "You are just saying that to cheer me up. I know what everyone is thinking."

"Rajam, why do you torment yourself? Have faith and you will become pregnant."

"It's easy for you to say. Do you know how bad I feel that I have not given Partha a child yet, after being married for so long?"

"But waiting for it always makes it take longer and just so much more painful. It's like waiting for a pot of water to boil. It always seems to take twice the amount of time when you stare at the pot. Just relax and let it happen."

"No, Sushila, I really don't think it will happen. I will never conceive a child."

"Shush Rajam; don't even say that. The Devas passing by will say 'asthu asthu' — (So be it), and then your fate will be sealed. You are still so young. Seventeen is hardly the age when you stop trying and give up totally. Come on, keep your spirits up; everything happens in good time."

"I know, but every month I wait and nothing happens. I feel that God has forsaken me."

"Never lose faith, Rajam. Just knowing you will have a child will make it happen. Sankaracharya said you would have a child. He does not waste his words. If he said it, then it will happen."

"But see. I'm here languishing in this room. It didn't happen."

"Maybe not right now, but it will soon. Think of what happened to me, Rajam. I lost the baby in the seventh month of my pregnancy. Which is worse? Not getting pregnant or losing a baby before it is born?"

Rajam felt ashamed. She had been so self-absorbed, not even pausing to think of Sushila's plight. "Oh, Sushila, forgive me. I have only been thinking of my own situation. I know your plight is worse than mine. I'm so sorry for behaving so badly."

"Don't fight your destiny, just have faith. If you are so highly strung, it will prevent you from getting pregnant. And I'll tell you another trick: after you do it, don't get up immediately. Lie down for an hour at least."

"Is it? But what about bathing?"

"That can wait for an hour. My friend told me that getting up immediately and washing yourself is a sure way of avoiding pregnancy. So I guess lying down will improve your chances. What do you say?"

# When the Lotus Blooms

That was useful to know. It had been so ingrained into her that sex was polluting and you had to bathe immediately, she had done so without questioning, like all the zillion other things she did. No one ever questioned the elders. If you were told to do something, you just did it unfailingly. Even if one were to question anything, no one had an answer because everyone did what their parents told them to. All of these rituals and practices must have had some justification once upon a time but over generations they had somehow lost the original validation. There were so many of them she could think of off the top of her head: lighting lamps at sunset, washing the front yard with cow manure, washing after sex. She could think of one for every waking minute of the day. So many practices that defined the culture they lived in. They were blindly followed but rebelling against them would raise eyebrows and cause a stir in the family; and Rajam was unwilling to take that risk. The practices and rituals lingered and endured over centuries, remaining almost identical perhaps to the time when they were first prescribed. Only men had the leeway to fine tune these, just like her father did in his household. No one really questioned him because he decided what went on in his house. But as a woman, she could never refuse to do anything that had been the practice in her household or her husband's household. It was not her place to question why and the thought of doing so never ever entered her mind.

The cramps subsided and the pain of not being pregnant waned. She felt drained of all emotions and when she lay down and stared at the moon and the stars through the open window, she lost all sense of space and time and drifted off to blissful sleep.

Almost like clockwork, her eyes opened even before the first rays of the sun peeped over the horizon. She sat up and looked out through the open doorway. The household had not stirred as yet, which meant she had enough time to use the bathroom and clean up before anyone awoke. It was pitch dark outside and because she had just awoken, her eyes were not yet accustomed to the darkness. The petromax lamp was at the foot of her bedroll and she groped for it blindly, catching it just in time before it tipped over. The box of matches was right next to it. She pumped vigorously and lit the wick, the brightness blinding her momentarily. Then, wearily, she found her way to the bathroom.

She stopped just outside as she heard the noise of water. The parayan had come early to clean the latrine. Nagamma was not going to be too happy about that. No one had used the toilet as yet, and smell would become unbearable by tomorrow when he returned once again to clean. The latrine sat on a raised platform with three steps leading to it. Every morning the *parayan* crawled through a small side door and scooped away the stinking remains that lay underneath. Rajam watched in silence as he poured water and washed out the filth. As he crept out from the aperture beneath the toilet, he gave her a toothless grin. He wore a dirty undershirt and had his veshti tied almost like a loin cloth. His hands and clothes were covered in the muck that he worked with all day.

Rajam felt repulsed and sorry at the same time. What a job! All day he toiled in the filth and dirt, making the world a cleaner place to live in. She wondered if he realized how important his job was to them. If he missed coming to clean even one day, it became impossible to use the toilet without gagging. Still, she could not bring herself to come anywhere near him and stayed rooted to the same spot till he finished collecting the garbage and exited through the back door into the street that only parayans could use. He too, sensed how his presence revolted her and left the house as quickly as he could. She was a Brahmin woman and he was a parayan, an untouchable. He knew his place and did not want to transgress the strict rules governing his presence in the Brahmin quarter.

He had absolutely no clue that his life or his job was of any value to anyone.

# CHAPTER 37 – VELANDI — THE PARAYAN
## VIZHUPURAM

He was not just 'the parayan.' He had a name, Velandi, and his loved ones called him Velu. His family had lived in the area from the beginning of time, never thinking of moving either occupation or residence in spite of the squalor and abject poverty that was their lot. In many ways, he never realized he was underprivileged or that he deserved better. He was just happy because he knew no better. This was his life, this was his home and this was his job.

Today he had come early to finish his work because he had to fetch water from the river. It was a long trek to the *ghat* where he and the other untouchables were permitted to fill their pots of water. Almost three miles downstream, it took him the better part of an hour getting there and even longer getting back, his pace halted by the weight he carried. Normally, his wife, Muniamma, took care of this chore but Muniamma was ill. She had just given birth to their fourth child and was still weak from the aftermath of childbirth. They had three other little ones to care for and Muniamma was not yet strong enough for the task. The childbirth was difficult and the considerable loss of blood left her anemic and weak. No doctors or vaidhyars visited the parayan quarter and the women used ancient herbal remedies to help their own. Muniamma was lucky to escape death. Just last week the wife of Velandi's neighbor, Chandar, had succumbed to childbirth and he was now left with seven children to care for, seven mouths to feed. If only they were allowed to dig their own well, then no one would have to walk this distance to fetch water and life would become so much easier. But the Brahmins and other upper castes would not hear of it. The ghat where they filled their pots was at the narrowest point of the river. Now the water level was high but Velandi

268

knew how much they suffered as the summer approached, when the waters narrowed down to a thin brown stream, teeming with germs. But no matter what the difficulty, under no circumstances could they draw water from the wells in other neighborhoods.

Thirst was something every man in his caste understood and lived with. Sometimes when there was absolutely no water, they cut the thick stems from cactus plants and squeezed precious drops of fluid down their parched throats.

Last year, his neighbor Chandar was so overcome with thirst, he dared to attempt stealing water. Chandar paid dearly for stealing one measly potful of water from the well near the merchant's quarter. He was beaten so badly the welts from the thrashing did not heal for three months and the water he stole was thrown onto the dry earth right before his eyes.

Muniamma weakly raised her head as Velandi walked into the hut. "Did you fetch the water?"

"Not yet Muniamma; I will leave right away."

"What about food?"

"It was too early. No one had kept out any old food for us. But I went through the garbage," he said cheerily. "I found two apples. Let me cut out the overripe parts and you can eat the rest."

Muniamma took a bite out of the half rotten apple. "Leave the rest for the children, I have had enough." In spite of her health, Muniamma could not bear the thought of eating while her children went hungry. They would wake up soon and she didn't know if she had any food in the house to offer them.

"Eat it, Muniamma; you need your strength. I will go back to the Brahmin quarter later. Someone is sure to give me some food." Guiltily Muniamma ate the rest of the apple. It was still dark when Velandi reached the ghat. The river was full and flowing fast. He stepped in, scrubbing himself thoroughly, dipping his head below the surface several times. The water was fresh and cool and he allowed himself a few moments of indulgence. He was washing himself after a whole month and the caked dirt had become part of his skin. He took a lump of wet clay from the waterbed and rubbed it over his body, letting the rough earth remove all the encrusted grime from his body and head. Once he was clean, he filled the four pots, balancing three on his head and holding the fourth with one hand as he began the long trudge home. His black, oily, freshly scrubbed skin shone in the morning sun. He smiled, sure that Muniamma would have trouble recognizing him. When he reached home, the children were already awake. Last night he had soaked a handful of cooked rice in a large pot of water. Fermented overnight, this would provide the nourishment for the family for the rest of the day. Most often, they ate this starchy breakfast if they were lucky enough to have cooked rice at home. After the children ate, none was left over for Velandi but he was not worried — a cupful of water would keep his hunger at bay.

He loved winter because people were extra generous at this time of year, perhaps because of the various festivals that took place. Velandi was lucky he cleaned Brahmin homes, as they would rather give away old food than eat it. Not everyone worked in the Brahmin quarter but hunger would bring them here, as old food was almost guaranteed. Almost every day he got leftovers from the previous day's cooking — that is, if he was lucky enough to get to it before the dogs and rats ate it up. Unfortunately, the women wrapped the food in banana leaves and left it outside the back door. Sometimes, he picked it up almost as soon as he saw them place it outside but if his timing was not right, others would beat him to it, including stray dogs and vermin. It was too late to go back, so he decided to try his luck elsewhere.

It was the holy month of Ramzan, so at the end of the day, there was excellent food available in the Muslim Quarter. He would take his oldest son and wait in line outside the mosque before sunset. It was important to get there early. The unfortunate who were caught at the back of the line were stuck without food and left to wait a whole day before another chance at a meal. Velandi slept on an empty stomach many times but it bothered him that his children occasionally slept hungry. He wanted to be able to provide for them and every day presented a new challenge.

Having children was a boon and he provided for them only with God's grace. Sometimes God would question his faith by making life difficult but Velandi was steadfast in his belief. He was born into this wretchedness because of all the sins he had committed in his previous birth and was determined to use this life to change his karmic balance. No matter how desperate his situation he did not change his faith and he did not steal. When he was a child, a drought had lasted for five years and almost every year he lost a family member. The polluted river water and subsequent outbreak of cholera took three of his siblings in the very first summer. Death saved them from the cruelty of the next few years that ravaged the rest of the family, while nature played havoc with their lives and the lives of all the people that populated the land.

Every morning they looked up towards the sky in the hope of seeing the rain clouds gather, in a desperate prayer for the monsoon to arrive, but all they saw was the harsh and blistering sun that parched the earth and made the crops wither, causing pain and suffering to one and all. Even the wells in the Brahmin quarter were drying up and the toilets could not be cleaned without water. Women were reduced to washing their clothes in the river and soon, the utter scarcity of water made the river bed their toilet. That was when cholera broke out and it did not spare anyone. The wealthy at least had their doctors but in the parayan quarter, death and doom had devastated every house. The trees were bereft of leaves; and even the wild berries withered in the blistering heat. Velandi and his brother learned to set traps for snakes and rats, which they skinned and roasted on the fire to assuage their hunger.

Many families moved out of town, making the long trip to take refuge in the neighboring state of Kerala, which had more opportunities and definitely much more water. Some took sanctuary in the church, where, by accepting Jesus Christ as their savior, they got one square meal a day and a cupful of water. Velandi's uncles begged him to come with them to the Mission, saying the Hindu god was cruel and did not deserve loyalty. *Hesu Christhu* (Jesus Christ) was much more benevolent and in the mission they were treated as equals but Velandi's father would never convert. They pleaded with the family, saying all they needed was to change their name and food was guaranteed but Velandi's father was ready to face hunger rather than give up his faith. This situation to him was just God's way of testing their faith and only the weak succumbed to the pressure. Velandi believed that, too, because in the end the rains did come but not before taking away his only sister, the last sacrifice to the wrath of Mother Nature.

When he married Muniamma, she was only eight years old, so thin you could literally count the ribs sticking out through its perfunctory skin cover. But with the rains came the harvest, and very soon the waters in the river were flowing again. The Brahmin women once again kept out their leftovers, and Muniamma filled out and slowly became a

271

woman, and now was the mother of four children: three boys and a girl.

Velandi sat down to go through the garbage. He loved doing this because it was full of surprises. The garbage told him many stories about the homes he cleaned, providing small details, like the menu for the day and sometimes letting out untold secrets, like the time he discovered the blood soaked rags from the Raman household. He knew exactly what had happened but was not about to volunteer any information. He knew the word of a parayan had no value.

He carefully separated the glass bottles, papers and rags and piled them up in separate jute bags in the corner of his shack. Next week he would sell the bottles and paper in town and then maybe the family would enjoy a good chicken curry. Muniamma stitched all the rags he found into clothing for the kids. By the time he finished with the garbage, only rotten food was left over, which he piled in a corner of his garden to fertilize his small vegetable patch. Nothing was ever wasted. Last week he found a torn pair of slippers, which he repaired and proudly used when he went on long treks over rough terrain, such as the one he would undertake today to reach the mosque.

They were late and it was early afternoon by the time they left. It took twice as long because they had to walk around the outskirts of town avoiding the local neighborhoods in order to reach the mosque, which lay diagonally opposite to the north. But neither Velandi nor his son Nandanar (Nandu) complained. They could not wait to reach the mosque and taste the delicious, succulent mutton biryani soaked in rich spices. By the time they reached the mosque, the line had wrapped itself twice around the building. Velandi was not despondent and merely went to the end of the line and sat down cross legged to patiently wait for sunset. The evening prayers began at sundown, probably after six o'clock and after the congregation ate, food would be doled out to the waiting multitude. Knowing they would be here for the next couple of hours at the very least, Velandi looked around him to see if he saw any familiar faces. To his surprise, he realized he did not recognize anyone, which meant that many had come from other villages. Nandu was tired after the long walk and now his stomach was growling in anticipation of an excellent meal. He hated the thought of waiting and indolently leaned against his father, his eyes half closed.

"Appa, I'm bored. Tell me a story."

"Which one?" Velandi was tired and hungry too and a story would help while away the time.

"The Nandanar one." Velandi had named his oldest son after the legendary parayan, Nandanar, whose life story was a source of hope and optimism for all the underprivileged. He was renowned as one of the great devotees of Lord Shiva and his story always gave Velandi hope of salvation, especially when times were bad. Velandi's own father had told him the story many times and now, continuing the tradition, he told his sons the same story to instill in them the same feelings of sanguinity.

He began dramatically, in his inimitably flamboyant style, which made him the best story teller in his village.

"Many years ago in a village outside Chidambaram was a parayan like you and me ..."

"...whose name was Nandanar." Knowing the story so well, Nandu finished the line for him, preempting his father at every opportunity, much to the latter's chagrin.

"A great devotee of Shiva, he always visited a temple near his place of work. He worked all day in the rice fields for a landlord who was not terribly cruel but at the same time not exactly kind. From dawn to dusk, poor Nandanar toiled in the hot sun, tilling the land for a handful of rice. But he never complained because as long as he could go to the temple every evening, his life was complete. Every single day without fail he would go to the temple..."

"And do *pradakshanam*." Velandi tried not to show his annoyance when his son completed his sentences. "Yes. Without fail he went around the temple walls almost five times, doing pradakshanam to the God within its walls. Once he finished, he would stand outside the main gateway and peer in to see if he could get a glimpse of the beautifully decorated Shiva lingam, but always..."

"Nandi was in the way." Nandu completed.

"Yes exactly. Nandi the bull is always in front of every Shiva lingam in every Shiva temple." By this time a small crowd had gathered around Velandi, children and adults eager to hear the story. Emboldened and encouraged by his audience, he continued even more vibrantly.

"Nandanar was unshakable in his devotion. He wanted so badly to see the Lord that he sat down, singing in divine ecstasy. As you know,

273

when we go to the city we have to ask permission before we enter the street so that high caste people can get out of the way." Knowing this all too well, several heads shook vigorously in assent, and the crowd increased, listening in mute amazement.

Velandi continued, "So he was used to shouting '*Varugalamo?*' for permission to enter before he stepped onto a street and he used this word in the first line of his famous song." So saying, Velandi attempted singing although completely off tune but no one seemed to mind it. "*Varugalamo... ayyaa...*" He knew the first line and made up the rest as he went along, hoping no one would notice.

"Shiva was so pleased, he moved Nandi several feet to the right and Nandanar saw the beautiful Shiva lingam in all its glory, gleaming in the radiance of a thousand lamps. Even today we can see the Nandi in the temple to the right of the main deity — that is, if we were allowed to enter the temple." Velandi paused dramatically for the oohs and aahs from his audience.

"But Nandanar was not satisfied. He also wanted to see the Lord at the Chidambaram temple because that was one of the few temples where the Lord could be seen in human form as he danced the cosmic *Thandava*. He kept telling everyone he would make that fateful trip to Chidambaram and soon people were making fun of him. But Nandanar was too simple-minded to get offended by what people said and continued to ask his master for one day off from work so he could make that trip. But the Jameendar always made some excuse not to send Nandanar, laughing at his dream, saying that parayans would never ever be allowed inside a temple, particularly the Chidambaram temple, which was controlled by three thousand Deekshathars — priests who were so conservative that the thought of a parayan entering the temple was unthinkable. But Nandanar was adamant. Finally, the landlord agreed on the condition he till forty acres of land in one day. Nandanar was despondent because he knew this was an impossible task. Even forty men working together could not complete that much in one day. But a miracle took place that night. When they awoke the next morning, forty acres had been tilled and on top of that, the crop had grown and the grain was ready for harvest!"

At this point the audience was in raptures, extolling the virtues of a God who never lets you down, seemingly oblivious to their own wretched situation. Velandi waited till they quietened down before continuing.

274

"When Nandanar reached Chidambaram, as expected the Deekshathars would not let him in. After realizing this was the boy for whom the Nandi had moved, they agreed to let him in if he would walk through a wall of fire. A huge crowd gathered and the priests brought in lots of firewood. All the while Nandanar sat in meditation chanting the name of Shiva, *"Om namah shivaya om namah shivaya."*

"Then what happened?" Velandi was speaking way too slowly, elaborating on too many minor details and they wanted the story to climax; but Velandi prolonged it unnecessarily, enjoying the attention he was receiving.

"It was evening and the temple was beautifully decorated. Everyone waited as the head priest brought out a flaming torch and lit the dry wood. As soon as it caught fire, the flames streaked upward toward the heavens. Nandanar then stood up and with resolve, walked slowly but with determination, towards the fire. As he stepped into the blaze, the crowd closed their eyes, not wanting to witness the public annihilation of an innocent devotee of God. The smirking priests thought to themselves that this would be a lesson for any who dared question their rules. One less parayan would make no difference to the world. To their utter astonishment, Nandanar emerged from the other end unblemished, with not a single burn on his body or clothing. The last thing they saw was Nandanar running towards the sanctum sanctorum." Velandi paused for dramatic effect before concluding his story.

"For a while no one could move; they were awestruck by this miracle unfolding before their eyes but in a few moments the crowd followed him into the inner temple. No one was there — no body, nothing. He had become one with the Lord."

The deep silence that followed the story was broken by the mullahs calling the faithful to prayer. Not wanting to lose their place in line, everyone hurried back to their former spots. It was just a matter of time before dinner would be served. After Nandu ate, Velandi swallowed only one mouthful and packed the rest for his wife and children. Tonight a cupful of water would have to suffice. Muniamma's need was far greater than his.

# CHAPTER 38 – RAJAM
## VIZHUPURAM

The heads of more than twenty women could be seen bobbing above heaps of flowers, in the central courtyard of the temple. Marigolds, roses, lilies and blue December flowers were all piled in neat mounds. Today women from Rajam's street had gathered to make garlands for the temple deity. Every day, a different group met at the temple, everyone volunteering their time depending on their household schedules. No matter what their personal commitments were, they helped out at the temple at least once a week. Of course, everyone did so with the ulterior motive of accumulating the grace of the Lord, even though it was one more opportunity to get out of the kitchen and socialize. Making garlands was an art these women had learned from the time they were children, placing two flowers flat on the string facing opposite directions and then looping the thread around in order to fasten it. The more experienced taught the novices to loop it skillfully with just the right tension, as leaving the thread too limp allowed the flowers to fall and too tight to cut the stem. The red roses had such a strong fragrance that after making the garlands, Rajam's hands smelled of roses all day. She was making rose garlands and it reminded her of her marriage ceremony, when the whole house smelled of lilies, jasmine and roses.

At the time of her marriage, her father brought in special flower experts skilled at garland making from the town of Salem. They arrived four days prior to the wedding and deftly wove garlands from morning to night. Once a garland was made, they wrapped it in wet muslin to preserve it. When they opened the muslin bundle four days later, the garlands still smelled as fragrant as if the flowers had just been just picked off the trees. Inspector Swaminathan spared no expense for his daughter's wedding. All the saris came from silk houses in Aarani and Kanchipuram, the best flowers from Coimbatore and the whole house was covered with a colorful pandhal. He rented a beautiful white Dodge car from his friend Muhammad Salih for the groom's wedding procession. It was a grand wedding and over the three-day ceremony, food was served to over five hundred people. Five years later, he was still repaying his debts. Luckily, he was able to raise the money for the wedding through his friends, so there was no fear of high interests if he could not pay back on time. He knew of many stories of those unfortunate enough to borrow from money lenders, the arrears multiplying over time, making repayment of wedding loans a lifelong process, sometimes even passing their liability as a legacy to their children.

The conversation in the temple was lighthearted and generally centered on those not present to defend themselves. Rajam described her visit to meet Sankaracharya in Chidambaram and soon the conversation turned to holy men, with everyone adding their two *pice*[2] about their own experiences with saints. The discussion moved from holy men to impersonators and then converted into a heated discussion on theft and burglary, though how the conversation got there, no one knew. Rajam found out that Muthu Mami had sold the house and set off on pilgrimage to the Himalayas. Poor thing. After Revathi's horrible death and Raman's even more horrific one, she had no reason to live here. She prayed that Muthu Mami eventually find some peace and redemption.

Of course this led to expert advice on pilgrimages, since every Hindu dreamed of making a pilgrimage and visiting the holy cities situated in the Himalayas, along the banks of the river Ganga. Bathing in the ghats of Benares (Kashi) redeemed a person of all his sins and ensured freedom from the cycle of karma and rebirth. Rajam listened closely to several anecdotes of beautiful temples and hermitages in sacred locations like Hardwar, Hrishikesh, Badrinath, all the way to the source of the Ganga in the glacier of Gangotri. Each person tried her best to outdo the previous story but there was no denying that the journey to Gangotri was supposed to be remarkable, replete with a sense of being one with nature and with God. Rajam wondered if she would ever make that fateful pilgrimage.

---

[2] A former Indian coin worth one sixty-fourth of a rupee

Rajam lifted a pile of garlands to deliver to the priest, who had a small room at the back of the temple, where he lived with his wife and two-year-old son. He was not there but Rajam found his wife watering the plants in the tiny garden.

"Leave them in the corner. I will put them away," she said with a smile. She had just bathed and her hair was still covered with a thin towel. Rajam had never found an opportunity to meet her earlier and decided to use this chance to speak with her. She seemed to be around the same age and looked friendly. *"Namaskaram,"* she began. "My name is Rajam and I know you are Savitri."

"Yes, Rajam, I have seen you many times at the temple but we never had the chance to meet."

"You have a really beautiful garden," Rajam said looking around, admiring the tiny garden.

"It's not very big but I really enjoy talking care of it. I have jasmine, hibiscus and roses, all the flowers I need for my daily pooja. Of course the temple flowers are sent here by the merchant, so we don't really need to worry about that."

Rajam's eye caught sight of two unusual looking plants in clay pots in a corner of the garden. "What are those? I have never seen leaves like that before."

"Oh that. I really don't know what they're called. Muthu Mami, do you know her? She gave them to us before she left on pilgrimage. Apparently she got it from some friend who went on a pilgrimage to Kashi but it only brought her bad luck. I'm sure you know her story better than I do. Somehow when these things come to the temple, just being here in this holy area energized by positive energy from chanting mantras changes its luck. In fact, the day after I got it, I realized I was pregnant. Strange how something is misfortune to one and good luck for another."

Rajam felt a momentary pang of jealousy when she heard Savitri was pregnant. As soon as the thought entered her mind, she forced it out, telling herself that she should not be jealous of other people's fortune or children. She bent down to look at the plant. "My God, what a strange plant! The leaves grow out of leaves."

"I know. And just last month, I plucked a leaf and put it in the soil . . . and see how it has grown."

"Remarkable. You must have green fingers."

"No, not really. I did nothing other than water the plant."

278

"You found you were pregnant as soon as you got the plant?" The words slipped out of her mouth before she could stop them.

"Yes. Why do you ask? Do you have children?"

"No," said Rajam, careful not to sound dejected and divulge her innermost thoughts.

"And you want a child, isn't it?" Rajam said nothing but her silence revealed all.

"I tell you what; you take one of the plants."

"No I couldn't."

"I insist! It might bring good luck just as it did for me."

Somewhat hesitantly, Rajam took the plant. It was ridiculous what she was ready to believe in order to have a child. First, she thought sandalwood from a saint would get her pregnant and now she was taking a droopy plant home in the belief that it would change her fortune. But she was desperate and willing to try anything. Having a baby would change everything. It would change how she felt and maybe her mother-in-law would demonstrate some respect for her. The whole world viewed a young girl so differently from a mother of a child. Yes, this plant would bring her the luck she needed. She would water it every day, just as she watered the sandalwood and she would have a child soon. Very soon.

## CHAPTER 39 – RAJAM
### THE BRAHMAKAMALAM BLOOMS

The Brahmakamalam grew amazingly fast. It was now almost three feet tall. Rajam had taken the plant home less than a fortnight ago, and already there were many new jade green leaves. On closer inspection, it looked as if a bud she spotted a few days ago sprouting from one of the leaves was ready to bloom. She lifted the pot and walked up the back stairs. The open terrace upstairs was a wonderful spot to keep this plant, a celestial adornment to an otherwise almost bare concrete rectangle. She placed it in the northern corner, turning it so the bud got maximum exposure to sunlight. A *charpoy* stood on the other corner, a woven jute bed on a wooden frame covered with thin cotton bedding. Sometimes in the hot summer months, the men slept on the open terrace to avoid the scalding heat inside the house, which made sleeping indoors impossible. Rajam ran down to the well and filled a copper pot with water, which she then carried gingerly up the stairs, pouring the water onto the plant with deference, like gentle rain on a warm summer day, mindful of its inviolability, its pure sanctity.

Ever since the plant came into her life, she sensed a shift in her mood. Gone was the depression, the fear, the anxiety and the stress, and in its place a smile, an expression of pure joy for no apparent reason. She was like a mother caring for this plant as if it were her progeny, counting each new leaf and lamenting each withered one. Today she felt an elation she had not experienced for a while. It was amazing how being close to nature brought you so close to godliness, the flowers and leaves just a gentle reminder of the cycle of never ending creation. Being with nature brought hope for the future, of exciting new prospects with each blossoming bud.

Her happy thoughts were rudely interrupted by Nagamma's raucous voice. She was screaming at Sushila. That was surprising! What did Sushila do that was so bad to make Nagamma raise her voice at *her*, of all people? Rajam knew it was better to stay out of it but curiosity got the better of her and she found herself moving involuntarily towards the kitchen. Sushila had ignored the food on the stove and the delicate pieces of *podalangai* were now charred bits of charcoal.

Nagamma continued endlessly, "How could you ignore the food like that? What was so important that you had to forget about the stove? Have I not taught you anything in all the years you have been here? Look at the dish! Now we will have to break our hands cleaning it."

'*Not you,*' thought Rajam to herself, '*Sushila or I will be assigned the task.*' But she did not speak, merely hid behind the door watching Sushila squirm for a change. From her position, she was hidden from Nagamma's view and could see only Sushila, crouched down on the floor vigorously slicing the podalangai on the aruvaamanai, probably imagining it was Nagamma's head on the curved knife instead of the inert vegetable. She looked annoyed; her lips were drawn into one straight line and her brow knit. Rajam could see she was fuming, focusing on the task at hand, so she would not lose it and shout back. Rajam could not help rejoicing to see someone else at the receiving end of Nagamma's tirade. She felt a little guilty thinking so but she was so tired of always being the victim.

Nagamma continued relentlessly, "Did your mother not teach you anything about the kitchen or about looking after the house? Now see, everything is going to get delayed. It's almost time for lunch and no curry is ready. Do you think I am a magician that I can bring vegetables on the banana leaf just like that? What were you doing anyway that was so important?"

Sushila mumbled something about washing clothes and Rajam chuckled, thinking she should have said, '*No, not a magician, a witch*'. At least today things would be different; it would be Rajam consoling Sushila and not the other way around. She walked into the kitchen and swiftly picked up the leftovers from yesterday's meal, leaving the room just as speedily, not wanting to get caught in the crossfire. She went out the back door and looked around as she placed the food on the floor but the street was empty except for a couple of stray dogs. The parayan had not yet come but he would be here any time. He had better hurry or the dogs would beat him to it. Then she suddenly remembered she had to discard of one of Partha's shirts that she burned while ironing, so she ran back in to fetch it and put it outside with the food. She knew the parayans appreciated anything they got and the shirt was practically new except for the burn. She barely put the shirt down when Nagamma yelled for her in her rasping and surprising genteel tone. "Come, Rajam. Your friend, Savitri, is here."

Ever since she gave the plant to Rajam, the two women had become friends and Savitri dropped in often to visit Rajam, a welcome breather, breaking the monotony of the day.

"*Yenna*, Rajam? What are you up to?" Savitri waddled in holding her son at her waist. Rajam loved playing with him and enjoyed listening to his baby talk. Balu ran out as soon as he heard Savitri's voice and tried his best to entice little Ramu to come and play with him, but Ramu was shy, and it took some persuasion to make him leave the cozy comfort of his mother's lap. "Have you made plans yet for Pongal?" Savitri asked as soon as she squatted next to Rajam on the floor in the outer thinnai.

"Not really." Things were always so hectic dealing with only mundane chores that Rajam did not realize Pongal was around the corner. Savitri actually did her a favor by reminding her about it. There was so much work to prepare for the festival. The most enjoyable part was shopping, which she looked forward to. "Maybe this weekend I will go with Sushila and buy new clothes and all the supplies."

"Why don't you come and help me at the temple? We are expecting many devotees and I need some help with the *prasaadham*."

Pongal was a harvest festival, very important for farmers. For Tamils, it was a big occasion, with lots of preparation and festivity. Initially a celebration of the winter harvest, for farmers who toiled all year in the fields, Pongal celebrated the bounty of nature with great fanfare. As usual, a festival meant special food items had to be prepared, which on this occasion was called Pongal. Not being particularly fond of sweets, Rajam did not like *shakkarai pongal*. She looked forward to eating the more savory *venn pongal* with pickle and curry on the side.

"No one leaves the temple that day without prasaadham and we are expecting quite a crowd as usual. I haven't really involved myself in celebrations at the temple so far and I'm not sure how much to make.

If you make a big pot of shakkarai pongal, that would make four large pots, as I have already asked three others. Then two people are making venn pongal. That should be enough, don't you think?"

"That sounds fine. You can look at the crowd and adjust the helpings. I can definitely do my bit," said Rajam, who knew they would be cooking pongal that day. It was just a matter of making a larger quantity and cooking food for temple prasaadham was a blessing. But then she remembered something. "Savitri, I may not be able to help you at the temple. I will have my period that day."

"How can you tell that you will be 'out of doors' with such precision? I am always late and my period always disrupts everything. I can never plan on anything. Not that I need to worry about that now." Savitri rubbed her swollen belly as she spoke.

"Oh, Savitri, I can tell with conviction. It comes like clockwork in twenty-four days but I will tell Sushila to help you." Savitri stayed for a while, then left after enjoying a hot cup of coffee, much to Balu's disappointment.

The evening meal finished, Rajam prepared the bedrolls in the large inner room. Today Siva and Sushila would have the bedroom, so Balu was to sleep next to Rajam and she kept his soft pillow on the mattress right next to her own. The moon had risen high in the sky by the time the men came inside. The weather was so nice that the men sat upstairs on the terrace till late. Normally, they did not sleep outside in winter because of the *pani*, the cold dew that settled in the early hours of the morning. Their bodies were so accustomed to the heat that even the slightest drop in temperature made them feel extremely cold; and in the mornings they would cover their heads in monkey caps and wrap warm woolen mufflers around their throats to keep themselves warm and prevent a cold.

Rajam was happy to use Balu as a buffer between her and Nagamma because sometimes the snoring was overwhelmingly loud and sleeping became next to impossible, especially when Nagamma's face was six inches away. Partha made sad faces at her peeping over his mother's back and Rajam covered her mouth to stifle her laughter. Unfortunately, Partha would have to rely on his pleasant dreams to comfort him today as the bedroom was occupied. The rhythm of the snoring somehow lulled Rajam to sleep.

# When the Lotus Blooms

She didn't know how long she had been sleeping when she felt someone shaking her awake. As she opened her eyes, a hand went softly over her mouth, preventing her from speaking. It was Partha. What on earth did he want at this unearthly hour? She fluttered her eyes open, slowly adjusting to the darkness around her. Partha tugged on her arm and helped her stand up. She looked at him half dazed, still swaying from the effect of her deep slumber. Partha held her hand and the two of them tiptoed out the back into the open thinnai. The evening breeze was light and the backyard was bathed in moonlight. She finally whispered, *"Yenna?* What happened? What are you doing? Where are you taking me?"

"Shh…" was his only reply. She shuffled along as he led her up the back staircase onto the open terrace. As she stepped onto the terrace, her eyes fell on the flower pot in the corner. The bud looked full and ripe and gleamed in the moonlight. She couldn't focus clearly but it seemed as if it were about to bloom any time. She looked up and soaked her being in the expanse and brilliance of the celestial ceiling. It was not full moon yet but the moon still shone as bright as day. On a cloudless sky, the stars twinkled brightly, like a million flickering candles. It was quiet — just her, Partha and the heavens. She turned to question him again, when his intentions suddenly became clear. He pulled her gently into his arms and smothered her with hot kisses. Rajam panicked. *"Yenna,* stop! It's open and anyone could come."

"Don't spoil it. It's perfect and no one will come. Just relax and enjoy the moment." Partha put his arms around her and gently unwound her sari, twirling her till she stood a few feet away from him, her face glowing with excitement, her eyes half closed in anticipation. Like a dream unfolding, he walked towards her and as he came close, he reached his arm forward to move a wayward strand of hair away from her perfect forehead. Cradling her face in his hands, he looked at her, not needing to speak one word to express his love, merely communicating in the consciousness that pervaded her senses, echoing his every thought and emotion. And as his lips moved down to meet hers, she closed her eyes, drinking in the madness of the moment of forbidden intimacy. Their bodies swayed and shuffled onto the charpoy, his weight crushing her and making her gasp for air. The bedding on the charpoy was thin and Rajam felt the jute rasping against her skin but she didn't care. Her whole body was suffused with heat, rising from a glowing ember in her loins and gushing upward into

284

her body, till it flushed her face, her heart beating uncontrollably. The flagrant desire was mutual, like an all-consuming fire, inundating reason and making them oblivious to anything but the pleasure of the moment. As their bodies writhed in unison, their breath coming in shallow, starving gasps, she reached towards him with every cell of her being, moving to meet and complement his every pulsating move. Their naked bodies were covered in sweat. A gentle winter breeze cooled their heated bodies outwardly but was unable to quench their inner fire. Arms and limbs entangled to create a single body, restless and thrashing in passion. And then, a thousand lights burst all around her, a thousand stars came rushing towards her all at once, a thousand colors, a thousand shapes integrating into a kaleidoscope of ecstasy, and she submitted to this heavenly bliss, experiencing an intensity of passion she had never felt before, with wanton abandon, hardly aware of her physical surroundings.

After a while, Partha moved off her and the two of them lay in close embrace, not wishing to move, lest they spoil the moment. No sound broke the stillness of the night, other than crickets, who seemed to chirp in rhythm to their labored breathing. Rajam looked up at the moon and stars and felt an inexplicable connection with the cosmos and nature around, a joy and elation she had never experienced thus far. She knew she must awaken from this languorous slumber and wash herself but when she tried to wriggle free, Partha only held her closer. Unable and unwilling to fight, she slipped into a languid sleep, and when she slept she dreamed.

*She was running in a green valley, the wind in her face, her soft feet treading on grass which was softer than the softest silk. The setting sun shone down on her, yet its angular rays were warm, gentle and caring, almost as if they were caressing her being. As she ran, the breeze moved her thick black locks up and away, till they settled in a tangle around her face. When she stopped moving, she looked around to admire what she beheld. The view was panoramic and spectacular. All around her were snowcapped mountains, and exotic birds in vibrant colors were flying everywhere. Birds she had never seen before, in brilliant shades of yellow*

*and purple, creating a colorful collage in a myriad of effervescent hues defying description.*

*Then, she saw the flowers.*

*White bunches of Brahmakamalam in full bloom, their soft white inner petals a gentle yet pronounced contrast to their spiky outer ones. She sank to her knees and touched the delicate flowers and the perfume entered her nostrils, filling her being with its potent fragrance, exhilarating her. The scent was like none she had ever smelled, almost as if it were a special heavenly concoction made for her sensory pleasure. She sighed in contentment, drinking in the heavy sensory overload.*

The jangling of cowbells from the street below disturbed her sleep and she sat bolt upright, horrified to see her own nakedness in the morning light. With lightning speed, she dressed herself and rushed towards the stairs but something in the corner of her eye caught her attention. In the crook of the terrace around the flowerpot were soft white petals.

The Brahmakamalam had bloomed at night.

She couldn't believe she had missed it. She ran to the plant and scooped up the soft white petals and held it to her nose. Then she breathed in deeply, taking in the mystical aroma of the perfume that dreams are made of.

# Part XIV
# Dharmu

# CHAPTER 40 – KANDU
## RANGPUR – JANUARY, 1935

"Why not?" questioned Kandu, irate and almost screaming at his mother, who just could not understand his urgency.

"Kandu, for the last time, don't argue with me. No means no."

"But tell me why. You can't just say no. You have to tell me why."

"I don't know why, but you can't keep plants in your room and that is final." Dharmu had been arguing with Kandu all evening but he would not take no for an answer. He came back every five minutes to ask again, hoping to wear her down, but she was resolute.

"But why?" badgered Kandu with the same question, almost as if he had not heard the conversation all evening.

"I told you, Kandu, plants give out bad air at night. Go ask your father if you don't believe me."

Kandu clenched his fists, his arms ramrod straight on either side of his body as he stormed out of the room. His brow was deeply furrowed and his eyes narrowed down to small slits. He was really mad! He had been caring for the plant his grandfather had given him and now there was a bud ready to bloom. Kandu knew he must watch it carefully or he would miss it blooming but silly Mummy was not willing to listen. He had to keep it by his bed, didn't she see that? Honestly, girls were so silly! They just said things without any reason. What bad air was this plant going to give out anyway? Daddy was sitting outside in the verandah when Kandu ran up to him purposefully. Angrily, he plonked himself on the chair opposite his father, his arms crossed unyieldingly across his chest, his lower lip sticking out in a pout.

"What happened, Kandu? You look so angry the moon got scared and went behind a cloud." Kandu glanced up at the sky to verify the

288

statement but he saw the almost full moon peeping out from behind a cloud. "It's Mummy. She won't let me keep the plant in my room."

"What plant?"

"The Brahmakamalam that Appanshayal Thatha gave me. The plant has a bud. Come, come with me and see." He pulled his father to the corner of the verandah to show him the plant. Crouching down beside it, he gingerly pointed to the pinkish swollen bud, which was almost ready to split open.

"See this pink bud? It has been there for four days now. I have been looking at it ever since it first appeared after the New Year and I am quite certain it will flower tonight. If I don't keep it in my room I will miss it blooming. Don't you see I have to keep it next to me so I can watch it? Pleeeease Daddy, can I pretty please keep it just this night?" Kandu pleaded in an ever so gentle sweet voice, his hands folded, using every known ploy to get what he wanted.

"Don't be silly, Kandu, you can see it in the morning. It's not going to disappear."

"Noo…" moaned Kandu now suddenly infuriated at having to explain his rationale for the hundredth time. "It blooms only for a day and only at night. I have to keep it with me but Mummy says bad gas comes out of plants at night."

Mahadevan had been on the brink of capitulating but he saw that Kandu was playing him. "That's right Kandu, at night, plants give out carbon dioxide and that's why we don't keep them indoors. You don't want to breathe in carbon dioxide."

"Oh God, Daddy, a little *carbul diox eye* won't kill me," said Kandu, almost getting a handle on the word.

"Kandu, if your mother said no, then it is no; you can't keep the plant with you when you sleep." This was the last straw. Kandu let out a long loud wail and left the room sobbing, hurling himself onto the bed, sniveling about evil, uncaring parents who didn't know anything. By the time Rukku popped in to see what was up, he had pummeled the overstuffed pillow so hard, cotton feathers were coming out of it.

"Kandu, what happened, why are you crying?" she asked.

"Shut up and go away," he shrieked and hurled the pillow at her, sending the fluff all over the room. "Hey!" he said in astonishment and then jumped all over the bed, trying to catch the rebellious fibers. In the meantime, Rukku hurled the pillow back at him and more feathers got released into the air. In no time a full-fledged pillow fight had developed and the two were squealing in excitement, hurling the now droopy pillow and then throwing more feathers into the air. When Mahadevan walked into the room, it was a sorry mess. The air was misty with fluff and both Rukku and Kandu were covered in feathers. They stopped in their tracks and turned towards their father, staring at him, their eyes wide open in fear, waiting for the admonishment to commence.

"He/she, started it," they accused simultaneously. To their surprise, Mahadevan burst out laughing. It was so nice to see the children playing together and they really looked so comical. With their hair almost white and their clothes bathed in fluff, he did not have the heart to shout at them. Such impetuous moments came by only once in a while and he would leave it to Dharmu to do the bad parent routine.

Of course, Mummy entered soon afterwards and the *Jamadar* was summoned to clean up. With small children around, it was a great help to have a cleaner at your service twenty-four hours a day. The room was cleaned but not before Kandu rubbed a handful of feathers into the Jamadar's head.

After dinner, Kandu waited until Mummy and Daddy went into the living room, before surreptitiously sneaking into the library to search for the flashlight. If Mohammed could not go to the mountain, then the mountain would come to Mohammed. Daddy said that all the time and now he understood what it meant. He knew exactly where to find the torch, in the second drawer in his father's desk. He tested it, all the while nervous about getting caught. He knew he would be in terrible trouble if caught and he also knew he was not allowed to play with the flashlight, which had been a special gift from England from one of Daddy's friends. He knew that batteries were not easy to come by but he needed that flashlight tonight. His mind was ticking with a zillion things so that 'Mission Bloom' would be accomplished. He tucked the flashlight into the front of his pants and peeked out of the door. All was clear. Like lightning, he streaked across the open hallway and into his room, stashing it under his pillow.

Well, that was done. Now he had to get his bedroom door open, a very difficult task. The verandah ran all the way round the house and could be accessed from all the rooms. He didn't dare to open the front door, so his best bet would be his own bedroom door. All the doors had three sets of bolts: two on top, two on the bottom and one across. He had already undone the bottom and middle bolts but the problem now was getting to the ones on top. Why did they have to build such tall doors anyway? It wasn't as if some tall monsters lived in the house. His cupboard was about two feet away from the door but he didn't know how to get on top of the cupboard. A long time ago he had tried climbing up and the whole cupboard came toppling down on top of him. It was a miracle that he was not hurt. A step stool from the kitchen would get him to the third shelf but the dilemma was getting the stool into the room without alarming the family. He went into the kitchen and was surprised to find the servants had already left. Mummy and Daddy were in the verandah, so they would not hear the sound of the stool scraping against the wooden floor of the dining room. Only nosey Rukku was the problem. He crept up to their room and stood outside noiselessly, peeking through the curtains. To his joy, Rukku got up to use the bathroom. In seconds, Kandu was in the kitchen hauling the stool back to his room. Meera usually slept with Kandu and today he would have to make sure she did not see the stool. He inched the stool in the space between the cupboard and the door, out of plain sight. It was dark and Meera was not about to go snooping behind the cupboard.

Kandu closed his eyes tight and pretended to sleep when Mahadevan came to tuck him in. He pulled the sheet over his head when Meera entered with the lantern. In a while, the household was silent. Kandu lifted his head and peeked over the side of his bed. Meera was snoring softly. Hopefully, she was tired and wouldn't hear the noise. He opened the doors to the cupboard and slowly pulled out the stool an inch at a time so no one would hear. In the dead silence of night, the squeaking of the wooden stool against the stone floor was unbelievably loud. Finally, he had the stool where he wanted. Tucking the flashlight into the front of his pajamas, he climbed up the steps and was overjoyed to find he could touch the top of the cupboard. He must have grown recently. He took out the flashlight and placed it securely on top of the cupboard and then hauled himself up. Now, all that was needed was to open the bolt. He hoped against hope it would not squeak. If it did, then all this trouble would be for naught. He lay flat on his stomach and reached out and to his utter amazement, the bolt slid open noiselessly. Someone must have oiled it recently. Like the *doors to Krishna's prison*[3], the way was clear for him. He grabbed the flashlight and climbed down one step at a time, catching his breath when he heard Meera move.

The evening was almost as bright as day when he stepped outside and he didn't need the flashlight after all. All that work for nothing. The moon was almost full; only one side looked as if someone had taken a small bite out of it. *'I wonder if the moon is really made of cheese,'* he thought to himself, as he tiptoed to the front verandah. In the moonlight, he could see the leaves of the Brahmakamalam gleaming like dull jade. The bud had lifted a little and looked as if it were ready to open any time. Kandu sat down and stared at the bloom. It was just a matter of time. He was prepared and was not going to miss it. In a while, his eyelids involuntarily drooped. He pulled a cushion from one of the sofas outside and put his head on it, now looking up at the bud. It was only a foot away from his face and he could see every crease of its petals. *'I bet no one has ever seen this plant flower from underneath,'* he thought to himself. Just then, he heard a dull roar from the distance and shivered in fright. What if a tiger came? He listened closely waiting for the sound to repeat. In a few moments he heard it again, only this time it was more distant. Feeling safe, he got back to his comfortable position under the bud. He stared at it for so long his eyes got crossed with sleep. Kandu panicked! He had to stay awake a little while longer, so he decided to count the petals One, two three, four. *Hey! The petals moved. It's blooming!* But it was just his head that had shifted, or maybe his eyes had momentarily closed.

Sometime in the next hour, from sheer fatigue poor Kandu fell asleep and when he slept, he dreamed.

*He was running in a green valley, the wind in his face, his soft feet treading on grass that was softer than the softest silk. Animals of all kinds moved around him: giraffes, elephants, monkeys and birds, all grazing in the valley and curiously looking at him. "Hello monkey, hello peacock," he greeted them one at a time . . . till he saw the girl. She was calling him,*

---

[3] The miracle of Krishna's birth, when the prison doors opened, allowing his father, Vasudeva, to safely take him to Brindavan, away from the clutches of his evil uncle, Kamsa

*beckoning him to follow. Bathed in a sheath of light, she was dressed in traditional clothing — blue pavadai and chattai — and her eyes were sharp and bright. Who was she, and why did he feel as if he had known her for many lifetimes? Why did she look so familiar? Was it those eyes that he had seen before? He wasn't sure, but he followed her anyway, running as fast as he could down the valley, till he lost sight of her. But then the scent of something heavenly wafting past his nose distracted him. That was when he noticed the flowers. White bunches of Brahmakamalam in full bloom, their soft white inner petals a tender yet manifest contrast to their spiky outer ones. He reached out to touch the delicate flowers and the perfume entered his nostrils, the fragrance like none he had ever smelled, a gift from heaven. "Hmmm…" he sighed out loud, unable to contain himself. Smiling, he drifted into an even deeper sleep.*

Mahadevan woke up early, hoping to enjoy the cool morning before the events of the day unfolded. As he stepped out, he smelled a perfume so different from anything he ever smelt, somewhat like jasmine but not quite. He followed the scent and came to the corner of the verandah.

There under the plant was young Kandu fast asleep, a smile on his face, his head nestled on a cushion. In his hand, he was clutching a flashlight. All around his face were soft white petals fallen from the plant, which loomed above his sleeping face. Mahadevan scooped him up and carried him indoors. Then he returned almost immediately to the verandah to collect the fallen petals, which he took back to Kandu's room and arranged on his pillow all around his head. He watched his son, innocent in sleep, with a smile on his face.

'*Sleep, my darling and continue to dream; and may all your dreams come true. May love surround you like these soft petals at all times.*'

Kandu opened one eye and looked at his father, then turned and sank into an even deeper slumber.

# CHAPTER 41 – DHARMAMBAL
## RANGPUR— JULY, 1935

Dharmu sat outside in the corner of the verandah, drying her hair. The whole ritual of *dhuno* complete, she rested with her hair almost like a halo around her head, enjoying the warmth of the morning sun, as it dried out every last bit of moisture. The air was drier than usual although it was almost noon, so she was determined to make full use of that. She sorted through the mail and was thrilled to find Amma's letter. Her writing was difficult to read because Amma had no formal education and she wrote phonetically, just as if she were speaking. Tamil was a complicated language and did not have a phonetic base, so what one wrote was quite different from how one pronounced it. Reading the letter became a very complicated process, requiring her to decipher what Amma intended to say but Dharmu didn't mind that. She loved getting letters from home.

*My dearest Dharmu,*
*I know you left this time with a heavy heart. I wish that circumstances had been different and I was not forced to share my secret with you. I hope you did not tell anyone about it, especially not the children. They are too young to understand and I want them to respect their grandfather no matter what. It was wrong of me to break down like that and burden you with things you cannot begin to understand.*
*As for me, life goes on. I have trouble reading and the bright lights upset me. I had thick curtains put up in my bedroom window and I stay in my room in the afternoons, which keeps the headaches away. I keep myself busy with household matters. Your father is here at least three nights a week and I cherish my time with him. He is good to me — what more can I*

294

*ask for? I went to the jewelers in Dindigul and chose a beautiful uncut
ruby necklace, which I am sure you will love. He bought it for me for
Pongal.*

*Don't judge your father too harshly. He is a good father and a good
husband. Just because he has another wife does not mean he becomes a bad
father. He has always taken very good care of you and Venkat, and you
must always remember that. You are fortunate to have a very good
husband, which keep in mind, your father chose for you. He always has
your wellbeing foremost in his mind. Don't fret about me, I will be alright.
Now that I have shared my thoughts with you, I definitely feel lighter. You
don't dwell on it. Occupy your time and mind with your family. I long to
see you again.*

*Your loving mother,*
*Gayatri*

Dharmu put down the letter. Amma was right. It was almost as if
she could read minds. Ever since her return to Rangpur, Dharmu
thought all the time about her father, hating him for doing this to her
mother, hating the thought that she had brothers and sisters who were
not born of her mother. But Amma was right about him being a good
father. Never did she lack anything in her life. She was blessed in her
mother's and her husband's home. She should not think of him with
so much revulsion. If only she could talk about it to someone she
might feel lighter but she had no one; no friends or close relatives, so it
stayed in her heart festering till it erupted in anger, always directed
towards her children. Her mood had been deeply affected after her
return to Rangpur. For one, she did not like being here, and then all
these things happened in Dindigul, which she had to keep bottled up
inside for more than six months, adding to her already depressed state.
She certainly couldn't shout at Mahadevan, so it was the kids, especially
the girls, who bore the brunt of her anger. Poor things, it was not their
fault. She told herself that from now on she would be more patient and
not lash out inconsiderately. Just then, Vani walked into the verandah
with tears streaming down her cheeks. She was playing nervously with
the end of her hair and wiping away tears that would not stop flowing
down her pallid cheeks.

# When the Lotus Blooms

*What now?'* thought Dharmu to herself. She felt irritated and wanted to shake Vani and say, *'Stop it, stop crying! What is it you want from me?'* But thankfully, the words stayed only in her inner mind.

"Mummy, I am bleeding. I think I have my menses," she said, a look of terror in her eyes as she resumed crying.

It was almost on the tip of her tongue to say, *'Call Meera,'* but she bit the words back. She needed to take care of this. This was one job she ought not to delegate to Meera. No matter how hard it was, she had to get up and comfort her daughter. For all these years she had become so accustomed to other people around her taking care of things, she did not know what to do. Dharmu got up and held Vani close, till her small body calmed down and then the two of them walked to the bathroom. Once Dharmu reached the bathroom, she had to call Meera, because she had no idea where to get the cloth and what to do next.

"Meera, *kahaan ho?*" she yelled.

"No Mummy, don't tell Meera. I don't want anyone to know."

"Vani, if we were in the village, then we would have to call the whole village and tell them about your condition, so be thankful it is only Meera."

Once Meera arrived, with her usual efficiency, she found plain cotton cloth from a discarded petticoat and showed Vani what to do as Dharmu mutely watched.

The children were growing up. They really needed to move away from Rangpur soon. They needed formal education and soon Dharmu would have to look for a suitable boy for Vani. The very thought was too overwhelming and Dharmu needed to lie down. With Vani in Meera's confident care, Dharmu escaped to the sanctuary of her own room and lay down. She didn't quite understand what she felt, an inexplicable sadness, a gloom that nothing seemed to alleviate. She could not complain about anything lacking in her life. She had everything but still she felt a void, an empty space with no noise, no music and no movement, which left her listless and unwilling to do anything. If she could only figure out what it was that made her so sad, she might find some remedy but she hadn't the first idea what it would take to make the day brighter. The girls annoyed her. They seemed to want something all the time. Why couldn't they just leave her alone? Did Vani have to choose this particular time to get her period? Even Kandu's sprightly presence irritated her. She had no idea what was happening but she knew she did not feel all right. At night she would wait to see if Mahadevan reached out for her, but these last few weeks he came home so tired from work he went to sleep almost immediately after dinner. Every evening she would dress up and wait for him but he scarcely noticed her. Was this how it was with every married couple? She had no idea and no one to clear her own clouded mind, which was filled with a million nebulous questions.

She got up and walked into the living room, thinking about what she could do next. On top of the rosewood side board her gaze fell on a decanter of whiskey. The light streaming in through the window shone directly on the cutglass bottle, its bright reflections dancing around the room. So many times Mahadevan had offered her a glass of wine with her meal but she never wanted to take it and he never insisted. The one time she tried a sip of wine made her sick to her stomach. But today, she didn't know why, she moved without her own volition towards the bottle. For some time, she just looked at the bright lights and the colorful reflections. Then she took out a glass and poured a little whiskey into it. She lifted the glass almost in slow motion and brought it up to her nose. The pungent smell almost overpowered her and she turned her face away in revulsion. No way could she drink this disgusting stuff! Her arm moved to place the glass on the table, when suddenly she brought the glass up to her lips and swallowed its contents in one gulp. The alcohol burned her throat and she could feel the fiery sensation follow its route through her gullet to her stomach. She was shocked at her own impetuous act and scared about what might follow. Her heart was hammering and her face felt flushed and hot. Almost immediately her legs felt wobbly and as she took a few tremulous steps, she needed to hold onto the cabinet to steady herself. Then, in slow, shuffling, unsteady steps, she found her way back into her room. As she lay down, she noticed a certain lightheadedness. The pain racking her soul just a few minutes ago seemed to wane into oblivion. She felt as if she were floating. Dharmu closed her eyes but the swaying continued, almost as if she were on a boat, buffeted in stormy waves. But inside, a sudden calm took over her, obliterating everything else. Suddenly, it did not matter if her children existed or her husband made love to her or for that matter if her father slept with half the women in the village. She felt good, suspended on the edge of reality, swaying to a new undiscovered rhythm and she found herself humming a tune, something she had not done in weeks. Everything was fine, everything was all right. This was wonderful. As she sank into a deeper stupor, her lids felt heavy and she succumbed to this heavenly feeling of floating into a deep, dark slumber.

## CHAPTER 42 – KANDU
### RANGPUR – 1935

"Give up? ... Give up?"

Kandu pinned the chowkidar on the floor and sat astride on top of him, with his toy gun held to the poor man's head. They had been playing *chor police* for the last hour and of course Kandu was always the good guy, although judging by his behavior lately, he should have been the "chor." Twice he tore up Rukku's homework and was punished because he drew a moustache and beard on all of Vani's Women's World book covers. The women looked silly anyway, with their yellow bobbed hair and the moustache was really not such a bad idea. This morning, the bearer's wife complained that baba had put two cockroaches into her pot of boiling *dal* and of course, Mrs. Bowler also was at the receiving end of Kandu's unstoppable mischief. It was particularly bad for her because cockroaches were Kandu's latest discovery and she was scared stiff of them, which made her an easy target. Everyone was petrified of them and Kandu was having the best time of his life. That was until last night when Daddy gave him a sound beating after Rukku dashed hysterically into the room after discovering two live cockroaches under her covers. It was getting impossible to control him. Mahadevan could not figure out what was happening of late to make Kandu's behavior so incorrigible.

Kandu wandered into the house shouting for Mummy but as usual she was fast asleep on her bed. Kandu scowled as he shook her, trying to awaken her. But she would not stir, no matter what he did. He was angry that of late Mummy was always sleeping, always tired, always nursing a headache, always telling him to go find Meera. He didn't want Meera, he wanted Mummy. When Daddy came home, it was so

299

late he was almost asleep and could not be with him. Vani and Rukku always told him to get lost, but where should he go? With no other friends, he lived in a state of perpetual boredom. Maybe if he put cockroaches in Mummy's bed, she would wake up and take notice of him but he didn't dare do that. Not after the beating he got last night. Despondently, he walked into Vani's room, hoping she was in a good mood but he was out of luck.

"Vani, will you play with me?"

"Go away, stupid, don't bother me," she said harshly. Her romance novel was way too interesting to tear herself away.

"Go away, stupid, don't bother me," he aped, and ran to find Rukku. She was still mad with him after the cockroach incident.

"Don't you dare come near me, or I will hit you with a stick," she threatened.

"Sorry, Rukku, I won't put cockroaches any more in your bed. Please play with me," he pleaded. He was really bored and very sorry about his behavior.

"Why? Where is your dear Mummy?"

"Sleeping again," he replied dejectedly.

"I know, isn't it strange how much she has been sleeping lately?"

"I'm tired of her 'Go find Meera, go find Meera.' She doesn't say anything else."

"Welcome to our life. We have been finding Meera for a long time."

"Come, let's play."

"What do you want to play?"

"Hide and Seek?"

"Ok, you're it," and saying so, Rukku ran out of the room to hide.

"One two three...hundred," said Kandu, reaching one hundred surprisingly soon. Anyway, Rukku was out of the room and couldn't hear him. He walked into the study and almost immediately spotted Rukku's feet sticking out under the drapes. Both of them screamed in delight and then it was Kandu's turn to hide. He went into the living room and hid behind the sofa. Almost immediately, he heard a noise and crept down low, knowing someone was in the room. It couldn't be Rukku; she would have called out his name by now. He peeped out and saw Mummy. He almost called out to her but something stopped him. Mummy was by the rosewood side table, pouring the colored drink from the decanter into a glass. She gulped it down and poured another shot. What was she doing?

"Mummy," he cried out. "What are you drinking? Is it whiskey?" Kandu knew the decanter held whiskey because he had seen Daddy drink from it on many previous occasions. Whenever he asked if he could have some, Daddy always said children could not drink whiskey. So then, how come Mummy was drinking whiskey?

"Kandu, what are you doing surprising me like that. I am not drinking anything," she said swaying a little, her speech slurring.

"Yes you are, I saw you drink two times."

Dharmu was annoyed that she had been caught. For two weeks now, she had taken a drink, then another and today, she was here drinking for the third time. If Mahadevan found out about her drinking like this during the day, he would be furious. He offered her wine on many occasions but he drank only one glass and that too, as a social drink before dinner. Mummy knew Kandu was a blabbermouth and needed to be shut up.

"Come here, Kandu. See here, you can't tell anyone what you saw. It is a secret between us. Okay? Just you and me."

"Not even Vani and Rukku?"

"No, not them, and definitely not Daddy."

"What about Mrs. Bowler?" Kandu now unnecessarily facetious.

"Now why would you want to share this news with Mrs. Bowler?"

"I don't know, supposing it slips out of my mouth?"

"No, Kandu, this is a special secret between us and you can't tell anyone."

"Ok, then will you play with me?"

"Go find Meera," said Dharmu weakly. Her legs were trembling, her head was hammering and she was in no condition to talk, let alone play.

"Go find Meera, go find Meera. You always tell me to go find Meera. I don't want Meera, I want you." Kandu realized he had the upper hand and was trying to get the best bargain, but Dharmu's head was throbbing and she didn't want to deal with Kandu.

"I'll play with you later," she said weakly.

"No!" screamed Kandu almost in her face, making her head hammer more painfully. Almost by reflex, Dharmu slapped him hard across his back. For a moment there was a stunned silence. Looking for Kandu's hiding place, Rukku, had observed everything from the doorway. She came and put her arms around Kandu, an accusing gaze locked on her mother.

"Oh no," thought Dharmu, this was getting out of control. She could bribe Kandu but the girls were a different story. Now god only knew what Rukku had seen or overheard.

Kandu didn't cry; he was too stunned. Never before had Mummy slapped him and now she had hit him with full force on his back. He looked at his mother in disbelief. His tender skin had four welts, red and angry, and he tried to reach the spot on his stinging back. Rukku turned her attention to him. "Does it hurt? Come let's find Meera, she will know how to make it better. Leave Mummy alone." She put her arm around Kandu and led him out of the room but he turned to throw one last bewildered look at his mother.

Dharmu sat down on the sofa, her head in her hands, crying uncontrollably. What had she done? What was happening to her? Mahadevan was sure to see the welts in the evening and there would definitely be a showdown. She could not hide her new habit forever. Now young Rukku was being the mother, while she had just behaved like a petulant child. She had to stop drinking. Maybe telling Mahadevan was not such a bad idea. Maybe he would help her to stop this disgusting habit. She was so absorbed in self-pity she cried continually till she passed out, right there on the sofa.

Rukku kissed Kandu's injured cheek as she pressed a damp cloth against it. "Poor Kandu, are you better now?"

Kandu nodded, enjoying the attention.

"I love you, Rukku," he said hugging her tight.

She hugged him back even tighter.

# Part XV
# Rajam

# CHAPTER 43 – RAJAM
## VIZHUPURAM – JANUARY, 1935

All preparations for the Pongal festival were completed. Sushila and Rajam had been busy all week getting things ready. They bought clothes for everyone in the family and enjoyed buying new saris for themselves, even though it was not customary to get new clothing for this particular festival. The whole town wore a festive look and homes were bustling with activity. Streets were swept and gutters cleaned and the town looked as if bathed by the first rains. Every dusty corner of each home now shone with cleanliness. New grain and produce arrived from Nagamma's land, although the quantity had dwindled significantly. The pongal would be cooked with new rice and lentils, while the old grain was stored in separate *kudhirs*. This was the time to check supplies and replenish the store room. The harvest was a bumper crop this year, and for a change the kudhirs all over town were overflowing with fresh rice, wheat, ragi, lentils, pulses, chillies and spices. All week, women had been busy clearing out and organizing their storerooms. Once that was done, they turned their attention to other parts of the house. Every room was dusted and scrubbed, cobwebs brushed, curtains washed and windows cleaned, and if they could afford it this year, they had their home whitewashed. Finally, the day before the festival, as in every home in town, the front thinnai was swept and washed, and fresh cow dung spread on the floor.

On the morning of the festival, the women were up before daybreak as usual and after a bath they went out to the front entrance and began the long and intricate task of making complicated kolams. The design for each kolam was unique, extending all the way across the street, and the women in each household competed against one another to see who had the most elaborate kolam. The planning began weeks in advance, getting all the materials together and deciding on the basic design. This year, Rajam and Sushila designed their kolam in the form of a lotus, decorating each petal with different colored rice, lining the outer shell with rows of dung lamps filled with oil. In the evening when they lit the lamps, the whole outline of the lotus would be illuminated. The men tied fresh banana leaves on either side of the front entrance, and in between garlands of mango leaves and orange marigolds formed a canopy. After sunrise, the clay pot with the rice and lentils would be put to boil. Nagamma was the major domo, busy barking directions to everyone. "Rajam, did you wash the clay panai nicely? Partha, move the garland a little to the right. Pattu, stop singing and cut the vegetables for the seven-curry *kootu*."

Finally everything was ready just the way Nagamma wanted it: the clay pot washed and anointed with turmeric and kumkumam, sugarcane leaves tied around it, the kolam completed except for a few final finishing touches, the banana leaves and marigold garlands hung, the seven vegetables cut and stewing in a rich, spicy, coconut curry, sugarcane chopped and ready to be eaten. The family had gathered in the back thinnai around the clay pongal paanai.

Everyone except Rajam. She was in the bathroom for the tenth time since she woke up this morning, checking to see if her period had come. Her stomach had been feeling queasy all morning and she was expecting to get her period, but so far her petticoat was unstained. This was really strange. Every month her period came like clockwork and it should have come three days ago but so far there had been no sign of it. She seemed to be cramping and felt an empty sick feeling at the pit of her stomach. She had been unable to drink her morning coffee for two days now, which was unusual, because as far back as she could remember, she never skipped her morning coffee. Somehow the coffee churned her stomach and she felt like throwing up. She probably had a bug from the food but there was no diarrhea, only this churning and emptiness in her stomach. Normally she had pain in her thighs two days before the onset of her period but so far she felt nothing. She was terribly anxious and felt a headache pulsing at the nape of her neck. As she stepped out of the bathroom to wash her feet, she heard everyone calling out her name and rushed into the thinnai to take her rightful place next to Partha.

# When the Lotus Blooms

Nagamma had already put the rice and lentils into the pongal paanai and Sushila added the jaggery. The fire beneath the pot was flaming, burning bright and strong as the men kept adding more firewood so the pongal could boil faster. Balu had his brass plate and spoon ready and waited impatiently for the pongal to boil over. The water simmered as Nagamma added the milk. She turned to the family. "Pray all of you that as this pot of pongal boils over, so does our life boil over with good events and happiness." She barely finished speaking when Balu noticed the pongal rapidly rising to the top of the clay pot.

*"Pongalo pongal!"* he yelled gleefully, hammering his spoon against the brass plate. Everyone shouted in unison, *"Pongalo pongal!"* clapping their hands and shouting as loudly as they could. Rajam stuck her tongue half out of her mouth, rapidly moving it from side to side in a warble louder than Sushila's. Balu looked at her and tried to mimic her, but no one could hear his soft voice amidst the din. Rapidly removing some sticks of the firewood from under the pot, Nagamma reduced the intensity of the flame. The evil spirits hovering around the house were sure to have been frightened away with the racket they made. Rajam closed her eyes and prayed for all bad events to end and for new happy moments to surround their lives. In her mind she knew she was only praying for that one elusive event to take place.

The day was going to be extremely busy. Since Rajam had not yet got her period, she decided to spend a few hours at the temple helping Savitri serve the temple prasaadham. But first, the pongal had to be made at home. The women went into the kitchen to finish the rest of the cooking. Somehow cooking for a festival was always enjoyable. For one, they prepared different food items than usual, which gave them a break from the mundane cooking. Today there would be no rasam and sambar but instead they would eat delicious veṇn pongal, shakkarai pongal and the seven-curry kootu. Just thinking of it made Rajam hungry but they could not taste a morsel until they placed the food in the altar and offered it to God.

Before noon, Rajam and Sushila were at the temple, carrying between them a large pot of shakkarai pongal that they had promised Savitri. The line for the holy prasaadham was long and the temple was milling with devotees all dressed in their new clothes. Everyone talked at the same time and the excitement and positive energy in the atmosphere was palpable. The temple was radiant, decorated with flowers — and just being here made one feel peaceful. The deity had been decorated with special care in a new maroon Kanjeevaram silk sari, adorned with temple jewelry. The air was thick with the smoke from the incense and camphor.

Savitri had been up for hours preparing the prasaadham for the devotees and she looked tired. She waved to Rajam and indicated with her eyes that she needed assistance. Rajam and Sushila took over the task for the next hour, allowing Savitri some respite. By late afternoon the temple doors had closed and Rajam and Savitri sat on the stone steps, exhausted from all the work. The silence was strange but definitely welcome after the hectic activity of the morning. Finally Savitri spoke. "How come you're here? You were so sure you would not be able to help me."

"I know, I have been waiting all morning to get my period but since it did not happen, I thought that I would come and help. Hey, I thought you would be grateful for the help."

"That I am. Where did Sushila go?"

"Back home I think."

"Oh gosh, I don't think I could eat another morsel. I have had about six helpings of shakkarai pongal already and I feel sick."

"So do I," said Rajam massaging her lower belly.

"Really? You feel sick? You don't think..." Rajam knew what she was about to say and she did not let her complete her thought.

"No I don't. I don't even want to hope. I know by the evening it will come, so don't say anything." Savitri was not convinced and continued to probe, not realizing Rajam was terribly superstitious and felt if you said something, just the opposite would happen.

"I don't know Rajam. How many days are you delayed by?"

"Three."

"You said you are never late."

"Maybe I have reached menopause. I feel old with all I have been through."

"Come on, Rajam, it's not that bad. Seriously, somehow I feel maybe this time..."

"Please Savitri don't say anything. I hate the disappointment that follows."

"I know, I won't say anything. Okay? Happy?" Savitri conceded, pinching Rajam's ample cheeks.

Rajam felt a twinge of pain at the base of her stomach as she got up to leave and she rushed out of the temple. She knew it was sinful to be anywhere near the temple if you had your period. As she walked into the side street, her stomach churned and she felt the bile rush into her mouth. She doubled over by the side of the road, holding the wall for support and all the pongal she had eaten found its way into the gutter by the roadside. She groaned loudly, holding her aching belly. The churning stopped but her legs felt weak and her head was spinning. She stood up slowly, waiting for the sensation to pass and then walked towards her house with slow, deliberate steps.

'*I should make a ginger kashayam to settle my stomach,*' she told herself as she entered the thinnai.

# CHAPTER 44 – VELANDI
## VIZHUPURAM

"Muniamma... Muniamma... wake up!" Velandi called out to her, softly rubbing her clammy forehead, pushing the damp hair away. Muniamma stirred and tried to open her eyes but her lids felt too heavy and she allowed them to droop, closing them once again. The fever had broken, leaving her weak and exhausted, unable to wake up even to eat. Velandi poured a few sips of water between her lips but Muniamma was hardly aware of his actions.

"Amma... Amma... get up, Amma!" Muniamma was barely aware that her little boy had been calling her repeatedly, trying to wake her up. Velandi's eyes filled up with tears. What was the point in feeling sad either for himself or his children? Until Muniamma recovered, he would have to take care of everything. Velandi picked up his youngest son and took him outside. He touched the child's forehead with trepidation but thankfully he had no fever.

"Nandu, Amma is not well. What do you need? Food?"

"I'm hungry. Tell Amma to wake up and make something to eat."

What could Amma make? There was nothing in the house. Velandi had to take care of his wife and could not go out to get any food. He had sent a message to Muniamma's mother, telling her to come as soon as possible but four days had passed and she had not arrived. It was hard having to do it all, working and feeding the small children, as well as taking care of Muniamma, and Velandi was drooping with fatigue. Only now he realized how much Muniamma did in the home, how many things she took care of. Not only did she do housework, she also worked in two homes, cleaning vessels and sweeping. Now ever since the baby, she had not gone to work and there was less money coming in. The children were amazingly patient, but they were young and needed their mother. Muniamma's breast milk ran dry and he gave the baby to a neighbor who recently delivered a baby and still had plenty of milk. Nandu, his oldest, was a great help but he was still a child and he could do only so much. If Muniamma's mother did not arrive soon, the situation would become unmanageable. Velandi closed his eyes and prayed fervently for Muniamma to recover.

"Amma needs her rest. Today is Pongal. I will bring back some delicious shakkarai pongal for you. Just now, drink water and go to sleep, and before you wake up I will be back with your food." Velandi hoped he was not too late to get food. Today, everyone would be waiting like hungry jackals to get the food before anyone else got to it. He knew he should hurry or he would be too late.

Velandi looked sadly at his wife. After the birth of the child, she had been confined to bed. She had been bleeding constantly and the old Amma from the next village came to see her. She gave her some kashayam to drink but nothing seemed to help. Muniamma was weak from hunger and malnutrition. Velandi felt tears well up in his eyes. What was the point of it all? How could he call himself a man? One month had gone by and no one in the house had eaten properly. The children were uncared for and he was so tired from everything that he was sometimes short with them. Why was everything so difficult? Why could life not give him some semblance of happiness? Just when he thought things were going well, everything changed, making mere existence a misery. He was so happy Muniamma's childbirth had gone well but now she was not recovering. What was he going to do? Why was God testing his faith? He did not ask for much. All he wanted was food at least once a day for his children but instead, every day became a challenge, with a scramble for one square meal. Sometimes he wished he did not have children so there would be no stress about food. But almost immediately he felt ashamed that such thoughts had entered his mind. His children gave him so much pleasure; it was a crime to wish they didn't exist.

God alone knows why such an evil thought entered his mind. Perhaps it was the constant hunger gnawing away at his insides, playing tricks on his mind. Hunger was strange. It began as a mere rumble in his stomach and then his insides churned, making it impossible for him to think straight, until it felt as if an enormous, unending gnawing pit had replaced his stomach. No matter how much he ate, the hunger was back like an evil spirit to haunt him the next day. No amount of food could exorcise this insatiate spirit. It was an evil curse his kind cohabited with. Living with hunger constantly made him wonder if hunger was his friend or enemy. Its unappeasable pangs constantly tore away at his innards but yet, whenever he ate, he had so much appreciation for the Almighty who blessed him that day with a full stomach. Hunger he could live with but he could not think about what life would be like without Muniamma. As soon as the thought entered his mind, he pushed it into the farthest recesses of his subconscious, not wanting the angels to dwell on such a chilling predicament.

He washed his face, ridding himself of this distasteful thought and prepared to leave for work. It was early but he needed to be in town at daybreak to be guaranteed food. He walked into the hut one last time and crouched down next to Muniamma. Her forehead was cool but her breath was coming in sharp, shallow gasps and her stomach heaved with each strained breath. Today he would send another message to her mother. Why had she not come as yet? Once he left, there would be no one with the children till noon. He soaked a piece of cloth in cold water and woke up Nandu.

"Nandu, keep this on your mother's forehead and keep wetting it and putting it on again every few hours. And don't forget to give her water."

"Appa, is there anything to eat?"

"Soon, Nandu, I need to go to work and bring back some food. Take care of your mother till I get home."

With a heavy heart Velandi walked briskly toward the Brahmin Agrahaaram. After the gloom in his wretched hut, the village looked bright and clean. He spent all of last week cleaning the village along with his fellow parayans and everything looked so festive, a sharp contrast to his state of mind. He could hear the cries of *"Pongalo pongal"* from several houses. He had to wait until after the families ate before he could hope to get any leftovers. Almost mechanically he made his way down the street cleaning latrine after filthy latrine, soiling his hands and body as he made things sanitary for others. He just finished cleaning the latrine at Nagamma's home and from the back he saw the family congregated in the thinnai. How happy they looked. What did they do to get all of this? He was angry with the whole world for having so much when he had nothing. He watched the child, chubby and well fed, with plump shivering jowls as he vigorously banged the

311

spoon against the plate. He was quite sure this boy never knew the meaning of the word hunger. He thought of his own children, gaunt and filthy, scantily dressed in soiled tattered clothing and another wave of anger swept over his whole being. He looked at the beautiful young girl standing behind her strapping husband. She was so beautiful, like an *apsara* in *Indra's* court. She was kind too. Many times she left clothing for him along with the leftovers. He saw her turn and head for the bathroom and he ran out, not wanting to get caught spying on the family. Just as he closed the back door he heard her call out to him.

"Velandi, come back in an hour. I will have food for you." And she was true to her word. He was back in an hour and only had to wait a few minutes before she came out and kept the folded banana leaf on the floor. He waited till she left and pounced on it tearing the leaf in his urgency to see what she had given him. There was venn pongal, kootu and shakkarai pongal; just the sight of the food brought saliva painfully into his mouth and he was tempted to take a small bite but then his self-control prevailed and before he was hit by another wave of temptation, he picked up the food and ran home.

When he entered the hut, it was dark. The children were still sleeping. He went up to Muniamma and picked up a handful of pongal.

"Muniamma, wake up, see what I have for you." But she wouldn't stir. He tried to pry open her mouth but he could not get her to open it. He was too late. Fever, weakness and malnourishment had laid prior claim on Muniamma's life.

*A cold fear gripped him and he felt his bowels release.* The pongal slipped from his hand and splattered on the floor. He let out a long, unending wail. The only sound that could be heard in the hut was his heart wrenching, lamenting.

# CHAPTER 45 – SUSHILA
## VIZHUPURAM – FEBRUARY, 1935

"Sushila, Sushila, where are you?" Siva returned home early from work and appeared agitated as he searched for Sushila. His voice sounded urgent and his face wore a worried look. Recently, he had been travelling a great deal in his new job as a salesman. His work took him to remote villages in Tamil Nadu and he was away from home for over twenty days in a month. He constantly complained that, considering the amount he travelled, his remuneration was a pittance, which was a problem, especially since a large portion of the financial burden of maintaining the family was his.

Somehow Sushila felt uneasy when he travelled. Twice she had seen kumkumam stains on his white shirts. She herself used only a deep maroon color and these stains were in different colors. In her mind was that niggling doubt about his fidelity but she was too scared to even allow the thought to express itself. Fidelity was a rare breed and women needed to live several lives and gain good karma to get a man who was completely faithful. She was Siva's second wife and knew she was not his first woman. She accepted that he had shared the bed with his previous wife, but prostitutes? Just the thought made her shiver. All kinds of debauched images of street prostitutes and devadasis dressed in gaudy *mitthai* pink saris drove her crazy every time she saw the telltale kumkumam stains. She was too scared to broach the subject with him, fearing his response. It was easier to merely ignore that part of his life. Pretending she did not know dulled the pain of rejection. When he slept with her, her mind was filled with images of him coupling with fat prostitutes and she hated that part of her life. But what was the point of knowing the squalid details of his meanderings? It would only intensify her pain and make it impossible

313

for her to talk to him normally but more importantly, continue to respect him. The kumkumam marks and the cloying smell of cheap perfume on his unwashed shirts made her sad and angry simultaneously. She knew he had a roving eye but there was precious little she could do about it.

Siva obviously didn't particularly care if she knew, or he would have taken care to remove all overt signs of his unfaithfulness. Not that she could openly discuss and air her doubts. Doing that would only confirm her suspicions, making it a reality and not just a figment of her imagination. In any case, how would it benefit her to know? Could she leave him or make him stop doing what he did? No, that was not possible. Some people were born with these tendencies and no matter how good or beautiful their wives were, they would still go to other women. It was like a disease or addiction. If he continued on this path, it was only a matter of time before he contracted some dreadful disease. Every time she slept with him, she waited for boils to appear in her groin but she had been lucky so far. It was peaceful when he travelled, even though she knew what he was doing. But when he returned, the tension became intolerable. Why was it that only men could take lovers? Why could she not do the same? But it was no use thinking about such things. Here under Nagamma's eagle eye she could do nothing except suffer in silence. *'One day,'* she told herself, *'I will make him suffer the same pain.'*

"Sushila, where the hell are you?" Siva sounded annoyed that she didn't respond to his first call. She hurried outside, wiping her hands on her sari.

"Come on. How many times do I need to call you?"

"My hands were dirty and I needed to clean them," she said apologetically.

"Come to the terrace, I have something to discuss with you," he said leading the way up the stairs.

*Discuss, not instruct?* She thought to herself. *This is a first.* They sat on the charpoy making sure no one was snooping around to overhear their conversation.

"I have got a job in Madras with a Japanese company and I join next month."

"But what about your parents?" Sushila knew the eldest son was primarily responsible for the family and this news would break the family apart.

Siva looked visibly annoyed at her question. He knew very well he was abandoning the family at their time of need. "I can't take them. I have run this household for so many years, now let Partha take care." Siva did not want to answer her questions. What he was doing was selfish and there was really no justification to his actions.

"But why the urgency?" In spite of everything, Sushila did not want to be the one to break the family apart.

"Amma has lost all her money and she wants me to sign the insolvency papers."

"So? Why don't you sign them?"

"Are you stupid? If I sign them then no one will hire me again and my entire future will be at risk."

"But how can we just abandon them? What will they do?"

"I don't know and frankly I don't care. I am tired of supporting this household and I need a break." Sushila was shocked at his rationale. "*Yenna*, that is not correct. After all, your mother has cared for you for so many years."

"If you love her so much, then you stay. I have made up my mind. I leave in two weeks."

"Have you told her about this?"

"Not yet, but I will. I wanted to tell you first." If Siva wanted her approval, then he was in for a surprise because she could not support him openly and still hope to be part of the family.

"You said we would discuss it, but it looks like you have made up your mind, so what is the point of talking further? I feel guilty abandoning the family. What will they do? Partha does not earn enough." Siva was quiet; he felt guilty too but he was tired of being the sole supporter for the family.

"Let us go to Madras first and then I can think about my brothers. But first, I have to think of myself and my interests."

"*Yenna*, we can't break this family up. Whatever happens, you are the oldest and it is your responsibility to take care of the family."

"While my father sits around doing nothing?"

"Forget your father; he's old. Think about your mother and your brothers."

"Okay, okay, stop lecturing me. I don't need my wife to tell me what to do." Sushila became silent. Siva looked troubled. This was a difficult decision and he had to make a tough choice. His mind was racing. "I won't sign the insolvency papers. Let Partha do it." He looked quizzically at her. But Sushila said nothing.

"I will talk to Amma in the evening. I leave in two weeks and you can join me in a few months when I find a house." Siva departed, leaving Sushila confused. She sat down, her thoughts in turmoil. On the one hand, she was excited about leaving the village and moving to the city. Moreover, she would have her own home and be free from Nagamma's clutches. But then, there was this overwhelming sense of guilt at abandoning the family. Anyway, this was not her decision to make; it was Siva's and if anyone should be guilty it was he. If he felt no remorse, then why should she care? She was going to be free.

Her thoughts were interrupted by the sound of someone retching. She peered over the side and saw Rajam bent over throwing up. What was wrong? Was she sick or was it possible…? Mentally she counted the days back to when she had spoken to her the last time she got her period. It was over forty days.

Good heavens! Rajam was pregnant!!

# Part XVI
# Dharmu

# CHAPTER 46 – MAHADEVAN
## RANGPUR – AUGUST, 1935

Mahadevan poured himself a scotch and water and was on his way to the verandah to enjoy a drink when he noticed a substantial drop in the level of the whisky decanter. He looked closely again. Yes, the level had fallen by at least four inches. That was strange! Last week he noticed the same thing but Dharmu said the servant had tipped over the bottle while dusting. He did not remember drinking after topping up the decanter the last time, so how come the low level?

"Dharmu where are you?" he yelled, walking into the bedroom, only to find his wife fast asleep. He glanced at his pocket watch. It was a little past nine. "What? Sleeping again?" He muttered a few expletives under his breath, turned around and walked towards the kitchen, thinking that he may as well ask the bearer what had happened. Fool, dropping precious whiskey!

"Gautam… Gautam…" he called out, his voice visibly irritated.

*"Aaya Saab,"* was the reply as Gautam rushed into the living room.

"Did you drop the whiskey bottle again this week?"

"No Saab, I am always very careful while dusting. I have never dropped it."

"Then have you been drinking from the bottle?"

Gautam's face turned red with indignation. He had tried the whiskey once and found it too smooth for his liking. Frankly, he preferred the strong smell of country liquor.

"No Saab," he said pulling his earlobes, "I would never touch it."

Mahadevan was so busy arguing with Gautam, he didn't notice Kandu saunter into the living room dressed for sleep in his crisply starched and ironed white pajama-kurta. For a while, Kandu did not

318

pay attention to the heated conversation but it didn't take him long to figure things out.

"Daddy, what happened?"

"Nothing to do with you, Kandu. I am trying to solve the mystery of my whiskey disappearing."

"What mystery? Mummy drinks it." The words slipped out of his mouth before he could take them back. Kandu knew he had put his foot in it and now Mummy would be mad with him for telling tales. He covered his mouth with his hands and looked soulfully at his father, his eyes filled with remorse at his own impetuousness. A stunned silence followed as Mahadevan digested this piece of information. Kandu fibbed at times but his response was almost immediate and by the look on his face, Kandu was not lying. But Mahadevan still needed to be sure. "What do you mean Kandu? Don't talk nonsense."

"No Daddy, it's not nonsense. I have seen her drinking from the bottle many times. If you don't believe me, ask Rukku." Kandu was too petrified now to speak anything but the truth. Mahadevan realized that and he sat down on the sofa, stunned and speechless.

On cross examining Kandu, the story emerged and unfolded. The drinking, the sleeping suddenly made sense. When Kandu showed him the fading red welts on his back from when he was beaten, Mahadevan was truly distressed that he had not noticed it earlier. What happened in the last couple of weeks to affect Dharmu in this disturbing way? How did it totally escape his attention?

Mahadevan was nonplussed. How should he react? He could not believe that in such a short time Dharmu had drunk so much whiskey. No wonder she slept so much. If he had come close to her, he would have smelled it on her breath but these last couple of weeks were so busy he returned home way after Dharmu had retired to bed. By the time he came to bed it was early morning and he had no inclination to do anything but sleep. He was angry with her for behaving this way. After all that he did to provide for her: giving her a large house with a retinue of servants. Her only responsibility was to be a good mother and care for the children. How dare she drink so heavily? How dare she beat Kandu? He got up from the sofa and strode out of the room, ready to wake her up and beat some sense into her.

Kandu recognized his intention and ran after his father wailing loudly. "Daddy, no Daddy, don't get angry with her… Daddy leave her alone." Kandu was on the floor holding on to his father's leg, weeping uncontrollably. Mahadevan stopped in his tracks and stooped to pick up his son, hugging and kissing away the tears from his face. In between hiccupping and the tears, Kandu pleaded with his father.

"Daddy, don't get angry with Mummy. She will know… th…that I told you… and then … again she will b… b…beat me."

"No Kandu, don't cry. I am not angry. I won't say anything to Mummy. Don't ever think you will be in trouble if you tell me the truth. No one can ever punish you for that." Mahadevan rocked him gently in his arms and carried him to bed. Kandu's arms were tightly locked around his father's neck, forcing Mahadevan to lie down next to him.

What a mess! A disturbed child, a wayward mother and an absent father.

As Kandu slipped into slumber, Mahadevan unlocked his son's limp arms from around his neck and slowly got up. Dharmu's snores from the other room disgusted him. She had slept through all of this. In a way it was a good thing Kandu had stopped him from waking Dharmu, given his mental condition at the time. He would surely have slapped her in front of the child and that would have traumatized Kandu further, creating more complications. He was not violent by nature but knowing that his wife, a conservative Brahmin woman, could actually drink till she was intoxicated, made him furious. He was not opposed to drinking *per se*, and had offered Dharmu a glass of wine on many occasions, but knocking back a couple of pegs of whiskey was a far cry from downing half a bottle. Maybe it was his fault. After all, if not for his influence, she wouldn't dream of drinking. Heavens, this was terrible! How should he deal with it? What should he say? His confusion was unfamiliar. Normally so clear thinking, he couldn't imagine reacting as emotionally as he was doing right now. Work was work and one could be dispassionate about it — but family? That was much closer to the heart.

Despondently, he sat down on the rocking chair in his study and began chanting verses from the Bhagavad Gita. He needed to calm himself, to get some perspective or else things would go out of control. Tomorrow he would tackle the situation with a cool head.

## CHAPTER 47 – DHARMAMBAL
### RANGPUR – THE NEXT MORNING

Dharmu could barely open her eyes but the hammering in her head woke her up, making her sharply aware of the pressure on her bladder. With much difficulty she staggered to the bathroom, each agonizing step tempting her back to the comfort of her bed. The chamber pot was full and the toilet smelt disgusting! Somewhere in the deepest recesses of her brain, she could hear the birds chirping, the sound wafting in through the window, but each sound jangled and reverberated in her throbbing brain. She recoiled at her image in the mirror: her bloodshot eyes, messy hair and coated tongue disgusted her. Her grey tongue looked and felt as though layers of muck had settled on it. Walking painfully to bed, she opened the drawer and took out the balm for her headache. Its strong camphor scent would help relieve the pain.

Still early in the day, she could not hear any noises from the kitchen. Heaven knew what the exact time was, but no one in the household had stirred. The hammering in her cranium sounded as though someone were playing a *mridangam* and *thavil jugalbandi* inside her head, except that everything was out of sync. Each side of her brain seemed to be acting independently of the other, making her heart beat at two different rhythms and the cacophony was driving her crazy. And to her agony, she wanted to urinate again. If only she could go back to sleep. She wanted to sleep forever because waking up meant encountering Mahadevan and she was in no condition for that. Why was life so complicated? What if Kandu had mentioned yesterday's incident? A shiver went down her spine. She hoped against hope that Mahadevan hadn't seen the angry welts on Kandu's back. That foolish child had a big mouth. He was sure to tell his darling father. She

321

groaned loudly. It hurt even to think. Maybe she should have another shot of whiskey to ease the pain.

She stepped out of her room, stopping to listen for any sounds, as she made her way to the living room. In addition to the darkness, her eyes were foggy and unfocused but she could still perceive the outline of the decanter. Divine sleep inducing whiskey! What a discovery! Capable of obliterating any pain and drowning you in deep, comforting sleep. She could hear the sound of breathing coming from the study. She tiptoed across, swaying and confused, and peeped in. Mahadevan was fast asleep in his rocking chair, his mouth slightly open and his head askew. What if he woke up? No, that wouldn't happen. She would be as quiet as possible. It was one measly drink anyway. After this, she would never drink again. Just this once it would be nice to feel the exhilarating liquid burn down her gullet and then in a bit, she would be fast asleep.

The living room was darker than she hoped and she was wobbly, hung over and sleepy, and to her horror, she bumped into the corner table. Damn! It made a piercing noise as the legs of the table creaked across the wooden floor. Dharmu held the table to steady herself, not daring to breathe. Damn, damn, damn! Why did she have to bump into the table right now? Why was it so dark? Was it her imagination or did sounds become louder in the dark?

She waited, half bent over the corner table, straining to hear if the noise had woken Mahadevan. She could only hear the comforting sound of even breathing, and emboldened, sure that no one had been disturbed, she walked to the side board and slowly pulled on the crystal cork. Dharmu reveled in the sound of the pouring whiskey, similar to the waters of the Kutralam Falls. Yes, sounds were definitely much louder in the dark.

She brought the glass tantalizingly to her lips, when a hand clamped her wrist. She looked up, stunned to see Mahadevan, who pried the glass out of her quivering grasp. Dharmu stared at him, shaking uncontrollably and then, thankfully, the whole world went dark.

When Dharmu opened her eyes she was lying on her bed and Mahadevan was dabbing her hot forehead with a damp cloth. She cringed in shame. And the quivering resumed with greater intensity. She waited for his admonishment but he remained silent and completely calm.

"Say something," she pleaded.

Mahadevan's eyes were clear and cold and he knew that now was not the best time to chastise her. "No, Dharmu, not now. You sleep. We will talk later."

"Later? No, not later. Please say something. Slap me! Do something! Oh, dear God, please take me away." The tears of self-pity flowed down her pallid cheeks, wetting the white pillow cover. Just then Meera walked in with a drink.

"Come drink this; it will take the headache away and make you sleep."

She swallowed the nasty liquid in one gulp and convulsed into a bout of coughing.

"Sleep now. I will see you in the evening." Mahadevan pulled the curtains close and instructed Meera to watch over Dharmu.

"Sleep? I can't sleep. I want to die," she said burying her head in the pillow in shame.

"No Dharmu, you won't die, not now at least, but you will sleep, and when you wake up, you will feel better."

She did not know how long she slept but when she opened her eyes she could see the rays of the setting sun making designs on the ceiling as they bounced off the glass panes. "Meera?" she called out, and Meera was in the door almost as soon as the words left her mouth. "Has Saab returned?"

"No Memsahib, but he said to give you some ginger tea when you woke up. Shall I bring it now?"

"Yes, and bring me something to eat too." Her stomach was growling. She had not eaten for a whole day. She sat down in the verandah and stared vacantly into the distance. She felt empty. No thoughts, no feelings, just emptiness. Meera came in with a tray and set it down. Dharmu glanced at the tray. As she stared at the hot ginger tea and tomato sandwiches, the saliva painfully rushed into her mouth and she took her first ravenous bite.

She must have been sitting and nibbling for the better part of an hour when she heard the phaeton pull up at the gate. She tried to get up but her legs felt weak and she slopped down on the chair, helplessly gaping as the phaeton pulled in and Mahadevan stepped out. Her bloodshot eyes were filled with fear and remorse but she had no choice except to wait for what would follow, like a lamb to the slaughter.

323

Mahadevan came in and sat down next to her. The silence was uneasy and Dharmu, already nervous, broke out into a cold sweat.

"Banu is coming at the end of the week to be with you. I know you are waiting for me to shout at you but I am going to disappoint you. I realize that the fault is not yours, it is mine."

"Yours?" gulped Dharmu. "But I was the one drinking."

"I should have realized how unhappy you were. I should have been more caring but I have been so preoccupied with work. I know that it is a poor excuse for a negligent husband. I should have realized how lost you were, left all alone in this alien world. You sought release from your misery in a wrong way but all is not lost. I will help you get over this bad time and together we will make things better."

Dharmu could not believe what she was hearing. She had been dreading the worst but suddenly the dark clouds lifted and sunshine was pouring in. She let slip a nervous snicker and then realizing that she ought not to be laughing, unexpectedly found herself crying. Mahadevan sat next to her and cradled her head on his chest, rocking her back and forth as he urged her to calm down.

From the corner of the verandah, Kandu and Rukku watched, unnoticed by their parents. And they smiled at each other.

# CHAPTER 48 – MEERA
## RANGPUR

Meera could barely breathe. She held him in a close embrace, their hips locked, even after the passion had abated. She ran her arms across his smooth shoulders, feeling every muscle, drowning in the languor that set in after an almost violent act of copulation. Copulation. Just that. Not lovemaking, copulation. Two bodies, two motives but one single, burning, overwhelming desire. His body, which had been so enjoyable as he thrust lustily into her, was now dead weight and seemed to be sucking the life out of her as it lay limp across her naked form. She put her hands on his muscular shoulders, urging him to move so she could breathe.

"*Shoro... ogo shoro... jete hobe... shunchho?*" (Move...Hey move over. I have to go...can you hear me?)

Still recovering, he groaned and unwillingly moved off her, mumbling incoherently, "Meera, Meera, you drive me crazy." Then in a few minutes he was fast asleep.

She looked at his inert body and the mere sight of his black oily nakedness, his rugged, half shaven young face with its strong protruding jaw line, his tight and hard stomach muscles, his muscular thighs and his engorged manhood, made the heat spread once again in her loins. She turned her head away hastily, knowing that she needed to get back to the bungalow. She had stepped out only to use the bathroom when he accosted her, a pleasant and invigorating bathroom break, but she was in a rush to get back in case Kandu baba woke up. She put on her sari and blouse and quickly glanced at the mirror, smoothing down her unruly hair, forcing it into a tight bun. She stared at herself in the broken mirror as she attempted to reapply her *bindi* with red *sindoor*. In the heat of the lovemaking, the sindoor had spread all over her face and there were remnants on her cheeks and to her horror, on her white sari. But under the cover of darkness no one would see her now. She examined her unlined brow, her soft almond shaped eyes, her smooth tawny skin and her full lips. Yes, she still looked desirable, especially after the passion of the last few minutes. She was young. She still had beauty, zeal, ardor and love burning inside her. She was still alive!

When she entered Kandu baba's room, he was fast asleep. Thank God! She had been taking many chances lately and was lucky not to have been caught. Initially, she had delved into one wayward, exhilarating instance but this last month, she had been slipping out at least two or three times a week. He was like a drug and no matter how much she got, it was never enough; she wanted more. She lay down on her bedroll and as soon as her head touched the pillow, she felt that uneasy sensation again, a gnawing feeling at the pit of her stomach and she sat up gasping. Since Kamala died, nothing made sense anymore. She felt a nibbling emptiness eating away at her insides and whenever that happened, a violence erupted within her, making her want to smash everything around her. Of course, she couldn't; she merely fell back into bed, hammering her pillow repeatedly, crying till her tears dried out completely.

Meera had been unable to come to terms with Kamala's violent end. Death she was used to but every time she closed her eyes, the scene of Kamala's final moments flashed across her mind's eye. The pain, the fear, the sheer terror the child must have experienced would explode in her mind in images so real she could not tell if she were sleeping or awake. Knowing that her child had suffered so much made her death all the more difficult to bear. She tried to be brave and immerse herself in her work but the demons appeared at night when the household was quiet. She loved the children and Kandu baba's antics made her forget her own pain but the nights were unbearable. Everyone had been so compassionate with her initially but soon their patience for her melancholy had died out. No one wanted to hear about Kamala any more. Whenever she tried to talk about Kamala, they would make excuses about getting back to work . . . and soon enough, she got the message and stopped talking about her unfortunate daughter. Life was strange. Only a few months ago, Kamala had been living and breathing and filling her life with happiness, and now she had faded into a memory. Not talking about her could not erase Meera's pain. Kamala was her only child and now her life felt like an empty photo frame.

As her mind raced through the painful flashbacks, Meera locked her arms around herself and rocked back and forth. She had seen around nine harvests when she was married to her husband, who was several years older than she. No one really kept any account of a person's age, which was counted by the number of rice harvests they had seen. Meera's husband had seen nearly forty harvests and Meera was his second wife.

Almost immediately after marriage, he wasted no time in claiming his conjugal rights, tearing her so badly that Meera was sent home for six months till she healed. Her mother had little compassion for her pain, having gone through the same ordeal at about the same age. All children were married young and in these parts the girls stayed with their husbands, never going home until their first confinement at the time of childbirth. When Meera returned, her husband showed a little more consideration and was gentle with her. She had only had her menstrual period twice before conceiving Kamala. The birth of her daughter was the happiest time of her life, and comforted by a cooing baby strapped to her back, she didn't mind the housework and toiling in the fields. Somehow after Kamala's birth, she didn't conceive again. Everyone said she was infertile but she knew it was because of her husband's inability to perform, although she could not share this information with anyone. Now that she was in the prime of her womanhood, her husband had become infertile, impotent and old.

Hard work and a meager diet take its toll on people in these parts and they aged very quickly. Repulsed by her husband, Meera was thankful he had stopped forcing himself on her. His sunken cheeks and eyes made his nose stand out like an eagle's beak and the loose skin of his hollow chest hung over his protruding ribs. He ate only *kanji* and soft fish because he had lost most of his teeth. Heaven knows what disease caused this but his body was that of a man who had seen a hundred harvest moons.

When Meera left the village to find work in the city, she knew her husband was grateful for one less mouth to feed. Every month Meera returned, eager to spend a few precious hours with Kamala, but now that was gone and since Kamala's death, she had no desire to return to her village. Neither her presence nor her absence made any difference to anyone there. Here in the bungalow, nothing happened without her; one always heard Meera this and Meera that. She felt good to be needed. The children loved her but these were not her offspring. The mere thought that she had none of her own any more made her even more depressed. How nice it would be if she could only have another child; but how could that happen? When she was alone, thoughts of her loneliness and longing for a child consumed her and strangely, as these thoughts obsessed her, she found herself driven towards Kalia.

The gardener's aide spent hours toiling in the hot sun every day, his skin burned to an oily ebony — hence the name Kalia. Meera was so absorbed in her own misery, she hadn't noticed him until a few months ago. One night, she stepped out of the bungalow and was making her way to her hut when she saw someone drawing water from the well — someone powerfully built and very young. The subtle movements of muscles rippling under his sweaty skin as he pulled on the rope mesmerized her. She couldn't take her eyes off him, staring and taking in every part of his glorious body, as if a magical spell were cast over her. All these months of loneliness had suppressed her emotions, creating a sort of violence bubbling within her like a volcano waiting to erupt. She found her body suffused with heat, rising from her loins and rapidly spreading — an unfamiliar sensation that seemed to obliterate her pain and melancholia. She found herself walking towards him like a zombie. Alerted by the tinkle of her anklet bells, he looked at her for the first time. The moonlight shone off his body and he seemed a celestial gift, a heavenly offering against her pain. She dropped the *pallu* of her sari and exposed herself as his eyes undressed her. The chemistry was instant and unambiguous. He lifted her up, carried her into her room and then coarsely pulling up her sari, he pushed her up against the door and forced himself into her. Meera's head was swimming, caught up in the madness of the moment and even after he put her down and left the hut, she couldn't believe what had just happened. That was the first of their many rendezvous, stolen moments of passion, with the moon and the stars as their only witness. But Meera felt no guilt. She owed no one anything. She belonged to none. All she had to deal with were her own feelings, her own conscience. And nothing else could have felt more right.

# Part XVII
# Rajam

# CHAPTER 49 – RAJAM
## VIZHUPURAM – JULY, 1935

Rajam shielded her eyes from the strong rays of the setting sun as they pierced through the leaves of the banyan tree, blinding her momentarily. The summer had been unbearably hot and with the additional weight of the baby, she had low tolerance for heat. But on a more positive note, she had been relieved from the burden of heavy housework. Nagamma's benevolence was uncharacteristically thoughtful, stemming from her elation that her favorite son Partha was soon to be a father. This delight thankfully filtered down to Rajam, who incidentally happened to be carrying her grandchild. But Rajam wasn't going to complain. After so many years of harsh words, snide remarks and downright malice, this was a welcome respite. Nagamma was so thrilled when she first heard the wonderful news that she bought Rajam a new single stone diamond nose ring, even though she herself continued to wear a vepalai twig in her nose. Times were hard and almost all the land she owned was gone. They were very close to insolvency and there seemed to be no way out. To add to her problems, Sushila and Siva had moved out of the house and now Siva gave a paltry thirty rupees to Nagamma to run the house. Nagamma's son, Thambu, was still young but she was urging him to quit studying and find a job, as Partha earned very little as a schoolteacher and there were so many mouths to feed. Some days the family ate only *thayir shaadham*, rice with watered down yoghurt and pickle, but Nagamma always made a small portion of vegetables just for Rajam. The growing fetus needed nourishment.

Frankly, the expectation of a new arrival in the family was the single ray of sunshine in an otherwise cloudy sky. Nagamma took extra care of Rajam and although her manner was brusque and her comments indifferent, yet Rajam could tell that her feelings were real and her happiness heartfelt. In her own bizarre and constrained manner, Nagamma was exposing a softer side of her nature. Sometimes Rajam could not understand how someone who in the past had taken such pains to hurt her could alter so drastically on hearing the news of her pregnancy. Still, Rajam remained on guard, never knowing when this new behavior would drop and uncover the real Nagamma!

The best part was that she was spared from the cow dung routine, as Nagamma did not want to expose her to any infection in her delicate condition, unfortunately for Sushila who had consequently inherited this unpleasant chore. Now that Sushila was not around, Nagamma actually did it herself, making Rajam feel guilty but not guilty enough to offer to do it. If Rajam felt any negative energy at all, it was from Sushila. On hearing the good news, Sushila was quick to hug her and congratulate her but in her eyes, Rajam caught a glimpse of something else. She could have sworn it was jealousy but Sushila had no reason to be jealous, having such a nice husband with such a well paying job. Now she even had her own home and her own kitchen and was finally free from Nagamma's clutches. If anything, she should have felt compassion for Rajam for having to suffer Nagamma's presence through her pregnancy. Human nature has minimal appreciation for what one has and covets what is out of reach. Many times in the past Rajam had to remind herself of her good fortune whenever she was depressed about not conceiving. She had been so preoccupied with conceiving that now she felt as if she had nothing to do and even less to think about.

Her father sent her harmonium to her and she spent many hours practicing music and singing. Music was supposed to be good for the baby and if she sang a lot during her pregnancy, then the baby would imbibe the talent even before birth. Even Nagamma enjoyed the sound of the music and often when Rajam took a breather, she would hear Nagamma's booming voice asking her why she stopped. Rajam hoped that this change in their relationship would persist even after the birth of the baby.

The new leisure time provided many opportunities for Rajam to be alone with Partha, a rare privilege in the past but now commonplace. This evening they had strolled out to the calm and bountiful mangrove, where family problems were left behind, at least for the moment. A few weeks ago she had felt soft butterfly movements inside her stomach, an extraordinary fluttering sensation, reminding her of the tender life growing in her womb. Partha was terribly excited to feel these movements and constantly badgered Rajam to allow him to touch her stomach, stressing her out because of the family's constant presence. But here alone in the mangrove, Partha gleefully cradled his head in Rajam's lap and enjoyed a different sort of intimacy, this time with his unborn child.

"Hello, Kamu… can you hear me? I am your Appa," said Partha, attempting to send a message through her navel to his child, whom he affectionately named Kamu, short for Kamakshi.

"Don't come so close, it tickles. *Yenna*, how can the baby hear you?"

"Why? If she can hear your music, then why not my voice? I want her to know me. She is so close to you but she doesn't know her Appa yet, so I need to talk to her."

"But don't put your mouth on my stomach; it tickles," she said gently pushing him away. Reluctantly, he turned his head in Rajam's lap, looking up at the sky through the leafy foliage.

"After Kamu is a year old, we will have a baby boy and I will call him Karthik," boasted Partha.

"Don't plan so much. Let this baby be born and then we will think of another. And can you get off my lap now? It's so hot my thighs are wet."

"Ooh… let me see!" exclaimed Partha, enjoying Rajam's embarrassment whenever the conversation turned sexual.

"*Yenna*, you are so shameless," repeating what she must have said a million times over, pushing him off her onto the soft grass.

"Let me enjoy being with you here at least and stop pushing me away. I can't come near you at home in the day time because everyone is wandering around, and at night if I try anything, you push me away saying that it will harm the baby. I want to be near you and touch you. Is that so wrong? Why do you constantly push me away? Anyway, when you go to your parents' house next week, god knows what I will do till you return. I will probably be a raving lunatic by then."

Rajam felt bad. She didn't push him away to reject him. It wasn't acceptable for people to demonstrate their affection in public and pushing him away had become a habit. She saw his sulky face and burst out laughing.

"Come on now! Don't get angry with me. Did I tell you Amma wrote to me? She is so excited about celebrating my *Valaikaapu* ceremony, she has been making all kinds of preparations and is planning to invite the whole city. It's going to be so exciting. Kunju and the kids will be there and in any case, you will be there very soon for a whole week for the *Seemandham* ceremony, so why are you complaining?"

"But half the time will be spent celebrating the Seemandham and I won't be with you. Besides, I don't understand why you have to go so early."

"Amma says that the Valaikaapu is always performed in the seventh month. Unfortunately, Amma and Appa have moved to Chidambaram. Had they been here, I would have gone to their house for a week and come back home for the Seemandham. As it is, traveling is a risk, although I must admit that I have a good feeling about this baby. I have crossed the fifth month and things don't often go wrong after that."

"That's another thing: August is only your seventh month and I don't like you being tossed around in a vilvandi, even if it is only to and from the train station."

"Didn't I tell you? Appa has arranged for a police van, so I will arrive in Chidambaram like royalty with police escort."

"Ha! Trust him to pre-empt me. Looks like he's more concerned for you than I am."

"Of course, after all I am his *chella kutti*." The evening was very pleasant with a light breeze rustling the leaves and for a while no one spoke. Instead, they soaked in the energizing splendor of the outdoors, drenching themselves in the calm it created within them, though neither of them was especially aware of it.

"*Yenna*, what is insolvency?" Rajam asked voicing her thoughts.

"It means that you are bankrupt. That you have no money to repay your moneylenders."

"Have we borrowed from someone?"

"Yes from many 'ones,' but don't worry your head about it. You have the baby to think of. Let Amma and me handle that part."

"Have we lost everything?"

Partha paused before replying. He knew this was no time for Rajam to worry. She needed to be calm and happy no matter what.

Yet, he couldn't lie to her. She was his wife, his predicament was hers and she had a right to know what the future held in store for them. With reluctance, he answered her. "Yes."

"The house, the lands?"

"Yes to both."

Rajam looked worried. She had been hearing this word for a while but had no idea what it meant and what it would signify for the family. She had always been well off and never had to deal with poverty, the very thought of which petrified her. Now it all made sense: Siva running off, refusing to sign the papers and leaving the family in the lurch. Now her life, which was on the threshold of completeness, was teetering on the brink of ruin. How ironical. What would happen? Would she have to sell her vessels and jewelry? Where would they live and what would they do? What about the baby? How were they going to manage? Everything around her seemed to be crumbling and she didn't quite understand the ramifications of insolvency. All she cared about was the future of this child in her womb and now that seemed to be in jeopardy. Involuntarily, her hands went to her stomach in a protective gesture. She put her fingers under Partha's chin and turned his face up sharply to face her. "Are we poor? Tell me, are we going to be in the streets?"

"No Rajam, in fact we're rich." This was stupid. Here she was dead serious and Partha was joking and playing with her again. Rajam didn't understand what he meant till he qualified his statement a moment later.

"We have each other. That is enough. God will take care of the rest."

'Yes,' thought Rajam. 'That was true.' They were a family, and together they would face every challenge. Whatever happened, they had each other . . . and God, who was always there. After all, God never gave you a problem you couldn't handle. They would solve everything together and make this whole financial business a small, surmountable hurdle, and while doing so, they would enjoy themselves. The future promised to be exciting with so much to look forward to. Maybe the time for change was imminent. A new baby, a new home, so why should she be so fearful? Surprisingly, excitement had replaced her worry. What an amazing difference one reassuring statement could make.

# CHAPTER 50 – MANGALAM
## CHIDAMBARAM – AUGUST, 1935

Mangalam gasped in horror as looked at herself in the mirror. She had used too much turmeric powder while cleaning her face, creating an unnaturally bright yellow. She picked up the bottle of talcum powder and applied it feverishly, hoping to change it to a lighter shade of yellow. This was terrible! Today of all days she had to use turmeric. So many people were coming and she was going to look like a clown. She looked once again at herself and now her face had become a patchwork of yellow and white. This would never do. She couldn't face her guests looking like this. Now she would have to wash her face again. What a waste of time! As she ran out the back, she could see Parvathi busy in the kitchen speaking to the cook. Thank goodness for her. Heaven knows how she would have managed without her. The house was full with Kunju and her six children and Rajam. Parvathi was remarkably efficient and took over much of the housework. Thanks to this blessing, Mangalam could take complete care of the children, something she loved doing, so Kunju got a break from the bathing and changing and feeding. Mangalam grabbed the tin of shikakai and went across to the well, moistening the brown powder in her palm and then scrubbing her face till it turned raw. Wiping her face, she ran back in to her room to finish dressing.

At least seventy women were coming for lunch to celebrate Rajam's Valaikaapu — the Bangle ceremony that was celebrated in the seventh month of pregnancy — and they would be here in less than an hour. Rajam had bathed and worn her sari and was waiting for Mangalam to give her the jewelry. She wore a black Kanjeevaram sari with *jarigai oosi*, thin lines of woven gold thread. This was the only

335

occasion when a woman could actually wear a black sari, the color to ward off the evil eye and ensure a safe delivery. Satisfied that she had chosen a gorgeous sari, Mangalam also bought some complementary jewelry — a set made of black beads and gold. These black beads were considered auspicious, especially for married women. She had asked the bangle seller from the market to bring his best selection and Rajam and Kunju had a grand time selecting bangles. All sorts of glass bangles sparkled in the tray, some with gold work on them, some cut, others embossed, yet making the choice mind boggling but enjoyable. During the ceremony the older women would adorn the pregnant lady with glass bangles, which she was supposed to wear till her pains began. The clinking of the glass bangles was meant to have a calming effect on the baby but it would make sleeping difficult for Rajam, who cradled her head on the palms of her hands while she slept. In any case, Mangalam assured her that by the time delivery came around most of the bangles would have broken, making the load lighter. After picking the bangles for Rajam, they had bought a few extra to give to their guests.

Delectable, tantalizing aromas wafted in from the kitchen as the ladies walked in the door. Mangalam had invited all the ladies from the neighborhood, including some ICS wives and she didn't want anything to go wrong. Today Rajam would be the center of attention. She was seated in the middle of the mutram on a chair and she glowed with the morning sunlight beaming down on her. Her inner happiness radiated from every pore and the excitement of the function completed her contentment, making her doubly radiant. Mangalam looked at her younger child. She had grown up so much since her wedding. She knew Rajam had been stressed out because of her problems with Nagamma, but now all visible signs of anxiety seemed to have vanished, replaced with sheer sparkle and joy. After so much prayer and of course the unforgettable benediction of Sankaracharya, she was blessed with this pregnancy. She looked so pretty; she was sure to have a female child. Sankaracharya had said that she should be named Kamakshi and everyone already referred to the baby as Kamu. Hopefully, it would be a girl; no boy would appreciate being named Kamu. She took a little *mai* from her eye and smeared it on Rajam's cheek, not wanting any evil eye to fall on her precious child, especially since she had spent the last few minutes admiring her. People said a mother's pride and admiration was especially harmful. '*So ugly, so ugly you look, Rajam,'* she muttered under her breath, hoping to counteract the effects of her recent compliments.

The function went off beautifully with all the elders anointing Rajam with turmeric, chandanam and kumkumam and of course putting the bangles on her wrists, which was the main purpose of the ceremony. After everyone had gone home, Mangalam walked into her room, when suddenly she felt the whole room swim. She tried to hold onto her bed, but then everything darkened around her. When her eyes opened again, she was on the bed and both Kunju and Rajam were fanning her, their eyes wide with trepidation. "*Yenna aachu?* What happened?" she asked, attempting to sit up, only to be pushed back down by both girls simultaneously.

"Nothing Amma, you lie down. You fainted, that's all. I think you have worked too much and the heat must have affected you. Appa is bringing the doctor."

"Doctor? There's no need for that. *Oh Perumala!* This is embarrassing!" Mangalam had never been to see a doctor before. In fact, she had never fallen seriously ill. Common colds and stomach ailments were always treated at home with herbal kashayams and the thought of going to an English doctor was appalling. No respectable Brahmin woman appreciated being touched by another man, even though he was a doctor and she couldn't believe her husband was going to subject her to this. Just then, Swaminathan walked in, holding the English doctor's black valise. "Come Doctor, this is my wife, Mangalam."

"*Yenna,*" she reproached him. "How can you bring him here? How can you allow him to touch me?" But Swaminathan summarily dismissed her. She had been unconscious for a long time and somehow he knew everything was not right. The situation looked dubious, an emergency calling for drastic measures. He knew how Mangalam felt about English doctors and he would not have resorted to this extreme step if he didn't think it absolutely necessary.

Much to Mangalam's horror, the doctor listened to her heartbeat with some strange instrument touching her body, which was unpardonable, and she held her breath as he took her blood pressure with some apparatus that hurt her arm. After he finished his examination, he took Swaminathan out to talk with him.

"Your wife has very high blood pressure. She may have had a minor stroke; her responses are not too good." Swaminathan had no idea what he was talking about and the Doctor attempted to explain it as best as he could. "What shall we do, Doctor? What medicines can we give her?"

"Unfortunately, I cannot recommend any medication, other than less salt in her diet and lots of rest." He wrote something on a piece of paper, a draught to be prepared by the pharmacist to calm her down and help her sleep.

Swaminathan was really worried, especially after the doctor explained to him what might have happened to Mangalam. All his life she had just been around, his constant companion and he always expected her to be healthy and outlive him; most women did. This piece of news gave him a real jolt. For the first time in so many years of marriage, the thought of her mortality entered his mind and it scared him. Mangalam was the backbone of this home and he couldn't bear the thought of anything happening to her.

"*Yenna*, what did the doctor say?"

"Nothing serious; he wants you to rest and eat food with less salt."

"Less salt? Oh no! It's better not to eat. I can never think of eating food without salt."

"We'll talk about that later. Now you rest." Swaminathan left the room with the girls, instructing the children not to disturb their Paati. He sat outside in the thinnai on the easy chair. What a day it had been; such a wonderful celebration and now this. He shook his head and sighed loudly. The gate creaked as the postman came through with a telegram. Swaminathan felt uneasy. No one sent telegrams unless they had bad news. Fearing the worst, Swaminathan opened the telegram.

It read: *Panchu serious. Stop. Send Kunju immediately. Stop.*

This was terrible. Kunju had arrived a week ago and now she would have to go back to Bangalore. Naturally, he would have to accompany her. But how was he going to leave Mangalam and Rajam with six children? Besides, Mangalam was already sick; how would she react to this news? He had to make arrangements for Kunju and himself to take the night train and he called his orderly, instructing him to buy tickets. Parvathi would take care of things. She was like an iron pillar, especially in times of crisis. He tried to think if Kunju had mentioned anything about her husband's condition. Kunju had said that Panchu had some trouble with digestion but she did not seem worried about it; at least she had not mentioned anything alarming. What could have happened now? He closed his eyes and prayed. Kunju had six children! If anything happened to Panchu, then they would be his responsibility. His own son, Mani, was still unmarried, and Swaminathan's responsibilities were far from over. And now he might have the additional burden of caring for six more. He prayed fervently that everything would be all right soon but he didn't feel at ease. A niggling doubt popped into his mind that this time around prayer might not be enough. He was a strong person and his police training gave him the ability to deal with crisis, but he found it difficult to control his emotions when it came to his children. Kunju was still young. What was going to happen?

Swaminathan suddenly became aware of his inner turmoil and he jerked himself out of the vicious cycle of emotions. Whatever happened, he would deal with it. He entered the house and went into the bedroom to check on his wife. Mangalam was fast asleep on the bed and next to her on either side were Kunju and Rajam, each with one arm thrown protectively across their mother. His eyes moistened with emotion. He walked out, not wanting to disturb such a touching, tender moment.

## CHAPTER 51 – NAGAMMA
### VIZHUPURAM – SEPTEMBER, 1935

The house was quiet. It had been so after Sushila and Siva left but with Rajam away as well, the silence was deafening. Tearfully Nagamma stared at the jewel in the palm of her hands. Red rubies set in the design of a snake — a *Nagara*, a hair accessory that she was going to present to Rajam on the occasion of her Seemandham. The setting was intricate, with tiny rubies and two small emeralds for the eyes of the snake. Nagamma watched her uncontrolled tears drip onto the jewel, like a superfluous adornment, misting the eyes of the snake until the green emeralds could scarcely be seen. She was not given to emotional moments but the events of the last few months and the ensuing stress had been too much for her. Siva abandoning her when she needed him the most was the worst — such a stab in the back. She always prided herself on the way she brought up her children, instilling in them the utmost respect for authority and family values. Sushila must have been the negative influence; he could not have thought up such a morbid plan on his own. He was her eldest son and had always been someone she could rely on. How could he abscond, leaving her to deal with this mess?

"*Chi chi,*" she murmured under her breath, trying her best to reign in her uncontrolled feelings. She did not want to cry. After all, what was the worst that could possibly happen? That she could die? And until that happened she could not give up. Still, no matter how hard she tried, she could not deal with the idea that all her efforts over her whole life had come to naught. She was too tired and had no more energy to go on. She strived so hard for so long and when she needed the most support, Siva had left. It tore away at her flesh to see her son leave like that. She could not believe her own son would kick her when she was down — tell her that her problem was hers and he could not involve himself any more. What if she had said the same to him when he was a child nursing at her breast? Your hunger is your own and I can't be bothered? Why were the rules different for mothers and offspring? What was it that turned a child against the mother? Was it because he was solely responsible for the finances in the home that he resented his mother and siblings? Maybe that's why he took such delight in putting them in a situation where they would be forced to fend for themselves. How could he bring himself to utter such harsh words that pierced her soul, language so hurtful that she would carry them with her into her next life? Did he not see that his mother's blessing shielded him, protecting him from bad karma? What demon had entered and captured his mind, making him willfully capable of divorcing his family?

While Siva had wildly accused Partha of escaping his duty, Nagamma was filled with pride to see her younger son stand tall, ready to accept any responsibility. Completely calm, Partha told his brother to leave in peace. He was ready to sign insolvency papers, throwing caution to the wind, not caring about the outcome. The future, he said, would take care of itself. The heated exchange, the bitter words, reason and rationale lost in the fire of resentment and aversion — sheer insanity! She saw the futility of trying to reason with madness, in trying to change the unshakeable; the effort had left her weak and emotional, and she couldn't afford that. Now she needed to harness every remote resource, every accessible reserve of energy, and see the family through this crisis. For so many years she held the fort all by herself, secure that the money from her lands would put food on the table. But then she was young, strong and infallible. She was always so proud of her achievements but more so of her family. How could she be on the brink of complete ruin? She simply could not accept it. The tears involuntarily welling in her eyes, she buried her head in her lap and cried loudly. Tears saved up from months of anxiety and stress flowed freely down her wrinkled cheeks. Her husband was sitting outside, but he was fast asleep in the easy chair and the sounds of her lamenting didn't reach his deaf ears. She was alone… as usual.

When the tears abated, she walked to the well and washed her face and sat down again to admire the jewel in her hand. She had sold her last piece of jewelry, her diamond earrings, to make this hair piece, a

341

gift for Rajam, who should never lack anything, especially during her pregnancy. Nagamma's earrings had been an heirloom in the family for hundreds of years, passed down from mother to daughter. They were the size of pigeon's eggs. 'Blue Jagger Diamonds' they called them. She touched the ordinary pearl earrings that replaced the coin sized earrings and tears welled up in her eyes again. Everyone identified her by the large earrings, which had adorned her ears for as long as she could remember, and the last thing she wanted was for others to feel sorry for her. No, instead, here she was feeling sorry for herself. Fate had brought her down from grace and she would no longer be able to hold her head high and walk the streets of Vizhupuram. The grand, proud, striking, imposing lady had been ousted from her self-styled pedestal. She could imagine the neighbors discussing how Nagamma had no house to live in any more. No house? Why, she had no food to give her children. For the last few months they had eaten only thayir shaadham and pickle, and just the week before, she sold the last of her silver vessels to buy a bag of rice.

"*Maa kuru dhana jana youvana garvam harathi nimeshath kaalah sarvam,*" she recited an ancient Sanskrit verse out loud, one that her mother explained to her in detail several times in her youth, but which signified nothing until now. How true that Sanskrit *shloka* was. One takes so much pride in one's ancestry, family wealth and youth but time takes it all away, leaving you wondering what you were proud of in the first place and if in fact it was ever yours.

Nagamma walked into her room and opened the almirah to put the Nagara away. Next to it sat another small blue velvet box. Gingerly she opened it, revealing a small seven-stone diamond nose ring. She took it out of the box and for several minutes watched it glimmer in the evening sunlight. Then, very purposefully, she unscrewed it, pulled out the brown dried vepalai twig from her nose and threw it on the floor. Then with resolve and pride she replaced it with her new diamond nose ring and looked at herself in the mirror.

No. The queen was not yet vanquished. She still reigned supreme.

## CHAPTER 52 – RAJAM
### CHIDAMBARAM – SEPTEMBER, 1935

Two weeks had passed since Kunju left. The Seemandham went on as usual, remaining a simple family affair. For this function, the main purpose was the actual chanting of verses in front of the holy *yagnas* and not a single ritual was left out. Mangalam did not want anything to be postponed and was grateful that no bad news had come thus far from Bangalore. Besides, Partha and his whole family had already planned their visit to Chidambaram and she was happy that the function went smoothly. The house was incredibly noisy, with babies crying, children screaming and yelling from all corners, just confusion compounded. Partha was tired of the noise and after dinner coaxed Rajam to the front thinnai to sit and talk peacefully. He had been speaking for a while when he realized that Rajam was preoccupied and hadn't paid attention to what he said. "Where are you? Lost in thought?"

"Nothing. I am worried about Kunju, that's all."

"Me too. I hope Panchu recovers soon."

"Yes. Six children."

"And they sound like twelve."

"You get used to the racket. In fact, I have hardly noticed it the last few weeks; they went by so fast. *Oww!*" she exclaimed, holding her belly.

"What? Did the pains start?" said an alarmed Partha. Rajam felt an elbow or knee press painfully against some organ and she winced in pain. Half of September had passed but the head was not fixed yet, although the baby was very active, especially at night.

343

"Looks like your baby is also in the mood for creating a ruckus," said Partha in relief. He touched Rajam's swollen stretched skin, feeling an ungainly lump on one side.

"Must feel strange having something alive inside you."

"It's like a butterfly; it flutters. This must be the best time of my life. Other than the first two months when I had the vomiting, I have never felt as good as I do right through my pregnancy. I only hope the childbirth won't be difficult."

"What does Chithi say? When does she think the baby will be born?"

"Ten months on the lunar calendar takes me to the end of October. But she feels it will be closer to the tenth of October because that is *Krishnapaksha*."

"So?" Partha didn't get the significance.

"Chithi says that babies are usually born closer to full moon and moonless nights. So either I will go beyond my date or come early. By the shape of my stomach, Chithi is sure it will be closer to Krishnapaksha; so maybe you should plan on coming then."

"I can't get leave. I'll lose my job. Don't forget I am the sole breadwinner."

"I know. What happened about the papers? Did you sign them?"

"Yes," said Partha sighing loudly. "That's what happened all of last week. You can see how pulled down Amma looks."

"Yes, I was shocked to see she sold her earrings. The pearl earrings don't look right on her. I have never seen her without those huge rocks on her ears."

"But she is proud of wearing the nose ring once again."

"She sold it to buy me the Nagara, didn't she?" Partha was silent.

"I knew it. She shouldn't have done that. I should return it to her."

"No, no, don't do that. She will be terribly insulted. It is her blessing for the baby. Later, when I get a better job, I will buy her another pair."

"What about the house? What are we going to do?"

"I have already found a two-room house. It's not in the agrahaaram but at least we can afford the rent."

"That is terrible. How will Amma bear to live outside the agrahaaram?"

"She has no choice. She has to accept it."

344

Both of them turned and watched Nagamma through the open door as she sat in the thinnai with Mangalam and Chithi. Her face looked wan and her eyes were filled with sadness. She had lost a lot of weight, making her already large nose much more prominent.

"She looks terrible; she has really taken it hard. I wish I could help her," Rajam said wistfully. "But I have to stay here."

"She knows that. This is her problem and she will work things out, and while she does we need to be patient. She is a very proud woman and cannot stand people pitying her. You know that."

Partha glanced at Rajam, who was still staring at Nagamma, her erstwhile nemesis, still in disbelief at the transformation of character.

"Don't look sad. Good and bad things happen all the time. We go through everything secure in the knowledge that things change all the time. Today we have no home but tomorrow is another day and a new sun will rise. See how happy I am just waiting to hold Kamu in my arms. She will change our luck and life will become good again, so cheer up."

"You are so positive, Partha."

"It's my way of coping. I have my life ahead. I know that right now I am not earning well but I have great hope for the future."

The creaking of the gate interrupted their conversation as the postman entered. Rajam's heart sank. She knew what a telegram at this hour meant and seeing the grave look on Partha's face as he read it confirmed her suspicions.

Good news, bad news. How strange life was.

# Part XVIII
# Dharmu

# CHAPTER 53 – BANU AND KANDU
## RANGPUR – SEPTEMBER, 1935

*"Neeye nao Maa, kee bhalo kaaj... neeye nao."* "Take it, look at this excellent work... take it," urged the sariwallah, but Banu was not easily swerved from her resolve to get the best price.

*"Naa, naa, daamta khub beshi."* "No, no the price is too high," she insisted, trying to press him to reduce it even further.

Banu enjoyed haggling with the sariwallah, who loved making this annual trip to the bungalow because he was sure of a big sale, especially with Banu here as well. East Bengal was famous for Dacca[4] muslin — cotton thin as gossamer, perfect for this humid and hot September. Dharmu watched in awe, amazed at Banu's grasp of Bengali and her skill in striking a bargain. Some people just had a knack for learning languages, an ability that boggled her own mind. She had chosen five saris — two for Meera and three for herself — and Banu selected a half dozen. The sariwallah came from a weaving loom in Dacca, the state's capital, one of the few that had survived the British textile tax, imposed to promote cheap English cotton and prevent people from buying the far superior Jamdani muslin. The weavers had lost so much business that several looms had closed, nearly killing this art of weaving, another successful attempt of the foreign masters to strike and vanquish the local economy.

After haggling the price down by two rupees a sari, she was satisfied she had the best deal for these invaluable garments. Dharmu ran in to get the money while Banu made small talk with the salesman. Banu's presence had changed the ambience in the house. Just knowing she was around made Dharmu wake up each morning in anticipation

---

[4] Modern-day Dhaka, Capital of Bangla Desh

of a fun-filled day. Banu did not know exactly why Mahadevan had called her here but she was shocked to see Dharmu looking so pale and withdrawn. Dharmu hoped that Banu would not talk with the servants, who would need little encouragement before spilling the real story. But Banu's behavior did not indicate she knew anything.

The girls loved having their aunt here, who did special things for them, such as tying their hair in an *anju kaal pinnal*, a braid made by separating the hair into five separate strands. She also put makeup on them, which was such a special treat, as Dharmu used no cosmetics other than talcum powder. Vani spent hours pouting before a mirror, admiring herself in bright red lipstick and imagining that she was a Hollywood star. Just as the satisfied sariwallah left, counting the money over and over again to reassure himself, Rukku came and sat at Banu's feet with her comb, ready for the day's beauty treatment.

"Today I want a French chignon," she declared.

"Oh my gosh you girls! You want to be film stars or what? You are beautiful enough to be one though." She pinched the cheeks of both girls and as she finished with Rukku, she turned her attention to Vani, who was holding an English magazine and hoping that Banu Mami could copy the style from the picture.

"Vani, I have to oil your hair; it's so curly, just like your mother's. I can't do anything with it." Dharmu watched her girls chattering away gleefully with their aunt, who filled them in with all kinds of stories from their younger days at the Jameen. Dharmu never spoke to them much about her childhood and the children enjoyed getting the inside scoop from their aunt. Right then Kandu walked in, brown from head to toe after wrestling with Rover on the wet grass for the last half hour. He poured himself a glass of lemonade and then, after checking that no one was watching, helped himself to seconds. But he had not finished playing, so his bath would have to wait. While the girls were getting dolled up, he ran up and down the stairs chasing lizards. Somehow he always found some inane pursuit, which kept him completely engaged. If he wasn't playing with the dogs, he was ordering the chowkidars around, catching butterflies or setting traps, but chasing lizards was his favorite pastime. Dharmu watched his strategy, smiling at his cunning. He would approach the lizard and in one swift movement swoop it up in the palms of his hands. Then for a few minutes he would pet it and then let it go. Some lizards were smarter, making the chase all the more enjoyable as he ran up and down and behind the stairs and across the grass till he cornered the hapless creature. Once cornered, the lizard would freeze up in fear, allowing Kandu to pick it up, only to pet and release it. What joy he got from this activity was unfathomable, but not a day went by without the lizard-chasing routine. He ran up the stairs and reached for some more lemonade.

"Uh uh… no more," said Banu Mami. "Just drink water." Annoyed, Kandu turned, ready to run into the kitchen with his muddy shoes only to be hauled back by an alert Banu Mami, forcing him to walk around the verandah to the kitchen. He was back soon, brushed and combed, with his bright yellow watering can in his hand ready to care for his favorite plant. He did this religiously, which was strange for a boy of almost six years. Kandu lost interest in most things quickly but with this plant he had been faithfully attentive for a whole year. He scrunched down, peering at the poor wilted plant and murmuring to himself. Having watched this ritual every day, Banu wanted to learn what interested him in this flaccid potted plant, which had no flowers, only sad droopy leaves.

"Kandu is this your plant?" she asked.

"Yes, this is my special plant because Appanshayal Thatha gave it to me as a present."

"Oh I see, but why are you looking at it so intently?"

"See this small thing here?" He said pointing to an insignificant bump on the stem that was barely noticeable to the naked eye. Banu tried to examine the miniscule nodule on the stem but it looked so unimportant.

"It will become a flower," Kandu added in delight, his eyes bright and alert.

"Really?" she responded, believing this to be a childish fantasy.

"Yes really, and maybe you can see it with me. I'm sure it will bloom soon."

"Okay, that sounds super. I would love to." Banu knew this was just a small malformation of the stem but she indulged him anyway, not wanting to dampen his fertile imagination. "So why is this so special?"

"Oh," said Kandu, his eyes wide and wistful. "It has something to do with my future. Thatha said and it will bring good luck and plan my destiny."

"What big words from such a small child. Where did you learn words like 'destiny'?"

"Destiny means future. If I water the plant, it will flower and tell my fortune. I can make another plant for you if you want it to tell your future and bring you lots of luck."

"That's lovely. Is that my special present? Because I have a special present for you." Kandu got excited as soon as he heard the word 'present'. His birthday was on the eighth of October, and Mahadevan had asked Banu to bring some goodies for him.

"You will be very surprised," she said hugging him so tight that he gasped out loud.

"Oh, can I see it now?" He asked, a little breathless after the chest-squeezing hug.

"No, you have to wait two more weeks, but I won't give you yours till you give me mine." Excitedly, Kandu ran out to get a pot for Banu Mami's plant.

Banu smiled. *'Silly boy, believing that a plant can bring good luck.'* But she didn't want to spoil his excitement. In reality, she had no idea about the power and potential of the plant and the significance of its next blooming in Kandu's life. How could she? Not even Kandu would understand its esoteric message. She looked at the nondescript nodule on the stem, shook her head in disbelief and walked inside the house.

# CHAPTER 54 – MEERA
## RANGPUR – SEPTEMBER, 1935

Meera was feeding Kandu baba rice and fish curry. He was full and kept insisting he didn't want any more but she persisted. His cheeks got progressively larger, stretching beyond normal proportions as each spoonful added to the previous, all tucked into the corner of his mouth. Meera was lost in thought and her attention was not focused on Kandu. She was merely following a feeding rhythm without bothering to look at him, so when she stuffed in the next mouthful, his mouth reached its maximum capacity and he gagged, bringing up everything onto his plate and the floor. She suddenly awoke from her reverie and in sheer reflex slapped him on his back. Almost immediately she realized what she had done and was horrified. She was only the maid and had no authority to hit the child. Heaven knows what had got into her that she completely lost control like this. She was terribly nervous. If Sahib found out, that would be the end of her job. She was at a loss; she did not know whether to calm Kandu down or clean the mess. Any moment she expected Memsahib to walk in, and she had no explanation for her behavior. Coming to her senses, she yelled for the Jamadar to come in and clean the mess on the table and the floor.

Picking up Kandu, she ran into the bathroom and carefully shut the door after her. She cleaned him up and changed his clothes and all the while he cried and screamed at her. He loved Meera so much and couldn't believe she had hit him. Just recently Mummy had hit him and now Meera. He felt as if his whole world were crumbling. All the people he loved were slapping him. Meera's slap was a reflex action. If she had been thinking, she would have recoiled in horror at such an idea. Kandu was not crying from the pain but was livid that she actually had the gall to strike him. He was completely traumatized, as was Meera. She always cared so much for the children. Never even in a weak moment had she ever struck them. She changed him into his night clothes and then gathered him up in her arms and took him to the back porch, where she was sure no one would hear him. Memsahib and Banu Memsahib were sitting in the front verandah and they hadn't heard anything. Thank heavens!

Meera had been feeling terrible these last few months. She hadn't been herself. To Meera it felt almost as if a ghost of some self-seeking temptress had entered her body, making her behave in ways completely contrary to her character. *"Kande na baba kande na,"* she said soothingly, urging him to stop crying and calm down.

"Put powder on my *ooa*," said Kandu woefully, referring to his stinging wound. Meera, as always, made it better by putting cooling talcum powder or cream on it.

"Show me where your *ooa* is," said Meera lifting his kurta. Kandu was so fair his skin had reddened but thankfully, she had not hit him hard enough for it to form welts. She brought the talcum powder and sang to him softly as she rubbed his smarting back.

"Baba, don't tell your Ma and Baba what happened. Okay? Let it be our secret."

"Why? Asked Kandu, wondering why everyone wanted him to keep secrets, especially when it came to telling about him being slapped.

"Because then Ma and Baba will get angry and tell me to leave the house. Then who will sing songs for you, play with you and sleep in your room?" Kandu saw the logic in that. In any case, his wound was more psychological; the pain had lessened considerably after Meera attended to it and it didn't bother him anymore.

"Okay, he said crossing his fingers, a twinkle in his eye. But only if you give me *mishti doi*." Meera went into the kitchen to get his favorite dessert, yoghurt sweetened with molasses. She fed him, this time paying full attention, something she should have done earlier. Kandu ran off and Meera went into the kitchen to eat her dinner. In no mood to eat, she toyed with her food, her mind going over the wretched events of the last few months. Finally, her appetite non-existent, she left the kitchen to lament and wallow in self-pity in the safe haven of her room.

She had not got her period for three weeks, and even though a part of her rejoiced, she feared that God had really answered her prayer. Now she was in a terrible dilemma. In a few months her pregnancy would swell and show and Memsahib would know that she had done some *gondogol*. What explanation could she offer? She had not been home in six months, so Memsahib knew she hadn't seen her husband. Soon the servants would gossip and talk behind her back and label her as wanton, which she was; temporary lunacy that left her feeling ashamed. She searched with little success for some rational justification for her behavior but in her heart she knew her actions were purely instinctive. A few moments of stolen passion leading to a lifetime of regret. But now what was she going to do? Just the other day she saw Kalia flirting with the cook's daughter. She was a spring chicken; compared to her, Meera felt like an old hag in spite of being in the prime of her womanhood. Kalia was never going to marry Meera. She was just his whore and nothing else. In any case, how could she marry him when her husband was alive?

Her husband!! That was another problem. What was she going to say to him when she went back to the village? He knew he could do nothing; and how would he react to being cuckolded? Would he accept this baby as a gift from God? And if he didn't, where would she go? Who would help her through childbirth? She couldn't go home. Her parents were dead and she had no contact with any of her sisters or brothers. What was going to happen? She banged her head repeatedly against the wall shouting out loud, "Silly fool, silly fool, oh *maago*, why did you not think of the future? You should have thought of all this before you acted like a whore, wanting to fill your womb. Now what will you do, Meera, what will you do?" Crying hysterically, she let out all of her frustration, hitting herself repeatedly on her head, trying to slap some sense into herself. After a while she calmed down and thought about what she could do. But her psychological tumult merely churned out morbid solutions, which to her were the only salvation, true repentance for committing sin in the eyes of Banobibi.

She had only two choices: she could either kill the baby or kill herself. To kill the baby she would have to find some medicine woman who would give her a potion of crushed berries. Many in the village had used the remedy, which worked sometimes but more often the baby was born deformed. What was she going to do with a deformed baby? It would only add to her problems and certainly would be no replacement for Kamala. No, no, she could not do that. Maybe she should kill herself. She deliberated about what would be the best way — drown in the Ganga or hang herself. She was not crying anymore. Her racing mind considered different ways to end her life. Looking up at the ceiling, she saw the wooden rafters that ran along the length of the room and she had her answer. She would hang herself from the ceiling above her bed, an appropriate location, the perfect repentance for her sins, ending her life right above the scene of her crime. She tied two saris together and then standing on the bed threw one end over the rafter. Securing the knot, she tugged on it to test its strength. It would have to do. She stood at the edge of her bed and placed the noose around her neck. Her mind was a blank. She had exhausted every emotion. Now all she wanted was to be united with Kamala. She closed her eyes and thought of her darling child as she stepped off the edge of the bed.

The noose was tight around her neck and she couldn't breathe. Lights exploded inside her brain and she felt the struggle as her windpipe closed. Her arms and legs flailed, her lungs begging for air and she became sharply aware of the flashes, the tightness and the loss of control. She wasn't sure how long this went on until she felt something give. The noose around her neck loosened its death grip, allowing fresh oxygenated air to pour into her deprived lungs, even as she fell to the ground hitting her shoulder hard against the mud floor. She lay there sucking in the air, breathing in deep wheezy gasps, grappling with the realization that she was alive. She loosened the sari from around her sore neck and gazed up at the ceiling, wondering what had just happened. A few seconds passed before she realized that the rafter had broken, having rotted with age. She couldn't believe it! She couldn't live and she didn't die either.

This was definitely a message from Banobibi, telling her that this was not her time to die. This was not her solution; her repentance must come through facing the consequences and raising this child. She curled into a fetal position, submitting completely to will of the divine Mother, silent tears pouring out of her dazed eyes.

# CHAPTER 55 – MAHADEVAN
## RANGPUR – SEPTEMBER, 1935

Mahadevan kept reading the letter over and over again. He was a little peeved to say the least. He had been expecting a transfer to a big city like Calcutta or Delhi, so this transfer order back to Sylhet was disappointing. He had done an excellent job in Rangpur, was definitely in line for a promotion and was thunderstruck with this lateral move. The farther he was away from Calcutta, the longer it would take him to climb the ladder. 'Out of sight out of mind' was a pertinent axiom when it came to Civil Service transfers.

The previous month had brought many important changes for the country. The second Government of India Act of 1935 had been passed in the British Parliament, resulting in many administrative changes in India. Some lands which had originally belonged to Burma were transferred into the state of Assam, which was where Sylhet was located.

The whole administrative service had been abuzz with rumors flying around about possible amendments. There were long debates, both official and unofficial, in intellectual circles and much derision over the British pandering of Jinnah and his Muslim cause. As Mahadevan had expected, almost all of Jinnah's recommendations had been accepted, testimony to the cunning policy of Divide and Rule. The new Act also held special provisions for the unconquered princely states to accede to the Federation with representation in the Government. Instead of presenting a cohesive front, each state was furthering its own petty interests. Of course this angered the Nationalists, who saw this Act as another instrument to further demolish the unity and integrity of the nation. But these situations were peripheral to the news of his own transfer orders — an inopportune corollary of the Act itself.

He knew that Dharmu needed a change and a move to Calcutta would have been so welcome. Banu would have been there for moral support and Dharmu's social life would have been much more colorful. More pertinently, his personal visibility would have increased, opening new avenues of growth in the service. But what was the point in talking about or thinking about what was not imminent? It only caused turmoil and disappointment, both of which disturbed his customary sanguinity; as a result, dismissing his thoughts seemed the best tactic. He would have to break the news to Dharmu and the children and he knew they would not be very happy. Sylhet lay east of Rangpur, which made it even farther away from home. The people there spoke either Assamese or Burmese, and Dharmu, who was already at her wits end with Bengali, would now have to deal with two new languages. She had made no attempt to learn either when they had been posted there earlier and Mahadevan had not insisted on anything at the time. The children were young then and Dharmu had spent most of her pregnancy in Sylhet before she left for Dindigul to have Kandu. But now the children were older and the question of their education bothered him. Still young, Kandu would benefit from private tutoring, but Vani was growing up and needed some formal education. He would have to think about some way of tutoring her on par with an education in the city.

Mahadevan had so many conflicting thoughts that he hardly noticed the ride home and soon the phaeton was pulling into the gate. Dharmu and Banu were sitting outside drinking their evening tea and he wondered if he could break the news in front of Banu. Dharmu had put on a little weight and her cheeks sported more color. Banu's visit had definitely done her good. The recent episode over her drinking resulted in a poignant realization for Mahadevan; he saw that hard work and the office could only be a part of one's life. The main purpose of a married man was to have harmony in his home and that could only come when husband and wife were intimate. Physical intimacy was a prerequisite for spiritual communication and the latter was crucial if any relationship was to endure and be fruitful. He had ignored that aspect of his life thus far and had immersed himself in his work, which, unfortunately, had resulted in this lateral move to Sylhet.

If only he had invested as much energy in his marriage, there might have been greater gains and satisfaction from life. Maybe that would have prevented Dharmu from drinking. He could not get over how the intimate touch of a woman lifted his spirits and made him feel invincible. How much time had been lost and how much damage done he did not know. In hindsight, it irked him that this realization had not come sooner. The children sensed a difference in their relationship, resulting in a more positive and upbeat change in the atmosphere at home.

After drinking tea and scones in the verandah, Banu accompanied Kandu on his ritual watering of the plant and examined the burgeoning bud, participating wholeheartedly in his enthusiasm. Seeing that she was out of earshot, Mahadevan decided to quickly broach the topic before Banu returned, giving Dharmu some time to digest and accept the news before reacting. Banu's presence would have made further debate on the topic improbable.

"Dharmu, I got my transfer orders."

"Really? To Calcutta?"

"No, to Sylhet." There he had done it. He told her.

"Sylhet? Why? Why not Calcutta?" Dharmu looked crestfallen.

"Good question, one that has been bothering me too, but Sylhet has just become part of the Indian dominion, so I will have to be there for at least the next two years."

Dharmu's heart sank. Two more years away from the comfort of civilization. But she had no more time to think, because Banu came back, saying something about Kandu and the plant but Dharmu didn't quite hear anything.

"Yes," said Mahadevan trying to behave as jolly and normal as he could. "He was very sad he missed the blooming the last time. You know he slunk out of his room at night and I found him sleeping here in the verandah in the morning."

"Well, he says it normally doesn't bloom twice a year, so he won't miss this one. He has his heart set on seeing it," said Banu, indulgently looking at Kandu.

Mahadevan left the ladies and went in to freshen up. He knew Dharmu was sad but she would come around. Next week while Banu was still here to care for the children, he would take Dharmu to Assam for a visit. The area was in a beautiful part of the country, nestled in the hills with the River Surma nearby. Picturesque tea plantations dotted the landscape, and the climate was definitely much cooler and drier than Rangpur. Mahadevan wondered how two towns with such different climates could be geographically so close together. The children could learn horse riding, and maybe he would find good teachers there, since many ICS officers were being transferred there. Kandu ran in chattering nonstop just as he had changed into his lounge clothes. "Kandu," Mahadevan finally got a word in edgewise, "we are going to move from Rangpur next month."

Kandu raised both his arms up and shouted "Yay!" at the top of his voice. "Where are we going?" He added, bobbing up and down on his father's lap, the conversation not meaning much to him.

"To a place called Sylhet," said Mahadevan, wondering why he was telling the child anything. He wasn't sure if Kandu understood much. Perhaps he was looking for some approval, some positive feedback from someone, even a child.

"Sylhet, what a silly name. Do you wear silly hats there?" And Kandu burst out laughing, loving his own joke, as he jumped off his father's lap chanting "Silly het silly hat...Rukku..." He yelled, running out of the room to search for his sister.

As his voice faded away, Mahadevan smiled to himself. Children gave you so much more perspective in life. He had been overwhelmed at the thought of moving to this remote place, but Kandu found the name funny and he feared nothing.

Adults fashioned mental torment for themselves by creating fears and apprehension where none existed. They were merely imagined problems, arising from the fear of the unknown, from moving out of their comfort zone. Children were so much more real and practical because they functioned from the heart, living totally in the present. It amazed Mahadevan how much he was learning from them.

He sighed aloud. Everything was going to be fine. His career would take off, his children would be educated and his wife would be happy. Life was going to be beautiful. He knew it because he felt it in his heart. And for the first time in his adult life, he would follow his heart.

# Epilogue: The Lotus blooms

# OCTOBER 11<sup>TH</sup>, 1935

Rajam felt her belly hardening and she tried to move into a more relaxed position, but no matter which way she turned she was still uncomfortable. Finally, unable to sleep, she sat up and to her surprise her stomach softened. Thinking that this was a better position to sleep in, she piled up a few pillows behind her and settled back in a half seated position and closed her eyes. She could not have been dozing for more than fifteen minutes when she felt her belly hardening again. The pressure on her bladder had built up this past week and when Chithi felt her stomach, she confirmed that the baby's head had fixed . . . whatever that meant. She got up slowly and went to the bathroom for the fourth time this night, hoping that the relief from emptying her bladder might ease the hardness. Rajam hated using the bathroom at night. She had to take a lantern and there were so many cockroaches creeping around at night that it made her jittery.

It was not daybreak yet and everyone was asleep. Chithi was sleeping in the open thinnai with Kunju's six little children next to her. Rajam peeped into Amma's room and from the doorway could hear her gentle snoring. She was sleeping by herself, as Appa was still not back from Bangalore. Kunju's husband, Panchu, had died a fortnight ago and Appa was with Kunju completing the ceremonies, after which he would bring her back to Chidambaram. Rajam felt the tears well up in her eyes as she thought about Kunju being a widow. Would they have cut her hair and made her wear a white sari like Chithi? She hoped not. Her father did not believe in those rituals and had protested when Chithi lost her husband. But unfortunately, he was young at the time and did not have much say in such matters. Besides, he was totally outnumbered and forced to keep his counsel to himself. But Kunju was his daughter, and Rajam was sure that he would never allow the priests to perform all those cruel rituals reserved for widows. Poor Kunju . . . she was so young . . . why did she have to face widowhood now? Rajam felt like weeping but suddenly a sharp pain gripped her lower back. She bit her lip to prevent herself from crying out and in a few seconds the pain had subsided. She breathed in deeply, filling her deprived lungs. Kamu must have pushed against some already squished organ, something that happened once too often nowadays.

It was so different being pregnant. All of her insides felt squashed, and she could not eat much at one sitting, throwing her digestion completely off track. A constant burning sensation in her upper stomach, especially at night, and her inability to move her bowels regularly made her feel even more bloated. Right now she was so huge that she probably measured the same vertically and horizontally. '*A round ball,*' she thought to herself and giggled, half asleep. She must have dozed off because the next thing she knew Chithi was calling to wake her up. Rajam stirred and unwillingly crawled out of bed. Every act was so complex now, even sitting and sleeping had become a painful chore. She couldn't wait for the birth of the baby, her darling Kamu. When, oh when would the pains start?

She didn't have to wait long. The first pain began in earnest during her bath, a strong contraction hardening her stomach and radiating to her back. She gasped out loud and held the wall for support, staggered by the sheer force of the pain. Unable to stand any longer, she hastily wrapped the sari around her wet body and stumbled out of the bath area, calling for her mother and Chithi. She was halfway across the courtyard, when to her horror, she felt herself urinating. She gaped dumbstruck at the hot fluid gushing down her legs. She couldn't believe she had lost control. It was odd, because she had just used the toilet and felt no pressure, no urgency to go. Chithi heard her, and recognizing the panic in her voice, walked briskly towards her just in time to see her standing, her feet wide apart, in a pool of pinkish fluid. Her waters had burst. It was time to prepare for delivery.

"Mangalam," she yelled. "Come quickly, it's time. I told you that the baby would come around Krishnapaksha."

Rajam stared at her vacantly, unable to fathom what just happened. "Chithi . . ." she began, her voice rising up into a crescendo as another contraction commenced, choking her words back. Chithi herded her into the front room, the official childbearing room. Then she lay her down on the bed and carefully removed the last of her bangles.

Partha had returned home from school a while ago, and the house was quiet without the usual sound of women chattering away in the kitchen. Nagamma had become reticent and spoke only when spoken to. It felt oppressive and crowded with so many of them packed into two rooms and Partha enjoyed the brief reprieve, soaking in the feeling of space on the small open terrace. His eyes fell on the Brahmakamalam. Rajam had insisted that he move the plant to the new house and water it regularly. He had done the first but omitted the second. Thank goodness for the rain. Guiltily he ran down to get a pot of water. When he poured the water on the droopy leaves, he noticed the bud. The full purplish bud was frothing at the tip, ready to burst into bloom. Inadvertently Partha found himself smiling. The plant was going to bloom. Rajam had been desolate the last time when she missed it blooming. Well, today he would stay up and watch it bloom. He would enjoy telling her one more tale of what she missed by staying away from him.

Velandi stared at her face, an empty manic look in his eyes as he looked at her but didn't actually register her presence. Every time she appeared before him, her face would morph into Muniamma's and he would cry out in anguish. He never wanted to remarry but the village elders had persuaded him to get a woman to care for his little ones. In his heart was a special place reserved only for Muniamma and no one could replace her. He was like a madman working mechanically, not bathing, barely eating, his hair unruly and his eyes red in anguish. Sindhuri, his wife of two months, was an adolescent herself, scrawny and restrained, terrified of making a wrong move. His nightmares jerked her into a fearful awakened state at night, and his agonized expression during the day tormented her, leaving her puzzled, constantly wondering what she had done wrong. He could not embrace Sindhuri into his life. It was too soon. Hardly aware of her terrified presence, he wandered off to the banks of the river to the spot where he had cremated the remains of Muniamma. He had no money to pay the *Chandala* for wood at the burning ghat to burn her body, so he and Nandu painstakingly collected branches and twigs from the forest floor and cremated her on the banks of the river. He had sat by the dying embers, watching the eerie glow through the tortuous night, almost in a trance. Then, when the heat of the fire had abated, he collected the ashes and bits of bone and immersed them in the river, his final act of service to his wife. As he sat down, he remembered the scene so clearly; it was almost as if it were taking place in the present moment: the ashes and bone fragments floating, hovering on the surface of the water only for a moment before mingling and dissolving into the running current, taking her last worldly remains back to its source.

"*Muniamma!*" he screamed, his voice reverberating inside his own head. No one else heard him.

Mahadevan had been depressed after hearing of his transfer to Sylhet. No matter how much he tried to rationalize, he could not come to terms with this move. He should have had that promotion by now. It would have made a world of difference to his morale and would have given Dharmu something to look forward to. Thirteen years away from the power center, away from urban civilization, except for his brief sojourn in Madras, way back in 1926. He would just have to grit his teeth for a few more years and wait and hope. His own rise in the hierarchy was not of paramount importance to him. He could think of so many more concerns: his children's education and their future being foremost. The girls were growing up, and how would he secure a good match for Vani when he lived in the back of beyond? In any case, the girls were familiar with Sylhet and Dharmu had become reconciled to moving there. She had a soft spot for Sylhet because Kandu was conceived there. Maybe moving there would rekindle those good moments. The job would be less taxing and he would have more time for his family.

He sighed, momentarily distracted as his newly hired assistant, Vaithee, walked into the office with the day's mail. Mahadevan indicated with a snort that he put the mail into a folder. Vaithee spoke Tamil, which was a welcome respite from constantly speaking Bengali. What made him come so far from his home for employment was a mystery and Mahadevan didn't probe too much. He was efficient, spoke minimally and that was good enough. His eyes however, were always bloodshot and wore a haunted look, making Mahadevan wonder what dark secret was trapped inside his head. But he never asked him about it. Instead he turned his attention to the mail folder.

It was hidden under some long routine memos and he didn't get to it right away. However, seeing that the envelope contained the Imperial stamp, he opened it immediately and in complete disbelief read its contents. The earlier transfer orders were rescinded. He was being promoted to Additional Deputy Secretary in the Industries and Labour Department and would have to report to duty on April 27th in New Delhi. In the interim he would be stationed in Nadia District, north of Calcutta, as Magistrate and Collector.

He dropped the paper down, unable to register and digest this information, unsure that what he had just read was not just a figment of his imagination. Picking it up, he read it three times over. No, this was no mistake. What a turn of events! He felt his energy rise and soar heavenward. Then he leaned back in his chair, threw his head back, and laughed wholeheartedly.

Mangalam returned to her daughter's side, mopping her sweaty forehead. Dusk had cast its dark mantle over the house and the lamps had to be lit. Chithi had kept a hot stove ready with a pot of boiling water bubbling over it. The pains were strong and the head had almost crowned but the baby was taking her own time to come into this world. Rajam had been in labor all day and was weak from the pain. Chithi felt her stomach. Rajam would be ready to push very soon. Hopefully she wouldn't bleed too much. She had spent the last few hours preparing all kinds of kashayams from a combination of ground and boiled herbs to ease the process. Just then, Rajam screamed as another contraction tore through her belly. "Enough, Amma, no more... make it stop. Never again, never again will I ask for a baby," she sobbed. Chithi had seen so many women say the same thing, swearing never again to have another baby. But the following year they would be back with swollen bellies ready to undergo the same torture to hold a bundle of joy in their arms.

Mangalam gave her a sip of water, soothing her, holding her gently in her arms. "Soon Rajam, hold on, it will be over soon."

"Banu Mami… come here…. hurry up. The flower, it's going to bloom!" Hearing his desperate call, Banu dropped her sewing and walked out, amazed at how closely Kandu was observing the ripening of the bud, awaiting the elusive bloom. She wondered if the story about the flower blooming only once a year was a figment of his imagination but she humored him anyway. The plant was actually quite ugly and the bud uglier still, but she hid her skepticism from him. The stem had taken a "U" shape, rising upward and the once limp bud had lifted up. Kandu squatted comfortably, admiring the bud, slapping his arms at intervals to get rid of the swarming mosquitoes. The swarms were at their peak at dusk. Banu wrapped the sari around her shoulders and hunkered down next to him.

"See, the bud is slightly open; its tips are white," he said, marveling at the latest transformation. The two of them sat quietly admiring the unsightly pregnant bloom.

"What do you think this means? The Brahmakamalam blooming? Is something wonderful going to happen to me?" Kandu was reading too much into an ordinary event, ready to fire his already fertile imagination, Banu replied with a laugh. "Oh didn't you know? The love of your life, your special friend will be born somewhere in this world. And she will wait to meet you and marry you."

Kandu frowned, not appreciating her response. Girls? Marriage? That wasn't exciting. He didn't like girls anyway but somewhere in the deep recesses of his mind, he tucked away this seemingly unimportant piece of information.

Sushila sat in the easy chair in the thinnai, waiting for Siva to return home from work. She had only to cook for three people and had plenty of free time to sit and ponder about her life. Moving to

Madras was supposed to have been the 'Great Escape,' but surprisingly, she actually missed the bustle of living in a joint family. She missed the excitement, the gossip, constantly having to attend to little things, chores which at the time she considered tedious and cumbersome. On the other hand, she enjoyed the freedom, the space to think and breathe, to do things that only she wanted to do. Siva had settled into his new job but the guilt of abandoning his family had worn him down. He hardly slept at night and his eyes had dark patches underneath them. His tossing and turning disturbed Sushila's sleep as well and only when he decided to wake up and sit outside, could she actually fall into a deep slumber. His mind was terribly disturbed, although he never openly admitted it.

That evening, from the thinnai, she could see him walking down the road, briskly for a change.

"Sushila, good news, I finally managed it." Siva was breathless as he entered the courtyard.

"Managed what?" Sushila asked, amazed at his joyful appearance, a refreshing change after his recent depressed state.

"I got a job for Partha and Thambu in the same company. Isn't that wonderful? Now they can all move here."

"Move here?" Sushila wasn't so sure this was exactly the news she was waiting for.

Swaminathan watched his daughter stare vacantly out of the window. Kunju was still numb after the events that had taken place recently. So young to be a widow. Heaven knows what karma was playing out that she had to face this sorrow at such a young age. They had not spoken since they boarded the train to Chidambaram. What was there to say? Swaminathan sighed deeply. His mind jumped from one thought to the next. He was due to retire in three years. Maybe now he would have to ask for an extension. How was he going to manage such a large household on his meager pension? He hoped he wasn't too late for Rajam's delivery. A new child in the house might lift Kunju's spirit. Had Mangalam rested enough? Caught in a quagmire of emotions, Swaminathan found himself unable to focus on a single thought as his mind moved from one problem to the next. Too much had happened this last month and his shoulders ached as he physically took on the burden of his family. Maybe things would not be so bad. Maybe the joy of being surrounded by his sprightly grandchildren would alleviate the burden of responsibility. Maybe. He gazed out the window, just like Kunju.

His thoughts were interrupted by a large, noisy group of men dressed in white cotton, entering the bogey. By their conversation he gleaned that they were returning home from an INC meeting in Bangalore. Swaminathan turned away and once more stared out the window, his expression soulful, as he watched the landscape fade in the setting sun. Morchas, meetings, marches ... how long will they go on before the sun sets on the British rule? When will a free India become a reality — one year — ten years? — And Kamu? Will she have the privilege of living in a liberated Bharat? Will she ever understand what we endured for her sovereignty? Will she value freedom? — Maybe.

Dharmu sat on the verandah combing Rukku's hair, listening to her idle chatter, patiently responding and laughing at her comments — something she had not done for such a long time. So much had changed this last month. Mahadevan had become so loving, attending to her every need. It was almost as if some miracle had taken place. She had not even thought about drinking in over two weeks and her face looked brighter with color in her cheeks. For a change, she spent time with her daughters and not just with Kandu. But she knew that Kandu was special, her only son, and he would always occupy that unique, hallowed place in her heart. Sylhet was not going to be so bad. After all, she and Mahadevan had shared some intimate moments there and that's where Kandu was conceived. Her thoughts were interrupted as the front gate opened and the phaeton noisily came to a stop at the foot of the stairs. Mahadevan was out in a trice and climbing up the stairs two at a time, waving a piece of paper in his hands.

"Dharmu, Dharmu, you are not going to believe this," he said breathlessly, a smile lighting up his face, making his wide jaw line even more pronounced. One by one faces lit up, and smiles turned to laughter, followed by whooping and yelling with everyone hugging one another, tears of joy streaming down their cheeks. Nothing could have been more welcome than these astonishing tidings.

Meera watched the family unite and celebrate, bringing into sharp focus her own sorry plight. They were going to leave Rangpur, causing her to wonder what she was going to do. They were the only family she knew, and she could not go with them, not with the baby growing in her womb. Part of her longed for the happiness a new baby would bring but the other half was lost, searching for some inkling, some brainwave about how her future would unfold. Where would she go, and who could help her with this new baby? Should she return to her husband and beg his forgiveness, or go to her mother's village and make up some story, hoping for acceptance? She went back into the dim comfort of her hut and sat on her bed, her arms locked around her as she rocked back and forth trying to comfort herself. Something would work out. If Banobibi had brought this baby into the world, then she would have a plan for her. She softly sang to herself a lullaby her mother used to sing, her sweet melody cutting through the darkness that enshrouded her.

Rajam squatted on the floor, leaning back against her mother, the pain exploding in her brain. Chithi was in front urging her on, now that she was ready to push.

*"Mukku,* Rajam, *mukku."*

"I can't any more. I just can't push. It's not coming out." The contraction passed and Rajam leaned back in Mangalam's arms, turning her head to swallow a few sips of water to soothe her parched throat. She was consumed by the effort, her whole body covered in sweat. She had no idea that childbearing was so difficult. Mangalam held her in her strong arms, rubbing her lower back and whispering in her ear, "It's almost out. The next push you have to put in all your effort and the baby will be out. Come on, Rajam, you can do it."

But Rajam didn't think she could. She was half dazed, in pain, and terribly uncomfortable. The effort of pushing in a squatting position tired her now shivering thighs. She leaned back, slumping her quivering body against her mother's supportive one. She closed her eyes, grateful for the respite between contractions and suddenly had a vision, a feeling of déjà vu, almost as if she were sinking into the comfort of a familiar dream.

Partha led the retinue up the stairs, carrying a lantern to shine some light on the dark terrace, which was deprived of illumination on this virtually moonless night. When he told them about the imminent flowering of the Brahmakamalam, the whole family wanted to see it. After dinner they followed him in single file up to the terrace. All except his father, whose snoring provided the background music for this motion picture: the flowering of the Brahmakamalam plant. The moon was a sliver in the sky and in the muted darkness, the radiant glow from the white flower delighted its enthralled observers as they crowded around the half opened bud.

"Aha!" exclaimed young Kannan totally in awe. "I can actually see the Shivalingam inside."

"It's beautiful. Why didn't Rajam tell me anything about this?" wondered Nagamma. Rajam hardly told her anything but Nagamma did not realize that.

"There!" exclaimed Thambu. "Did you see that? I saw it opening."

"Yes, yes, that's right! I saw it too," added Kannan excitedly. The flower was blooming right before their eyes, an incomparable sight, almost a touch of heaven on earth. Comfortably seated on the terrace for a while, no one noticed the passage of time, so engrossed were they in the proceedings. Nagamma had barely finished chewing her paan when they realized that the bloom was completely open. The heady scent was all consuming. No one spoke. Words were inadequate to describe the experience. They were lost in the marvel of nature, in the beauty of creation, submerged in the intoxication of this unique experience. No one was ready to break the poignancy of this moment with something as mundane as spoken words. They watched and marveled, completely united in expansive joy.

# When the Lotus Blooms

With no warning, like a whiff of perfume in the wind, the thought crystallized in Partha's brain. He knew that the moment had arrived. He knew that he was a father. He knew that Kamu must be born.

Rajam closed her eyes, submitting to the vision unfolding within her.

*She was running in a green valley, the wind in her face, her soft feet treading on silken grass that was softer than the softest silk. The field was lush and green and the heavily clouded sky blocked the sunlight. She was back in the memorable verdant meadow surrounded by blossoms of Brahmakamalams waving gently in the breeze, dancing as it were in unison. White bunches of Brahmakamalam in full bloom, their soft white inner petals a gentle but pronounced contrast to their spiky outer ones. She stood still in amazement, with the gentle wind caressing her face as she submitted to the intoxication of the fragrance, which danced around her nostrils and settled in her wavy locks. She turned slowly around, her body responding to an unheard rhythm, reacting to the joy brimming within her, when she saw the child. Straight black hair cascading over her shoulders, reaching her small waist. Her narrow unlined forehead, soft plump cheeks and pert nose complemented her large sparkling eyes. Just then the clouds parted and the glorious rays of sunshine shone down, lighting her up, as her radiant face broke into a smile, which travelled from her lips to her doelike eyes, illuminating them as though they were fired with a torch from heaven. Eyes with a twinkle of mischief that exuded her joy for life, though she didn't say anything. She just smiled, but Rajam heard her unspoken words clearly as if they had said,*
*"Amma, I'm ready."*

With a mighty push from her mother, Kamakshi entered the world, her petite arms and legs flailing frantically, her tiny face screwed up as she let out a prodigious wail announcing her arrival.

"It's a girl!" yelled Chithi in joy as Rajam's exhausted face broke into a smile. "Kamu," she said softly.

Mangalam held her in a gentle embrace. "Yes, Kamu. All your desires and yearnings have been answered. Sankaracharya was true to his promise. You are a mother now." She helped her to her feet and led her to the cot to rest and then joined Chithi with the newborn, checking to see if everything was normal. Ten fingers and ten toes. Once they were satisfied, the baby was washed in warm water, covered in a blanket and placed in Rajam's waiting arms. She looked at this wrinkled, squirming bundle of life in her arms, and tears of joy and disbelief rolled down her cheeks. All at once, Kamu stopped crying and opened her eyes for the first time, allowing Rajam to stare deeply into her soul. Those eyes... with a twinkle in them? She knew them from somewhere, but she couldn't recall exactly where. The vision emerged like a distant memory from a misty dream.

◆❖◆❖◆
### *The Lotus had bloomed.*
◆❖◆❖◆

Miles away in Rangpur one satisfied six-year-old boy hugged his pillow tight, a smile anointing his face as he slept soundly after an exhausting evening watching his flower, the Brahmakamalam, bloom. Everyone, including Meera and the servants, had spent the evening in amazement as they watched the burgeoning bud burst into bloom. Sinking deeper and deeper into sleep, he dreamed the same familiar incomprehensible dream.

◆❖◆❖◆

*He saw her once again running down the hillside towards him, a red rose in her hands. She stopped a few feet away from him and smiled.*

*"I'm here," she whispered, her voice soft and sweet. He stood firm, his brow furrowed as he looked at her questioningly, trying to figure out who she was. His short pudgy arms akimbo, he demanded to know who she was.*

*"Your friend, didn't you know that already?" was her cheeky reply.*

"*My special friend?*" *asked Kandu, the words slipping out on their own volition. She smiled and said nothing, merely turned around, ready to return from where she had come.*

"*Wait,*" *he called out, eager to stop her.* "*Come back. Don't go so fast. If you are my friend, then let's play.*"

*She shook her head.* "*Not yet, it's not time yet.*"

"*Then when? When will you come back?*"

"*Soon,*" *she said, shrugging her tiny shoulders.* "*I'm still small, I have to grow.*" *Kandu didn't quite understand why she had to leave so soon, and if she had to go so fast, then why had she bothered to come? But he wanted a special friend very much.* "*Will you come back for sure?*" *he asked again, eager to meet her once more.*

"*You know I will,*" *she said as she turned again to scamper off.*

"*But you will have grown; so how will I recognize you?*"

*She placed the red rose gingerly in his hands and then turned, swiftly making her way back towards the mountain, her dainty anklets jingling as she carefully stepped in between bunches of Brahmakamalams.*

"*A red rose. Will you have a red rose with you?*" *He yelled out, needing to know but she was out of earshot, so with determination he ran after her. She stopped and turned around smiling at him, her eyes dancing and sparkling with mischief. He ran as fast as his short legs would carry him, but he tripped on a fallen vine and fell heavily to the ground before he could reach her.*

Sheepishly Kandu picked himself off the floor, rubbing his sore behind. He must have fallen from his bed. Climbing back onto the bed, he wondered why he had such a strange dream. He sank back onto his pillow when he realized that he had been clutching something tightly in his fist. He opened his fist and looked at what lay in the palm of his hand.

A red rose.

# The End

Kanchana Krishnan Ayyar

# When the Lotus Blooms
## Glossary of Indian words

| Word | Meaning |
| --- | --- |
| Aarathi: | A Sanskrit word for a ritual to prevent bad omens and ward off evil |
| Abhishekham: | A Sanskrit word meaning a sacred shower to a Hindu deity using water, milk, honey, etc. |
| Achkans: | An Urdu word for the long, formal upper garment used by men from north India |
| Adais: | A south Indian crepe made out of soaked and ground lentils |
| Agrahaaram: | A Tamil word to denote a village square lined with houses - traditionally occupied by upper class Brahmins |
| Almirah: | A Hindi word for closet |
| Alur Dom: | A spicy potato curry; a delicacy from Bengal |
| Amma: | A Tamil word for mother |
| Ammi Kallu: | A Tamil word referring to a granite stone to grind chutney |
| Angavastram: | A Sanskrit word to denote a top cloth draped around the shoulders for men |
| Angrez: | A Hindi word meaning foreigner |
| Anju Kaal Pinnal: | A Tamil phrase for a braid made with five separate strands |
| Anthim Samskara: | A Sanskrit phrase for the last rites performed by the eldest son of the deceased |
| Appa: | A Tamil word for father |
| Appalaam: | A South Indian delicacy, a thin and crispy deep fried snack |
| Apsara: | A Sanskrit word meaning a nymph in the celestial court of Indra |
| Aruvaal: | A Tamil word for a sickle |
| Aruvaamanai: | A Tamil word for a kitchen instrument used to cut vegetables |
| Avamaanam: | A Tamil word for shame |
| Ayah: | A Hindi word for nurse/babysitter |
| Ayurveda: | A Sanskrit word for a branch of Indian herbal medicine |
| Baba: | A Hindi suffix with several meanings: Father (Bengali) or an endearing reference to a young boy |
| Bandobast: | A Hindi word meaning arrangements for a function |
| Bangla: | A Hindi word for main house, corruption of the word bungalow |
| Banobibi: | The local female deity in the jungles of the Sunderbans |
| Banyan: | A Hindi word for undershirt |

375

# When the Lotus Blooms

Bearer: A word from colonial India for a valet

Beeda: A Tamil word for areca nuts wrapped in betel leaves (Paan in Hindi)

Besari: A Tamil word to denote an ornament worn on the nose

Bhakti: A Sanskrit word for devotion

Bhetki: A river fish common in Bengal

Bhiksha: A Sanskrit word meaning alms

Bidi: A Hindi word for a rolled tobacco leaf

Bindi: A Hindi word for a small dot worn as a forehead, decoration to ward off evil and to protect the pineal gland

Biryani: A Hindi word for a spicy, rice preparation

Brahmacharya: A Sanskrit word meaning bachelorhood

Brahmin: A Sanskrit word denoting the priestly, learned caste

Chaiwallahs: A Hindi word for tea vendors

Chamakam: A Sanskrit chant in praise of Lord Shiva

Chandala: People belonging to a caste that work in cremation grounds

Chandanam: A Tamil word for sandalwood

Chandhai: A Tamil word for a village fair

Charpoy: A Hindi word for a bed with jute fibers woven on a wooden frame

Chattai: A Tamil word for shirt/blouse

Chella Kutti: A Tamil phrase meaning "favorite child"

Chinna Veedu: A Tamil phrase to denote the home of a mistress—literal meaning "small house"

Chithi: A Tamil word for Aunt—Mother's younger sister

Choppus: A Tamil word meaning toy pots and pans

Chowkidars: A Hindi word for guards

Chowky: A Hindi word for police station

Coolie: A Hindi word for men who carry luggage in train stations

Dak: A Bengali word for mail

Dak Bungalow: Rest house for Government travelers

Dakshina: A Sanskrit word meaning fees given to a Brahmin for performing some ceremony

Darshanam: A Sanskrit word meaning sacred viewing

Davara: A Tamil word to denote a cup like utensil to hold a tumbler with hot coffee/tea

Dayakattam: A board game–precursor to chess.

Deekshathars: A class of priests

Deepavali: A Tamil word to denote the Festival of Lights (Diwali)

Devadasi: A caste where the women are temple dancers or courtesans

Devas: A Sanskrit word for Gods

| | |
|---|---|
| Devi: | A Sanskrit word meaning female goddess |
| Devistotra: | A Sanskrit chant in praise of Devi, the female goddess |
| Dhuno: | A Bengali word for incense |
| Dhotis: | A Hindi word for the traditional lower garment for men |
| Dosai: | A pancake made with ground rice and lentils; a South Indian delicacy |
| Divan: | A Hindi word of Turkish origin for a sofa |
| Durbar: | A Hindi word for a royal court |
| Ganesh: | Hindu elephant-headed God who is the son of Shiva and Parvathi |
| Ganga Snaanam: | A Tamil word to denote a bath in the holy river Ganga |
| Gayatri japam: | A sacred religious Hindu chant, considered to be the holiest verse of the Vedas |
| Ghat: | A Hindi word for steps and platform on the banks of a river |
| Ghee: | A Hindi word for clarified butter |
| Gilli Danda: | A game played by children using two sticks. |
| Gondogol: | A Bengali word for trouble or getting into mischief |
| Gopuram: | A Tamil word to denote a monumental tower at the entrance of a temple in south India |
| Grahastha: | A Sanskrit word to denote the second stage in a man's life, that of a householder |
| Gyanamudra: | A Sanskrit word for a ritual hand position for meditation where the index and pointer touch while the other fingers are stretched out |
| Idli: | A Tamil word to denote a soft steamed rice and lentil cake |
| Idli paanai: | A Tamil word for a pot for steaming idlis |
| Jaggery: | Unrefined sugar |
| Jameen: | Plantation |
| Jameendar: | Plantation owner |
| Japamala: | A rosary for chanting often made using beads from the Rudraksha tree |
| Jarigai: | A Tamil word for gold embroidery |
| Jarigai Oosi: | Thin lines of gold weave |
| Jhal Muri: | A Bengali delicacy/fast food made with puffed rice and sold by street vendors |
| Jimikis: | A Tamil word to denote hanging earrings |
| Jugalbandi: | A Hindi word to denote a combined performance by two soloists on equal footing |
| Kakakuli: | A Tamil word to denote a quick bath like a crow; in and out of water |
| Kalchatti: | A Tamil word to denote a metal pot used in south Indian cooking |

# When the Lotus Blooms

Kali: Hindu Goddess to whom blood sacrifices are sometimes offered

Kallipaal: A Tamil word for poison from a cactus which is combined with milk—used for female infanticide

Kamakshiamman: Goddess Kamakshi - Consort of Lord Shiva

Kanakambaram: Crossandra- a plant with orange flowers

Kanya: A Sanskrit word meaning virgin child

Karma: A Sanskrit word meaning Fate

Karthikeya: Hindu God; son of Shiva and Parvathi; Commander-in-chief of the Gods

Kashaayam: A Tamil word to denote a medicinal concoction of herbs

Khansaama: A male cook from the northeast of India

Kolam: A Tamil word for a geometric design drawn using rice flour, as decoration in front of the house

Krishnapaksha: The fortnight denoting the waning phase of the moon used interchangeably to denote moonless nights

Kriya: A Sanskrit word meaning an action, deed or rite

Kudhir: A Tamil word meaning a rice granary

Kudumi: A Tamil word to denote hair worn in a top knot

Kurta: A Hindi word for the male top garment.

Kumkumam: A Sanskrit word for vermillion powder

Kutralam Falls: A place in South India with many water falls; a well-known tourist attraction

Lathi: A Hindi word referring to a baton used by policemen

Lathi charge: Dispersing a mob using batons

Leela: The Lord's celestial game

Lingam: A Phallic symbol representing Shiva the Destroyer

Loochi: A Bengali delicacy; fried bread made out of flour

Maamsam: A Tamil word for meat

Maaplai: A Tamil word meaning son-in-law

Machaan: A Hindi word referring to a platform built on a tree for tiger hunters

Madisar: The traditional nine yard sari worn by Brahmin women

Mai: A Tamil word for eye liner

Maidanam: A Tamil word meaning an open field (maidan)

Maali: A Hindi word for gardener

Mama: A Tamil word meaning maternal uncle

Mandi: A Hindi word for market

Manthravadhi: A Tamil word meaning magician

Maargazhi: A Tamil word for the lunar month usually from December 15th to January 15th

| | |
|---|---|
| Marwari Seth: | A Hindi word referring to a business man from the state of Rajasthan |
| Masiyal: | A Tamil word for a puree of any vegetable |
| Mazhalai: | A Tamil word for baby talk |
| Memsahib: | A colonial word referring to the lady of the house |
| Mirazdar: | A rich land owner |
| Mishti Doi: | A Bengali delicacy; yoghurt sweetened with molasses |
| Mitthai Pink: | A very bright, hot pink |
| Moksha: | A Sanskrit word for salvation |
| Molahapodi: | Brahmin common usage for Milagaipodi—chilly powder |
| Mookuthi: | A Tamil word for nose ring |
| Moothram: | A Tamil word for urine |
| Morai: | A Tamil word referring to a palm utensil for husking rice or wheat |
| Morcha: | A Hindi word meaning a demonstration |
| Mozham: | A Tamil word referring to a measure used by flower-vendors (from elbow to tips of fingers) |
| Muhurtham: | A Tamil word noting the auspicious time according to Indian astrology |
| Mundu: | A white lower garment used by natives of Kerala |
| Muri: | A Bengali word for puffed rice |
| Muriwallah: | A vendor who sells jhal muri, a delicacy from Calcutta |
| Mutram: | A Tamil word referring to a courtyard inside the house—generally open to sky |
| Nagara: | A bejeweled hair ornament shaped like a snake. |
| Nalangu: | A Tamil ritual on auspicious occasions, where designs are made on hands and feet using fresh turmeric |
| Namaskaram: | A Tamil word referring to bending down and performing an obeisance, seeking the blessings of God or elders |
| Nandi: | The Bull; the vehicle of Shiva |
| Nehru topi: | A Hindi word referring to a flat white cap popularized by Jawaharlal Nehru, who went on to become the first Prime Minister of Independent India |
| Nila Shaapaadu: | A Tamil word referring to dinner eaten under the moon |
| Odiyaanam: | A Tamil word referring to a gold belt worn by women |
| Oru kai: | A Tamil phrase literally meaning "one hand" |
| Oonjal: | A Tamil word for swing |
| Otha Brahmana: | A Tamil phrase meaning the lone Brahmin — considered a bad omen when venturing out |
| Paan: | A Hindi word for betel leaf |
| Paanwallah: | A Hindi word for a betel leaf vendor |
| Paati: | A Tamil word meaning grandmother |

Palaangozhi:    A game similar to Mancala using shells and a wooden board

Palaharam:    A light evening meal

Pallu:    A Hindi word for the flowing free end of a sari (Thalapu in Tamil)

Panchamrutham: A Sanskrit word referring to a sweet mixture of fruits with honey

Panchayat:    A committee of five well respected village elders, chosen to settle local disputes

Pandhal:    A decorative tent used to cover the area for social gatherings

Pandi:    A Tamil word referring to a game like hop-scotch

Pani    A Tamil word meaning early morning dew

Panjakacham:    A Tamil word referring to a unique style of wearing the veshti or lower garment by men

Parayan:    A Tamil word referring to the lower caste untouchable

Parvathi:    Consort of Lord Siva

Pavadai:    A Tamil word referring to a long skirt or petticoat worn by girls

Payasam:    A Tamil word meaning rice pudding

Pazhayadu:    A Tamil word referring to left over rice soaked overnight in water

Podalangai:    A Tamil word for the vegetable snake gourd

Pongal:    A Tamil Harvest Festival celebrated on January 14th

Pongal Panai:    A Tamil phrase referring to the pot in which the rice preparation Pongal is cooked

Ponpaakal:    A Tamil colloquial word referring to the official viewing of the girl for marriage

Pooja:    Prayers offered as per traditional injunctions often in a pooja room

Poriyal:    A Tamil word for vegetable stir-fry

Potlam:    A Tamil word referring to a folded packet

Pottu:    A Tamil word referring to the vermillion dot in the center of the forehead

Pradakshanam: Circumbulation of the sanctum sanctorum in a temple

Prana:    A Sanskrit word referring to life force which sustains the body

Prasaadham:    Sacred food first offered to God; then distributed to devotees after prayers

Ramayana:    A famous Indian epic about King Rama, an incarnation of Vishnu

Punkha:    A Hindi word for fan

Punkhawallah:    The person who pulls on ropes to make the fan work

Rasam: A tangy, spicy liquid dish—traditionally served with rice in south Indian cuisine

Rexine: Faux leather popular in Brahmin homes where leather couches are not permitted

Rudraksha: Prayer beads or rosary of Hindus - generally threaded into a garland of 108 beads

Rudram: A Sanskrit chant in praise of Lord Shiva

Saamiyaar: A Tamil word for mendicant

Sambar: A spicy lentil-based dish served with rice in South Indian cuisine

Sammandhi: A Tamil word referring to the in-laws

Sankara Madham: A center for Vedic learning established by Sankaracharya

Sanyasi: Final stage in the Hindu social cycle where men renounce worldly life

Sari: Traditional Indian garment for women using six yards of cloth

Seemandham: A ceremony performed by the boy's parents for the daughter-in-law's safe childbirth

Shaivaite: A sect that believes in Shiva as its main preceptor

Shakti: Female divine force also seen as the consort of Shiva

Shakkarai Pongal: A sweet rice preparation made during the festival of Pongal

Shanthi Kalyanam: A ceremony of nuptials in South Indian weddings

Shastra: A Sanskrit word for laws in religious scriptures

Shikakai: A Sanskrit word for soap nut used to wash hair

Shikar: A Hindi word for hunt

Shiva: One of the Hindu trinity—The God of Destruction, the other two being Brahma & Vishnu

Shloka: A Sanskrit chant

Sindoor: The red vermillion which married women of Bengal wear at the parting of their hair

Sojji-Bajji: Traditional snacks consisting of vegetable fritters and a sweet dish served on special occasions

Sumangali: A married woman

Terylene: A polyester material

Thandava: Cosmic dance of Shiva

Thalapu: The flowing end of the sari

Thaali: A gold chain and pendant given to a girl at the time of her marriage

Thatha: A Tamil word for grandfather

Thavil: A barrel shaped drum

Thayir shaadham: A must in south Indian meals; rice with yoghurt

| | |
|---|---|
| Theetu: | A Tamil word referring to the first three days of a woman's period considered unclean |
| Thinnai: | A Tamil word referring to a raised platform, bordering the front of the house |
| Thogayal: | A colloquial Tamil word for chutney |
| Tiffin: | A light afternoon meal |
| Tulasi madham: | A platform built for the sacred basil plant |
| Tumbler: | A metal utensil to drink water/coffee |
| Upma: | A dish from South Indian cuisine made from semolina |
| Vadaam: | A Tamil word referring to a crispy deep-fried snack in south Indian cuisine |
| Vadai: | A Tamil word referring to fritters made out of ground lentils |
| Vadama Iyer: | A superior sub-sect of Iyer Brahmins |
| Vaidhyar: | A Tamil word for doctor |
| Valaikaapu: | A bangle ceremony performed in the seventh month of pregnancy |
| Vande Mataram: | A rousing slogan/song during the Indian freedom movement meaning "Bow to Thee - O' Mother" |
| Varan: | A Tamil word meaning a matrimonial match |
| Vathakozhambu: | A well-known south Indian, spicy, tamarind dish |
| Vedas: | Four ancient Indian Sanskrit texts: Rig, Sama, Yajur and Atharvana |
| Veda Pathashala: | A school where the Vedas are taught |
| Venn Pongal: | A savory rice preparation made on the occasion of Pongal |
| Vepalai: | Leaves of the evergreen Neem tree with medicinal qualities |
| Veshti: | A Tamil word referring to the thin cotton lower garment for men |
| Vibuthi: | A Tamil word referring to sacred ash; typically worn on the forehead |
| Vidudhalai: | A Tamil word for freedom |
| Vilva Tree: | A tree whose leaves are offered to Shiva during worship |
| Vilvandi: | A Tamil word meaning covered bullock cart |
| Vishnu: | The Preserver in the Hindu trinity |
| Yagna: | A Sanskrit word to denote fire sacrifice dedicated to some deity |
| Yecchal: | A Tamil word for saliva |

Kanchana Krishnan Ayyar was born in New Delhi, India, and currently lives in South Florida, with her husband and her two daughters.

When the Lotus blooms is her first novel.

You can contact her at www.kanchibooks.com

Printed in Great Britain
by Amazon.co.uk, Ltd.,
Marston Gate.